# Praise for
# Royal Heirs Academy

"Lindsey Duga has taken what I love most in YA novels—romantictension, royal drama, and family secrets—and swirled them together with my favorite setting: a European boarding school. At times suspenseful, swoony, and heartbreaking, *Royal Heirs Academy* will keep readers flipping pages (and alliances) until the very end."

—Kristy Boyce, bestselling author of *Dungeons and Drama*

"Readers will swoon and ache at points, only to rage and cry at others. The blending of these emotions will ultimately keep them turning pages.... Fast, engaging, and addictive." —*Kirkus Reviews*

"An intense rivals-to-enemies journey, in which four royal heirs must decide how far they're willing to go if they want to rule a kingdom. No one is who they first appear

to be. Everyone has a secret. Filled with backstabbing and betrayal, this book will surprise readers in the best ways possible."
—Jodi Meadows, *New York Times* bestselling coauthor of *My Lady Jane*

"Deftly combines competition intrigue with the romance and friendship drama of standard boarding school settings, making for a twisty contemporary tale."
—*Publishers Weekly*

"*Gossip Girl* meets Katharine McGee's *American Royals*.... The unfurling romantic entanglements provide ample fodder for readers of the genre.... Duga has clearly created a developed world within the castle walls that invites readers to feel like they are a part of all the drama." —*SLJ*

# ROYAL LIARS

## A ROYAL HEIRS ACADEMY NOVEL

Lindsey Duga

Christy Ottaviano Books

**LARGE PRINT**

This book is a work of fiction. Names, characters, places, and incidents are the product of the author's imagination or are used fictitiously. Any resemblance to actual events, locales, or persons, living or dead, is coincidental.

Copyright © 2026 by Lindsey Duga

Cover art copyright © 2026 by Deanna Halsall. Cover design by Patrick Hulse. Cover copyright © 2026 by Hachette Book Group, Inc.
Interior design by Carla Weise.

Hachette Book Group supports the right to free expression and the value of copyright. The purpose of copyright is to encourage writers and artists to produce the creative works that enrich our culture.

The scanning, uploading, and distribution of this book without permission is a theft of the author's intellectual property. If you would like permission to use material from the book (other than for review purposes), please contact permissions@hbgusa.com. Thank you for your support of the author's rights.

Christy Ottaviano Books
Hachette Book Group
1290 Avenue of the Americas, New York, NY 10104
Visit us at LBYR.com

First Edition: January 2026

Christy Ottaviano Books is an imprint of Little, Brown and Company. The Christy Ottaviano Books name and logo are registered trademarks of Hachette Book Group, Inc.

The publisher is not responsible for websites (or their content) that are not owned by the publisher.

Little, Brown and Company books may be purchased in bulk for business, educational, or promotional use. For information, please contact your local bookseller or the Hachette Book Group Special Markets Department at special.markets@hbgusa.com.

Library of Congress Cataloging-in-Publication Data
Names: Duga, Lindsey author
Title: Royal liars / Lindsey Duga.
Description: First edition. | New York : Little, Brown and Company, 2026. | Series: Royal Heirs Academy ; book 2 | Audience: Ages 14–18 | Summary: "Four teenage royals team up to defend their beloved boarding school from a mysterious threat, risking their futures and their hearts in the process." —Provided by publisher.
Identifiers: LCCN 2025037329 | ISBN 9780316585675 trade paperback | ISBN 9780316585699 hardcover | ISBN 9780316585705 ebook
Subjects: CYAC: Boarding schools—Fiction | Schools—Fiction | Love-hate relationships—Fiction | Interpersonal relations—Fiction | LCGFT: Novels
Classification: LCC PZ7.1.D83424 Rp 2026
LC record available at https://lccn.loc.gov/2025037329

ISBNs: 978-0-316-58569-9 (hardcover), 978-0-316-58567-5 (trade paperback), 978-0-316-58570-5 (ebook), 978-0-316-61041-4 (large print)

To Kelly,
I found you in high school and I'll keep you forever.
(But not, like, in a creepy way. Love you!)

# PROLOGUE

## LEANDER

W<small>AR IS INEVITABLE</small>.

That was Leander's recurring thought as he read the report, his thumb accidentally smearing a pink tinge of crimson across the page. The blood was appropriate, albeit annoying, considering the paper's contents.

His fresh tattoo was still bleeding and likely wouldn't stop until he applied some ointment. However, the wound would need to wait. Zuri Aquila had just left, he needed to review this report, and he had a call he could not miss.

*The days are getting shorter,* Leander thought as he wiped the remnants of blood on his black slacks, *with every year I am king.*

Reading the report was not of vital consequence, considering that the call he'd received from Captain Kendrick was what had triggered his tattoo in the first place. He'd known for hours that Operation Peaceful Sea was successful the moment it had happened. As commander in chief of all Ashlandic military forces, Leander was the first person to receive the call—the *only* person who truly mattered.

Still he wanted to read the report anyway. He felt like he owed it to the dead.

Never mind that they'd been trying to steal his crown. Never mind that they had been planning a coup that would put one of the other ancient Ashlandic rival houses on the throne, throwing the country into *another* civil war after forty years of unprecedented peace and economic prosperity.

The traitors were still human beings and Leander was no monster. He was simply a monarch willing to do what was necessary for the benefit of his people. Though this operation could've been avoided if he'd been merciless years ago when he'd first learned that the Scealans were still alive. But with experience came wisdom, and he was finally eradicating the threat now.

His gray eyes scanned the paper, reminding himself of the intelligence gathered from his various sources that had led to this swift, tactical extermination. A man had emerged with the name Scealan and held plans for several choice attacks on energy plants, military bases, and ports, to weaken the country's infrastructure, military, and economy. The culmination of the conspiracy was his infiltration of Heres Castle and the forceful removal of Leander's crown along with his head.

The insurrection was quite well strategized, actually.

If Leander were to stage his own coup, this would be how he went about it.

"Pity," Leander muttered as his gaze raked over the confirmed casualties in the conspirator's seaside home of Farach, where the royal intelligence team had found the rebels and eliminated them permanently.

Pity that Scealan man had been power-hungry enough to use his genius for treason. He would've made a good general.

Leander skimmed through the report's midsection, explaining all the tactical maneuvering, any errors (naturally there were none), and the extraction as well as the staging for civilian law enforcement. No need to make the public aware of another rebellion quashed. They needed stability. So it would be staged as a break-in where men had been doing nothing but relaxing, drinking, and playing cards. It was a nice house. There wouldn't be much suspicion. Besides, the tactical team was very good, covering up their jobs as easily as performing them.

It was when he got to the conclusion of the report that he paused.

His tattoo burned, and, absentmindedly, he stroked the cuff of his dress shirt, now tinged in blood.

The rebel had a wife and child.

He'd known this, of course. It had all been a part of his plan when he set Operation Peaceful Sea into motion. But it was a tragedy nonetheless.

Unfortunately, the wife had to go. She likely knew of her husband's plans, and Leander was nothing if not thorough. But the child... the child was innocent.

He would set the child up with a new home. Likely an aunt or a close friend on the mother's side. Someone willing to raise the child as their own out of love but with enough fear of the regime to keep the adoption a secret. It was easy to arrange such things.

Leander's gaze flicked to the chair opposite his desk. The one Zuri Aquila had sat in mere minutes ago, asking about the fourth applicant to her beloved Almus Terra.

Ironic that she'd arrived mere minutes before he received the name of the child in this report.

*Aurelia.*

He liked it. It was strong. Beautiful.

The child could keep their name. At least partially. It would involve paperwork, a lot of it in the adoption process, but this was a small token he could bestow.

A knock sounded at his door and the guard poked his bald head through. "Your call is on line one, Your Majesty."

"Thank you, Kendrick," Leander said with a sigh, opening his desk drawer and filing the report into the folder for special covert military operations. His chief secretary had been nagging him to go digital for a long time, but he was wary of computers. Hackers seemed to be getting craftier every day. At least this way, if someone stole these documents, he'd be able to look his traitorous subject in the eye, rather than a faceless nobody overseas.

He reached over and picked up the phone, sliding it between his ear and his shoulder. "Leander."

There was a beep, and he gritted his teeth. A king should not be kept waiting on a call, and, yet, here he was. Waiting for a man who had more money than God and was somehow considered a relatively "young" billionaire.

*I wonder*, Leander thought as the second beep sounded and there was the whisper of wind in the receiver, *if I should have gotten into business rather than politics.*

"Afternoon, Leander," the smooth voice said over the phone, sounding much too casual.

It was the second time today he let the rigid royal decorum slide. "Rhett. How are you?"

"Better than the Americans."

Leander lifted his gaze to the ceiling in annoyance. *Rhett* was American, yet the man seemed to believe he transcended nationalities.

"But not great," Rhett continued. "This one is going to hurt us all."

Leander kneaded his temple. "So it will."

"News is that the US government is going to seize control of Fannie Mae and Freddie Mac."

"Mmm." Leander had not called to talk about the housing market collapse in the United States but the failure of banks and mortgage lenders was currently tanking the American stock market. Unfortunately, that kind of crisis rippled into a worldwide one. Last year the European Union, Australia, Canada, and Japan had all banded together to inject liquidity into credit markets to stabilize the rapidly failing lending markets.

"Leander," Rhett grumbled, "this does not bode well."

Leander stood, shoving his free hand into his pocket and walking to the window. The storm was finally calming now. He could see a break in the clouds in the gray-scaled horizon. "It is what it is. You don't like it because this proves corporations and banks must rely on governments in crisis. When all else fails, a government remains standing."

"That's rich coming from Ashland's king," Rhett drawled, "I wouldn't call your country's history of government exactly stable."

True. He *had* just quashed a rebellion.

"Maybe so. But my reign has yet to fall. Now, have you considered my proposal?"

The billionaire was silent for a long time. The question was not about whether he'd considered it, but whether he was willing to go through with it.

"I...am not opposed to the idea. It is messy, however."

"Messes can be swept under the rug as long as no one is watching."

Rhett chuckled as a seagull cawed in the

distance, and Leander assumed the man was on his yacht, looking out at a very different sea, with a very different view.

"I suppose that's fair. You're certain this... institution can give me what I want?"

Leander thought of his grandchildren, his legacy, and the future of Ashland. He thought of the deposits he just put down. "What you want, Rhett, is the future. So yes, it can."

The other line was silent, then, "Very well, then. We should meet in person. Expect me in forty-eight hours."

Then the line went dead. Leander would've been offended, but that was yet another indignity he was willing to overlook. The man was, after all, agreeing to a plan that would make Ashland *quite* rich.

He placed the phone back in its cradle and sat in his desk chair, glancing at his drawer with the report of Operation Peaceful Sea. He did not need to check his watch to know how long the call had lasted. In rare form, he was actually ahead of schedule, and he was not one to waste time.

Opening his notepad, he began to draft a new memo for his secretaries to review and implement. In his superior penmanship, he scrawled *Ashland's National Merit Scholarship Program.*

# 1

# ALARIC

*Seventeen years later*

Was it a left at the naked mermaid statue or a right?

Alaric didn't recall the exact directions the servant had given him a few days ago. He went with his gut. Left.

His sleek black Oxford shoes, the ones he was forced to wear at every formal event, padded softly and silently across the deep cobalt rug. Not that discretion really mattered. The fireworks from the traditional summer reenactment of an epic Ashlandic sea battle off the cliffs were a good distraction.

Alaric glanced over his shoulder to see if anyone was following him. They weren't.

In his time at Heres Castle, Alaric had picked up a few clues about its layout and decorative styles. Marble floors were pathways to state rooms, while living quarters, studies, and personal offices had thick rugs and plush carpets leading to their thresholds.

Whether it was a good thing or a bad thing, he *was* getting better at navigating these halls. Ever since becoming an Ashland heir, he'd felt out of place in every castle he'd been in. Which, weirdly, was more than one. His school, Almus Terra Academy, was also in a castle, though a vastly different structure than this one. While Heres Castle had become more of an amalgamation of royal architecture from across Europe, Almus Terra was classically medieval. Though it was now a fortress of learning rather than a fortress of protection for some long-dead Roman Catholic noble.

Sadie would know exactly which noble most likely.

No, *nope*. He was not going to think about Sadie—his rival, the heir apparent, and the girl he could not get out of his head for the life of him, despite the fact that she was dating his *cousin*.

Alaric shouldn't be thinking about anything except the mission before him.

He walked faster. It had already taken him

too long to get back inside the castle. The royal courtyard on the Durah cliffs could be seen directly below most of the balconies facing east, but there were hundreds of steps carved directly into the rock between the castle and the courtyard. A lift had been built years ago, but it was manned by guards and Alaric did not want to risk being seen returning when he was *supposed* to be enjoying the national holiday with the rest of the Ashlandic Court.

Finally, the long corridor ended in what looked like a half-moon drawing room. He must've entered a tower. That sounded about right. The servant he'd bribed with a few banknotes from his royal allowance had mentioned that all the princes and princesses had each been given a tower upon their birth, and that his mother, Crown Princess Rhea, had received the northeastern. Not that he knew where northeastern was at this point, but it *felt* right.

He tried the ornate wooden door on the left. Locked.

"Yeh think in a palace riddled with guards the security inside would be lighter," he muttered to himself as he pulled out the tools from his jacket pocket.

Before becoming a prince, Alaric had been...

the extreme term would be *delinquent*. But his criminal activities were fairly benign, all things considered. A couple of minor break-ins at run-down businesses and old warehouses. A few fights. Well, not a few. A lot. A lot of fights. Some underage drinking. But that's it. Nothing serious—no drugs, no stealing, not even petty theft. Everything he'd owned, he'd earned. Even from a juvenile age, he'd understood what things cost. What *life* cost.

Still, he knew how to pick a lock.

Flipping the case open, he selected his torque wrench and slid the tool into the lock. With a quick couple turns he was able to determine the direction of the key. Next, he inserted the pick, the curved metal facing upward to push at the pins and test their movement. Once he was confident they'd slide upward, he removed the pick and then inserted his final tool, the rake, slowly lifting each pin and applying pressure through the wrench. Ear pressed against the door, he listened for the sound of the pins falling through the lock mechanism. The technique of raking usually took multiple attempts, but Alaric got it on his second.

Sure enough, the pins clicked and the lock disengaged.

Blowing out a breath, Alaric pushed the door open and slipped inside the darkness, shutting the door behind him. For months, he'd plotted to break into his father's suite, and he was finally here.

He didn't pause to take stock of the room. He didn't care what it looked like or how his father lived. All he cared about was...

Alaric's gaze landed on the massive mahogany desk and the laptop sitting unguarded on top.

"Bingo," he muttered.

Crossing the room in long strides, Alaric took out the external drive from his jacket pocket. After plugging his drive into one of the ports, he opened the laptop and was faced with a login screen. Tongue between his teeth, his fingers flew across the keys, pulling up the command prompt and using the hacking script he'd been practicing in his Cyber Security class all last semester.

It was a ridiculous amount of typing. But he was rewarded when the black screen full of his code disappeared and the simple blue screen of his father's desktop took its place.

Clicking on the first folder he found, another password prompt popped up, and Alaric swore harshly.

Of course Mikael Erickson would have double

encryption on everything. It was smart but obnoxious. At least Alaric was prepared. Typing out another command, he began copying the computer's files onto his external drive. That alone was not an easy task either. There was a security protection in place to prevent copying and Alaric had to dismantle it. Over and over.

Minutes ticked by, but he kept typing, taking down every security feature that was triggered as the files were slowly, but surely, downloaded. Later, he would be able to hack into the folders themselves, but he was already creeping up on two hours of absence from the party.

As the last of the folder downloads reached 80 percent, his phone vibrated in his pocket. Without even checking the ID, Alaric slipped on his earphones and answered the call.

"Yo."

"How goes the break-in?" Jacob's voice came through all cheery, his mouth stuffed with some snack. Alaric was going to guess cheese puffs. The kid was addicted.

"Not swell," Alaric grumbled. "The chancer's got all the files double-encrypted."

Jacob barked out a laugh, the sound in Alaric's ears making him wince. "Your dad is a piece of work, my dude."

"Tell me about it," Alaric said as the files finally finished their download. He unplugged the drive and slipped it into his jacket.

Jacob was a fifteen-year-old American, four full years younger than Alaric, but super freaking smart and Alaric's best friend at Almus Terra. He was studying robotics and aspired to help build Mission to Mars tech. Alaric didn't doubt he would achieve it.

"Are you going back to the party?" Jacob asked.

With his prize safely in his coat, Alaric ducked out of his father's room. "Not sure I'd call Ashland's ceremonial sea battle reenactment a party, Jake. Ilsa mentioned they spent twenty-five million on the ships and gunpowder alone."

"Is there booze?"

"Yeah."

"Then it's a party."

Hard to argue with that logic.

He was about to head back down the hall when his gaze snagged on the other door.

His mother's room. He knew there was nothing to be gained by going inside, but his legs were already moving.

This door did not have a lock to pick. It clicked open with a simple twist of the knob.

Jacob must've heard the sound because he piped up again.

"You still in your dad's room?"

"No, my ma's," Alaric mumbled as he stepped inside. Wisely, Jacob stayed quiet as Alaric took it all in.

The moonlight shone in through the several large windows, highlighting his mother's dark room in silver. The furniture looked pristine, and it didn't surprise him at all that they would keep the crown princess's quarters perfect in both her life and death. Though the decor was not what he expected. It seemed to follow Rhea's style. She had posters of '80s rock bands, bohemian-style rugs, and gauzy curtains with astrological symbols. But the furniture was like everywhere else—ornate, heavy, old. A massive cherrywood dresser and desk, a canopy king-size bed with accented throw pillows of... Trolls and Care Bears.

It was then he'd wished he hadn't answered Jacob's call, because this had become unexpectedly personal. His throat grew uncomfortably tight. His eyes burned. His mother had seemed... *cool*. It was clear she didn't give a shit what real princesses should have on their beds. She liked what she liked and was unapologetic about it. Like Alaric.

For the first time in a long time he'd wished he'd known his mother.

"Alaric? Dude?" Jacob's voice was tentative.

Alaric cleared his throat. "Yeah. I'm here."

He made his way through Rhea's quarters, taking in every detail, even pulling out his phone and snapping a few pictures. Though now that he knew what this place looked like, he'd be back.

When he got to his mother's desk he stopped dead in his tracks. "I'll call yeh later, Jake."

Before Jacob could reply, Alaric tapped his earbud to end the call, then picked up an ornate gold picture frame. It was a photo of Rhea and a baby—him. He was maybe one year old, if that. There was nothing special about him as a baby, but his mom—*his mom*—looked radiant. She looked over-the-moon happy. Cupping his chubby baby cheeks, holding him to her face and laughing into the camera, she was incandescent.

For a brief blip in his nineteen-year-old life, he had been loved. Deeply. Setting the picture down with a shaky hand, he picked up the next framed photo. This one showed Rhea holding him on her knees, ready to bounce him. She wore a Tears for Fears sweatshirt, and her raven-black hair, curly and unruly, so much like Alaric's, hung from a messy ponytail. There were more photos. More of

Alaric as a baby, and a few more of her—one when she was quite young, maybe his age now, and then another of her when she was a little girl, wearing a tiara and a fancy dress—probably the only image where she played the princess role.

Hungry for more of a past he thought he'd never know, Alaric started to open the top desk drawer. But then his phone buzzed again. Short and quick this time, thrice in a row.

> Emmeline:
> **GET**
>
> Emmeline:
> **BACK**
>
> Emmeline:
> **NOW**

"Shite," he cursed, and slipped his phone into his pocket, then hurried back through Heres Castle. The return trip was easier because he didn't have to remember exact directions. He could find a landmark and reorient himself toward the cliffs. Finally he located the servants' hallways, found the steps down into the courtyard by going around the lift, then took all damn near two hundred of them.

The torches surrounding the courtyard, held by ornate iron sconces attached to the surrounding columns, eventually came into view and by then he was sweating in the late-August evening air under his suit jacket. Before Alaric even had a chance to scan the crowd, to see what he'd missed, Emmeline was right next to him, shoving a glass of champagne into his chest.

He took it but didn't drink, his gaze landing on the raised stone dais with King Leander and his chosen royal dynamic duo—Sadie, heir apparent, and Titus, the golden-boy prince and boyfriend.

They, and the rest of the court, all clad in gorgeous dresses and suits, were watching the conclusion of the sea battle. The ship *Maiden Eldana* pierced the hull of the *Serpent Scealan*, cannons in the form of fireworks exploding across the ship's side. It was a summer holiday in August known as Eldana Day, a significant turning point in the country's history that ended a fifty-year-long civil war back in the 1600s.

"Learn to be more discreet," Emmeline hissed between her teeth as a lord, a distant relative whose name Alaric hadn't ever bothered to learn, passed by them, nodding respectfully. Emmeline gave him a charming smile. "Lovely night, Lord Faust."

Alaric ground his teeth together. "Why don't yeh just tell me what yer dying to. Did anyone notice I was gone?"

Emmeline could be annoying, condescending, and pretentious, but she was the only family he had that he didn't want to strangle. She had this weird way of looking out for him. Even if she threatened him afterward.

"Ilsa asked where you were," Emmeline replied, taking a sip of her own champagne. "I covered for you."

"Told her I had a bad case of the runs?"

Emmeline snorted into her glass, then looked shocked she could even make such a sound. She jabbed him hard in the ribs with her pointy elbow. "I'm not doing it for you again. You may not be heir apparent, but you're still a prince. Your absence *will* be noticed."

Alaric's tone was dry. "I'll keep that in mind."

"I'm *serious*, Alaric. Do you think you'll have a place in this family if you cause trouble? You're a spare royal. There's a fine line between noticing when you're gone and caring if you don't come back."

The words stung, but they shouldn't have. He'd known for years that he hadn't mattered.

*But I mattered to Ma. Once.*

"This family," Emmeline said, her gaze locked on her own parents across the courtyard—her mother scrolling on her phone, her father drinking deeply from a whiskey highball glass, "will chew you up and spit you out."

It was then that the ship *Serpent Scealan* exploded with fireworks, signaling its defeat against the *Maiden Eldana*. Smoke and sparks and more rockets going off into the night, reflecting the multicolored pyrotechnic stars on the dark waters of the Labrador Sea.

Sadie was dressed in a gold shimmering gown, intricate jeweled beadwork shining like stars across her slim form. Her strawberry hair twisted into a curled mass down her back with braids woven around the delicate tiara on her head.

She was stunning.

Just like she'd been for the last eight months. Breathtaking and untouchable.

Then his cousin leaned down and kissed her. Titus pulled back after the too-long kiss to smile at her, all handsome and adoring. Always the perfect prince.

Alaric tossed the entire champagne flute back in one swig, feeling the external drive shift against his chest with the movement.

At least he'd managed to steal one thing tonight.

# 2
# EMMELINE

Emmeline wasn't entirely sure when it happened. Like most instances of falling in love, it had snuck up on her. But somewhere between last winter break and this summer, Emmeline had become smitten with her country.

It was impressive, considering she hadn't set out to do so. Unlike other plans that Emmeline excelled at executing, this had happened by accident.

It was a good thing, a necessary thing, for a princess to love her country but ruling over Ashland had never been her prime objective. Winning over her family had.

And look where that had gotten her.

Emmeline strolled along the shore of Wellowhale Bay, the fierce Ashlandic sea wind whipping her hair around her face. After the first week back in Ashland for summer break, Emmeline had given up on trying to prevent the gusts from raking through her honey-colored waves and creating a rat's nest that only the strongest of detangler serums could calm. Even tight fishtail braids had proven largely useless against the sea-salt gales, so she let it fly free.

Her handler, Cliff, kept a fair distance behind her. Another effort she had abandoned: convincing Cliff to join her on these walks. He insisted he could better protect her by assessing threats from his vantage point behind her.

Emmeline had resisted the urge to bite back, *What threats?* Would a shark leap out of the water like a freaking dolphin and tear her to shreds?

With a sigh, Emmeline paused in her walk, her rain boots—or wellies as the locals liked to call them—crunching on the pebbles. It was a lovely day in Ashland. Light blue sky with wisps of stratocumulus clouds streaking above the coastline. Clusters of people were out with chairs and blankets, enjoying the sun. A rare treat for Ashlanders, even in late August.

Wellowhale Bay, a small inland bay off the coast of Durah, was one of Emmeline's favorite places she'd discovered so far. It reminded her a bit of the Long Island Sound back in New York. The choppy Atlantic was a beautiful wild backdrop to small cottages and huts selling seafood like lobster rolls, fried cod tongues, and Ashland's infamous sea urchin stew made with bits of white fish and hearty potato.

She'd learned a lot about Ashland and its unique culture over the summer. Unfortunately, she'd had plenty of free time to do so. With Sadie as the heir apparent, it was *her* face that was required at all the PR events, *her* butt required in the seat of all the advisory council meetings with the king. Well, her and Titus, since the two were glued at the hip most days.

They were both so... perfect. Sadie, especially, had practically become a different person. Her posture was regal, her smiles were charming, her clothes and makeup were immaculate, her conversations were engaging.

All of which pissed off Emmeline to no end. Because the light laugh, the tilts of her chin, the hair flipping over her shoulder—it was all like looking into a mirror. Sadie was *stealing* Emmeline's mannerisms. Copying her to be the perfect royal because Sadie had been nothing but a commoner and you don't get that good without someone to emulate, especially in such a short amount of time.

Sadie hadn't simply been watching Emmeline, it seemed, she'd been *studying* her.

At one point over spring break, following a state dinner with several lords, Emmeline had cornered Sadie, intending to shame her into admitting it. She'd said, "It's pathetic, you know. How you've just been copying me."

Sadie gave her a blank look, then said, "And, yet, I'm the one with the crown. You only have a tiara. At least it's pretty, Emmie."

Emmeline had almost slapped her right then. The only thing holding her back was that King Leander and a few other lords were nearby.

Now, eight months after Sadie had been named heir apparent, she was every bit the person Emmeline *should* have been, and Emmeline saw no way of crossing the Rubicon that now lay between her and her goal.

"It's the princess!"

A voice called from a few yards away, farther from the shoreline where the tiny shells and pebbles gave way to softer earth, perfect for locals or tourists to enjoy the sunny day.

Emmeline lifted a hand to her face to shield her eyes and get a better look. Sure enough, a woman with her children was waving down at her, nearly jumping in her excitement. Emmeline smiled and waved back.

Which turned out to be an invitation for the young family.

"Let them approach," Emmeline told Cliff, who'd already started toward them, all tense and brooding, preparing to intercept her incoming subjects.

"It's not wise, Your Highness."

"It's a woman and her children, Cliff. If they take out a shiv and stab me, you can say I told you so."

Cliff grumbled something about making his job harder, but she ignored him and plastered on a big smile as the small group approached.

"Good afternoon, Your Highness," the woman said, nearly breathless, curtsying, the small boy in her arms bobbing up and down with the movement. The young girl, on the other hand, looked at Emmeline with narrowed eyes. She couldn't have been more than eleven or twelve, but already she seemed to have the countenance of a teenager.

"Good afternoon," Emmeline said with a smile.

"I can't believe you're here, Princess. We thought the heirs would've been back at school by now."

"We leave tomorrow actually," Emmeline

said, ignoring the brief pang in her heart at the mention of Almus Terra. "It's such a lovely day, so I thought I'd take a walk in one of my favorite places."

The woman beamed, proud of her home. "You like Wellowhale Bay, Your Highness?"

"I love it. It reminds me of—"

"Then please tell the king not to give that evil company permission to drill," the young girl snapped.

"Jana!" The mother scolded. "You will apologize right now."

"That's all right," Emmeline said, forcing a placating smile onto her face. Virin Corporation. She knew all too well about that "evil company."

"I understand how you feel, Jana, but oil is complicated. Until we can find more alternatives, it is a vital energy source and will bring a lot of wealth and jobs to our economy."

"Pah is a fisherman. What will that mean for his job if an oil spill kills our ocean life?" the girl continued.

"Enough, Jana." This time the mother grabbed her daughter by her shoulder and shoved her back. She curtsied again, then stepped forward and pressed a business card into Emmeline's hand. "It was a privilege meeting you, Your

Highness. Perhaps you can stop by our restaurant one day. It would mean the world to us."

*Translation: It would be great marketing if you filmed an endorsing clip for social media.*

Emmeline smiled and nodded, giving the woman a small wave as she ushered her daughter back up the shoreline. Clearly they weren't the biggest fans of the monarchy, but still the woman came down here, swallowed her pride, and advocated for her family's benefit.

Emmeline had to admire the woman's hustle. She pocketed the business card and turned to Cliff. "I'm ready to head back. Call the car."

No texts, no DMs, no calls, no emails—nothing.

It seemed every time Emmeline checked her phone a chip of her heart would break off. It was nothing new, considering the last lonely semester, but still. She hadn't gotten used to it.

With a disgusted sigh, she threw her cell back on the bed. It bounced off the mountain of throw pillows the staff insisted on staging every morning while Emmeline was taking a shower. If she had it *her* way, she'd kick them all off and have the bed an unmade chaotic nest so at any moment, she could burrow into the gigantic comforter and five-hundred-count Egyptian cotton sheets and never leave.

"Your Highness?" Camille asked meekly behind her.

"Yes?" Emmeline answered without turning around, seriously debating crawling back into her bed.

"Would you like us to pack the Celine blazer and wide pants?"

"Were those on my list?"

"N-no, Your Highness. But Georgianna—"

A flare of anger coiled and sparked in Emmeline's gut at the gall her mother had to use her personal secretary, Georgianna, to send *her* maids orders.

"Does Georgianna dress me?" Her voice was dangerously cold.

She felt Camille back away behind her. "No, Your Highness. We will stick to the list."

Immediately, Emmeline felt bad about snapping at Camille and the rest of the maids that were assigned to her quarters. But she was tired of her mother dressing her up like a doll. At first, Emmeline had hoped that Lady Chloe's obsession over her daughter's appearance was how she showed affection. Unfortunately, she quickly learned that the extent of her mother's love was skin-deep. Literally.

Forcing Emmeline into Chloe's own styles, her own preferences, without caring to find out what Emmeline *already* liked... the audacity of it made her claws unfurl.

And they were already out. Waiting to shred someone—anyone—to pieces.

Well, no, not anyone. One in particular.

Sadie Aurelia had ruined Emmeline's life. Not just by taking away her crown but by obliterating her friendships. Oakley, Danica... Oliver.

Emmeline snatched up her phone again and scrolled to the last messages she'd had with them. It was her own form of punishment, the way she constantly reminded herself of her social obsoletion.

The last text from Oakley, nine months old, read: **Something came up at home and I have to jet out early. Ace job with Hibernia, girl! It was a real ripper! XOXOXXXX.**

The night of Hibernia burned through Emmeline's mind, and she pressed her phone to her forehead, like the memory physically caused pain. The worst night of her life. All that she'd worked for, all that she'd *done*, not just to make ATA's traditional winter ball a success but for her whole *life*—came crashing down in just a few seconds.

And in eight months, she hadn't managed to build herself back up.

The words from her grandfather still haunted her.

*"Sadie Aurelia has proven to be just the young leader I was looking for. I am pleased to announce her as Ashland's heir apparent."*

Emmeline would never forget how she'd felt in that moment. When her eminence in the Eldana family slipped through her fingers. The crown should've been hers. No one deserved it more, no one cared as much as she'd cared, achieved what she'd done, sacrificed what she had.

With a sigh, Emmeline navigated to her last text string with Oliver. **Thanks again for suggesting me to the committee. You're a true friend. Good luck tonight!**

And then ice-cold silence. When she returned for the second semester, Oakley, Danica, and Oliver all refused to even acknowledge her existence.

It made sense. There was no going back from what she'd done to Sadie.

Oakley was a really good person, with a strong moral compass, and she had abhorred Emmeline's actions.

The fight that came when Oakley found out

what Emmeline had done over winter break and then returned to their dorm the following semester had been...brutal. Every so often Emmeline would replay it in her mind, like an endless hell loop, which she could feel herself slipping into now.

"Is it all true?" Oakley had asked, her expression like carved stone.

There was a part of Emmeline that wanted to play dumb and lie, lie, lie. But, as terrible as this was going to be, a small part of her was...relieved. She would no longer live in fear of Oakley finding out who she really was anymore.

"Yeah. Probably."

Oakley had stared at her. "Probably? What does that mean?"

"It means," Emmeline said, just as sharply, "I don't know what she told you and I don't know how she told you. She could've exaggerated and played the victim, or she might've told you exactly how it went down. Probably either way, you'll be pissed."

"She is the victim, Emmeline. You burned her father's journal!"

Was that what Sadie was most upset with? What about Titus or Trang? It was just a journal. Emmeline didn't have a single thing from her parents so she *wasn't sure she could understand the sentiment—and maybe she was a little jealous of that.*

Emmeline nodded. "And what else?"

"You stole her laptop."

"She can't prove that, but, fine, yes I did."

"What the hell, Emmeline!" Oakley gasped. "This is Calixa-level poisonous. Have I been friends with a heartless bitch this whole time?"

Emmeline threw up her hands. "Yeah, I guess so, Oak! Does that ruin the perfect moral version of yourself? That you were friends with an evil bitch who stepped on others to get what she wanted? Well, you have the luxury of having a loving family and a clear path on what you're going to do with your life. Good for you. It's easy to see the world in black and white when you know who you are. But I am NOTHING to my family if I am not the best. Do you understand that ninety-nine percent of the time, my parents forget I even exist? What do you want me to say, Oakley? That I don't care about that? Well I do! I care. I care so much I am willing to crush that girl and my own cousins to finally be seen. To finally be LOVED."

Emmeline hadn't realized she was now nearly screaming at this point. That tears were in her eyes and her voice was cracking.

Oakley stared back at her, eyes so wide Emmeline

*could see the white all around her irises. For a long moment, the two girls said nothing. Oakley dropped her head, and after a couple of minutes, she looked back up, shiny tear tracks down her pretty brown cheeks.*

*"I loved you, Emmeline."*

*Loved.*

*It took everything in Emmeline not to let tears fall. There weren't any words left. She couldn't allow herself to apologize or offer remorse for what she'd done. She wasn't defending her actions or claiming that they had been good, but they had been what she'd chosen to do.*

*When the silence lasted too long, Emmeline knew what she was conveying, without saying it out loud.*

*Your love wasn't enough.*

*Oakley seemed to hear those unspoken words, too, because she took a deep breath and shook her head. "There's something... wrong with you, Emmeline. Something broken. And until you figure it out, don't talk to me. Or Danica. I don't want you hurting us again."*

"Your Highness?"

Emmeline was yanked from the memory she had relived a hundred times in the last eight months. She had purposefully avoided Oliver at all costs, so she had no awful memory to revisit with him. Thankfully. That might *truly* break her.

Camille had another piece of clothing out to pack that Emmeline had not approved—surely the work of her mother—and Emmeline merely sighed.

"Pack whatever, Camille. I don't care."

Actually, she cared far too much. But she was still relieved that at least Lady Chloe hadn't entirely forgotten her existence. Maybe wardrobe control was the best parenting Emmeline could hope for.

Emmeline hated how pathetic that was. But, if she was going to be pathetic, might as well lean into it. Today was her last day in Ashland and they were catching the flight out to Toulon tomorrow morning. Her mother was shopping in Amsterdam, but her father was home.

"Finish without me, Camille. I'm going to say goodbye to my father."

Camille straightened, arms full of Emmeline's blouses. "Right... right now, Your Highness?"

"Yes," Emmeline said, slipping on her shoes.

"Maybe you should wait until tomorrow morning."

Tomorrow morning, he would likely be gone

again. She knew he was home because of a cricket match he'd wanted to attend this afternoon. Now might be the only time she had.

Annoyed at being forced to confront that her father had so little time for her, she snapped back to Camille, "Maybe you should finish packing."

Finding Prince Frederick's tower was not very hard. She'd memorized the path to her parents' rooms the first time she'd come to Heres last year during the fall break. Just in case she worked up enough courage to go meet them. Or if they showed even the slightest bit of interest in her.

This was her first time actually making the trek.

The sitting room of the tower, done in a half-moon that held two doors to her parents' suites, consisted of a fancy couch that did *not* look comfortable to sit on, a coffee table with a vase of flowers, and several marble statues of Viking-looking sailors.

Emmeline scoffed at the idea of her father ever taking up a sword like the stone guardians of his tower. Without knocking, she passed through the right door. It was unlocked and her feet were silent across the carpet of the living area. Another couch, looking just as uncomfortable and ornate, a massive desk that seemed entirely untouched—the whole scene reminded Emmeline of one of those staged period rooms, frozen in time, that tourists view in castles and manors.

She bet her father lived his real life in a stylish apartment in Paris or... God, don't let it be Manhattan. If he'd been just twenty minutes away all her life... she did not want to know. Did not want to destroy another piece of herself at the hand of her parents.

This looked fake and yet clearly, he slept here. She could hear voices coming from the bedroom.

Familiar voices.

Her father's and... Ilsa's. Ilsa Halvorsen, royal secretary to the heirs. A woman who was supposed to be at Emmeline's beck and call, and one of the king's many trusted staff.

Emmeline stopped breathing as she closed the final distance to the crack in the bedroom doors. Thank God her father was out of view, but she could see Ilsa... buttoning her blouse, her short blond curls wild and mussed. She was saying something as she bent over and grabbed her pencil skirt and shimmied into it, and Emmeline knew, *knew* that the strategic thing to do would be to listen. Learn. Use.

But. *But.*

Emmeline was going to be sick. Hoping her frenzied steps stayed as silent as before, Emmeline raced from the rooms, down the hall, and promptly threw up in the first potted plant she found.

It had been one thing to know. Another thing to witness. Her father wasn't just screwing a nameless maid or some model, but the staff member closest to Emmeline.

And she knew, *knew* that it wasn't about her. It was never about her. Never. Her father probably didn't even know what Ilsa *did*. She doubted he stuck around long enough in court to know. But somehow... that made it worse.

Emmeline wiped a shaky hand across her lips and stood, backing away from the variegated monstera.

*I'm not surprised. I'm not disappointed. I'm fine.*

She could repeat those words a thousand times and they still wouldn't even be remotely true. Revulsion burned inside her, as corrosive as the bile in the back of her throat.

*I should've listened to Camille.* How many of the staff knew?

Her maid had *known* and had tried to stop Emmeline. How public was it that her parents' marriage was a sham? Why was she working so hard for their approval when they didn't know the first thing about love, or even honor? Not that she knew much better.

Thoroughly disgusted, with herself and with her father, she turned on her heel to head back toward her suites. Leaving the ruined thousand-dollar-plant for someone else to find.

# 3

## SADIE

Sadie wondered if there was a way for her to sleep with her eyes open. If yes, surely she would've found it by now. With how long these advisory council meetings lasted, and how boring they tended to get, she'd had plenty of hours to practice. Luckily, she and Titus had developed a system. Whenever one of them started to feel like they were drifting off, the other would reach over and pinch, pinch, pinch.

This fail-safe elicited severe looks from the king (because it usually involved chair scrapings and loud gasps), but it was much better than snoring while Lord Dorren droned on for ninety-two minutes about a new tariff they were trying to enforce on the United States and Canada. Another ancient lord, ironically approaching age ninety-two himself, *had* fallen asleep and started snoring while Lord Dorren explained the reasoning behind his 15 percent tariff. Only then to have Leander immediately nix the proposition repeating, for the fiftieth time, that he had no interest in a trade war. Which was about the only economic policy that Sadie agreed on with her king.

Today, however, they were talking about something far less interesting: citizenship visas for wealthy investors.

*Who. Cares.* She wanted to scream. Put a dollar amount on it and call it a day! One million, great. Five million, brilliant. Just move on to something that really and truly affected the people struggling to pay grocery bills and cover medical costs.

There was a medical bill that she was desperately invested in sitting on their agenda—and that had been there for the last three council meetings. Somehow it always got bumped down the list.

"It is simple, Lord Sigfried, if the number is too high we miss losing out on those who could afford the lower price point."

"My dear good sir, the appeal of this is exclusivity. If anyone could pay a million dollars, why would they want it?"

Sadie seriously considered banging her head

on the table. Partially out of frustration for the man's insufferably loquacity, and also to wake herself up.

They had been in the advisory council meeting for four hours already with only two fifteen-minute breaks. Either these old crotchety men weren't drinking enough water, or they had catheters strapped to their calves. King Leander had left nine times already for some reason or another.

Titus reached over and drew something on her notepad. It was a fried egg.

Sadie glanced to her left, three chairs down the long shiny mahogany table.

Lord Silas Edgerton, or Lord Silent Eggfarts as she and Titus had secretly named him, was nodding off himself.

She snuck a glance at her fake boyfriend and tried to smother her smile.

He caught her gaze and returned it with a small wink before clearing his throat and sitting forward in his chair. "Excuse me, Lords, I wonder if I might call for a ten-minute recess?" Titus asked, rapping his knuckles on the table. Lord Silas snorted and jolted in his chair at the sound, and Sadie ducked her head to cover a laugh.

Lord Sigfried, the advisor on foreign trade,

frowned, but with a glance at his white-haired counterpart in foreign relations, he nodded. "Yes, I suppose we can take a short break."

The glorified stenographer paused in his typing, looking relieved at the interruption as he shook out his fingers and flexed his wrists. The young man was so detailed that his notes took on the format of a book, if that book was really, really boring.

Titus leaned back, giving Sadie a smirk. "You owe me on that one."

With a scoff, Sadie flipped her leather-bound notepad closed. "You did that for your benefit as much as mine." Though it was an unfortunate truth that the council accepted Titus's interruptions and calls for recess with much more grace than when Sadie asked. Her requests were met with nothing but eye rolls and judgment.

Oh, the misogyny was strong in this group, but Sadie tried to tell herself they were merely victims of their generation.

"I could've lasted at least another fifteen minutes," Titus muttered. "I was actually playing a game in my head."

"You mean counting how many times Lord Sigfried used the words *deficit reduction*?" Sadie guessed.

"Bingo." Titus shot her a finger gun and she laughed.

They had come a long way, she and Titus.

It was not exactly friendship, but maybe a tentative partnership. That was the best way Sadie could describe it.

Nine months ago, Sadie thought she'd hate him forever. Titus had been dating her just to get ahead in their heir-apparent competition, and he'd broken her heart by using her.

But being trapped in their fake relationship had forced her to work with him and slowly, very slowly, she had given up her anger. As much as she'd hated to admit it, she needed Titus's princely endorsement for the advisory council to accept her. As Leander had warned her, they had barely acknowledged Sadie in these meetings or when she shadowed the king. But with Titus by her side, they seemed to listen to her comments and answer her questions without rolling their eyes. As long as he was there, she was tolerated.

It did help that Titus seemed to get riled up on her behalf. More than once, he'd even stood up for her. But he was careful not to fight her battles *for* her. Instead, he gave her the strength to fight her own.

What did he get out of it? Sadie wasn't entirely sure. Perhaps he was simply happy to learn beside her, biding his time until Leander switched their titles. Titus as heir apparent, and Sadie as dutiful consort hoping to share in the responsibilities of ruling. Except it didn't feel that way exactly. Often his concern for her felt...genuine. Which was as frustrating as it was beguiling.

Their fake relationship had felt like a prison in the beginning and she still didn't like it, but Titus had spent many, many of their fake dates attempting to properly apologize for his hand in hurting her. She'd never once accepted his apologies, but she'd gotten to the point where she no longer wanted to hear them.

The truth was, the deeper she fell into her role as heir apparent, the more she realized that she would go to almost any lengths to remain first in line. If Titus had been as desperate as she was... well, she supposed she couldn't fault him for that.

And at times, when he held her in front of the cameras...she could almost imagine them before Hibernia. She could recall the stomach-swooping feeling as he leaned in to kiss her, and often she swore that she saw real tenderness when he looked at her.

He'd even, on more than one occasion, tried to convince her that this time it was *real*. That his feelings for her weren't some publicity stunt anymore. That he cared about her.

But Sadie would be a fool to believe him and she was *always* quick to put a cap on any of that, shutting him down anytime he even tried to mention actual feelings. She was getting better at compartmentalizing and found she was quite talented at shoving down thoughts or emotions that could hurt her.

Maybe she'd inherited the skill that day when the last piece of her parents burned into little flecks of ash. But that crucible of her past had only made her stronger. Like a phoenix, she had emerged from those ashes.

Because even without the express endorsement of Leander's advisory council, Sadie was crushing it with the press.

Ashland *adored* her. It was that simple. As one of them, she had risen to royal family status and then *surpassed* the blood heirs. She had over ten million followers on her social media platform and thanks to her passion for sea life, her favorite nonprofit, the Ashlandic Sea Mammal Conservation, had doubled its endowment in less than six months.

And yet... Leander kept treating her like she was a nuisance.

"What's that?" she asked Titus pointedly as she caught sight of his laptop screen. It was a dashboard full of graphs and statistical analysis that looked vaguely familiar. That's when she recognized the number at the top of the screen. "Is that last year's census data?"

Titus frowned, massaging his knuckles and fingers as he shifted from foot to foot behind his chair. Sadie had noticed he did that a lot. As much as he claimed he called breaks for both their benefits, she observed that he was more antsy than she was—by a lot. Not that his movements seemed anxious, per se. He always gave the appearance of being cool as a cucumber.

"It is... Don't you have it?"

Sadie's face heated. "If I did, do you think I'd be asking you what it was?" she snapped back.

It was moments like these that shook their very precariously balanced partnership. Moments where it was so obvious the powers that be were grooming Titus far more than they were grooming her.

Deeply frustrated, Sadie cast another look at the end of the table. Leander had left the advisory council session over twenty minutes before and hadn't returned.

"It's the last council meeting before we leave, Sadie," Titus started, reading her thoughts. *Meaning, don't give them a reason to hate you even more than they already do.*

"Thank you, Captain Obvious," Sadie muttered, hands clenching and unclenching on the arms of her conference room chair.

All summer, Sadie had waited for something more than endless meetings. She'd been promised to "shadow" the king. She was sure that if Titus, Emmeline, or even Alaric had been selected as heir apparent, King Leander would've had them by his side 24-7. Instead, Sadie was left to fester in these endless meetings while her king—her mentor, technically—was somewhere else, *actually* running the country.

His advisory council was just that: a council of advisors. They helped draft and debate and devise laws, but it was Leander who spoke them into existence, who signed the executive orders, who determined the fate of the country and its people. Plus, from what Sadie had seen, he rarely listened to them anyway.

"Look, I'm emailing it to you now," Titus said, bending over the table to forward the census data to her.

"Save it," Sadie said before grabbing her

Gucci blazer off the back of her chair and slipping it on.

Titus glanced at the empty council room, waiting for the old men to return to their seats. "I'll... think of a cover story for you, shall I?"

"Or you can tell them I don't give a shit what they think. Just like their king," she growled before she stormed out of the room, her ginger waves flying behind her.

Captain Kendrick bolted up from his desk chair, saluting Sadie as she strode into the antechamber of the king's inner sanctuary, the office that he hardly left most days.

"Good evening, Your Highness. Please wait a moment while I announce you."

"No need," Sadie said, continuing toward the door, faster than Kendrick could stop her. "I'll announce myself." She shoved the door open. "Princess Sadie Aurelia, heir apparent," she called out.

Leander looked up from writing something on his famous red leather notepad. More times than she could count, he would jot a memo on those pristine ecru pages and then lo and behold, a new policy would go into effect.

Slowly, he put down his fountain pen, his mouth flattening into a thin line.

"I'm so sorry, Your Majesty, she just—"

"It's all right, Kendrick. Leave us."

Captain Kendrick bowed low, and backed up, shutting the door behind Sadie.

"Something the matter, my dear?" King Leander asked.

"I was promised shadowing, Your Majesty," Sadie said, walking over to one of the chairs in front of his desk and plopping down. "Yet the only time I really see you is at ineffectual meetings you end up ditching."

He folded his hands on his desk, his steel eyes flashing. "What did you expect?"

Sadie stared at him. "Ex... Excuse me?"

"You forced my hand, Sadie. You were not my first choice, or even my third. And I have seen nothing remarkable from you since that night, nothing to persuade me to actually train you."

"That's because you haven't given me a *chance*—"

"You shouldn't need one," he said, gruffly. "Leaders makes their own luck."

Sadie's blood boiled. She could feel it simmering under the surface, staining her easily erubescent skin. But she said nothing in response, letting their tense silence stretch on until it bordered on uncomfortable.

A knock sounded at the door and Captain Kendrick popped his head back in. "Pardon the interruption, sir, Lord Erickson would like to see you."

Of course he did. Alaric's "father" always needed to talk to his king about *something*.

Leander glared at her, but Sadie didn't budge from her seat. With a sigh, he stood and nodded to the door, telling Kendrick, "I'll see him out in the hall."

It was a small victory, not being forced to leave, and she would take it. Crossing her arms, she waited as Leander stood from his desk and left his office to meet with his chief financial advisor outside.

For a minute, Sadie did absolutely nothing. She just sat there, stewing, wasting time as she waited on him yet again.

*Leaders make their own luck.*

Well... this could be a chance, couldn't it?

Quickly she ran it through the WWED test, the *What Would Emmeline Do* test. Emmeline had been the obvious choice for heir apparent before Sadie had turned the tables, so she assumed Emmeline and Leander were cut from the same cloth. Not to mention, mimicking Emmeline had helped her quickly master the etiquette required for Ashlandic Court. Because, as loath as Sadie was to admit it, being a princess came naturally to Emmeline.

With a glance at the door, Sadie quickly rose from her chair and circled behind the desk. She very much doubted there would be cameras installed anywhere in Leander's personal office. The man had five guards stationed at various points down the hall, and his chief secretary who waited on him was a military captain, for crying out loud. Video surveillance would be overkill, even for someone as paranoid as Leander Eldana. And she suspected he enjoyed his privacy.

Her gaze skimmed down the row of drawers. The first one was likely full of personal items like reading glasses and mints and letter openers and things like that. She reached for the second one.

Jackpot. It was a personal filing system, but with randomly coded labels like PEACEFUL and HORDE and GARDEN. If this was to delay intruders from knowing where to look—it was working. But she couldn't waste time trying to figure out what each label actually meant. She just had to make the most of this brief window. So she grabbed a handful of papers from each folder and spread them out on the desk. Heart pounding, she snapped a bunch of shaky pictures with her phone. Hopefully she'd be able to discern the contents later.

The muffled voices outside the door grew louder, followed by a hint of footsteps.

Sadie scooped up the documents, shoved them into their respective folders, closed the drawer, and fell back in her chair just as the door was opening.

"Now, where were we?" Leander muttered going back to his desk.

Sadie bestowed her prettiest, most Emmeline smile. "Giving me a chance, Your Majesty. Though…" She tapped the edge of her phone with those pictures within the pocket of her blazer. "I think you're right. I'd do best to make my own."

# 4

# TITUS

His phone dinged for the thirty-fourth time. Thirty-four text messages. Seventeen missed calls. This was borderline harassment. Could he get a restraining order against his parents without alerting the media? What were Ashland's laws regarding restraining orders?

Gritting his teeth, he finally slid open his messages and typed out: **I'm coming. The council meeting ran long.**

He was twenty minutes late, and it was for a very good reason. Unlike Sadie, he'd been forced to sit through the full session, waiting until Lord Eggfarts finished his rebuttal against Lord Cigarette's argument. One would think his mother would cut him some slack since this was all in service of *her* dreams.

But no, he was not heir apparent. He was a failure. A disappointment.

*And* he was broken, according to her.

Feet like lead, Titus made his way down the hall, nearing his parents' suites. He'd been here more times than he'd cared for, honestly. Anytime he was summoned to their rooms it was never for anything *good*. Not a "Well done at that court dinner, Titus. You charmed the pants off Lady Odora" or a "We're really impressed you memorized that entire speech for the children's hospital and kept going even though the teleprompter broke." What had they focused on instead?

His mistakes. Others' achievements. Sadie shined more brightly. Emmeline was more charming. Alaric commanded the room in a way he'd never be able to.

Finally, he reached his mother's door and entered without knocking. She'd fuss if he was polite—how dare he make her wait another two seconds when he should've been there half an hour ago?

As soon as he walked in, conversation stopped. Lady Calliope turned away from the two men by the window of her reception room and regarded her son with an arctic expression. But Titus didn't bother to deal with that, he was too busy staring at the men behind her.

Both of whom, unfortunately, he knew quite well.

"Titus," his mother said smoothly. "So you *are* alive."

He chose to ignore that barb.

"What are they doing here?" Titus asked, his gaze staying on the men in suits. Both were middle-aged, Caucasian, British men, though that's where the similarities ended. One was thicker around the middle with a glossy, rosy face and sandy hair; the other was taller, leaner, with a full beard, glasses, and dark hair.

Lady Calliope took a deep breath, her nostrils flaring with anger. He knew he sounded like a child, but in fairness he was being treated like one.

"Dr. Malcolm and Dr. Wallace are both here because I would like my own evaluation. I know you believe you have—"

She stumbled, actually stumbled on the words he'd used countless times over the last eight months. Oh, he'd talked to his mother plenty about his diagnosis while in Ashland during winter break, texted her whenever symptoms were especially bad at school, and then over the summer—whenever the opportunity presented itself, though it wasn't often—but she simply would not *listen*. Everything he told her, she dismissed. Just like every other time he'd expressed his own needs and wants.

"Rheumatoid arthritis," Titus said, striving to keep his voice level. He should be used to this. He'd had almost ten months of living with the diagnosis and another whole year prior dealing with her constant gaslighting. Frankly, her denial was often more exhausting than the RA itself—this constant self-doubt and hurt from his mother's heartlessness.

The only real support he'd received was from his doctor back at ATA, Dr. Sharrad. He'd been Titus's physician and, somehow, therapist, all rolled into one for almost a year. In addition to helping Titus determine the best medication regimen and dealing with the side effects of his steroids, Dr. Sharrad also *listened* to him. To his fears and worries about how this disease would take a toll not just on his body, but on his mind and will.

"Yes, that," Lady Calliope said with a roll of her eyes.

That tiny gesture alone was like a stab in his chest. Why didn't she care? Had Titus disappointed her so much so that she no longer had any love for him?

"But Dr. Malcolm has been your doctor since you were an infant. And Dr. Wallace is a highly renowned specialist in holistic medicine. I trust them far more than some hack at your school—"

Titus surged forward, his shoes treading across the plush carpet, one hand going up to stop her, as if he could not, *would* not, hear another word.

"Don't you dare, Mother. Don't you *bloody* dare. Dr. Sharrad is the first one who ever listened to me. I refuse to let you speak ill of him."

For the second time in his life, Titus registered shock on his mother's face. He knew she hadn't expected such defiance. Especially with an audience.

Most of his life he'd cowered under her sharp reprimands and thinly veiled insults about his ineptitude. It was likely a surprise to her that he had any backbone at all. To himself as well, honestly. Standing up to his parents was an entirely new concept for him. Telling his mother off at Hibernia had been the first time he'd ever even attempted such a thing.

There was a long moment of awkward silence. A beat where no one spoke and the doctors shifted nervously—the doctors whom Titus had come to despise for their constant dismissal of his symptoms, their belief that he was just a rich kid complaining, wanting Mummy and Daddy's attention.

"Darling," Lady Calliope began and the word startled Titus for a moment. She'd never used that to address him before. "Please, I only want to make sure that this...is real. What if you're stuffing your body with pharmaceuticals that could hurt you? Haven't you been having trouble with your stomach? What if it's been all for nothing? Don't you want more opinions before you're sure of such a thing?"

Maybe it was her tone—softer, placating, even...borderline gentle—that made Titus reconsider telling both of the doctors to shove off. Her words were painful, but he also...he also wanted to please her. He wished he didn't, but it was coded into his DNA. Following her orders, trying to be the perfect prince, it was ingrained in his subconscious. The instinct to obey was hard to fight.

When he got his RA diagnosis, he was scared and devastated, sure, but he was also *relieved*. Finally, there was an explanation for how he'd been feeling. Finally, someone was telling him, "It's not just in your head. You're not just making this up." He didn't want to go back to that.

But...he wanted to make her happy. He

wanted her to embrace him, smooth back his hair, and tell him they were going to figure this out. Together.

Bloody hell, he was tired.

Maybe, if she got her own assessment, and the diagnosis was the same, she'd finally accept it. Finally come around with the support he really, desperately, wanted.

Without a word, Titus took a seat and with a glance at the doctors, Lady Calliope followed suit, as did Dr. Malcolm and Dr. Wallace, until all four of them were at the table.

"I have an hour, then I have to pack," he said. Of course, she'd chosen to coerce him one day before they returned to Almus Terra. She'd had all summer to address this. But she was even better at deflecting than he was.

Lady Calliope nodded to the two doctors and Titus was then subjected to a long form of déjà vu. It was those useless appointments all over again, back in England before Almus Terra.

Their tone reminded Titus why he had doubted himself so much in the beginning. They asked him questions about his diet. About his activity—was he exercising enough? Eating right? They drew a blood sample that Titus didn't believe they would do anything with, and listened to his heart. They felt his hands, testing the heat of his inflamed joints, but declared they were no different than anyone else's. Because this was a *good* RA day, and Titus knew they'd never admit to such a thing anyway, he didn't fight them on it.

But as the questions went on, they became progressively more insulting, insinuating that maybe he was experiencing growing pains—because, why, look how tall he had gotten!

At last, Titus couldn't tolerate any more. With his fingers pressed against his eyelids, his shoulders hunched, Titus took one breath after another.

"I think we're done here," he said, his voice low.

"Far from it, I'm afraid," Dr. Malcolm said in his nasally voice. "During a weekend, you should take the ferry to Toulon and we can run a few tests at an actual hospital. I can get you in two weeks from—"

Titus stood, done with this. *So* done with this. "No."

His mother stood, too, her face flushing with anger. "Titus! If you want me to accept—"

"Accept *what*, Mum? Me?" he lashed back. "If you don't believe me, that's fine. If you don't want to accept the disease I have, fine. I can't make you. But if I have to hear one more time that if I just stick to a special diet or if I take these extra supplements or if I was just *patient* with my body, I'm going to lose it. So just let me deal with my illness on my own."

"On your own?" Lady Calliope scoffed. "Please, you have never done anything on your own. I don't agree with Lord Mikael's parenting choices, but at least *that* child learned some independence."

It was a low, unforgivable blow. For a moment, Titus couldn't do anything but stare back at her, disbelieving. Was she *really* comparing him to Alaric? Whose fault was it that Titus had never had independence? Whose fault was it that he lived under the weight of his parents' wishes, their own ambitions, and their very strict, insufferable orders?

Titus turned his back on her, literally, as he walked toward the door.

"Titus!" she snapped, her voice as close to breaking as he'd ever heard it.

He stared at the doorknob as he addressed the two doctors. "Dr. Malcolm, Dr. Wallace, thank you for coming. But I won't be seeing you ever again."

Titus shut the door on his mother's near-screech and walked calmly back down the hall. But to his incredulity, the sound of her heels followed him.

Unbelievable. He wasn't asking for much, just for her to stay out of this one facet of his life. Granted, it was huge, but he was managing fairly well.

He stopped when he felt her nails dig into his arm. "*Titus.*"

She pulled him into the study where she'd once thrown a teacup near his head.

"We're done talking, Mum," Titus said, the anger enough to strengthen him.

"We are *not* done talking. How dare you decide that? If you would only listen to reason, we wouldn't even be in this situation."

"*Me* listen to reason?"

"Do not interrupt me!" her voice jumped up an octave and Titus knew that if she had a piece of porcelain within reach to throw—she would.

"You are *young*, Titus. Barely seventeen."

"I am nineteen."

"Arthritis is an old person's disease. What you are going through—it's growing pains. Stress. Nothing more. If you'd just listen to Dr. Wallace, he has a strict regimen of dieting, exercise, and supplements that would alleviate all your...discomfort. I'm so tired of pandering to you, Titus, and I will not tolerate it anymore."

There were so many things wrong with what she'd just said, Titus's brain nearly short-circuited with a rage that he'd never experienced before.

Cold fury, fueled by the raw pain and devastation roaring inside him at his mother's insensitive, cruel words, made his next threat explode from his throat.

"Stop, Mother, *stop*. Leave this alone. If you try to insist one more time that I'm delusional and my pain isn't *real*, I am going to end this. End all of it."

Lady Calliope gazed back at him with equal amounts of rage. Like she wanted to reach out and strangle him with her acrylic nails. "End *what* exactly?"

"I will renounce my claim to the throne."

His mother stumbled back like she'd been physically struck, her eyes wide, her lips white. "You...you wouldn't."

"Try me," he whispered through gritted teeth. If this was his only leverage, the *only* way he could get his parents to leave him be, he'd use it. Despite his whole soul rebelling against it.

Because if there's one thing he'd learned

through these endless council meetings and study sessions about his country's infrastructure alongside Sadie, it was that Ashland was broken. His country needed help, and he truly believed he could be the one to help it.

Titus's threat was real, but it was hardly a gamble. His mother cared about seeing him on the throne more than anything else in her shallow world. She would cave.

Minutes passed before either spoke again, both of them breathing harshly.

"Very well, son," she said after a long moment. And once again, Titus recognized this was the first time she might've called him that. Ever. "Maybe it's best that we take a pause here. We can discuss this another time."

At that, she wrenched the door open and was gone. Without a goodbye or a "Good luck this semester." Nothing.

The moment the door clicked behind her, Titus slid his back against the wall and sank to the floor, ramming the heels of his hands into his eyes. They burned with the dwindling hope of ever having a mother who would love and support him unconditionally.

*Ha*, it was laughable he'd had any in the first place.

He may have won this battle, but he always lost with her. Always.

Ashland in the summer was surprisingly beautiful. Because of its northern climate and the rocky terrain off the coast, most of the year was dreary, cold, and wet, which wasn't something that Titus particularly disliked. Indeed, Ashlandic climate matched his personality quite well. But he couldn't dismiss the appeal of the stunning green hills and flowering fauna of the late-August day as a backdrop on their way to the Durah airport.

His companion in the back seat, however, wasn't partaking in the views. Sadie was staring at the tablet in her lap so hard it was like she was trying to turn it to stone. He supposed she'd lived through seventeen Ashlandic summers. It wasn't like she needed to marvel at it again.

"Any new takeaways?" Titus asked as she swiped through to the next dashboard page of the census data.

The census was an incredibly important element involved in governing a nation, since it determined not just how many people lived in the country, but also how to best allocate funds, like where to build hospitals or schools, and the laundry list of other ways for a government to care for its citizens.

"Only that the population is growing older and needing the pensions they get from the government while the people young enough to work, who actually need to lift up the economy, can't pay their bills because—" She stopped, taking a deep breath and glancing out the window.

There was a long, long moment as the car rolled by on the highway that definitely needed repaving. Titus was sure they'd hit at least five potholes in the span of their ten-mile drive.

"What are we doing?" Sadie said softly.

With her face turned toward the window he wasn't entirely sure he'd heard what she said.

"What?"

"It...fixing all this feels impossible. I'm not saying Leander has done a bad job. He's been more stable than anyone else in our entire history but there's still so much and we're not even out of school."

"Sadie, he's not going to die tomorrow. We have plenty of time to learn how to run a country." Though, even to his own ears, "how to run a country" sounded absolutely delusional.

At that, she glanced over at him and her scowl deepened. "Why are you smiling?"

Was he?

There was a part of him that warmed at her words. She'd said *we*. He wondered, rather, he *hoped* that she meant the two of them together.

He shrugged. "You said *we*."

Sadie narrowed her eyes at him. Then, to his surprise, she clicked off the tablet and turned fully toward him in her seat.

"You know we're not going to be in this fake relationship much longer, Titus."

He ignored the bite of pain in his chest at her words and slowly massaged his knuckles, a healthy habit he'd started doing to help his arthritic joints. "The council doesn't seem to have warmed up to you any degree over the summer, Sadie."

"Lately, your presence isn't exactly helping me. They are tolerating me and *grooming* you."

He couldn't exactly argue with that.

"Tell me how to fix it. I am open to your suggestions," he said with a sigh.

"Don't worry about me. I'll figure something out," she snapped.

"Sadie...," he said, dropping his cheek on his fist as he rested his elbow on the car door, preparing for the argument they'd had about a dozen times. "I know you don't believe me, but I really do care for you—"

"I do believe you."

He paused, looking over at her, and she was staring back at him, but her expression wasn't as haughty or as shuttered as before.

"I think I do anyway. So, kiss me. Now. Without anyone watching. Just for us."

Titus lifted his head, staring at her. He couldn't tell if she was serious or not.

She closed her eyes. As if to say, yes, she was.

With a frown, Titus regarded her, not sure what she was trying to prove. The only time they'd ever even touched, outside of the pinches in council meetings, was in front of cameras or their classmates. Other than the king, and perhaps Emmeline considering how she'd been the one to orchestrate Titus breaking Sadie's heart, no one else knew they weren't real. They had been very convincing.

Titus was good at turning on the charm and faking their happiness as a loving couple, though he wasn't sure what that said about him.

Now was his chance to prove that he wasn't faking. That *his* feelings, at least, were real.

Hope in his chest, he leaned in to cup her

face, his large hand warm and gentle on her skin. So close he could count the freckles on her nose, the number of eyelashes across her cheek. She was beautiful and...tense.

Her lips seemed to tremble, her shoulders and posture rigid, her eyes squeezed shut.

That wasn't anticipation for a kiss. That was dread.

Gut twisting with a mix of disappointment and revulsion, Titus dropped his hand and sat back. Every time he kissed her...she didn't want it.

Sadie was right.

This couldn't continue.

He couldn't keep putting himself through this torture of being with her but knowing she was never going to feel the same. Now that he felt that final nail in their relationship coffin, part of him wanted to call it off this minute.

Instead, he returned his gaze to the window. "You tell me when you want to end it, and we'll end it."

He owed her that at least. The fact was...he'd hurt her. Deeply. It had been arrogant to think her feelings would be so easy to change.

He didn't look at her for the rest of the car ride.

# 5

# EMMELINE

Yellow. So much yellow.

It was Emmeline's least favorite color, but she had to admit, she missed the sunny yellow of the mimosa flower. It was out of season now, but in the springtime, this mimosa grove had been alight with beauty, so breathtaking against the horizon where blue sky met teal ocean. Even a bit ethereal.

Emmeline knew her plants fairly well, and had purposefully sought out the vibrant mimosa shrub, this signature flower of the French Riviera, last March to calm her inner turmoil. Once native to Australia and brought over by English nobility in the late nineteenth century, the plant thrived in the rich soil and the temperate climate. Emmeline had even heard of certain French cities holding festivals in honor of the blooms.

They were an odd flower, clumped like

wisteria, but each tiny blossom more like a puff ball of minuscule petals. She wished she could stroke the satin-smooth texture and immerse herself in the fragrant, sunny yellow atmosphere now.

Sensory therapy. That's what she needed.

Seeing Oakley's name on her dorm door had sent her into a downward spiral of dread and complete panic. She couldn't go through another semester of silent treatment and angry glares like the last one. After Hibernia, her dorm life had been hell.

Living in such close proximity with three people who hated her? Maybe the old Emmeline could, but after her friendship with Oakley in those first few months at Almus Terra? She'd known what it was like to have real friends. To be cared for and... loved.

Staying in the same room where that very person now hated her guts? It was too painful.

Without thinking, Emmeline had bolted from the castle corridor, weaving her way in and out of incoming students finding their dorms and meeting their new roommates. She headed for the edge of Almus Terra, where she knew this mimosa grove had existed and tried to... breathe. And concoct a plan B.

She could talk to the administration. Surely it wasn't too late to change dorm rooms. No doubt Oakley would have the same issues, and Trang, and Sadie for that matter. After all, King Leander wasn't judging her anymore. She had failed him. He likely wouldn't care where she lived in reference to the heir apparent.

With that upsetting thought, Emmeline spun on her heel and stepped out onto the path, and right into a solid wall. Pain exploded in her nose, up her sinus cavity, and across her cheeks as she stumbled backward.

The wall moved with her, grabbing her around the shoulders before she could fall into the trees.

"Emmeline!"

The voice was deep. Deep and rich and familiar. Cupping her hands around her throbbing nose, she blinked and raised her gaze up the white cotton shirt across the dark-brown-skinned collarbone and throat to gorgeous, soft, intelligent eyes behind thick framed lenses.

"Oliver." It came out in a whisper across her lips and she hated how weak she sounded—saying his name.

His large hand had wrapped around her arm to steady her when she'd bumped into him, and she felt his gentle grip like he was holding her heart. She hadn't felt *anyone*'s touch in months. She glanced down at his hand on her arm and he quickly removed it.

But his thumb had swept over skin so purposefully that the sensation stayed there.

"Are you okay? I didn't even see you—why are you stepping out of the trees like that?" His brow furrowed as he scanned her face and then moved down her body. But not in a hot way, more like a concerned way. Not that she deserved his attraction, Emmeline reminded herself, much less his concern.

It was a little selfish, but she let herself take *him* in too. His raglan T-shirt was white with a navy neckline, and his favorite pair of Air Jordans stuck out from the hem of light wash jeans settled on a narrow waist. He wore a bomber jacket, and his hair was done in his usual style of twists but shaved on the sides.

He was so casual and attractive, it made Emmeline's heart beat double time. It didn't help that his scent was as she remembered it, like warm, damp earth, mixed with fabric softener.

Perhaps it was because she'd met him in the greenhouses, but she'd always associated Oliver with the gardens and flowers she loved so much. Full of sun, beauty, and with the potential to grow.

Unfortunately, she was more like a weed. Unwanted.

"I was—admiring the sea," she mumbled, looking down at the space between them, which wasn't much.

She sounded so foolish! The Mediterranean was hard to miss almost anywhere from the castle. But she'd sound even weirder if she told him she was *imagining flowers*.

"Oh, sure. It's..." He stopped for a very long time, his expression troubled. He was staring at her like he was trying to find words. Kind words, because Oliver was kind. He likely even wanted to try to put the past behind them. Or maybe he was thinking of a way to be polite without being *too* nice. So as not to give her false hope that he'd forgiven the horrible things she'd done.

So she wouldn't think she still had a chance with him.

"...pretty," he finally finished after the most awkward pause of all time.

*I can't do this.*

"I have to go," Emmeline dodged around him. Oliver was tall enough that she could just duck under his elbow. With a flip of her hair, she strode up the path, toward the castle ramparts, praying he did not follow.

Her heartbeat slowed when she didn't hear footsteps behind her.

She was so stupid to come here. Especially when there were no flowers to even take comfort in. It was right by the greenhouses, and she knew how he loved to visit them and work. Had her subconscious chosen this place on purpose just to catch a glimpse of him?

Well, mission accomplished. Was it not enough that her self-loathing made it hard to look in a mirror, she had to torture herself too by seeking out what she obviously couldn't have?

She feared the answer to *that* question.

The administration offices were packed. A rare occurrence considering the school was so well run. But on the first day they were full of students asking about class schedules, Elite or C-Suite privileges, scholarship details, and half of them complaining about the maximum five-suitcases rule. Emmeline had argued about that one too.

A frazzled Mrs. Khalid glanced up at Emmeline from her computer. "Yes, Emmeline, we received your request for a dorm switch."

Emmeline resisted the urge to say *And?* Attitude would not help in this scenario.

"But the headmistress denied your request."

For a second, Emmeline thought she'd heard wrong. Unfortunately, Mrs. Khalid kept on typing, then looked past Emmeline as if to summon the next student in line. Conversation over.

"But... but why?" Emmeline finally said. That didn't even make sense. Why would the headmistress take a personal interest in something as petty as a dorm room change?

"You'd have to ask her, dear," Mrs. Khalid said, though not unkindly. She was a nice older woman in a hijab, and Emmeline had always thought she had a comforting grandmotherly aura about her.

Emmeline wondered if asking was even an option, then... *ugh*, when had she become so docile? Being demure was overrated. Not so long ago, nothing had stood in her way.

Self-reflection would get her nowhere, but as she took the stairs to the corridor that led to the headmistress's tower, she couldn't help but admit that she was now fueled by sheer desperation. So here she was, barging into the headmistress's office unannounced, desperate for another dorm. For roommates who didn't hate her guts.

Who she saw down the length of the hall, sitting at the bottom of the headmistress's staircase, however, almost made her turn right back around.

Oakley looked up from her phone as Emmeline's clicking heels echoed down the corridor toward her. Immediately, she made *the face*.

Emmeline had gotten Oakley's disgusted face more times than she cared to count last semester. At some point, she got it twice, almost three times a day.

Ignoring the rip in her heart, Emmeline started up the stairs. But Oakley's arm shot out right in front of her shins, nearly tripping her.

"Oy, what do you think I'm doing just sitting here? I'm waiting for Headmistress Aquila. Get in line," Oakley snapped.

"I see that," Emmeline said. *Not demure.* "Just figured I outrank you."

Oakley's eyes narrowed to slits. "Wow. Wooooow. You are a piece of work, Emmeline."

Emmeline. Not Emmie.

It was sad how much that actually hurt. The nickname she'd always thought she'd hate would now never be used by her favorite person on the planet. Because as cold as Oakley was now, Emmeline still loved her former best friend.

Oakley hadn't been the one to do wrong. Emmeline had. And yet, the only defense she had to Oakley's caustic remarks was her own nastiness. She didn't know how to fight fire with anything other than... fire.

"Someone is in her office." Oakley turned her attention back to her phone. "You can't go up yet."

"Maybe it's another student whose dorm room request she ignored," Emmeline muttered, folding her arms and leaning against the staircase wall.

Oakley snorted. "Why do you think I'm here?"

"Why do you think we're *both* here?" Emmeline hissed back.

"You know, I pity your next roommate. Hopefully you won't burn any of *their* shit," Oakley fired off.

Emmeline pushed off the wall, face heating with what she would never admit to as shame. "I did what I had to do."

"That is such—"

The door suddenly opened above them, heavy and loud, echoing down the stairs with a sharp creak followed by two sets of footsteps.

Oakley moved out of the way as an older man in one of the most expensive suits Emmeline had ever seen came down the stairs—and Emmeline had seen a lot of high-end suits.

He was likely in his late sixties, with graying dark hair, brown eyes, a clean-shaven jaw, and a rather forgettable face.

Yet he had the countenance of a *someone*.

Headmistress Aquila was right behind him, and when she saw Oakley and Emmeline she rolled her eyes.

The man turned back to the headmistress and gave her an amicable smile. "It appears as though you have students who need you. I can find my way out, Headmistress. Thank you for seeing me."

Headmistress Aquila shook his extended hand. "Thank you for coming all this way, Mr. Croft."

"Of course. There is nothing I wouldn't do for Almus Terra. Good luck this year, ladies," he said, shooting Emmeline and Oakley a small smile. Oakley did not smile back, eyeing him with wariness as he disappeared down the next staircase.

Croft...Emmeline knew that name. He'd been in the news for a long time, sporadically. Some infamous billionaire with huge companies spanning multiple industries. If she remembered correctly, he was a big player in energy, media, and tech.

But why was he here? Emmeline would've remembered if he had a kid at ATA. Or maybe one was just starting? Except...she didn't even remember hearing if he had any children.

"All right, I am going to save time and answer both of you at once," the headmistress began and Emmeline could already feel her stomach sinking.

"Headmistress—" Oakley started.

"I am *talking*, Ms. Strider. Your requests to change dorms are denied. And it truly boggles the mind how you'd endeavor to reverse my decision."

With that, she turned to head back up to her office.

"Is this a punishment, Headmistress?" Emmeline asked.

Long braids swinging, Headmistress Aquila spun back around to face her students. "Do you two not understand what this school is *for*? This is not just a fancy boarding school. We are here to build relationships, to understand and empathize with people from all kinds of cultures and backgrounds and of all beliefs. I have no interest in the path of least resistance. If I must, I will disregard the wishes of my students in pursuit of this school's true mission."

"This isn't about global peace, ma'am! Emmeline is just a bitch!" Oakley exploded.

Emmeline felt like melting to the floor.

"Ms. Strider!" Headmistress Aquila's voice was close to a growl. "You are *both* poised to achieve great things and surely there is a lesson in diplomacy to learn here. I will be damned if I let you take the easy way out. Now, make it work. You are not *children* anymore, and I will not put you two in different playpens."

That shut Oakley up. Her hands flexed at her sides, balling into fists as she about-faced and power walked down the corridor.

Meanwhile, Emmeline wondered if her new life as a slime would be better suited for the castle dungeon.

# 6

## ALARIC

Alaric sneezed for the fifth time. There had to be something he was mildly allergic to in here. Not very surprising, considering they were in the greenhouses, basically an organized jungle.

"Feckin hell, Oliver," he muttered, then, like an old man, pulled out a handkerchief from his pocket and blew his nose. He now had to use his sleeve to wipe the sweat glistening on his brow from the heat and humidity levels carefully monitored by the student botanists. "Why don't yeh sit in the library like a normal lad?"

Oliver kept his gaze on his laptop. "It's brighter out here. I like it."

"It's hot as hell."

He shrugged. "My grandparents are from Louisiana, down in the southern states. Feels like home."

"I think I need gills to properly suspire," Alaric coughed dramatically. "Do people from the swamp come with gills?"

"Shut up and go away."

Alaric grinned, pleased that he'd finally managed to elicit a snarky response. It was a feat when talking to Oliver Jackson. The guy was *too* nice. He'd come to learn that over the last semester, as Oliver spent more time with Jacob and some of Alaric's other Scholar friends.

"I would, but yeh haven't done what I asked yet."

Oliver stopped typing and frowned. "For the last time, I'm not a hacker."

"Well, yeh can do... things," Alaric muttered. Like Emmeline, Alaric had deduced that Oliver had something to do with what happened at Hibernia and Sadie becoming heir apparent. Neither Sadie nor Oliver had explained what, exactly, had gone down but he remembered Sadie barging into that meeting of all the global leaders like a force of nature.

He still had so many questions about that night. How she'd stormed up to those closed doors like she was about to unleash pestilence and plagues. She must've done *something* biblical because the next minute, she was being named heir apparent by Ashland's king in an announcement that was very clearly unplanned.

He had questions about how she'd pulled it off. But he had *more* questions about what had caused the depth of pain in her eyes. Hurt was there, in her gaze, blazing like an inferno as she'd charged toward him, Oliver right behind her.

Alaric had suspected that Oliver had been there because of the portal he'd created. Something to do with his software coding genius. Which was also why he'd now come to Oliver for help to hack his way through some of his father's nearly impenetrable files. It had taken Alaric the better part of an entire night to get even halfway through opening one. He was beginning to think he'd graduate before successfully opening them all.

"Yeah, I can do lots of things," Oliver said with a smirk. "I'm just not a hacker."

*Well*, Alaric thought as he wiped his sweating brow with his sleeve again, *on to plan B*.

The first week of the new semester reminded Alaric why he'd stayed in the succession race to begin with. His classes were fascinating and even through his limited perspective, he recognized this was probably the best education a young adult could receive. In the world.

Courses like International Econ 200 and Epistemology 101 kept him reading late into the night. They were so far beyond anything he could get at a normal high school that he'd considered attempting to get a scholarship, like the rest of the Scholars, to stay on at ATA rather than participate in his grandfather's demented competition.

That, of course, had changed when he'd gotten to know his "father." Now he wanted to ensure that man—that monster—lived to see the bastard child he hated so much on the throne he so adored. Alaric knew it wasn't the noblest cause, but he couldn't bring himself to care that his motivations were shitty. It wasn't like he was inherently a good person anyway. He'd read enough David Hume and Immanuel Kant to know as much.

That self-deprecation was reinforced every time he saw Titus and Sadie together. Morally speaking, if he was a good person, he wouldn't feel like pounding his cousin into the ground like a Neanderthal every time they sat together at meals or walked to class holding hands. He wanted not to care. Wanted to ignore them entirely, but it was hard when every flash of gingery red hair in the corner of his eye had him glancing in Sadie's direction.

It was a moment like that, cutting through the bailey, on his way to his Cyber Security class, that had him wondering when he'd be able to move past this awful feeling. This inexplicable... *crush*.

He should be numb to it by now. It had been months of seeing them together. But every time, somehow it got *worse*.

Sadie sat on one of the stone benches under the apricot trees. Her hair was down today, long and silky, twisting into a slight curl at the ends. She had a heavy textbook on her thighs and a bag of crisps in her hand.

For one very stupid moment, Alaric considered stopping. Considered asking her how her classes were going. Considered asking her what Oliver had done for her. Even if they never talked and it would be awkward and strange.

Before he could stop it, his feet switched direction, taking him toward her. Three feet away, a shoulder brushed his. It wasn't hard, or forceful, but it was there. Like a warning.

Titus overtook Alaric's strides and stopped in front of Sadie, handing her a Frappuccino with whipped cream. She looked up at her boyfriend and gave him a pretty smile, tilting her neck back to kiss him on the cheek.

He'd seen such tenderness many, many times. Never got easier.

As Sadie leaned forward to lick at the whipped cream oozing from the lid, her gaze snagged with Alaric's. It was only a second, maybe two, but staring into her hazel eyes felt like much longer.

The last *real* conversation they'd had might have been the night where she'd gotten tipsy and he'd told her he didn't believe in her.

He'd said it because he was a selfish, awful person. He'd told her not what would lift her up, but what would tear her down. To dash her hopes of becoming one of these elites who were corrupt—evil and cutthroat. He'd wanted her to stay exactly who she was.

Yet she'd done the exact opposite of what he'd wanted. She'd changed.

Alaric didn't judge her for it. Nor was he disappointed. But it didn't stop him from mourning. Something had happened to her, and he hadn't—

Frustration, hot and swift, sparked through him for just standing there like an idiot. Thinking about her still. He tore his gaze away and turned back in the direction he'd been heading. Toward coding languages and encryptions. Away from heartbreak and regrets.

* * *

Unlike most classes, Cyber Security didn't have many lectures. Students were expected to study the tutorials available, learn the skills, and, then, during class, fend off attacks made by the professor in real time.

Currently, they were studying code-injection attacks, and Alaric was still twenty hours away from mastering SQL injections. After a full hour surrounded by clacking keys, his eyes were blurring from manually scanning his code for database vulnerabilities. So he didn't think much of clicking on a file sent to him privately from the class's message board.

Too late he realized his mistake.

He shot up in his seat, blinking rapidly. They had yet to cover Remote Access Trojans, known in the cyber security world as RATs, so it was extremely unlikely that his professor was testing him randomly. He'd never known a teacher to deviate from the curriculum, especially not for one individual student. Besides, Ms. Reyburn didn't exactly play favorites.

Alaric let out a string of expletives under his breath as his screen started flipping open with files and logins. How could he not have recognized a phishing scam—in a cyber security class of all things? RATs were basically files of malware and once they were downloaded it gave the hacker backdoor access to the computer's private network.

True experts in the world of cyber security are coders themselves—hackers that learn the systems and languages so well they can test and retest for vulnerabilities. But downloading malware wasn't a strategy he'd been learning, and he could only watch, helpless, as the RAT secured direct connectivity with the hacker's command-and-control center via a predefined open TCP port. The transmission control protocol—or TCP—worked with the internet protocol—IP—to pass the data through the network, the first dictating the order of delivery, and the other its transmission.

So, yeah, Alaric knew how they worked—for the most part—but how to stop one? Not exactly. He'd spent all of last semester learning how to bypass a login screen and get into his father's computer. He wasn't on this level yet.

Annoyed, Alaric glanced up discreetly from his computer. The hacker had to be in *this* class. The RAT file had come from the message board, after all. Unless, of course, they'd hacked into that too. But that was unlikely. Nothing got into these servers without their teacher's admittance.

All the students had their heads down, seemingly engrossed in their assignments.

Unfortunately, all his antivirus software would only help with prevention, not deletion of the RAT. Curling his fingers into his unruly waves, Alaric considered trying to quickly get an intrusion-detection tool going. It could automate some of the RAT's removal since it detects trojan packets within a computer's network.

But all of his truly important data and logins were well protected with multifactored authentication. If the hacker wanted to get into his email, or cloud, they'd need access to his phone to enter his security code.

More than anything, he was… curious. Who would attempt to hack his computer? More importantly, what was their purpose? Remotely accessing his computer reflected the qualities of a narcissist, not the desperation of a thief.

Sure enough, a message popped up on his screen, unprompted.

**HEY, HANDSOME**

Despite himself, Alaric smirked. Not at the compliment, but at the gif that followed. A cartoon Harley Quinn blowing a kiss at Batman.

Alaric waited a long few minutes, and when he realized the hacker was waiting for his reply, he typed out:

**BATMAN WOULD NEVER GET HACKED BY HARLEY QUINN**

The reply was immediate.

**WHO THE HELL SAYS YOU'RE BATMAN? CLEARLY...**

Instantly another gif popped up. This time, one from Christopher Nolan's *Batman Begins* movie with Christian Bale saying the iconic line "I'm Batman." Alaric snorted and typed back.

**CONGRATS, YOU'RE THE HERO WHO CAN'T TURN THEIR HEAD PROPERLY.**

Next, a Joker gif popped up. The old cartoon one that the legendary Mark Hamill voiced for years.

He avoided responding while he thought through his options. The hacker kept going though. Twenty minutes went by and they'd already sent a barrage of messages about who would win in a fight: Elsa of Arendelle or Jack Frost? Plot twist: enemies to lovers.

This hacker was pretty playful, so Alaric decided to lean into it. Flexing his fingers, knuckles cracking, he opened his incognito browsing window, hoping the hacker would think him that ignorant. Then he started digging into his old social media accounts, Reddit, Tumblr, TikTok. He had them (because Ilsa made him have "an online presence"), but he rarely used any. The notifications and tagging and comments had been overwhelming once he'd been revealed as one of Ashland's princes. So he'd let the accounts passively exist but deleted them from his phone.

He'd been wise enough to throw up some protection so the hacker couldn't *easily* gain access to them (though, of course, it was possible) and went about laying his breadcrumbs.

Where the hacker was unaware they were going was to a site from the early 2000s that his mate Kyle sent him a few years ago over Discord as a gag, covered by a carefully disguised URL. Once clicked, the site blasted a dumb American song called "Cotton Eye Joe"—the sped-up version that sounded like it was sung by hamsters.

He planted redirects of the URL carefully

among his accounts, so it would increase the chances of the hacker stumbling across it. Then he waited with bated breath.

He didn't have to wait long.

A girl with wild light brown curls in the second row, to the far left, suddenly jerked in her chair, ripping off her Boze headphones with little cat ears as she let out a feline hiss.

"Gotcha," Alaric muttered.

Fifteen minutes later, Alaric was one of the first to pack up and slip out of the classroom. The cyber security lab happened to be in a rather narrow corridor, which boded well for him. He ignored most of his classmates as they filtered out and straightened as Ms. Reyburn stopped in front of him.

A tall, striking woman with black hair, gray eyes, and a Scottish accent, Ms. Reyburn reminded him of the professor from Harry Potter who was always dishing out detentions. She wasn't mean, but she was strict, and calling on Alaric when he wasn't paying attention had to be a special talent of hers.

"I'm disappointed, Alaric. That RAT was an obvious trap. Do better," she said.

Alaric hadn't yet figured out how she did it, but she always knew *everything*. But then, not only was she the Cyber Security teacher, she was also head of IT for Almus Terra and worked closely with the headmistress on ensuring that ATA was a fortress of digital security and progress. She was relatively new though. She'd arrived in the second semester of their first year but had already made a lot of changes to ATA's IT and the Cyber Security course curriculum.

"Yes, ma'am," he answered as she passed him, too late to point out he'd been able to rat out the RAT in less than thirty minutes. But she likely knew that and just wasn't giving him any praise for it.

Two students later, the girl with the wild caramel curls came out and, with one step, Alaric cut her off.

To her credit, she hardly blinked. Or rather, her blink was slow, bored, exaggerated almost. Made all the more dramatic by the sweep of thick black eyeliner across her lids, ending in a sharp dagger-like points, Amy Winehouse–style.

"Took you long enough, handsome," she said, then rolled her eyes. "But 'Cotton Eye Joe'... really?"

Alaric jerked his chin toward the now empty classroom. "Let's talk."

The girl blew out a breath, her lips motorboating obnoxiously, then she rotated her wrist to check her vintage Mickey Mouse analog watch. "You have ten minutes."

Back in the classroom, the two servers blinked behind them like giant robots and the rest of the computer lab's monitors cast an electric-blue light in the dimness of the room. Neither of them bothered adjusting the lighting panels, while the hacker girl simply dropped her bag on the floor and leaned against the first row of desks, folding her arms.

Alaric wasted no time. He was *extremely* annoyed that some rando now had access to his computer. "Who are yeh?"

"My name is Ramona Vasquez," she said, faster than he thought she would. "But call me Romy. I'm from Puebla, Mexico. I'm a Scholar and a Sagittarius and my favorite movie franchise is *The Matrix*. My IQ is 147 and I'm an autodidact programmer who coded my first website when I was nine. I like long walks on the beach, and my favorite date is April 25th. What else would you like to know?"

From his spot leaning against the door, Alaric knocked his head back against the wood, his foot sweeping up behind him to plant against its frame. This girl was indeed amusing. It was a weird mix of a resume and a dating profile. "How much of that is true?"

"All of it," Ramona said with a wide, white smile. "I would never lie to you, Durham."

"Durham?"

"Rumor has it you prefer your old surname, not the royal one. Sorry, am I wrong?"

"No. Just wasn't aware there was a rumor."

"Oh, sweetie, there's a rumor for almost everything about you."

That was probably true too. "Okay, but the *entire Matrix* franchise? Even the last one?"

Romy narrowed her eyes. "Watch it, Your Highness. I could do terrible things to your laptop."

Despite himself, he grinned, liking this girl a little bit more with every verbal spar. "Am I really going to have to get a brand-new laptop?"

She shrugged, examining her checkerboard nails. "Of course not. I'll remove myself and you can watch me do it if you don't believe me. I was just trying to get your attention."

Alaric blinked. "My attention?"

Romy shot him a pretty smile. "What? Hasn't a girl ever hacked you to get a date before?"

"I...can't say they have, no."

"Did it work?"

Her smile was disarming, and Alaric couldn't remember the last time he'd been so intrigued by a girl. Not since Sadie.

Shit. *That* was a depressing thought. It would actually be nice to try to go out with someone. To *move on*. But then he thought of all his father's files that he still needed to crack.

"Sorry, I'm really busy."

"That, sir, is a god-awful rejection," Ramona said, cocking an eyebrow. "You can just tell me you're not interested. I'm a big girl. I can take it."

"No, I...seriously," Alaric insisted, frowning. "I've been trying...to..."

He stared at her. She was a hacker. A very good one. Had he just found his plan B?

"Actually," he said, tucking his hands into his pockets. "I have some double-encrypted files I need opening, and they are beyond my skill set."

Ramona raised both eyebrows this time. "Are you suggesting if I hack these files for you, you'd go out with me?"

Alaric frowned. He wasn't sure *what* he'd been

suggesting, if anything. This was why he needed to better plan ahead, to actually *think*, the way Emmeline was always nagging him to.

"Well, I…"

Suddenly Ramona stepped right into his space, pressing her nails into his chest, and beaming up at him with a catlike smirk.

"Because I am *totally* game."

# 7

# SADIE

Returning to Almus Terra was a bit like going back home. Ashland, for as much as she loved her country, no longer felt that way. At least, where she spent most of her time didn't. Heres Castle was more like a luxury hotel where people bought her clothes that weren't her style and cooked her food that was too fancy to eat at every meal. Some days she just wanted a hoodie and a ham-and-cheese sandwich.

But back at Almus Terra she could wear whatever she wanted (goodbye, pantyhose) and while their meals were still five-star, Sadie could also enjoy her favorite vinegar and malt crisps.

In other words, she'd missed her school, even if her dorm mates were less than desirable.

She and Emmeline were at odds (*duh*) and the two didn't even try to hide their obvious feud.

Oakley was fine. They got along well enough,

but after Sadie had told Oakley what Emmeline had done to her, Oakley seemed to be so crushed by Emmeline's moral failure that it felt a little bit like she blamed Sadie. Not that she'd consciously admit it, or even realize it. But Sadie imagined it was like hearing from your friend that they saw one of your parents cheating on the other. You would forever view that friend as someone who shattered your perfect reality. Even if that reality was, in fact, a lie.

Then there was Trang.

The night of Hibernia had caused an insurmountable rift between the two of them. Only later had Sadie realized the error of her ways, in believing Emmeline that Trang could do such a thing and then blaming her best friend without even talking to her. (Just another thing that Sadie could hate Emmeline for.) But it was too late to repair the damage. Once, she'd tried to approach Trang to clear the air, but Trang had dismissed her attempt at reconciliation.

Not that Sadie blamed her. To be honest, it was a crappy attempt. It was just difficult to walk back her accusation while still trying to sustain her new persona.

She hadn't just changed her mannerisms to appear more like a princess, she had changed entire aspects of her personality. Meek, timid, shy—any of those synonyms she tried to be the opposite of. In order to stand a chance among the king's advisory council, she'd realized quickly that she needed to be more opinionated. Louder. Unapologetic. Just...stronger.

So, over their second semester at Almus Terra, Sadie had made every effort to stand out in her classes. To be *seen*. Not that she needed to try very hard. Social media and the school forums documented everything about her, from how she did her hair and makeup, to what her nails looked like that day, to even how she subtly styled her uniform. She was the school's biggest celebrity and she and Titus were the golden couple on campus.

There was no place she could go, really, where she was not seen. Though it was her intention, it was exhausting. Sometimes her little top bunk was the only safe haven.

Which was where she was now, sliding through the pictures of the documents she'd snapped on her phone from Leander's desk.

The first week of school had kept her incredibly busy with all her new, very demanding classes and it wasn't until the next Sunday night that she could finally settle under her comforter and focus on the images.

Regrettably, many were too blurry to read. They were mostly handwritten memos. Pages from that legendary leather-bound notepad where Leander brainstormed all his laws and policies.

She stared at one in particular with a sort of reverence. It was the initial concept for Ashland's National Merit Scholarship Program—the very one that had landed her in ATA. The program that had always been meant to find another contender for the crown. If not for this little memo, scrawled in Leander's elegant handwriting...she wouldn't be here.

While this photo seemed sharper than the rest, the edges were slightly blurry and she didn't manage to capture the entire memo. If she zoomed in, however, she could see a name scrawled in the bottom corner.

Her name. Well, her last name at least. *Aurelia Sad—*

But then it was blurred, the letters in cursive were hard to make out. Aurelia, Sadie? She assumed so. Maybe Leander had put her name down when he had his Merit Scholarship winner. Kind of like a full-circle conclusion.

Pushing past all the feelings that the realization brought, she swiped to the next photo. This one was more out of focus than the rest and Sadie could tell that it was a typed report, maybe from a typewriter, though that seemed strange given the date: August 5, 2008.

"Who uses typewriters unironically?" Sadie mumbled to herself, zooming in on the image. She could glean the words *Peaceful Sea* up at the top and then there was a lot of tactical jargon. Wait...was she reading some military report? Like one of those Seal Team Six operations from American TV dramas?

Sadie sat up in her bed, her hair falling around her shoulders as she hunched over her tablet and tried to zoom in even farther.

Never had she even thought to consider the commander-in-chief aspect of running a country. After all, Ashland had been at peace her whole life. Were spies and covert military operations really a thing nowadays?

This photo was largely out of focus, but since it was typed, she could discern half its contents. It was all very tricky to follow with its military speak, but the word that made her pause was...

*Scealan*.

Every Ashlander knew that name. It was one of the old Ashland houses that had been constantly vying for the throne.

House Eldana was the last remaining family among the five that had fought and ruled Ashland for nearly a thousand years. The five houses had existed since the old Norwegian Vikings settled in Ashland and then, cut off from Europe due to terrible sea storms for decades, eventually merged with the natives, and became their own people. In other words, the five warring houses were about as old as the country itself.

At one point, all five Ashlandic houses were battling each other consistently, much like England's War of the Roses in the 1400s. Except these feuding families hadn't retired into the pages of history. At least, not until somewhat recently. The last of the Brehdals had been eliminated with the end of Ashland's most recent civil war, around the time of America's Cold War. The Thoranes and Reynars had disappeared in the eighteenth century, and the Scealans hadn't been heard from since the last heir died from tuberculosis in the early nineteen hundreds.

Only Eldana had survived.

Had Leander discovered some kind of Scealan act of treason? It seemed impossible. Like legitimately something out of a movie. Besides, no one had heard of the Scealan bloodline since the 1940s.

Unable to glean anything else, Sadie moved on to the next photo. This one was an entire spreadsheet of numbers with losses and gains and a line graph depicting the numbers moving drastically.

It looked like a stock portfolio. Which... sadly, wasn't Sadie's strong suit. She loved economics, but the stock market was her biggest weakness. More than once, she'd tried to get her personal tutor in Ashland to help her better understand the ins and outs of the stock market, but they shifted her focus to other things. Like international trade and tariffs and then governmental policy on health care and education.

At the top of the graph was the acronym AIF.

Sadie frowned. *Why was that so familiar?*

A quick Google search showed her it stood for Ashland Investment Fund. If it was what she thought it was... then she was ashamed to admit she knew far too little about it.

Suddenly the door opened, and Sadie locked her tablet. It was Trang, walking in with her headphones and throwing her bag on her bottom bunk.

The girls ignored each other. At this point, they'd lived like this for months. It wasn't awkward anymore.

*It just...*, Sadie thought, picking up her laptop to start on her Political Philosophy paper, *is what it is.*

"Sovereign wealth funds?"

Sadie nodded, standing in front of Professor Gupta's desk, cradling her laptop. Thanks to past experiences, she hardly went anywhere without it these days.

Professor Gupta glanced over at her tablet, where the semester's syllabus was pulled up. They were in International Econ 300 and while the course didn't focus entirely on stocks (there was a whole other set of courses for that), the credit markets were a large part of Economics. Especially International Economics.

"You're skipping ahead quite a bit," Professor Gupta said, tapping on the tablet's screen with one long crimson nail.

"Yes, Professor, but...well, Ashland has its own sovereign wealth fund and I'm trying my best to understand it as soon as I can."

Which wasn't a lie.

Professor Gupta nodded slowly. "Yes, I'm aware. The Ashland Investment Fund, correct?"

Sadie wondered if this woman knew every country's wealth fund off the top of her head.

She wouldn't put it past her. Professor Gupta had previously taught economics at Oxford and had published papers and books on international economics using complicated subjects such as game theory and Marxism.

"Well, a sovereign wealth fund is basically a stock portfolio for a country. A nation, in this instance, can be treated as an individual and be allowed to invest their money in corporations. They can buy and sell their stocks just like a real person investing could."

Sadie had learned that much from her cursory research into their class material, but there were details her professor could explain that a search engine wouldn't be able to teach her so easily.

"But where would that money to invest come from? The nation's treasury?" She asked. "People's taxes?"

"Like most government funds, it comes from a lot of different sources, Sadie. Centralized banks, money from taxes, people's pensions—"

"Pensions? Like, their social security? The government is using people's future retirement funds to play the stock market?" Sadie asked, appalled.

"Well, I wouldn't put it that way. It is a perfectly acceptable, safe, and legal practice,"

Professor Gupta explained, tapping her stylus on her tablet. "Sovereign wealth funds were originally conceptualized for countries with extra money to spend. Think of wealthy countries that make a lot from exporting oil, for example. It's a way to spend that money rather than having it just sit in a treasury, or have it disrupt the economy with things like inflation."

"So... it's a good thing," Sadie said.

Professor Gupta gave her a wry smile. "It can be. But remember, sovereign wealth funds are run by politicians. And different countries invest in different things. Look at Norway. They invest in green initiatives rather than defense spending."

Sadie's stomach twisted in discomfort at the last bit of Professor Gupta's lesson. These investments were made at the whim of politicians and, in Ashland's case, the whim of their king. That made her anxious. To know that taxpayers' money was being invested in something as volatile as stocks, and not to have a say in *which* stocks, didn't exactly make her feel at ease.

And yet, Leander had grown their economy in a way no one else had by bringing stability to the government, opening up foreign trade, and giving tax breaks to businesses local and overseas, among other initiatives. Their social class system—the divide between the poor and wealthy—was still far too large, but she knew that wasn't something that could be fixed overnight.

"Will that be all, Ms. Aurelia?" Professor Gupta asked, arching one dark eyebrow.

Sadie flushed and backed away from Professor Gupta's desk. "Thank you, Professor." Then she ducked out of the classroom and into the hall where Oliver was waiting for her.

He looked up from his laptop, giving her a friendly smile. "Hey. How'd it go?"

With a sigh, Sadie pressed her back against the wall and slid down the castle's cool stone. "It was...helpful."

Oliver nudged her shoulder. "Wow, that's convincing."

Out of everyone at Almus Terra, Oliver felt like the one person she could rely on to always be exactly who he was. And therefore, he was Sadie's favorite person at school. Ever since Hibernia, the two had developed an easy friendship. He'd admired her for what she'd done in giving all that money away to charity and standing up for her beliefs. And she, of course, had felt so grateful to him for helping her pull it off. After all, she wouldn't be where she was without Oliver

Jackson and his technical bravura in front of the world's leaders. Truth be told, there was a small part of her that felt like she didn't deserve his friendship.

Had she been a selfless person, she would've given *all* that money to charity. Even if it would have had dire consequences.

"It's a sovereign wealth fund, like I thought. But I wish I understood stocks better." She pulled out her phone to show him the photo of the document again. "I mean, this is practically gobbledygook to me."

"Ah. Gobbledygook, the secret language of traders," Oliver deadpanned.

"I *mean*," Sadie said, smothering a grin, "I can look at numbers and charts all day, but there's context I'm missing. Didn't you come up with your nonprofit investment idea based on the stock exchange?"

Oliver frowned. "I know the principles of trading, Sadie. It's not like I'm checking the Dow every day."

"Right, sorry," Sadie said with a shake of her head. Over the last eight months she had tried so hard to surpass Emmeline in every possible way and this was the one area where she'd always fallen short. The royal princess of the Eldana line practically lived and breathed the global stock exchange, especially the New York one.

She'd had little more than a week with these photos and already she could feel her "opportunity" slipping through her fingers.

"But... I can take a look," he offered.

Not for the first time and certainly not for the last, Sadie felt a surge of gratitude toward Oliver. Normally she would have told him not to worry about it, but she was at her wit's end.

Biting her bottom lip, she held out her phone. "Do you have your AirDrop turned on?"

# 8

## TITUS

"Helluvan agenda, mate," Sebastian said from the end of the long student council table. "You sure we'll be able to get through it all today?"

Titus didn't look up from reviewing his notes. "If we have no more interruptions, then I don't see an issue."

Sebastian rolled his eyes.

"Let's move on to the approval of the Twenty-third Amendment repeal," Titus said. As he spoke, he felt a surge of pride. It had taken no small effort to get where he was today. President of the student council. After the mess of Hibernia, his predecessor, Calixa, had to deal with the fallout with the school board, claiming that budgets needed to be cut due to the event not bringing in enough money as expected. Both Calixa and Kavi, the previous president and vice president of the student council, had been too bogged down with graduation and their failures that they had no meaningful impact on their succession. So, thanks to his relationship with Sadie, Titus had managed to achieve enough backing and popularity the following semester to win the presidency in hopes of ushering in some drastic changes.

Starting with killing the amendment that had caused so much unrest among the Scholars. The very one that had started his cousin's *ATA Is Messed Up* slogan.

Titus was glad, at least, that it was *his* work and not Alaric's that made its repeal a reality.

"All those in favor, say aye."

There was a chorus of "ayes" around the table and the secretary quickly went on to document the vote.

"The ayes have it," Titus said. "Moving on to the allocation of funds for this year's student organizations. I am forgoing the prioritization of Elite– and C-Suite–led groups, and instating an application format instead. Any organization that wants to receive funding for their activities must apply to be considered. It will then be approved by a committee composed of an equal number of Scholars, Elites, and C-Suites. I've asked Oliver to spearhead this application portal, so you can direct any questions to him."

Oliver gave a small half-wave to the rest of the council, then, looking embarrassed, dropped his hand.

Titus knew he was rushing, but Sebastian hadn't been wrong about the length of the agenda. Regrettably, he wasn't able to give Oliver's induction into the student council the attention it deserved, especially as he was the first Scholar in over fifty years to be a student council member.

But much like a professional politician, Titus knew he had to move fast in his first few days in office to get things done.

"All right, moving on to lab and art room schedules—" Titus said, tabbing through to his next slide of notes.

"Oy, hang on." Sebastian rapped his knuckles on the hard wood. "Are we not discussing this? There has to be an amendment where—"

"Article Fourteen, section B of the student council bylaws," came a clear feminine voice, "states that the president has the sole executive privilege of determining how student organization funds are allocated."

Everyone glanced over at Emmeline, who sat

bent over her tablet, stylus in hand. Considering how she was doodling some kind of fancy logo in Adobe Illustrator, no one had really thought she was paying attention. Especially given that she had been livid when Titus beat her for student council president, and she'd had to accept the veep spot.

Titus nodded to his cousin, hiding a small smirk, then he turned to Sebastian. "Calixa had another amendment in place, but this article supersedes hers. Therefore, a discussion won't be necessary."

Sebastian's dark eyes gazed coldly back at Titus. "You're going to ruin everything she built, aren't you?"

Titus switched back to the slide with the lab schedules heavily favoring the C-Suites and Elites. "That's the goal."

"You did well."

Titus *did* look up this time. Mostly because he was shocked that those words could ever come from that voice.

Emmeline leaned against the table next to him, checking her nails, her bag packed and slung over her shoulder.

"Oh...thanks," he said, honestly not sure

how to take a sincere compliment from her. He didn't think he'd ever heard one come out of her mouth. At least, not directed at him.

For a moment, they didn't say anything, letting the time stretch to mirror the awkward distance between them. Nine months ago, he'd hated her, convinced that she had ruined everything for him. Blackmailing him and going to such lengths to destroy Sadie and him right alongside her. But that resentment of Emmeline had faded as he tried to get Sadie to forgive him.

Because what he'd realized was that *he* had hurt Sadie. Emmeline just forced him to show her the truth. And in the end... the truth of *his* actions had been lethal. He'd started dating Sadie to use her, and he could not blame Emmeline for that forever.

"How did you get Oliver to join the council?" she asked finally.

*Ah.*

Titus looked back to his laptop and switched to his email, navigating to a message from Zhong Yiming, his liaison from the school board.

"Sadie convinced him before summer break. I'm assuming he was your top pick when you tossed out the idea of inviting a Scholar onto the council last fall."

Titus didn't need to look at her to know that she was blushing. Emmeline prided herself on being unflappable, but when it came to Oliver Jackson... all bets were off.

"You're the one who made it happen," she grumbled.

"Maybe so, but—" Titus stopped as the words from Mr. Yiming's email needled their way into his brain and down into his gut, making him suddenly nauseated.

"Damn it to hell," Titus said, staring and rereading the email.

Emmeline jolted at the swear words, her eyes wide. "What? What is it?"

"I have to go."

"Titus, wait—"

But he was already out the door and down the tower steps, the joints in his feet and knees complaining loudly as he went suddenly from zero to sixty. Normally he would take time to get up and slowly stretch his joints and muscles after two full hours of sitting to prepare for the long trek across the castle back to his dorm. For better or worse, outrage had propelled his body into action, taking the stairs so fast he half worried that he'd face-plant and break his neck.

Thankfully, he knew to take a shortcut

through the bailey to get to the school's administrative offices. Even though he hadn't visited the headmistress's office since his very first day at Almus Terra a little over a year ago, he found it easily. That hour had been ingrained into his mind as a core memory—something he would remember till he was old and gray.

Not only was he ignoring his body screaming at him to slow down, but he also ignored the most basic etiquette: He didn't knock when he stormed into the headmistress's office.

"Titus, did you really just waltz into my office like it's yours?" Headmistress Aquila leaned forward over her desk with the deepest scowl he'd yet to see on her.

"I'd actually describe this as more of a storm than a waltz," Titus said flatly. Oh, he knew he was being an arsehole, but he was shaking from the email he'd just read.

A snort directed his attention away from his headmistress for a brief moment and he was startled to find Trang Nguyen in one of the chairs across from the large mahogany desk.

She was watching him, her dark eyes alight with curiosity. Her silky black hair was pulled into a loose braid that hung over one shoulder, and she wore flared jeans, Converse, and a

T-shirt with some pro-wrestler fight emblazoned in beveled type, complete with lightning bolts.

"Don't think I won't give you detention, Titus Eldana. Even as the student council president, you are not protected from me."

"Looks like none of us are protected *by* you either, Headmistress."

Zuri Aquila stood then, blinking, like she couldn't believe the words coming out of his mouth. That any student at her school could be so brazen was shocking itself, but *Titus*?

"What exactly do you mean by that, young man?"

Titus didn't care that Trang was in the room. She didn't strike him as the kind of person who would immediately post gossip all over social media.

He held up his phone with the email from his school board liaison, Mr. Yiming, relieved that his arm was steady. "According to the board, scholarship funding will be eliminated at the end of this year. Is this really true?"

He heard Trang suck in a breath, but his focus was on Headmistress Aquila. Slowly, the headmistress lowered herself down to her chair, her face expressionless, her gaze made of steel.

"They should not have sent you that email."

Titus's heart sank. "Because it's true?"

"Because I will prevent it," she snapped.

Titus said nothing, taking in her hard look and flared nostrils and muscular arms tensed on her wingback chair.

Could she really?

The idea that the school board could eliminate the Scholars entirely seemed incomprehensible and yet... over the course of the last semester he'd learned from Calixa that the board held much more power than he would've thought possible over an institution like Almus Terra Academy. Even Headmistress Aquila, for all her authority, had to answer to the board. It was made up of the majority of the school's investors and, as much as ATA praised the student council's independence in running the school, not a dollar seemed to be spent without the board's express approval.

Titus turned back to his phone. "It says that they want to take the school back to its original roots. To reserve it for students with power and prestige. They want the school entirely composed of those with international wealth."

"Can the board really do that, Headmistress?" Trang asked, her braid swinging over her shoulder as she looked back at their school's sovereign.

"Not if I have anything to say about it,"

Headmistress Aquila said, her jaw working with annoyance. "If all you have to bring me is something I already know, Titus, you may leave."

"Headmistress—"

Her hand shot up in warning. "That's enough. I said, you are excused. You as well, Ms. Nguyen. Not to worry, your spot is secure."

"For this year at least," Trang muttered.

Dismissed, Trang got to her feet, shouldering her bag and shooting Titus an annoyed look, as if to say, *Thanks for getting me thrown out too.*

The moment they were outside the office, Titus turned to her. "What did you mean by that just now?"

Trang sighed and shifted her bag over to her shoulder, then started down the steps, Titus following behind her. "I'm switching over to a full scholarship student. My family's company isn't doing well and we can't afford the payment terms for tuition."

"Oh, I'm...sorry to hear that," Titus said with a frown. He truly was. Though he was surprised she was so readily admitting such a thing to him. He knew it couldn't be easy, especially for a once-great C-Suite family.

She shrugged. "It is what it is. My father still wanted to try to make the payments. I decided to speak to the headmistress on my own. He doesn't need to overextend himself if I'm smart enough to attend Almus Terra on my own academic merits."

They stopped at the bottom of the stairs and when he expected her to bolt, she lingered, nibbling on her bottom lip.

"Do you think Scholars will really be removed from ATA?" she asked.

Titus ran a hand through his hair, mussing up his golden waves. "I wouldn't put it past the school board. Seems like they're a bunch of technocratic arseholes."

"Takes one to know one, I s'pose," she fired back.

Titus couldn't even argue, considering what he'd thought of Sadie last year. "Touche," he said, shrugging. The word came out sounding like 'tush,' which made Trang wrinkle her nose.

"*What?*"

"Touche," he repeated, keeping his expression flat. Though it was difficult.

Trang narrowed her eyes. "Are you saying *touche*?"

"Now who's Elitest?"

She snorted again and rolled her eyes.

Instead of finding the sound annoying, it

made him grin. He had no idea what on earth had possessed him to try out the ridiculous joke from one of his favorite shows—a joke that had made him laugh for five minutes straight. But he'd just had a feeling Trang would like it. If her affinity for pro-wrestling was any indication, she might really enjoy a bit of ridiculousness now and then.

"You stole that joke," she said.

He smirked. *Wow, she got the reference.*

"It's a good joke."

"I'm leaving."

She took five steps before she turned back to him. "Do you think the headmistress can really stop it?"

That made his smile drop. It was the same question just phrased differently.

Titus thought for a minute, then answered honestly. "I don't know. But I do know I'm also going to do whatever I can to stop it."

Trang nodded, staring at her shoes. Then she looked up and met his gaze. "If you can think of a plan, I'll help."

Titus folded his arms, regarding her. There was something in her voice and expression that called to him. Matched his own love for this school. Almus Terra Academy had never been *his* choice for education, but the last year had been one of the best of his life, even with all its trials and pitfalls. He'd found a doctor who listened to him and classes that challenged him. Even friends he'd made on the student council, and Sadie, despite all her endless complications and emotions. At last, he'd finally started to crawl out from under his mother's manicured thumb.

Almus Terra was so much more than an institution—it was a belief system. A belief that this world could achieve peace and prosperity through the collaboration of young minds.

And he doubted very much that, when this school was founded on those values, they would only want students with the means and pedigree to be able to attend.

A suspicion poked through the back of his mind, sharp and insistent.

With a sigh, he moved his hands to his hips and stared hard at the marble floor. Thinking. He glanced up at Trang. "You're on the finance track, aren't you? How good is your bookkeeping?"

# 9

# EMMELINE

The door slam echoed in the student council room, the sound reverberating off the walls over and over, mocking her in its emptiness and isolation.

Emmeline was insatiably curious as to what Titus had read on his laptop. Surely if she had been in *his* spot, she'd be the one sprinting through the castle. After all, he had everything that Emmeline should've achieved: student council president, next in line as heir apparent once Sadie inevitably screwed up, the prodigal child in their grandfather's eyes...

Instead, she was simply...here. Left alone in the tower, surrounded by the elegance and prestige that had once impressed her so much and now served as nothing but a reminder of everything she'd lost.

With a sigh, she shouldered her bag and

glanced once at the words *Princeps Iuventutis* behind the table. *Leaders Among the Young.* Everything here seemed to taunt her.

Perhaps she should've tried harder to campaign for student council president, but she hadn't seen much of a point. Thanks to her falling-out with Oakley, Emmeline had lost a lot of support from Oakley's friends, of which there were many. Plus, Titus was too popular. His good looks, combined with the fact that he was dating the most popular student in the school, earned him the highest rung on the social ladder.

At last, Emmeline slowly made her way down the stairs. It was only because she was lagging that she didn't run into Oliver Jackson for a second time.

He'd been on his way up, coming around the spiral staircase so fast that Emmeline had to dart to the other side of the stairs to avoid a collision.

"Wow, I'm so sorry—again," Oliver said, taking a step backward, dropping down so his head was level with hers.

Emmeline quickly looked away, her honey-colored hair swinging. He must've forgotten something to be returning to the meeting he'd left only a few minutes before. Anyway, it had nothing to do with her.

"It's fine, but Titus already left if you needed him."

Praying to get by with her feelings unscathed, Emmeline pressed against the opposite side of the staircase and started to move past him.

"Oh, uh, well, I was looking for you actually. I was...hoping you hadn't left yet."

Emmeline stopped so fast she nearly tripped.

As if sensing that she was about to fall, Oliver lunged into her space, throwing his arm around her shoulders to steady her.

She'd caught herself in time. She hadn't needed his help.

But neither of them moved.

He stood so close his chest was against her arm, his face just inches from hers. In the dim light of the stairwell, the shadows cut lovely lines across his angular face, and it made him all the more ruinous to her heart. Especially with the way his gaze tracked her lips as she murmured, "Thank you, Ollie."

At his nickname, his eyes snapped up to hers and he quickly stepped back. "Yeah, of course. Uh, anyway, do you have a minute?"

"I...guess. For what?"

Oliver's cheeks darkened. "Um...maybe we could talk upstairs?"

It wasn't long ago that Oliver never would've even suggested talking in the student council room. Had he gained more confidence in his friendship with Sadie? Yet another thing to feel jealous about. Emmeline wanted to be the one standing by his side, encouraging him to step into his power. But no, it had been Sadie who had convinced him to join the student council. Sadie who likely gave him the confidence to feel like he belonged in that room alongside the C-Suites and Elites.

Truthfully, being alone with him scared her. Oliver trying to save her from tripping was enough to make her heart feel like it was bleeding out. If she faced his disappointment in her, or the anger he directed her way, she wasn't sure she could recover.

But, at the same time, she couldn't deny him anything.

So, she nodded and he gave her a small smile. Thanks to that smile, whatever came next... was all worth it.

She followed him up the steps and he opened the door for her, then closed it behind them. It was awkward and tense as they crossed to the table and took seats across from each other.

"Er... I promise this won't take long," he

started, pulling out his laptop, fumbling with his external charger so much that it fell from the table and he had to stoop down to retrieve it.

"Oliver," Emmeline said, tentatively touching the back of his hand. "It's fine. You're not taking any time I wouldn't be willing to give to you."

Again, his cheeks darkened, and he pushed his glasses higher on his nose. "Right. Well. I remembered you were good at stock markets."

Emmeline resisted the urge to correct him. She wasn't *good* at stocks. She was phenomenal at stocks. She'd been managing her own portfolio for fun since she was eleven. Living a few blocks down from Wall Street in Manhattan had ignited a distinct curiosity for their complexity, as well as a passion for their deep impact on both the national and global economies.

Everyone knew about America's Great Depression, but the 2008 financial crisis had been one of her yearlong projects back at her old school. When the stocks had plummeted so deeply from the housing market collapse that the rest of the world had to practically bail them out.

"I've dabbled," she said with a smirk.

That earned her another smile. "Okay, well, my dabbling is much lighter, I assure you. It's mostly only in the fundamentals and the trade market's operations. Actually, last year my software project was to replicate the stock market but exclusively for nonprofits."

Emmeline pursed her lips. Of course he'd figured out a way to invest in the goodness of humankind. What a very "Oliver" thing to do. Why every girl in school wasn't in line for this Black Clark Kent, she would never know, but she'd remain secretly grateful.

"But I don't follow actual activity on a day-to-day basis."

"Oh," Emmeline said, pulling out her phone and opening up several of her favorite stock market tracking apps. "There's loads of apps that will help you do that. I recommend—"

"Actually, I have some stock reports that I'm having trouble analyzing and was wondering if you could help."

Emmeline raised an eyebrow. That invited a whole separate round of questions.

"Did you...get your own portfolio?" she asked, unsure how to satisfy her curiosity without snooping into his personal business. Then again, he had asked *her* for help.

He gave her a funny look. "What Monopoly money would I have to make investments?"

Emmeline flushed. Usually she would lash

out when she felt embarrassed, but this was Oliver, so she managed to keep the impulse at bay.

"Right... sure, then what am I looking at?" she asked.

"Oh, yeah, I guess..." Awkwardly, Oliver got up and moved around the table, situating his laptop in front of her. With a few keystrokes, he quickly pulled up several complex reports.

Immediately, Emmeline's gaze went to the top right corner where the name had been blacked out. Okay, so this was a private equity investment report. Clearly. Not that it mattered very much. She and Oliver were barely on speaking terms, and he needed her for a favor, nothing more. They weren't friends. She shouldn't expect details.

And yet, she couldn't help feeling disappointed.

She slid her gaze over to the top left corner of the screen and her eyes widened—$1.9 trillion in the total holding market value. In other words, nearly $2 trillion in investments. If this mystery person or organization were to sell all their stocks the next day, they would have $2 trillion to play with.

How... was that possible? Whose stock report did he have his hands on? Jeff Bezos's?

She looked up at him and to his credit, he did look rather sheepish. Like... he knew that this was not a normal report.

Biting her lip, she glanced over to the next important number: Unrealized Gains or Loss. Again, unrealistically high—$2.37 billion.

Then she started skimming the list of current holdings. None of them were very surprising: Apple, Alphabet, JPMorgan Chase, National Bank of Australia, China Shenhua Energy, Banco Sabadell...

But the collection was familiar. So familiar that she could predict the next stock, one by one, down the long intricate list.

It wasn't as if she had an eidetic memory or anything, but she had been looking at this stock portfolio every day, for 382 days, ever since the day she'd learned that she was a princess of Ashland.

This was the Ashland Investment Fund. The sovereign wealth fund of Ashland, and the wealthiest in the whole world, quickly followed by Norway at $1.7 trillion, China at $1.3 trillion...

No wonder the total holding market value threw her off. She'd known the number by heart, of course, but had no reason to suspect that Oliver would be looking at a report from the AIF.

"Oliver," Emmeline said, slowly turning toward him, her knee nudging into his thigh. "Why are you looking at the Ashland Investment Fund?"

Oliver's eyes widened behind his thick frames. "Uh...why would you say that I am?"

Well, that was almost insulting. Emmeline knew her country's stock portfolio like the back of her hand. She knew they had a day trader who made financial moves in the stock market nearly by the hour. She also knew that in the last twenty years, King Leander had done many things to grow his economy—listening wisely and playing the stock market had been one of them.

"I look at these stocks every day, Oliver. What makes you think I don't know a report of the AIF when I see one? Wait..." Her gaze narrowed at him, the pieces falling into place. She knew Oliver and Sadie were friends. Hated that they were friends. Hated that Sadie literally had everything Emmeline wanted. "Did *Sadie* give this to you? Was she asking for your help? Why? She should have a tutor for stuff like this."

She literally had to bite her tongue not to say her next vicious words. How could the *heir apparent* not know how to read their country's stock portfolio?

Was there something she was missing?

She reached for the keyboard to tab to the next document when Oliver slid his computer away from her reach.

"Actually, on second thought… never mind. This wasn't a good idea."

As Oliver closed his laptop and shoved it into his bag, Emmeline gaped at him. He had come to her for help, and yet as soon as Sadie was involved, he clammed up and said this was a bad idea?

That *hurt*.

She didn't need reminding that Oliver was loyal to her rival. That he liked and respected Sadie and probably thought Emmeline was a poisonous bitch.

Oakley's words, not her own.

Though at her darkest times, while lying in bed and feeling the loneliness press in on her like the insides of a casket, she really did believe that. She was a poisonous bitch.

Emmeline just didn't need reminding.

"Tell Sadie that one report is not going to tell her crap," Emmeline said, unable to keep the hurt out of her voice. "Daily stocks aren't a snapshot of the health of an economy. She needs to monitor them and look at them over time. The trends and the patterns. When stocks are sold and when they're bought. She needs to understand what several days in the red *actually* means. If she doesn't look at that, I mean *study* the stock market, then she'll never understand how to keep our economy afloat. For example, I'll bet she doesn't know that the AIF contains the pensions of all Ashlandic citizens and if the AIF crashes, it will make the Great Depression of the United States look like freaking Shangri-La."

Oliver stared at her with wide eyes, his hands raised in front of him, like... he wasn't here to fight.

But that didn't make her feel any better. That made her feel worse somehow. He was here, playing the intermediary, when it should be Sadie coming to her with these questions. Not that she would ever, ever do such a thing. Emmeline wasn't even sure how she'd handle it if Sadie did. Would she use this newfound weakness against her rival or would she actually teach Sadie about stocks because she was heir apparent and needed to know these things to best serve Ashland, their country?

Ha. *That* was her whole problem, wasn't it? That she would so easily choose blackmail to get what she wanted.

Emmeline ground her teeth. "While we're on the subject, tell Sadie to stop *using* you. She should stand on her own. It's pathetic how she's gone to you for—"

"Hey." Oliver's face turned stony. For the first time in a long time, since January, there was anger in his gaze as he looked down at her. "I offered my help. And even if I didn't, that's what friends do, Emmeline. They lean on each other."

Emmeline waited for the inevitable line *and if you had any friends, you would know that.*

But it never came. Because Oliver was kind.

Oliver shouldered his bag, now seeming uncomfortable. "Look, I didn't mean to preach. I just don't want to betray—"

Emmeline threw up a hand, stopping him from saying another word. She didn't want to hear Sadie's name from his mouth.

"Don't. It's fine," she said, forcing her voice to take on its usual airy, casual tone. *This is nothing. This doesn't hurt me.*

God, what a lie. This might hurt worse than realizing that her parents hadn't ever given a shit about her. Because she hadn't known her parents. But she knew Oliver, and cared deeply about him and his opinion of her.

Which was so low he seemed to look at her with nothing but pity.

She glanced at the door. "You can go. Sorry I wasn't able to help you."

With the way she was feeling, she didn't want

to spend another moment with him. She didn't want to lash out and hurt *him*.

So even though she'd been more than ready to leave herself, Oliver pursed his lips and slowly backed up toward the door, his feet shuffling across the expensive plush carpet.

"See you around, Emmeline," he said with a small frown, then disappeared down the stairs.

Emmeline collapsed into her chair, taking deep breaths so as not to burst into tears. She was *not* about to walk through the castle with a tear-streaked face. She wasn't a goddamn child.

Thankfully, she'd just gotten her breathing under control and chased away the burn in her eyes when the door opened *again*.

But it wasn't Oliver returning. It was Titus and...Trang?

Titus stopped at the threshold of the door, staring at Emmeline. "Oh" was all he said.

A flush crept up her neck. She had no idea what Titus was doing bringing Trang up to the student council room, but just like Oliver and his little stock market project with Sadie, she knew that Titus wasn't about to divulge any details.

Left alone and in the dark once again.

"I was just leaving," she said, grabbing her bag and brushing past them.

She closed the door behind her and went down the steps.

Then...

She slipped off her shoes and padded silently up the stairs to listen.

This time she wasn't sure if she was there because she merely wanted to be included in *something* or if she wanted more information on Ashland's golden prince to use against him.

"That was awkward," Trang's voice said. "Is Emmeline going to care that a non-student council member is up here?"

"Probably," Titus answered. "But she can't do anything. Here. You need to be directly plugged into the server to get access."

Access? Emmeline frowned, ignoring the dig of *she can't do anything*.

There was a pause and some shuffling. "Are you *sure* this is sanctioned? Like, I won't get in trouble or anything?"

"If you're asking whether I'm allowed to give a regular student access to the school's accounting books, then I don't know. I didn't exactly check the bylaws before I brought you up here," Titus said in his dry British accent.

"Okay, I'm out."

"Bloody hell. You said you wanted to help.

This is helping. Also, what's the worst that could happen? You get kicked out? That's going to happen next year anyway, right?"

There was a pause, then Trang said, "You're kind of a dick, you know that?"

Titus sighed. "So I've been told. Do you want access or not?"

"Hold your freaking thoroughbred horses. Let me get my computer out."

Emmeline backed down the steps and slipped on her shoes, her head spinning. What on *earth* were they talking about? She knew about Trang's financial situation and could only wonder... was she no longer able to afford Almus Terra?

But, more importantly, why was Titus giving her access to the school's books? Did it have something to do with his reaction earlier? Not that he would tell her if she asked.

There was such a long list of people who either didn't like her or didn't trust her, and it was getting harder and harder to pretend that wasn't soul crushing.

# 10

## ALARIC

It was a struggle for Alaric to ignore the Discord messages pinging away on his phone during his Experimental Energy class. He'd silenced the sound, but the notifications just kept coming, all showing the avatar of a Korean-style cartoon of a girl with cat ears and dragon wings throwing up a peace sign.

Either Ramona had a study hall during this period, or she wasn't paying attention in her own class. She'd had his father's files a little over two weeks and every time he checked in with her, she practically bit his head off. *You will KNOW when I have something, Mr. Impatient.*

So he'd stopped. Now, though, it seemed that she had something. And he was desperate to know what.

Desperate enough to check his Discord during one of his most intense classes? It was excruciating, but he managed to resist the urge and turn his phone off entirely.

"Nuclear energy," Dr. Choi continued, tabbing through to her next slide, "is obviously the leading field in the race to renewable energy. Over thirty nations are using nuclear reactors for electricity generation, while sixty additional nuclear plants are under construction worldwide. With just over four hundred nuclear reactors in operation across the globe, twelve countries used nuclear energy for one-fourth of their electricity. Remember these numbers or don't, but—*hint hint*—they might be on an upcoming quiz."

Several students in the class chuckled, including Sadie, who sat in the front row.

She was in three of Alaric's classes this semester. In other words, impossible to avoid. Last semester, she'd been in only one—International Econ 201. It had been more than enough. It never failed to sting when Titus would pick her up from class while their classmates gushed about how adorable they looked together.

"As you know, I like to highlight the big names in each energy's respective field. It's important to look at not just *how* industrial energy affects everything from our economy to sustainability and fighting climate change, but *who* is making the change. Again—*hint hint*—it could be any one of *you*."

More laughter. Even Alaric smiled.

"So, a name in nuclear energy?"

Sadie's hand shot up. "Grace Stanke."

Dr. Choi beamed. "Ah yes, the former Miss America pageant winner now one of the best and brightest in clean energy. She is doing some amazing work. Very good. Any others?"

As other hands were raised, Alaric focused on his tablet and the upcoming syllabus.

When he'd signed up for this class, he'd been particularly interested in nuclear energy, especially since Ashland had invested in several nuclear reactors and plants. There were Ellis, Savnuc, Balway, and Krighton—rural towns in Ashland that could use the jobs. Of note, Balway was on the northwest coast, cold and more of a tundra than any other part of Ashland. Due to its harsh environment, the people there were resilient, but jobs were scarce. Their ancestors had lived there for centuries, and a nuclear plant had given hope for prosperous future generations.

Because of its success in Balway, nuclear energy seemed the obvious path forward, which was why King Leander's recent activities with the oil drilling by Virin Corporation didn't make sense to Alaric. He reasoned that diversification wasn't a bad move in any investment strategy. The concept tied right in to the last sections in the Energies curriculum. It also likely served to satisfy the powerful names in oil, who wanted another country's support in their war against clean energy.

That war was getting harder and harder to rationalize when there were other, cleaner, more powerful energy options gaining momentum by the day.

The zol battery, created by a Tanzanian Almus Terra alum by the name of Imani Nyerere, had shown a huge amount of promise in the last few years under Zolans Industries, a corporation based in Australia. Like most batteries, it held electricity but the chemical makeup that stored the energy was new and extremely potent. The battery apparently was being used in cars, and was rumored to hold a year's worth of power.

Then there was the latest laser, rumored to produce the strength of one million nuclear plants, acclaimed by SLAC National Accelerator Laboratory. The petawatt laser, with its ability to literally "shred matter" sounded like something straight out of sci-fi.

As the class continued, Alaric thought less and

less about his unread Discord messages and was therefore surprised to find Ramona at the door, waiting for him.

"Didn't you check your messages?" Ramona huffed, blowing a spiral curl away from her face.

"I was in class," he said, taking her arm and leading her away from the door. Just in case Sadie made it out fast.

"Can't you multitask?"

"Ramona—"

"Romy," she corrected. "My friends call me Romy. And my boyfriend especially would."

The guts this girl had. Alaric lifted an eyebrow. "I'm not yer wee boyfriend."

"Yet," she said with a smile that was all pretty white teeth.

"We haven't even gone on one date."

"A thing that will change by tomorrow evening, because I cracked several files."

"Aye? What's in them then?"

Romy placed a hand over her chest and made a mock gasp. "Do you honestly think I would snoop through your private files?"

"Yer *literally* a hacker."

"Fair point. But no, as much as I got the itch, I did not scratch."

Alaric felt a migraine coming on, while

simultaneously thinking that this might be the most interesting conversation he'd had in the last two months.

"See you tomorrow night then! TTFN! Ta-ta for now!" And she was turning on her heel and striding confidently down the hall before he could object. Not that he would've.

Ramona sent him her dorm room number that morning with a time range when he could come pick her up. He chose to err on the side of later, because he didn't want to have to wait around in case she wasn't ready.

Much to his annoyance, it was not Ramona who answered the door but three other girls.

"Blimey, he actually came," Oakley said. Her girlfriend, Danica, gave her a nudge in the side with her elbow. "No offense to Romy. But, you know, it's... *Alaric*."

"Oy, I am right here."

Bea, who Alaric had learned was Romy's roommate, beamed at Alaric and shot him two thumbs up. Apparently, Bea and Jacob were all for "Romaric," the couple name that Ramona had started and Alaric definitely sought to end.

"Sorry, sorry," Romy said, hurrying toward the door as she tugged on black combat boots.

"When I told Danica we had a date, she and Oak didn't actually believe me."

"Well, yeah, since he's been carrying a torch for Sa—"

Danica slapped a hand over Oakley's mouth, tugging her loudmouthed girlfriend back. "You two have funnnn," she sang.

"We will!" Romy sang back as she took Alaric's arm, which he never offered. He didn't mind, though. He was more than happy to let Ramona take the lead. By his calculations, he hadn't been on a date in almost two years. Relationships were too much trouble—and he hadn't found anyone worth it. Until…

He quickly shut that thought down. He was on a date with *another* girl for Christ's sake.

But, to his dismay, Romy led them down the pathway of greenhouses, out to the coast, with the little village's piers in sight.

It was the same beach where just less than a year ago he'd had detention with Sadie.

He wished he could say he'd forgotten a lot of that afternoon. How she'd almost fallen into the ocean, and he'd scooped her up and she'd cleaned his cut while laughing at him and calling him rude. He wished he could say he didn't remember almost every detail, but that would be a lie.

"It's kinda weird to have dates while at a boarding school, huh?" Romy said, flipping her mane of curls over her shoulder, though a few escaped in the sea breeze and danced around her cheeks.

She really was quite fit. Her skin so bronze and gold and satin-looking that she could've probably starred in a makeup commercial. She wore cut-off jean shorts and a mesh top that showed her curvy silhouette in a crimson tank.

Back in Dublin his goal would've been to get her back to his flat.

But that life... felt so far behind him.

"I mean, there's no cinema to play tonsil-tennis at," she continued.

He snorted. Cinema? Tonsil-tennis? "What are yeh, seventy-five?"

"I don't speak TikTok. I like to keep things retro."

"Says the hacker."

Romy nudged him, though her lips had curled into a proud smile. "Hey, I am more than my profession. And, for the record, I am not the kind of hacker stealing people's identities or credit cards. I am what you'd call a social activist hacker."

"Yeah? Give me an example."

"Remember that awful church in the States

that collected all those LGBTQ books and burned them, then sent hate mail to all the authors with their books' ashes?"

Alaric didn't keep up with every awful thing happening in the world, but he could definitely believe it.

"Well, yours truly traced half the congregation's IP addresses and leaked their search history. Spoiler alert: Those hypocrites had *so* much porn and I'll let you guess the type."

"Is yer goal to either scare me or to impress me into dating yeh?" Alaric asked.

Romy grinned. "Both. Is it working?"

He stuffed his hands in his pockets and bit back a smile. "I'm just relieved my own search history is relatively clean."

"Yeah, with the exception of your recent obsession with *Solo Leveling*, nothing very interesting at all."

"I thought yeh said yeh don't snoop."

Romy wrinkled her nose. "Is it *really* snooping when you're reading webcomics in Cyber Security class?"

Half his mouth tugged up into a grin. "I was done with my assignment."

"*Sí, sí,* I get it. You'll read manhwas during class but won't answer my Discord messages."

He rolled his eyes and was about to argue when she slipped on one of the wet rocks coated with salty sea spray. He caught her easily, lifting her to stop her from rolling her ankle in those massive platform boots.

He couldn't help remembering the feeling of grabbing Sadie, holding her against him, his hand on the branch while her soft fingers fluttered over his arm around her waist. She had a clean vanilla scent, but Romy's was more wild, like cinnamon and cloves.

"You really know how to sweep a girl off her feet," she said with a pretty red-lipped smile, easily looping her arm around his neck as he settled her back onto the pebbly part of the beach.

He felt like a proper tool for comparing them.

"I really don't," he said flatly. He wasn't his cousin. Not the golden prince of Ashland. True, a lot of his delinquent reputation had faded at Almus Terra, especially with someone as good and wholesome as Jacob as his best friend. But he didn't go around making girls swoon or performing valiant acts of service.

Did he want world peace? Sure, he wasn't some monster.

But Alaric's actions had always been more self-driven, rather than "for the good of the people," like Titus or Sadie. His bid for the crown wasn't even motivated by wanting to make Ashland a better place. He just wanted to ruin his father's life.

If he resembled either of his cousins, it would be Emmeline. She knew what she wanted and went after it.

Though she'd been more subdued as of late.

"Maybe not," Romy said, patting his chest as she regained her balance. "But that's why I like you. All strong and silent and brooding. Hot."

Alaric made a noise in the back of his throat, something between a cough and a scoff. Romy didn't hold back—he'd give her that.

Of course, neither had Sadie, really. She'd always been so forthcoming. Saying he was rude, calling him out for being a liar, spilling her guts after one little drink...

*Feck. I should not be here.*

"Listen, Romy," he said, stopping, the pebbles crunching under his sneakers. "What Oakley was trying to say back there, she's not entirely wrong. I feel like a chancer."

No way around it—he was being dishonest to himself and to Romy. Normally, he wouldn't care about being dishonest exactly, but not with a girl's feelings. Not with someone he actually liked and had respect for.

Loath as he was to admit it, he *was* still carrying a torch for Sadie, and it was pathetic that so many people knew about it. But try as he might, he hadn't been able to escape the growing feelings inside him, ever since they first went at it in their International Econ class.

Romy made a similar sound in her throat as she folded her arms. "And you think you're taking advantage of me. I appreciate your honesty, but do me a favor, Alaric, and give me some credit. I'm a big girl and I know what I'm doing. You're not leading me on. Especially when I'm the one who asked *you* out. If you don't want to go out with me, that's one thing, but are you having a good time?"

Alaric felt like he was walking into a trick question, but he gave a short nod. Yeah, he was. Romy was funny and interesting. If he could get over Sadie, Romy might be the one to help him do it.

With a satisfied smirk, Romy took his arm again. "See there, big guy? That's all today has to be."

The simplicity of that was a relief. And maybe he wouldn't feel so conflicted if he and Sadie hadn't walked down this beach, but it wasn't like there were a lot of alternatives. Romy was right.

A date at a boarding school, especially on an island, could be pretty limiting.

Even so, they made the most of it. They followed the beach through to the village and back up to the castle, taking a longer, meandering path. They talked about how each of them got into cyber security and their levels of interest in coding, they argued about the best current anime (*Kaiju No. 8* or *Solo Leveling*), they compared their Spotify playlists, and Alaric wasn't surprised to find her taste was all over the place, from Selena to a synthwave band called The Midnight.

Finally, they arrived at her dorm, and she reached into her back jean pocket and took out a slim external drive.

"Well, here you go. This has about half of them. All that I was able to crack in two weeks."

Alaric tried to temper the hunger in his gaze when he looked at the drive.

Romy twirled the drive in her hands. "I'm going to keep working on the others, if it's all the same to you. No more dates required."

"Yeh...really don't have to do that." Though today had been nice, he wasn't sure he could promise her another.

Romy shrugged. "It's my hacker's nature,

I guess. I want to finish the job. But I do have one... request."

"What's that?"

She crooked her finger at him and he bent down. Even with her platform shoes he had quite a few inches on her. With a sly smile, she tapped her red lips.

He leveled her a look.

She grinned. "Hey, I'm a positive person and a good kisser. Could lead me to date numero dos."

"Yeh know," he muttered, scooping his hand behind her jaw and tilting her face to his, "life coaches could make a fortune off your confidence."

Then, before she could say anything else ridiculous, he kissed her.

It was a good kiss. Her lips were warm and soft and she tasted a little bit like she smelled—like cinnamon Altoids. He hadn't intended it to last but for a few seconds. A relatively chaste, easy kiss.

But then Romy pushed herself up on her toes and drew her arms around his neck and parted her lips and it was too easy to give in.

It had been a heckuva long time since he'd had a good snog. The smooth, alluring touch of a girl's lips, the wet, hot brush of tongues, and the soft curves pressing against the hard planes of his chest.

The door opened behind Romy and Alaric pulled back.

His gaze immediately snagged on a pair of hazel eyes, surrounded by a flushed, freckled face.

Sadie stood next to Bea, who looked rightfully panicked. Sadie's eyes were wide, and she was clutching a stack of library books like it was her lifeline.

Alaric glanced down at Romy, who had a smirk on her face while holding out his external drive. With a scowl, he grabbed the drive and stuffed it into his back pocket.

His gaze sharpened as Sadie flattened herself against the wall, slid from behind Romy, and started walking down the hall toward her own dorm, which was a few corridors away.

Before he could think whether or not it was a good idea, he was after her.

"Sadie," he said, her name practically a growl out of his mouth.

Annoyingly, she just walked faster.

He wasn't sure why he was following her. It wasn't a good idea, she had a boyfriend, and yet his long legs doggedly pursued her.

Frustrated, he used the back of his fist to wipe his lips, hoping none of Romy's crimson lipstick had transferred.

"*Sadie.*"

Her name was harsh, impossible to ignore, especially when his looming presence came upon her.

She stopped and whirled around, right at the arch that led to the outside ramparts. He caught himself on the wall's edge, his large hand curling around the stone.

Without looking at his face, she hissed. "What? What do you want?"

Alaric was sure she hadn't really looked him in the eye in almost nine months. He would've remembered. Yep, not until thirty seconds ago when he'd just finished kissing another girl.

Why had he followed her? Why was he so stupid? Why, even after a good kiss, and a perfectly pleasant date, did his torch for her burn ever brighter? What was he expecting, chasing after her like a miserable little pox?

"I...nothin', cailín."

"Good, because I have a date," she snapped.

Once, in his earlier delinquent days, Alaric had been in a fight where he wound up in the hospital with internal bleeding, a broken nose, jaw, wrist, clavicle, a black eye, *and* a concussion. Yet somehow, this moment hurt worse.

If he thought nothing could top the emotional upheaval that had been his date with Ramona, followed by his run-in with Sadie, he had been sorely mistaken.

Because when he finally settled down in his bunk that night, after a long run and a cold shower, and opened the external drive with all the files and clicked on the first one with the label PATERNITY TEST, he found something that turned not just his world upside down, but Emmeline's.

His *sister's*.

# 11

## SADIE

It was meant to be a quick visit to Bea's dorm room to pick up some old reference books for their shared Linguistic and Cultural Anthropology classes, but then they got sidetracked by discussing their latest paper on the relationship between language and power.

Speaking of language...why hadn't she thought to *say* anything? Maybe because she hadn't been expecting to open the door and find Alaric with Ramona Vasquez's tongue down his throat.

When he'd started following her, she had not slowed down. Sadie had done a fantastic job of avoiding Alaric Eldana for nearly nine months and she wasn't about to break that streak now. Well, in the only way she *could* avoid him, considering they stayed in the same castle, had to attend multiple state dinners, court functions, and PR events together, as well as three classes this semester. She did it with vapid smiles, shallow conversations, and just generally never looking in his direction.

The truth—that she did not care to admit or examine—is that she'd never gotten over what he told her outside her dorm that night. That single, devastating *no*.

That he thought she could never be queen. How she'd embarrassed herself beyond repair in front of the one Ashland heir she had truly admired.

Titus may have broken her heart, but Alaric had shattered her confidence. Honestly, she wasn't sure which was worse in the long run.

Because while she felt like she deserved the title of "heir apparent," she wasn't able to say it was well earned. She had blackmailed the king into bestowing the title on her and while she'd been trying her best among the court and the king's council, not one person thought she was up to the job. No, that would be Titus.

So it was with grim satisfaction that she'd told Alaric she had a date. A fake date, yes, but he hadn't known that.

She and Titus were now set up in their normal little corner of the bailey, under the shade of the northern ramparts and surrounded by large fragrant gardenia bushes. It was the perfect spot because it allowed their study dates to be public enough for people to see them in passing, but it would be difficult for anyone to get within earshot without Sadie or Titus knowing.

Sadie despised statistics. It was too close to maths, and that had always been one of her weaknesses. Items like standard deviation, histograms, and box-and-whisker plots made her head spin, and she held her breath while Titus reviewed her statistics homework for any errors, praying there would be no mistakes. She'd spent over three hours on it, and she had no more time to spare.

While Titus bent over her notebook, all scribbled numbers and notes and data points, he massaged his knuckles.

"All clear," he said at long last, and Sadie blew out a relieved breath. He laid the notebook between them and gave her a small smile. "This attempt was better than your last."

No kidding. Her first attempt was riddled with red marks. He'd just kept scratching and scratching across the page.

"It came at great cost to other things, I assure you," she grumbled, flipping the page of her cultural anthropology book.

It had already been over a month back at school and nothing had really come from the photos on her phone. She was beginning to think it had been a colossal waste of her very precious time. Even if she could find out something that the king didn't want her to know, what was she going to do with it—blackmail him again? For what? To coax him into an early retirement? That would be hilarious.

"I hope not," Titus said, a frown in his tone. "It's not like you'll have this next weekend to catch up on anything."

Sadie winced. Right. Titus was referring to the upcoming United Energy Gala in Singapore. It wasn't as if she'd forgotten about the incredibly important weekend that only a select few C-Suites and Elites would be attending alongside their incredibly important parents. But other things had clearly gotten in the way.

The gala would celebrate the latest Chinese solar power plant, the result of hard work by the senior minister of Grenada, who was currently leading the efforts of COP28, the United Nations' Climate Change Conference under the Paris Agreement signed in 2016. It was going to be Sadie's first global event as heir apparent and she *had* to do well.

It certainly didn't help that Singapore was thirteen hours away and they would lose two days to travel. At least they got a note to be excused from their Friday classes.

"Speaking of which," Titus said, checking his phone, which had just pinged in his pocket.

Confused, Sadie finally looked up from her textbook. "What?"

He glanced at her, frowning slightly. "Ilsa's email. About the gala. Didn't you just get one?"

Sadie pulled out her phone. Just like the census report, it did not surprise her that she had no new unread emails.

"No," she said, her voice icy.

Titus hesitated, as if sensing they were about to get in a fight. A fight he believed wasn't *his* fault.

"Then look at mine. It's just some additional details on who's going to be there…"

"Forward it to me," Sadie demanded, voice cutting like broken glass.

Titus sighed and Sadie had the sudden urge to pinch him even if there were no boring council members to put them to sleep.

"There's no sense in getting mad at me about this," he muttered.

"Trust me, you are not the only person I am

mad at. But, yes, you deserve every ounce of my anger."

"Give me some credit. I share everything I get with you," Titus said through his teeth, in a rare moment of letting his frustration bleed through. "At least that levels the playing field."

"Because you feel guilty about what you did," Sadie shot back, "and there is no leveling the playing field, Titus. Not when I don't even know the rules of the game."

"That's bollocks, Sadie. If you'd trust me when I tell you I'm in this fake relationship to help *you*, not just get ahead, then maybe we could actually work together—"

"Enough, Titus! There is no working together. There is no future where we'll sit on the throne together. You need to get over that."

*"Excuse me."* His voice was more dangerous than Sadie had ever heard it. He sounded almost like his grandfather. "I told you. When you bloody well want to end it, we'll end it. But you're benefiting from dating me far more than I am you. So yeah, I am helping you and I think you know it and you're lashing out because you don't like feeling indebted to me. And I get it. But don't throw my feelings back in my face."

At that, Sadie went quiet.

Because, unfortunately, she had meant what she'd said in the car on the way to the Durah airport that day. That she'd been starting to suspect he really did have feelings for her. She'd asked him to kiss her to test the theory. And the fact that he *hadn't* kissed her actually, finally, made her believe it. He'd cared about her feelings—about what *she* had wanted.

But it was too late for them.

And Titus was starting to realize it too.

"You ask me to trust you," she said softly, "when I know you don't trust me either."

Titus froze, like he knew exactly what she was referring to. His secret. The one he had protected by creating that voice memo for Emmeline and shattering her heart.

Not trusting herself to say anything else that wasn't hurtful, Sadie began packing up her things. In her haste to get away, she accidentally knocked her notebook to the ground.

Titus stooped to pick it up and was too fast for Sadie to stop him. He scanned the page it had fallen open to and his blond brows furrowed.

She tried to snatch it back, but he jerked it out of her reach.

"Why are you researching the warring houses of Ashland?"

Sadie's face flushed. Another thing she couldn't trust him about. Ever since encountering that document about *Scealan*, Sadie had done her best to map out a full history of the old houses. Unfortunately, it hadn't amounted to much. Oh, she could list out some of the major battles won, and roughly who had power when, but their records were disjointed because the ruling family would get rid of any records from the previous family.

"No reason," she grumbled.

"Well, it's wrong," Titus said, passing it back to her.

Sadie took it, her mouth agape. "Excuse me? I know my country better than you do."

Titus's face darkened. "Ashland is my country too, Sadie. And I've had overbearing parents teaching me every single thing about Ashland's history from the best tutors money could buy. So I might, actually, know what I'm talking about."

Face flushing even deeper, Sadie snapped back, "What part is wrong then?"

Titus didn't have to glance back at it. "Leander defeating the House Bredahl in the last civil war, over sixty years ago, is obviously correct. It was eliminated when Leander returned from studying in America and ended the final civil war. Thorane and Reynar died out in the eighteenth century."

"In the War of Guress, which lasted for fifteen years," Sadie continued, "Hans Thorane was executed along with his sons and daughter in his home. Reynar's line ended when he tried to escape to Canada with his fleet. The ships were sunk with cannons. Every single one of them. And Scealan's last heir died from tuberculosis in the early nineteen hundreds."

"Wrong."

"I'm sorry?"

"I said, that's wrong."

Sadie stared at him. "Which part?"

"The tuberculosis story was fabricated for the public. The Scealans didn't die out."

# 12

## TITUS

Sadie didn't say anything for a long time, staring at him. She was likely debating whether or not to believe him about this particular slice of knowledge.

He couldn't blame her. It was a bold statement to make.

In some ways, the Scealans were to Ashland what the Romanovs were to Russia. So it was a bit like declaring that Princess Anastasia was alive with descendants. And if that kind of thing were true, it would be a secret that had been hidden by the reigning monarchy for over a century.

Slowly, Sadie sat back on the stone bench and narrowed her eyes, her fingers curling around the notebook.

"That sounds like a fringe conspiracy theory," she finally said.

Titus folded his arms and glanced at his own

pile of homework. It's not as if he had all the time in the world to convince her of this—she could believe him or not. Didn't matter to him.

As if sensing his indifference, Sadie quickly added, "It's not that I don't think something like that is possible, but it's hard to wrap my head around it. Will you tell me more?"

Titus lifted a brow at her request. It was the first time she was really asking him nicely for something. Most of the time she demanded things with hardly a *please* or a *thank-you*, and he never faulted her for it. He more than deserved her brusqueness for deceiving her and then breaking her heart.

But either she was starting to forgive him... or she really cared what he knew about this piece of protected history. Probably the latter, but again, he wondered *why*. Though he suspected that wasn't an answer he was going to get.

"Well, to be fair, I don't know a lot. I actually don't think I should've been told. So add that to the list of the things I wasn't supposed to know before landing at Almus Terra," he said with a shrug, acknowledging the fact that his parents had "broken the rules" on more than one occasion. What was one more?

"How it was explained to me was like the

opposite of Princess Anastasia of the Romanov Dynasty. For decades there was this rumor that Anastasia had survived the entire family's execution. A woman named Anna Anderson even claimed to be the youngest princess. But then a DNA test in 1993 revealed—"

"Titus," Sadie interrupted with a flat look, "are you really taking me on a side quest about Anastasia?"

He smirked at her. "Just in case you only saw the cartoon version."

"I know *all* the versions. Including the musical."

With a roll of his eyes, he continued. "Okay, well, it's the opposite of that. After Leander defeated the Bredahl monarchy and ended the last civil war, there were rumors that the final house, the Scealans, were still a threat. To ensure a smooth transition in his first years as king, the current regime fabricated a very believable news story about how the last of the Scealans died out to reassure the people of Ashland that there was no more threat to peace. To hide from the Eldana line, the Scealans let the story perpetuate and disappeared. Left the country, maybe changed their name."

"I guess...back then that would've been pretty easy to do," Sadie muttered.

"Naturally. This was way before the internet."

"So what happened to the Scealans? Where did they go? How did they survive?"

"Unclear. Or, at least, I certainly don't know the details. The prevailing theory was that they escaped to Iceland, but you can be sure there was at least some espionage strategy in order to keep tabs on them."

Sadie nodded slowly, her gaze locked on the notebook in her lap.

"Okay, I'll bite. Why the hell are you researching this?" Titus asked, now too curious to ignore it.

She stood again, though this time much more slowly. "No reason."

A punch of anger hit him in the gut. One she didn't quite deserve, but that didn't mean he still didn't *feel* it.

"Vicious liar," Titus said, his steel eyes narrowed on her.

He understood now that he'd lost his chance with her. Maybe if he'd been more earnest in his regret and his apology, some of her feelings for him could've been salvaged. But the truth was, he wasn't sure he wouldn't just do it all again. The only thing he *really* regretted was not seeing her merit earlier. Not truly developing feelings for her instead of dating her as a strategic ploy. Because for two lovely months he enjoyed their relationship. And he was bitter that the last eight had been nothing but heartbreak after heartbreak. Every time he kissed her for the camera knowing she didn't really want it...

Well, Titus was no stranger to pain. Inside his heart and all through his joints.

She looked at him so sharply it was like the strike of an arrow—deadly and impossible to escape. "How dare you say that to me."

Titus knew he shouldn't have baited her with that phrase so precious to them in the early days of their relationship. Normally, he would apologize and back down, but instead he rose and took two steps toward her until they were nearly chest to chest.

"I'm helping you and you're shutting me out, yet again. If you don't want my help, Sadie, that's fine. But then *release me*. What you're doing to me is as cruel as what I did to you."

Sadie reeled back like she'd been slapped, her hazel eyes wide as his words struck her in physical blows.

Because while she no longer had feelings for him, he was still trapped in his, unable to completely move on.

"Umm."

Both Sadie and Titus jerked apart to find Trang standing just beyond the gardenia hedges, her brows raised and her dark eyes darting between them.

"Is this...a bad time?" she asked.

Sadie shifted her bag on her shoulder and clutched her notebook tighter to her chest. "Not at all. What's up?"

"Oh..." Trang glanced at Titus, then back at Sadie. In the most awkward way possible, she pointed to Titus. "I actually came to talk to him."

A light flush crept across Sadie's cheeks. "Oh, okay." She started to leave, then stopped and looked over her shoulder. "Thanks," she said, meeting his gaze, "for the information. And the statistics help."

Titus gave a small nod. Though it didn't fix all their issues, this moment felt like a turning point. Like she would finally stop blaming him for everything.

"You're welcome."

With a flip of her ponytail, she was striding across the bailey.

"Well, that was awkward," Trang muttered, tentatively stepping into their little gardenia-walled alcove.

"Wonder whose fault that was," Titus said dryly, and sank back down on the stone bench, surrendering to his aching joints to let his body rest against the hard stone.

*Bloody hell.* He was so physically tired that he felt he could lie here for a week and still not get enough rest. Mentally, he felt like his brain was mush. Emotionally? He didn't even want to go there.

"Would you rather I wait behind the bushes like a creeper?"

"You could've texted me."

Trang gestured vaguely around the beautifully landscaped bailey. "I saw you out here, studying. I didn't think I'd be interrupting anything," she said, then muttered, "at first."

Titus ignored that and leaned back into the bench. "So? Did you find anything in the books?"

Trang smirked at him. "Of course. Why else would I be talking to you?"

The directness stung more than he thought it should've. "What did you find?"

"Evidence you're not just a dumb blond with a pretty face," she said, holding up her tablet and shaking it like it had the secrets to the treasure of Monte Cristo.

A spark ignited in Titus's chest. "Show me."

Which, by the way, that had nothing to do with the fact that she had just inadvertently called him "pretty."

Trang glanced at the space next to him on the bench and he scooted to the side. She took the spot, Sadie's spot, and opened up her laptop, balancing it on her knees.

"Okay, so I've been going through all the balance sheets. And you were right. Something is up with the accounting. Like, I *do* think that the school is getting rid of scholarships for financial reasons, not because they want to make it more *elite*," she said, wrinkling her nose in distaste at the word. "Or at least, both reasons could be true."

Titus nodded slowly, and though he should've been validated that his suspicions were correct, instead, he felt disappointment. How could a school with the support of billionaires and political figures across the globe be in financial trouble? It didn't make sense.

He waited for her to pull up the spreadsheets, to show the evidence of the discrepancies, but she didn't. She drummed her fingers on the side of her tablet.

"What's the holdup?"

"Well... it's not exactly black and white."

Titus frowned. "What do you mean?"

"Basically: The school is being ripped the eff off."

He stared at her. "You think we're overpaying...vendors?"

"Yeah, I really do. Take rent for this island, for example. It's two million...a month. The electricity. The food. Trash service. Equipment. Cleaning. Look, I calculated our monthly costs. Titus, these expenses are like what it would take to run a small country."

Titus scanned the spreadsheet she'd finally pulled up. And he had to admit...the prices were astronomical. Still, he had no way of knowing if that was normal for a boarding school such as Almus Terra. Considering there were none to compare it to.

"I know what you're thinking," Trang said. "How can we know what's a reasonable cost? The truth is we can't, really, but call it a gut feeling. I've looked over the books of my father's company hundreds of times and considering that the Nguyens run a power plant, I know the price of electricity and tech and I can pretty much apply it with a formula that figures in exchange rates and square footage. Check my math by all means, but trust me, we're overpaying."

It wasn't that he doubted Trang's knowledge of her father's company, nor the bills for it, but he was skeptical that she could reasonably compare it to a school. "By how much?" He asked finally.

She shrugged. "Half a mil, give or take a few thousand."

His brows flew up. "How confident are you on this?"

"Pretty dang confident, but I can see you're not. That's fine. I came prepared." She tabbed to another spreadsheet, this one full of green arrows and large amounts from donors and tuition costs. "This is our revenue. Before tax. Now look at the total for the year." She scrolled down to the bottom. "Then look at our expenses."

Titus didn't need to be an accounting major to see the issue. They were in the red. But it didn't make sense why they were in the red, and he finally understood now what Trang had been saying. While this issue *was* black and white, there were no errors in the bookkeeping. They were simply losing money. But how could they when the tuition and donation revenue was the price of a small government's budget?

"When...when did we start bleeding money?" he asked.

"I'm so glad you put it like that," Trang said, then pulled up a graph she had put together for revenue versus expenses over the years. The line of loss was subtle at first, starting fifteen years ago, but became dramatic in the last five years, as if ATA's expenses just became more and more exorbitant.

Titus didn't know what to say, nor did he know how to fix this problem. Should they look at other vendors? Or raise tuition? Were either of those things even within his power? It definitely felt like something the board or Headmistress Aquila would be addressing, and he assumed that she was. Or trying to, at least.

"Can you send that all to me?" he finally said.

"Already done." She was quiet as they both sat there, letting the news of the school's financial crisis really seep in.

"What are you gonna do about it?" she asked. "What *can* we do about it?"

Titus felt the ache in his neck, the stiffness in his wrists, as he dropped his head into his hands and sighed deeply.

"I have no bloody clue."

# 13
# EMMELINE

The tune of "Liz on Top of the World," played on repeat for the last two hours, was the only thing keeping Emmeline moving around the dorm, packing for the trip to Singapore tomorrow.

The United Energy Gala was sure to be an amazing event and something she would've reveled in last year. But nowadays she felt... pathetic. Like a wallflower, except one covered in thorns. Who would she talk to? Who could she charm?

More importantly: Did it even matter?

Her grandfather certainly would not care that she was there. Neither would her cousins, or any of her other C-Suite and Elite classmates. As usual, Emmeline was alone.

Always, always alone.

It was a wonder that she even got out of bed

nowadays. The only thing keeping her going was more of an autopilot response. What else was there to do except be perfect? She had lived her entire life by that code. It was the only way she operated now. She'd failed at being loved by her family, failed at making true friends, and she could not fail in her schooling. Could. Not.

Suddenly the music stopped, and Emmeline looked up from her packing.

Oakley was holding her phone and had obviously pressed pause on her music.

"Can I help you?" Emmeline asked flatly.

"My god, Emmeline. How loud were you listening to *classical* music? I've said your name at least eight times."

"Loud enough not to hear anything else. That's the point," she muttered, turning back to sorting through her makeup bag.

"Have you heard about the Scholars?"

Emmeline stopped, her mascara tube in hand. She didn't want to admit that no, she had no idea what Oakley was talking about. No one was including her on anything. Not Sadie, not Titus, not Trang... *not Oliver*.

But there was also no point in pretending. "Can't say that I have."

Oakley paused, as if surprised by this fact,

then clicked her tongue. "It's not schoolwide news yet. But Titus asked for my help...I kind of assumed you knew."

Emmeline tried to stop the flush of rage from creeping up her neck. Titus had already gone outside the student council for help by giving Trang access to the school's bookkeeping system, so she shouldn't be surprised that he'd contacted Oakley as one of the most influential C-Suites for help in...whatever was going on.

Still, it was so, so painful to know that she was *this* out of the loop. This disliked and distrusted.

"Do you have something you need from me, or not?" Emmeline asked, dropping the mascara into her makeup bag.

"Blimey, Emmeline. I'm trying to tell you that scholarships are being eliminated at the end of this year."

Emmeline fumbled with the travel bag, upending its contents and dropping everything to the floor. A special two-hundred-dollar bottle of serum shattered into a dozen pieces. She ignored it.

Oakley swore and bent down to mop up the mess with one of their hand towels. Emmeline didn't move. She was frozen in horror.

The Scholars were... leaving? They were being kicked out of Almus Terra?

*Oliver.*

"H-how is this possible?"

Oakley frowned and looked up at her. "Ask our stupid board. But, according to Trang, the school is bleeding money. Like, it can't be sustained without redirecting scholarship funds to the upkeep of the school. Ludicrous, am I right?"

"I... yeah," Emmeline muttered, her brain stuttering like a bad engine. If there was anyone who deserved to be here, it really was the Scholars. Alaric had been right. They had *earned* their access by merit, intelligence, and hard work. They were the backbone of Almus Terra.

Oakley stood holding pieces of Emmeline's broken serum in her hand towel. "You know what kills me, Emmeline? It's that you're brilliant enough to actually fix this. If only you'd put that chess-master mind of yours to good use. And I mean *good*. Ya savvy?"

Back when they were friends, Emmeline would've laughed at her *Pirates of the Caribbean* impersonation. But they weren't friends and what Oakley had just pointed out—that even though she *could* help, no one trusted her enough to give her a chance—stung worse than Oliver's rejection the other day.

With a pitying look, Oakley turned and dumped the glass in the trash, then left Emmeline to pick up her own broken pieces.

Alone, always alone.

Marina Bay Sands resort was an engineering and architectural marvel. Featured in pop culture, as well as being a key feature in Singapore's skyline, Emmeline had of course known of it, but to see it in person was something she'd never forget. Its three defining towers held over two thousand hotel rooms, a mall, restaurants, the world's largest atrium casino, and two floating crystal pavilions, topped by another world record: the largest cantilevered platform, which held the infamous SkyPark with its luxurious infinity swimming pool.

Which is where the United Energy Gala was currently being held.

Emmeline stood at the edge of the SkyPark, overlooking the enchanting night view of downtown Singapore. The wind off Marina Bay ruffled her gown and wisps of her silky honey-colored hair. She wore a dress made by Vera Wang and approved by her mother. It was dark navy and entirely

backless but had sheer long sleeves and a mermaid trail. As usual, she looked stunning.

But there was no one here she wanted to dazzle.

The crowd behind her, chatting and networking, drinking expensive champagne and eating celebrity-chef cuisine, all while half-watching the synchronized swimming show, was made up of the richest, most powerful people in the world. But the only people she wanted by her side were her parents. Oakley and Oliver. Even Alaric and Titus.

With a glance over her shoulder, Emmeline could even see Alaric engaged in conversation with an old Indian man who was explaining something that involved a lot of hand waving. Surprisingly, Alaric didn't look bored or annoyed. He seemed to be doing well.

So why couldn't Emmeline get it together?

After all, she was *made* for this night. Her governess, Heather, had molded her to be this breathtaking, clever, interesting socialite. To stand on the roof of this most exclusive venue in an $8 billion resort and charm the pants off the world leaders and billionaires.

Yet, unbelievably, her mind wasn't present. It

was back in her dorm-room bathroom, reliving her conversation with Oakley.

The entire plane ride, the entire day gearing up for this night, she had been unable to think of anything other than the news that the Scholars would be leaving Almus Terra. Her days with Oliver were numbered.

And no one had bothered to tell her.

Not that she had given them much of a reason to believe she'd do anything to help.

With that extremely depressing thought, Emmeline tossed back the rest of her champagne. It was only her first glass, so she still had her wits about her, but mentally she was calculating how much she'd be able to drink in order to numb her feelings and quiet her thoughts but not make a fool out of herself.

It would be a fine line.

"You look like you just got your favorite toy taken away."

Emmeline glanced over her shoulder to find Sebastian Bane standing just a few feet away. He looked like a young James Bond, dressed in a perfectly fitted classic black tux with his dark hair swept to the side. There was even a martini in his hand, for crying out loud.

She turned back to the skyline, her hands

tightening on the railing that separated her from the ground 660 feet below.

"Let me guess," Sebastian said, sidling next to her. "You heard about the Scholars."

Emmeline's head snapped toward him, her heavy waves swinging across her shoulder to brush against her lips. She peeled strands away from her glossy lipstick and glared at Sebastian.

"What do *you* know about it?"

Sebastian chuckled, swirling his glass and then lifting the rim to his lips. "Please. Do you think I wouldn't know anything that your prat of a cousin doesn't already know? He may be the student council president but my father is on the school board. I know all. Just like how your precious Oliver will be gone by next year. Miserable poor sod."

Emmeline tensed, feeling the urge to shove him into the swimming pool. "He's not my Oliver."

*He's Sadie's. Everything is hers.*

"Come now, Emmeline. It's obvious from the way you look at him. *Have* been looking at him for almost an entire semester. Even *he* probably knows."

It was a low point to realize that this observation about herself didn't even embarrass her.

Likely, she should've been mortified to know that Sebastian, half the school, and the boy himself knew about her crush on him, but she wasn't.

There was just...sadness. That, and a bone-crushing emptiness that had started when she was a child and just kept expanding and consuming everything inside her.

Why was she even standing here accepting this from him? She didn't need or want anything from Sebastian Bane anymore. She started to move away when Sebastian caught her arm.

"This isn't sudden, Emmeline. You remember last year after Hibernia where Calixa and Kavi had to make a ton of budget cuts for organizations? The school is tanking. It's us or them. And it won't be us."

Practically snarling, Emmeline jerked out of his grip. "I know the way the world works, Sebastian. But thanks for the lesson. Maybe you can teach children about world hunger next."

Before he could reply, Emmeline was striding away, dropping her empty champagne flute on one tray and picking up a full one as she wove into the crowd.

*It's us or them.*

She knew that. Practically speaking, it was the only way the world *could* work in many ways.

But... with education? Health care? Why weren't those things just a little easier for the less fortunate? Why couldn't opportunities like Almus Terra Academy be attainable for those with the drive and the talent to succeed, if only they were given a chance?

It seemed so—

"Unfair."

Emmeline stopped behind one of the palm trees that lined the rim of the infinity pool. She'd know her grandfather's voice anywhere.

"Is that really the word she used?" Another voice asked, one that Emmeline recognized vaguely. It was a man's voice, not deep or commanding, but distinctive somehow. Smooth and only slightly nasal. A clear speaking voice that sounded like it had been in the news.

"I am afraid so," King Leander said.

Emmeline inched closer to press her back against the palm tree. She knew there was no point in snooping—knew her grandfather would never let Emmeline take the crown after her mess-up with Hibernia and the way she'd floundered in the last nine months. If it wasn't Sadie, it would be Titus and then Alaric for the crown. Still, she worked hard to make out the conversation amidst the night wind, the ritzy music, the murmur of voices, and the splashes of the award-winning synchronized swimming team.

"That is disappointing. I once had such respect for the headmistress."

Her champagne glass nearly slipped from her hand. They were talking about Headmistress Aquila. Who else would her grandfather be referring to?

"As did I. But take the victory for what it is, Rhett. She is weakening."

There was a hum of approval from the other man. "It would certainly appear that way."

That's when Emmeline placed the voice beside the name. Rhett Croft, the billionaire Emmeline had seen coming from Headmistress Aquila's office on the first day back.

Why on earth was he talking to her grandfather and why were they *both* discussing Headmistress Aquila? What was the victory? What was she weakening on?

Of course her mind immediately went to the Scholars, but why would Rhett Croft and the king of Ashland have anything to do with the admissions decisions or financial workings of Almus Terra Academy? Neither of them were on the board. Emmeline knew from closely following the books of her country's treasury that King Leander had paid his grandchildren's and Sadie's tuition and entrance fee to Hibernia, and his donations to the school over the years had been modest at best.

Slowly, she backed away from the palm tree, determined not to be discovered having overheard this discussion.

Because if there was one thing she knew about Ashland's king: He was always working a deal. She was certain her strategic brilliance had come from her grandfather because a week rarely went by when she didn't notice some political, business, or trade alliance that was advantageous to their country in some respect.

So what was he working on with Rhett Croft that had to do with their school?

She didn't like the idea of Headmistress Aquila weakening on anything, even if it was somehow to Ashland's benefit.

As Emmeline stepped past the bright turquoise water's edge, the shimmering multicolored lights reflected in the infinity pool, Oakley's words rose to the surface of her mind like bubbles.

*"You know what kills me, Emmeline? It's that you're brilliant enough to actually fix this. If only you put that chess-master mind of yours to good use."*

"Ya savvy," Emmeline muttered under her

breath as she watched the hem of her mermaid tail dress skim the lapping water.

Could she put her mind to use? Was what she just overheard nothing... or *something*?

Emmeline had always believed in following her gut—though it hadn't served her very well over the last year—and her gut told her that this conversation was connected to what Oakley had said.

Piece by piece, a plan fell into place in her mind. It wasn't a *good* plan, at least not in the way Oakley meant. But it was a solid plan in terms of being able to produce results. Hopefully. *Theoretically.*

To be fair, her intentions *were* good, this time. But blackmail wasn't exactly condonable.

Picking up the excess material of her dress, she began to weave through the crowd, looking for a certain someone to be able to execute her plan.

It didn't take her long. Ilsa Halvorsen was never far from the heirs or her king at events like these. Emmeline backed up into a small table with empty glasses and waited a few minutes before the woman in a pale green evening gown and short blond waves headed in the direction of the restrooms.

Emmeline lingered a moment before she too

left her half-empty champagne glass and followed Ilsa into the bathroom. Sleek and modern, like the rest of the SkyPark, the bathrooms felt more like spas. Spotting the bathroom attendant in the corner, Emmeline jerked her chin toward the door. "Out," she commanded.

The attendant didn't hesitate. As the door closed behind her, one of the stalls opened and Ilsa came out.

The woman frowned at the sight of Emmeline, then crossed to the sink and began washing her hands as if the daughter of the man she was having an affair with hadn't just cornered her in the bathroom.

"Can I help you, Emmeline?"

Until this moment, Emmeline had wanted to forget what she'd seen a few weeks ago. She had wanted to go on pretending that her parents loved each other, even if they didn't love her, and that her father wasn't a skirt-chasing lush.

God, her naivete was pathetic.

"You can, actually," Emmeline said evenly. "I need something that I believe you can access."

Calmly, Ilsa dried her hands as she replied, "As long as your grandfather approves, I will be happy to provide you with anything you wish."

"That's the thing actually," Emmeline said,

leaning against the wall and checking her nails. "You'll have to be discreet. I need access to his personal memos."

At that, Ilsa's neck nearly snapped with how fast she whipped her head around to stare at Emmeline. "Princess, that's not...you know that's not possible."

"Oh, it is. All of his majesty's orders are executed as memos through his various secretaries, even the smallest commands like how he takes his tea. It would be easy enough to procure those receipts for me. And let's not pretend you can't do this surreptitiously. You and I both know you are *very* good at keeping secrets."

Ilsa stared at Emmeline in the mirror for a long moment. "I'm beginning to see it."

"See what?"

"Why Frederick is the way he is. You cannot simply be the king's children or grandchildren. You must find ways to surpass him...isn't that right?"

Emmeline took a step back, suddenly unsteady, her heels feeling much too high. "You...you don't get to say that to me."

Ilsa turned away from the mirror to face Emmeline fully. There was enough pity in her eyes to make Emmeline see crimson.

"I might be a loathsome creature, desperate for my parents' love, but at least I'm not sleeping with a married man," Emmeline whispered, blood rushing in her ears. "A married man who's the son of your boss. The *king*."

Emmeline was expecting at least a look of shock, but Ilsa didn't even blink. Instead, she sighed, like she was dealing with a petulant child. "You call what your parents have a marriage? Oh, Princess...No."

"Shut *up*," Emmeline said, her voice low and dangerous. "Or I will walk right out of this bathroom and tell my grandfather everything. Is that what you want?"

The confidence evaporated from Ilsa's face. "No, Your Highness."

"Good. Now get me what I ask for and, in return, I'll keep my mouth shut about your indiscretions." Then she left, before she could lose any more of herself in that damn bathroom.

She thought of Oliver and his love for moral philosophy books. Would she finally do something that he would be proud of or would he deem her next actions reprehensible?

*Well,* she thought, catching the bathroom door, *too late now.*

# 14

## ALARIC

Deputy Prime Minister Pujari was a nice man, but, boy, was he a talker. Alaric had asked one question regarding the recent Indo-Pacific Economic Framework trade agreements and it had snowballed into a full-on lecture about IPEF's four pillars.

"The second pillar—supply chain resilience—is perhaps the most critical. Economies across the world would stop. If you need evidence just look at what is happening with the Suez Canal. Attacks in the Red Sea have forced businesses into taking the far longer route around the Cape of Good Hope on the southern tip of Africa. This is a disruption of an increasingly fragile global supply chain. Or, for example, what happened a few years ago when the *Ever Given*, a four-hundred-meter-long container ship got stuck!"

"Minister—" Alaric tried to interject.

"Do you know how long it was stuck? Six days! It cost sixty billion dollars in disrupted trade, and seven hundred million in trapped cargo. If something like that were to happen again—for even longer—imagine the impact!"

Like the ill-fated *Ever Given*, Alaric was stuck, but he forced himself to stay the course. To be respectful. Minister Pujari was a knowledgeable and passionate man, and, to be fair, Alaric was learning a lot. Though if the minister were to pontificate on a pillar, Alaric would have preferred Pillar IV, the fair economy.

"Minister Pujari, I see you've met my other grandson," a distinctly deep voice said behind Alaric.

Alaric glanced over his shoulder and suddenly wished he hadn't. King Leander, Titus, and Sadie stood there.

*Feck.*

He'd been purposefully not looking at her this whole event. Because once he looked, he couldn't seem to stop. Like an absolute sap.

*Beautiful* seemed like a shallow word for Sadie tonight. Her evening gown was a pale pink with a sweetheart neckline and a bodice that hugged her curves and then fanned out in a simple silk skirt. What Alaric found most annoying—most alluring—were her sleeves. They came down in loose fabric that stopped at her delicate wrists, but they were sheer so he could see the outline of her arms and even the darker freckles that dusted her shoulders. With her hair drawn up in an elegant ponytail, her neck was bare, and Alaric had imagined kissing it more than once.

Not good.

"Yes, very smart boy you have," Minister Pujari said, clapping Alaric on the shoulder.

"I have more than one. Minister, this is Titus, and of course, my heir apparent, Sadie Aurelia."

"It's a pleasure, Minister," Titus said, taking Pujari's hand.

Sadie smiled and greeted him perfectly as well. But... Alaric could tell something was off. Her gaze didn't seem as sharp.

"And may I just say that your work in supply chains has been truly commendable," Titus continued. "The proposition you brought to the IPEF last week was brilliant."

"Ha!" the minister exclaimed. "That's just what I was telling this lad. Prince Titus, we should speak further."

"I would be honored, Minister."

"Then I will let you two discuss," King Leander said with a smile. "But I will be back to fetch him. I do know how you like to prattle on, Rahul."

Pujari chuckled good-naturedly. "That I do."

Golden Boy Titus immediately took over the conversation, outlining Minister Pujari's achievements in the latest IPEF agreements, while the Indian dignitary preened like a peacock.

It was easy enough for Alaric and Sadie to fade into the background of the conversation, as well as the scenery. The SkyPark of Marina Bay Sands was full of columns of palm trees or porticos, creating pockets of shadow between orbs of multicolored lights.

In his mind, he pictured the two of them in those shadows, his rough hands all over her soft silk sleeves, dying to get through the translucent fabric to the even smoother skin underneath.

*Boyfriend. She has a boyfriend. Get it together you fecking dope.*

"Has yer boyfriend been like this all night?" Alaric asked Sadie under his breath.

Sadie's lips tightened as she nodded. "With every person we've talked to."

Alaric kept his gaze focused on the opposite end of the pool as he brought his glass of watered-down whiskey to his lips. "How fun for yeh."

"I've managed."

But it was the unspoken words that Alaric heard instead. Titus had been outshining her in every introduction. Sadie's expression remained vacant, distant.

"Where are yeh?" Alaric asked quietly.

He could feel her glance up at him.

Alaric ducked his chin and met her wide-eyed look. "Where *are* you?" he repeated, altering his accent for extra emphasis.

Her expression shuttered and she looked away, understanding his meaning. She wasn't present—her mind elsewhere. Otherwise, she'd be kicking Titus's ass. He knew she'd prepared for this event backward and forward. He'd seen her flipping through flash cards with names of the guests before their classes.

"Mind your own business, Alaric," she said.

He knew he should, where Sadie was concerned, but he couldn't seem to stop. But he knew her well enough to know what buttons to push.

"Get it together," he growled. "Yer better than this."

At that challenge, Sadie squared her shoulders, her eyes flashing. With a swish of her skirts, she went off on her own in the direction of a group of men that Titus recognized as dignitaries from Italy, Spain, and the Netherlands.

As he watched her bravely introduce herself to the heads of state three times her age, Alaric's gaze caught on something that made his stomach seize.

Emmeline.

His *sister*.

According to a paternity test that had been taken from his father's computer, encrypted to high heaven, and broken only after a few weeks' worth of hacking by Ramona.

He was still having trouble believing it, and yet the results had been there in black and white. *"The alleged father cannot be excluded."* According to the STR loci, the short strands of DNA, Mikael Erickson was definitively Emmeline's father, with 99.99 percent repeating certainty.

And, for better or worse, his own parentage had been confirmed on the report's second page. He was, in fact, *not* a bastard. Instead, Emmeline was the illegitimate child.

The news had short-circuited his brain for nearly three days. He hadn't been able to sleep, let alone focus on his classes or anything else.

While Alaric had never given any real thought to Emmeline's parents—his aunt and uncle, technically—he'd thought about them a lot in the last week. Their marriage didn't seem to be a happy one by any means, and Lady Chloe seemed so young to have a teenage daughter. Not that he knew how their affair came to be (nor did he *want* to know). But, sadly, Alaric had no trouble believing his wretched father had lusted after a girl half his age, and Emmeline's mother, young and ambitious, was thrilled not only to have the attention of a prince but also the noble husband of Crown Princess Rhea, Alaric's mother.

It was all so, *so* messed up.

And yet, it seemed to be par for the course in this family. Part of him was actually disappointed that he *wasn't* a bastard. That Mikael Erickson's blood did truly flow through his veins. He didn't want to be related to such a monster.

Alaric had always hated him, but now he truly *despised* the man.

Not for what he'd done to Alaric. But for what he'd stolen from Emmeline.

Being a princess seemed to be woven into the fabric of Emmeline Eldana's sense of self. Out of all the Ashland heirs in the beginning, even more than Titus, she had taken to royalty flawlessly. Like she'd been born into it.

Ironically, she was the only one who hadn't.

Because Emmeline's parents weren't true royals. Lady Chloe and Lord Mikael had married into the Eldana family. They didn't have a drop of royal blood. And so, Emmeline didn't either.

It wasn't like Alaric knew his cousin—his *sister*—super well, but he'd come to understand her enough over the last year to realize this news would destroy her.

Lately, she'd seemed to be hanging on by a thread as it was.

He'd noticed changes about her in the last few months, as well as the previous semester. While Alaric had friends among the Scholars, Emmeline had disconnected from Oakley's circle and had spent much of her time with superficial groups of Elites and C-Suites. It hadn't been his business, and he never felt that it was his place to "check in," but now he wished he had.

She was his sister.

That changed things.

Maybe he should have always been a good guy who cared for people regardless of their relationship to him, but Alaric didn't have that in his bones. Years of orphanages and foster homes had stripped that generosity from him. Still, he'd longed for siblings from afar. One of his best friends back in Dublin, Kyle, had a little sister—Kaylee. Kyle had doted on Kaylee. Complained about how annoying she was, but loved her with his whole heart. He'd brag about her marks, buy her things when they were out, and protect her at all costs. Alaric had always envied their special sibling bond.

Now he had one. And he had no idea what to flipping *do* about it.

So he stood there, hesitating, unsure about whether to keep his distance or not. He was afraid if he walked over there, he'd say something, because while he knew he couldn't ever tell her, it was on the tip of his tongue... constantly.

But then someone else caught his eye.

The devil himself. Mikael Erickson stood by the edge of the SkyPark railing, his tall form backlit by the bright downtown Singapore skyline.

Alaric had suspected his father might be here, but he'd hoped he wouldn't have to see him. The whole point of breaking into his computer and its files was to take Mikael Erickson down. Ruin him because that was no less than the prick deserved. But what he'd found so far... outing Emmeline as his illegitimate child—*that* was not an option.

Unfortunately, that didn't stop a powerful surge of anger from ripping through him. How dare this man call Alaric a bastard when the hypocrite had sired his very own.

Before he could think of what he was doing, Alaric dropped his half-empty glass on a small end table, shoved his hands in his pockets, and strode across the open-air pavilion toward his father.

Mikael saw him coming and didn't bother to hide his grimace.

Lord Erickson stood in his black tuxedo and his graying hair and looked like one of those diabolical action movie villains.

"What?" he practically growled, lifting his glass to take a deep swig.

Alaric paused to take in the view. They were on the side of the SkyPark that faced the Art-Science museum—another incredible architectural feat. It was a building in the shape of a lotus flower, referred to by many as the "Welcoming Hand of Singapore" with sustainability features such as the collection of rainwater on the bowl ceiling to be used for the structure's restrooms.

He took a moment to admire it while he felt his father's irritation grow. Pretentious people just didn't appreciate marvels like this.

Finally, he glanced at his father with a small smirk. "Hey, Da, how's the craic?"

His father's lips pulled back against white teeth as the scotch—or whatever he was drinking—burned down his throat. "You know I don't know what that means. What do you *want*, Alaric?"

"Oh yeh know, just thought we'd have a little father-son chat. Catch up. I can tell yeh about my grades. The extracurriculars I'm into."

Mikael shot him a withering look. "I am not your father, Alaric."

"So yeh keep tellin' me," Alaric said with an irritating smile. This man's delusion must be stratospheric to continue denying something they both knew to be true.

But, Alaric reasoned, if you abandon a son you thought was a bastard for seventeen years and then, lo and behold, find out he actually was your flesh and blood, that's a huge mistake to own up to. Far easier to just...keep denying.

"I have to say," Alaric said, playing along like he didn't have the truth sitting on his laptop, "I really hope yer not my da, because yer one shitty father. Makes sense why Ma would cheat on yeh. Good for her."

Mikael's look of rage was one Alaric had seen many times back in the streets of Dublin. It was right before the first punch was thrown. But this was a fancy event with globally important attendees. There would be no fighting. At least not with fists.

"We're done," Mikael growled, and started to move, but Alaric stepped into his path.

"Not quite yet, Da. See, we could solve a lot of questions about this with a paternity test but I know why none of the Eldana royal family would want one. Because if it *is* true, then we'd have a gloriously high-profile royal scandal on our hands, now wouldn't we? Same could be said if I opened my mouth and blabbed to the press how a member of the royal family lived in orphanages and foster homes for sixteen years of his life, and wouldn't that invite all kinds of questions."

"You wouldn't dare—"

"I told you," Alaric enunciated, "I'm. No. Snitch. What I really want to know is why did yeh do it? It would've been safer to have me grow up as a kid with at least a guardian and a house. Yeh'd have less to cover up now, less to worry about. But...what? Yeh wanted to punish me? For just existing?"

Lord Erickson stared at Alaric for a long, long time, his eyes growing colder by the second. "I didn't care about you. I wanted to punish *her*. She loved you, and I wanted to hurt her."

Ice spread through Alaric's veins. *Her* meant Rhea. Alaric's mother.

"She...she was already dead, yeh psycho," Alaric whispered, hardly able to breathe through the pain searing in his chest like an infected wound.

Erickson's expression did not change. It remained frozen, neither pleased nor triumphant. "Even in death."

For a split second, Alaric wondered if he could do it. Push this man off the roof and see if he landed on one of the "lotus petals" of the museum below. This cruel, godforsaken monster.

But then he thought of his mother. That joyful woman in the photograph, nuzzling Alaric's puffy baby cheek with her own.

He was *her* child first. And she was not evil. In fact, she might've been the only good thing to come out of the Eldana line.

Alaric curled his hands into fists. He wanted to do *something*, though, and the desire to taunt this man with knowing the truth about Emmeline was just bobbing at the surface.

With herculean effort, he held his tongue.

He wanted to be a good brother. To protect Emmeline. And threatening their volatile father would not end well.

Showing restraint he didn't even know he possessed, he walked away.

God, he was so ready for this night to be over. Without caring what his grandfather would think if he ditched the event early, Alaric started toward the SkyPark elevators down to the resort's hotel rooms.

But he was unexpectedly intercepted.

The man who grabbed his arm came up to Alaric's chin. He had an average, rather forgettable face with graying hair, but his suit... from the man's cuff links alone, Alaric knew this man had to be as filthy rich as Bruce Wayne.

"Prince Alaric," the man said, dropping his hand from Alaric's arm and extending it for a shake. "It is a privilege to meet you. My name is Rhett Croft. I'm an acquaintance of your grandfather's."

Alaric shook the man's hand, but didn't reply. He wasn't really in a networking kind of mood, and if Mr. Croft was anything like Minister Pujari, he'd never be able to leave.

"I'd like to introduce you to someone if you have a moment," Mr. Croft said, cutting to the chase.

Before Alaric could even say yes, another man sidled into the conversation as if summoned telepathically by Mr. Croft. He was tall, Black, bespectacled, and wearing nothing more than simple khaki pants, a white button-down, a maroon cardigan, and loafers. He looked so out of place in the sea of black-tie and ball-gown attendants that Alaric was surprised he hadn't noticed him sooner.

"Prince Alaric, this is Imani—"

"Nyerere," Alaric finished, stretching out his hand to the young scientist. He remembered him from his coursework, though the picture had been of a fourteen-year-old, this guy looked closer to twenty. "You created the zol battery. I heard about you in my Experimental Energy class."

While Imani shook Alaric's hand, Mr. Croft chuckled. "Hardly experimental anymore, Alaric. The zol battery has quadrupled energy output in ways we've never seen from oil, gas, or nuclear. We have an entire small village in the Philippines running off a zol generator."

Alaric didn't know what to say to that. A simple compliment didn't seem sufficient. "Congratulations."

"Yes, we're quite proud of the work we're doing at Zolans Industries," Mr. Croft continued.

That's when it clicked: Mr. Croft likely *owned*

Zolans Industries and was showing off his shining star to everyone at the United Energy Gala.

"Would you do me a favor, Alaric, and give your friend Jacob Hewitt my card? We could use a robotics mind like his at Zolans. Have a good evening."

Too surprised to refuse it, Alaric accepted the card and watched the man stride back through the crowd, his scientist following silently behind him.

Mr. Croft wasn't interested in Alaric himself, but Alaric's friend? He was practically recruiting Jacob, and the kid was barely fifteen. More importantly, how did this man even know he and Jacob were friends?

Alaric stared down at the card, all black and sleek and simple. Just the name and an email address in silver, metallic print. Not even a logo or title. Even Croft's design aesthetic was arrogant.

He tucked the card into his inner suit pocket before the night's ocean breeze could steal it from his fingers.

# 15

## SADIE

W<small>HERE ARE YEH?</small>

Alaric's thick Irish brogue kept reverberating in Sadie's head as she moved from group to group. She chatted with the American secretary of energy, shook hands with several members of China's Political Bureau (the Politburo Standing Committee), listened to the vice president of Angola, admired the synchronized swimming team with a leading agricultural researcher from India.

All the while, she heard, *Get it together. Yer better than this.*

When he'd said it, she'd wanted to slap him. Now, however, she was more unsettled than anything. It unnerved her the way he could so easily tell when things were off with her.

It hadn't been the first time. Or even the third. The first time had been after their only class together last semester when she'd been about to keel over with menstrual cramps. Without even saying a word, he set a small bottle of painkillers on her desk. The second time had been at the end-of-year bonfire at the beach where she'd missed the line to get smoked kebabs and had been starving throughout the night until he gave her his unfinished plate. And the third time had been one of their first court dinners back at Ashland. She'd been freezing from the chill of the late-night sea wind off the harsh rocky coast and he'd dropped his jacket around her bare shoulders and walked away.

To be fair, a combination of these things would make most girls swoon.

But Sadie couldn't help seeing them as acknowledgments of her own weaknesses.

Alaric didn't think she could ever be queen. That she didn't have the strength, poise, or tenacity to rule. These small gestures, though kind and thoughtful, just reinforced his view of her. A weak, helpless creature in need of coddling.

It was a deeply jaded view to assume. But because she hadn't had a *real* conversation with him since that night outside her dorm where he'd crushed her tipsy, vulnerable self like an ant under his boot, it was hard for her to interpret his gestures as anything other than condescension. As if to say, *See, you can't even survive period cramps.*

Asshole.

But the whole reason she was off her game in the first place was because of another prince's words.

*Release me.*

Was Titus really in pain? Keeping him in this fake relationship out of spite and using him to get ahead—was it cruel, considering what *he'd* done to *her*? In her opinion, he could stand to suffer a little.

But had this gone on too long? She sure as hell didn't relish the idea of tormenting him.

"Did you hear me, Princess?"

Sadie snapped her head away from Alaric's tall retreating form and looked back at the small old man who had been telling her about the Greenland ice sheet and how its melting was affecting global sea levels.

"I—sorry, it was the splashing. I missed it. What was that again?"

The man, Hans Kleist, a leading environmental scientist from Greenland, adjusted his glasses on his nose. "I was *saying* that data is now showing that temperatures from the summer five years ago resulted in the melting of sixty billion tons of ice from our country. Do you know what that means? A single isolated incident caused global sea levels to rise by 2.2 millimeters in just two months. That's not even to speak of the Antarctic."

"Enough, Kleist, you're going to scare the poor girl," a wizened voice said from behind Sadie.

Kleist shook his head, muttering something about "kids these days," and walked off. Sadie turned to look at the older man who gently touched her shoulder, leading her to a private table under one of the large palm trees. He was *old* old, perhaps in his late eighties or early nineties. His elegant suit had likely fit once, but his body had shrunk with age. His appearance was still well-groomed, however—trim eyebrows and no rogue nose hairs—despite his wisps of thin white hair and liver spots.

"My apologies, Princess Aurelia," the man said in a thick Greenlandic accent, "Kleist means well, but he's a bit doom-and-gloom."

Sadie shook her head as the man lowered himself to a chair using her arm to do so. She took the seat next to him, politely choosing not to correct him about her first name. It wasn't worth correcting a ninety-year-old man about something he got half-right. Honestly it was a miracle he even remembered part of her name.

Studying him in the light of one of the hanging lamps, Sadie finally recognized him as Jeppe Rosing, the former prime minister of Greenland.

"I don't mind, Prime Minister. He's not wrong. We do need to understand the severity of the situation."

Rosing hummed in the back of his throat, as he situated his hands atop the head of his cane. "Perhaps. But I feel it is the duty of the older generations to protect the young. And yet, we seem to keep piling problems on you all. You are what, only . . . sixteen?"

"Nearly eighteen, sir."

"Still," he waved his old, wrinkled hand dismissively. "A child. I have lived for nine decades and been in politics over half my life. Every year, the world becomes more complex. Harder to govern, harder to heal. How can we expect the young to brave such complexity when their elders with the wisdom of time and experience do not see the path at our feet?"

"Is that because you let the past stand in the way of the future?" Sadie asked carefully.

The retired prime minister chuckled at that.

"Perhaps. It is hard to let go of things. And yet, without the knowledge of history, we will repeat it."

"I'd argue that happens anyway."

"Hmm. It's good you have a mind for politics, Princess. Though fate or God may have another plan in mind for us, we'd be fools not to try to prevent repetition. I think you'd agree that history and experience drive most of our decisions in government. Why, even your own king did his best to stop his country from an endless cycle."

Sadie tilted her head, not sure what he was referring to.

"An endless cycle, sir?"

Rosing yawned and nodded. "Oh, yes. The cycle of war. Ashland, the land of ash, of fire and fighting. Civil wars since its origin. Never more than five years of peace until King Leander. Like most rulers, he had to make many difficult choices through his reign. Though a choice that prevents war tends to be obvious, but not always easy."

Sadie's skin prickled with awareness. "Are you saying he...stopped another civil war, sir?"

The old man blinked watery eyes. "Oh, yes. Indeed. He came to me in confidence about it. That he did."

"What did he do exactly?" Sadie asked, leaning closer. The man smelled lightly of cigar smoke. "Did he stop something treasonous?"

"Mmm." Rosing squinted, as if he were trying to see through the fog of his decades-old memories. "You know of it then? I'm surprised Leander told you. But I suppose you are heir apparent and would do well to know your own history. It was treason, yes. One of those old bloodlines had returned."

"The Scealans?" Sadie asked, her voice nearing a whisper.

"Yes, that sounds right. They had a claim to the throne. Wanted to unseat your grandfather. They were planning a coup. Leander feared another civil war, so he took action. That is, sadly, one of the things the media often gets right about governments. We joke about spies and special operatives, but they are necessary, a vital resource. After all, the victories of preventing wars are never celebrated."

Sadie sat frozen in her seat, the image of the blurry typewriter document flashing through her mind.

*Peaceful Sea.*

*Scealan.*

It really had been a military report. Titus's

unbelievable Romanov comparison had been correct. The Scealans *had* survived, escaped, and disappeared, then returned to Ashland in hopes of taking back what they believed to be *their* country, *their* birthright.

Sadie wasn't sure how to feel about this. It was a lot to take in. To know that one day, strategic assassinations could be *her* job as well. Because what was the alternative? What would have happened if Leander had allowed the rebel group to continue to meet in secret and execute a plan that could hurt the public and cause another war? Was covert assassination the answer though? Why not a trial? True, it was treason. But killing off your enemies still felt morally wrong.

Sadie was so lost in her thoughts she nearly missed most of Rosing's next words.

"I supported him in his decision. But I know it was difficult. He was destroying a family. Orphaning a little girl. I sense his actions from that day still haunt him to some extent. I do believe he has tried to make up for it in you—" the old man started to cough then, wheezes racking his body.

Suddenly an attendant swooped in, one Sadie hadn't even noticed, standing in the shadows. The attendant produced a glass of water and a pill, and the prime minister took it without question.

"I'm afraid that this old body is ready to retire for the night," Rosing said with a chuckle, as he got to his feet with his cane. Sadie couldn't help but think that perhaps if he didn't smoke cigars his lungs wouldn't struggle so much.

"Have a nice evening, Princess Aurelia. I trust you will rule just as graciously as your predecessor."

"Thank you, sir. It was an honor to meet you," she said, her head spinning with all this new information.

She looked down at her own drink and suddenly wished she hadn't consumed any alcohol that evening. Because while she wasn't tipsy, or even buzzed, really, her head felt heavy from dehydration and standing most of the night.

The prime minister's words were a jumble in her mind that she needed to be able to sort through when she was less tired.

Desperate to keep a detailed record, she took out her phone and started to type out as many notes as she could.

"Sadie?"

Sadie jerked her neck up, quickly hiding her

phone, to find King Leander standing above her with a severe look.

"Why are you alone on your phone? Do you realize the optics?" he snapped.

"I was just with Prime Minister Rosing, Your Majesty."

"Did I ask who you *were* with?"

Grinding her teeth, her head pounding, and her feet blistering, Sadie stood and moved past her king, to the next group of politicians and business leaders that she was expected to charm.

*Yer better than this.*

She was better. But she wasn't sure she would ever be able to prove it to the only person who mattered. And she was scared to ask herself *who* that person really was.

# 16

## TITUS

The night was exhausting but strangely rewarding. The United Energy Gala felt like Titus's turn to prove his worth to his grandfather. King Leander stood by him proudly most of the evening, his large hand clamped on Titus's shoulder as they moved from politician to CEO to scientist.

Though his entire body felt like one large bruise. His feet throbbed with pain, while his knees and hips ached. From his lower back to the nape of his neck, there was a stiffness that made it hard for him to stand for long periods. While his fingers clutched a highball class of some brand of baijiu, which was a Chinese distilled liquor and one of the finest in Singapore, his knuckles itched to be massaged.

Not wanting his steroids and RA medication to mix with the spirits, Titus discreetly pretended to sip on the drink. Then, when no one was looking, he tipped some into the infinity pool. He sent a mental apology for his actions, but a bit of whiskey pollution would be better than his vomit.

Eventually, it felt like the event was winding down for the night and the king was finally gone from his side, making the rounds, saying his goodbyes to the people who mattered most.

"Enjoying the evening, Titus?"

A hand touched his shoulder, and Titus blinked at the tall woman with white-blond hair and pale skin.

"Madame DuPont," Titus said stepping to the side to give her room near one of the bridges across the infinity pool. "Yes, very much. We can't thank you enough for allowing us to use your charter plane to catch a ride here."

Madame DuPont was the aunt of a student at ATA and her company built the nuclear power plants that underwrote the cost of the jet that had flown them to Singapore.

"Think nothing of it. Anything we can do to absolve the profligate use of private planes. You definitely helped fill our seats."

Titus hid a smile behind the rim of his glass. The use of DuPont's plane had been Emmeline's idea, and he had to admit... he did admire her when it came to her passion about the environment. A thing that she and Sadie both shared—not that they would ever think to use that as common ground to get along.

"You know," DuPont continued, gesturing to the space with a wave of her drink, "this gala wouldn't be possible without the United Nations. But of course, our company owes them far more than that, so we're more than happy to introduce young prodigies to the importance of what we're doing here."

"You mean your company specifically owes the UN?"

Madam DuPont hummed in the back of her throat. "I mean our collective cause is indebted to the UN. Historically, the field of nuclear energy has been fraught with setbacks from governmental regulation. When we finally banded together, across borders, into the International Atomic Energy Agency, the UN took us in as a specialized agency and we've multiplied the impact of clean energy tenfold ever since."

"I...didn't know that. That's incredible."

Madame DuPont smiled. "Great things can be achieved when people across the world band together, young man. Don't forget that."

With that, she caught sight of another

dignitary and left his side. Titus looked back to King Leander and found that Sadie had joined him. She smiled charmingly as she tucked a piece of escaped hair behind her ear.

She looked gorgeous. As beautiful as a model or a movie star with her dusting of freckles, hazel eyes, and full lips.

Titus waited for the usual yearning pain to arise in his chest. While there was definitely a small sting... the longing was significantly less than before.

His phone went off in his jacket pocket and, feeling like he could finally check it, he slipped it out and the corner of his lips tugged at the short, blunt message.

> TRANG:
> **You're an idiot.**

Titus had a feeling he knew why she was calling him that, but decided to play along.

> TITUS:
> **Any reason you're just now coming to this conclusion?**

Instead of a message, he got a photo of a

T-shirt that said *It's Accrual World* next to a package from the company he'd ordered it from. He snorted, actually snorted, and quickly tried to smother his laughter. He was wondering when that would finally come in.

> TRANG:
> Do you expect me to wear this?

> TITUS:
> It's funny. Get it? Accrual vs A cruel?

She sent three eye-rolling emojis and Titus's smile widened.

> TRANG:
> Yes, I get the pun, Titus.

Perhaps it was stupid to get her the shirt. He'd bought it entirely on a whim. But he knew that she'd spent ages going through Almus Terra's books. And though she'd offered to do it, and she'd likely be offended if he suggested payment for her time, he still had wanted to do something that expressed his gratitude. Even if it was... idiotic.

TITUS:
I thought you'd enjoy a bit of accounting humor, since you are my unofficial accountant.

TITUS:
"My" meaning the student council's of course.

TRANG:
Thanks for the clarification. You didn't answer my first question.

TITUS:
You don't have to wear it.

TITUS:
But I think you want to.

TRANG:
...Shut up.

"What are you grinning about?"

Titus glanced over to find Emmeline standing a few feet away. Quickly, he tucked his phone back into his pocket.

"Nothing," he said, knowing full well she didn't actually expect him to answer.

Emmeline rolled her eyes. "It was Trang."

Titus stared at her.

"How..."

"You gave her access to the student council books, I saw you in the library with her, and every time she gets a text from you, she gets this smile and goes into the bathroom to respond."

"She does?" he asked, his brows going up.

Emmeline raised hers in return.

He quickly tried to school his features. *Shit.* He was supposed to be dating Sadie. How would it look if he was texting Trang and having any kind of feelings about it in front of Emmeline?

His cousin stared at him for a long time while he tried not to break out in a sweat. Emmeline was primed to threaten him about telling Sadie—not that Sadie would necessarily care, but Emmeline didn't know that.

Instead, she shook her head, looking tired. "Whatever. I came to tell you something."

He braced himself. "And that is?"

She crossed her arms and leveled him with a look. "Oakley told me about the school board eliminating scholarships. I want to help. Let me help."

For the second time in less than sixty seconds, Emmeline had shocked him.

"You...want to help."

"Is that so hard to believe?" she snarled, her nails digging into the sheer fabric covering her arms. Then she closed her eyes and took a deep breath through her nose. "I just...I'm your vice president. I care about this school as much as you do, believe it or not. I want to be in the game, not on the bench, okay?"

She seemed more than genuine, she actually seemed upset. It wasn't like Titus had been oblivious to the changes that Emmeline had been going through over the last nine months...he just didn't feel much pity for her.

In the same way that Sadie thought *he* deserved his own brand of torment.

With a hard swallow, Titus gave a small shrug. "It's not that I don't think you care, Emmeline. But can you blame me for not trusting you?"

"Figure out a way to trust me then," she said, her icy-gray eyes narrowing. "Because you need me on this."

Then she turned and left, her hair whipping behind her.

Finally, words from Emmeline he could agree with.

Titus was mid-drink when the jet hit a bout of turbulence. Hot tea, full of cream and sugar, sloshed down the front of his shirt and he jolted from his seat, the liquid scalding his chest. He swore colorfully under his breath while, next to him, Alaric opened one eye. He'd been listening to music with his eyes closed.

They were seatmates on the flight from Singapore to Toulon, and just like strangers on any other flight, they hadn't said two words to each other.

Alaric snorted at Titus's little accident, but then ducked under his seat and pulled out a spare shirt from his bag. It was a thin pullover athletic hoodie. Not Titus's style, but his size.

Titus blinked and took it. "Cheers."

Alaric just readjusted his headphones and moved his legs to the side.

Titus took the hint and headed to the midway point of the jet to change in the tiny bathroom. He ran his shirt under some cold water, then wrung it out and stared at his bare chest in the mirror. There was a bright red blotch on his skin, and he sighed as he wiped at the irritated skin with a cool wet towel. When he slid the hoodie over his head, the athletic fabric felt cool and comfortable against his chest. He wondered if it was made of bamboo fiber or something to enhance its breathability.

He'd always kind of judged blokes wearing

nothing but athleisure. But, bloody hell, maybe they were right.

On his way out of the bathroom, he almost ducked back inside. Sebastian was leaning against the little counter, flirting with a stewardess who was likely five years older than them, sipping at his own hot tea.

"Hey, mate," Seb said, glancing at him. Then he did a double take at Titus's pullover. "What the hell are you wearing?"

Titus lifted his soiled shirt. "Turbulence."

Seb smirked. "Smooth."

The call light went on and the stewardess left to check on a passenger toward the front of the plane.

"She'll be a nice ride when we land in Toulon," Seb said, brushing his black hair back.

Titus suppressed a grimace. "We're catching a ferry back to ATA immediately, Seb."

He shrugged. "We have weekend trips to Toulon."

"Whatever," Titus grunted, knowing for a fact that Sebastian was dating some C-Suite third-year from America. It would've been nice to stand and stretch his joints, but he didn't want to linger near Sebastian Bane, so he started to head back to his seat.

"Heard you were quite the prodigal prince last night," Seb said. "Well done, you."

The compliment sounded so belittling from Seb's mouth.

"How long until her freckled highness is kicked to the curb?"

Titus glared at him over his shoulder. "I don't know what you mean."

"Sure you don't. Well, you met the right people anyway. Saw your cousin talking to Rhett Croft. Good on him."

Alaric or Emmeline? It shouldn't matter either way, but Titus felt his skin prickle with irritation. Rhett Croft was a powerful person to know, but King Leander had neglected to introduce him, and it wasn't like he had a lot of time away from his grandfather during the gala. If either of his cousins got a chance to talk to Croft, there was a tiny bit of envy that he couldn't shake even if he'd clearly been the favorite last night.

In all honesty, he wished he wasn't like this. Even now, when he truly wanted to help Sadie, competitiveness always seemed to dominate his motivations.

He still preened when Sebastian had called him the prodigal prince. He'd still basked in the glow of his grandfather's attention. He *hated* that he was like this.

"I'm a little jealous," Sebastian continued, as if reading the emotion evident on Titus's face. "I wanted to speak to Croft myself."

*I'm sure you did.*

Rhett Croft was one of the biggest billionaires in the world, but that wasn't why Titus or Seb knew him so well. He'd been a guest speaker at Eaton one year, and his lecture was fascinating, even if the man was a walking economic crisis.

Rhett Croft was known not just for being an entrepreneur in major growth industries like energy, media, and tech but he was also a silent investor in so many companies it's like he owned a little bit of everything in every country. In not one but several nations, he had bought out layers of parent companies, creating monopolies and eliminating a competitive market. Almost all the natural gas in half of Europe was controlled by one of Croft's companies, and that monopoly meant the cost of gas was much higher than it needed to be.

His success was something to be admired and admonished.

"My father owes him his victory after all.

Ugh, I'm bored," Seb said, glancing back at the curtain, clearly tired of waiting for his stewardess. "Well, later, mate."

He clapped Titus on the shoulder and headed back to his seat, leaving Titus more than a little confused.

If memory served him, Rhett Croft had given his endorsement to the British prime minister's *opponent*. Not Sebastian's father. Titus ran a hand through his hair and curled his other into the folds of his soiled shirt. Maybe Sebastian was still hungover from last night.

Tired and sore, Titus took out his phone and pulled up the picture he'd saved from the last text he got before he boarded the flight. He might've looked at it a dozen times already.

Trang in front of a mirror wearing the shirt with her middle finger up and a smile on her lips.

# 17

## ALARIC

It was nearing nine o'clock that Sunday night when they took the ferry back to their island. The gentle rocking of the waves had most of the students sleeping inside on the plush couches, exhausted from their insane travel schedule. Two seventeen-hour flights in three days would wear anyone down. They were in the air longer than they had been on the ground.

Once they arrived at the docks, several carriages loaded them up and transported them back to the castle. Most of the time Alaric felt lazy using the carriages when the path up to the castle was barely three-quarters of a mile, but this time he was grateful.

Oakley, who was a member of the Equestrian Club, waited at the entrance to help take care of the horses and bring them to the stables that were located halfway back down the path.

He noticed Emmeline pass Oakley without saying a word, hurrying into the castle with her suitcase in tow.

The idea of his sister alone at this school, with no real friends since whatever falling-out she'd had with Oakley, didn't—couldn't—sit right with him anymore.

"Oy," Alaric said, walking up to Oakley as she stroked the neck of a large palomino.

"Hey, how was the trip? Did you meet my dad?"

Oakley's father owned the largest wind farms in Australia and New Zealand. It made sense for him to be at the United Energy Gala as well, but Alaric hadn't seen him.

"It was quality, no, and what happened with Emmeline?"

Oakley stopped petting the palomino and looked over her shoulder (and upward) to stare at him. "Blimey, Durham. What brought this on?"

Alaric shrugged. It hadn't been his business to ask. Now, he felt like it was. He felt dumb suddenly acting like the concerned older brother, but... he had to start somewhere.

"That's between me and her. If she wants to tell you, she can."

"She won't."

"Not *my* problem."

"C'mon, Oak," he grunted. "She's not all that ba—"

Oakley spun, shoving her finger into his face, nearly spearing his nostril. "Don't you dare. You don't get to defend Emmeline to me. You don't know what she did, nor what she's capable of. Considering you're obsessed with the girl she hurt the most, you'd be mad at her, too, if you knew. So, like I said, ask *her*."

Alaric raised his hands in surrender. "Fine then. No need to eat my head off."

With a huff, Oakley swung up on the carriage seat and the driver clicked the reins, pulling the horses ahead.

*Obsessed with the girl she hurt the most.*

He didn't like how she said that, even if it was, maybe, a little bit true. *Feck*. Was he *obsessed* with Sadie?

Groaning, Alaric slung his duffel over his shoulder and headed back to his dorm room. Sebastian was nowhere to be seen, Titus was likely walking Sadie back to her dorm, and Oliver was at his desk, glancing from his laptop to the girl sprawled on Alaric's bed, reading one of his favorite manga volumes.

"Romy," Alaric growled. "What are yeh doin'

here?" With the exception of when he'd talked to Sadie and his father, Alaric had tried to rein in his heavy brogue over the weekend, but now it came out in full force.

Romy lowered his third volume of *Death Note* and beamed at him. "Hey, welcome back."

"She asked if she could wait for you, Alaric. Said you wouldn't mind," Oliver offered, and though he didn't look angry, there was a hint of annoyance in his tone.

Alaric worked his jaw as he dropped his duffel at the foot of the bed. "Romy, it's almost ten-thirty."

"Right, but see, I cracked open some more files. And this time?" She raised her hands to her face, placing her fingertips under her chin and batting her eyelashes. "I couldn't help myself."

Alaric's eyes narrowed, but her smile just grew wider as if his anger gave her delight. He jerked his head toward the door. "Let's take a walk."

"You're the boss, muchacho. Bye, Oliver!"

Looking exasperated, but still somehow polite, Oliver gave her a small wave. "Later, Romy."

"Yeh could've texted me," Alaric said as she fell into step beside him down the corridor.

"And miss seeing the look on your face? Not

a chance, lance. I worked nearly eight hours straight on that last hack and I deserve my reward."

They went up the staircase and took the narrow corridor that led out to the ramparts. "So what did yeh find?"

"Noooo, we'll talk about your thing in a second. I want to know what you thought about our kiss."

Alaric coughed.

He was used to bluntness, but Ramona Vasquez seemed to operate on a whole other level than most people. Maybe another stratosphere.

"Yeh want to know... what I thought?"

She cocked an eyebrow and reached up to slide her fingertips along his jaw. "Yeah, like... do you want to do it again?"

Alaric didn't step back from her touch, but he didn't lean in either. "Ramona. I have no intention of dating yeh."

Romy grinned, shrugging. "Technically I wasn't talking about dating."

With a sigh, Alaric ran a hand through his hair. He couldn't deny that the kiss had been nice. Great, even. But no. He didn't want to repeat it. Not when he still felt the way he did about Sadie. Even though Sadie was dating someone else, and she likely hated his guts. Even though he'd been clear about his feelings to Ramona, and she hadn't cared.

It didn't feel right.

"Or anything else," he said finally.

Ramona pouted, but then stepped back and shook her head. "Ah well, can't blame a girl for trying." Then she cocked an eyebrow at him. "You know, it helps to get over someone by confessing and being able to get some closure. Maybe you should try that."

Alaric looked away. Maybe he should. But he wasn't ready for that yet. Wasn't ready to give her up. It sounded ridiculously sentimental, the kind of thing he'd read in some shoujo manga or romance novel. The simple embarrassing truth was that he wanted to hold on to these feelings a little while longer.

"Yeh said yeh found something?" he grunted.

"Okay, okay," Romy said, pulling out her phone from her back pocket. "Sorry for snooping by the way. I know I said I wouldn't do that, but once I saw the name of the file, I honestly couldn't *not* look at it." She glanced up at him from her phone screen with a frown. "You said this was your dad's computer, right?"

"Yeah, and don't worry, I already know he's an

arsehole. Whatever yeh find probably won't surprise me."

Romy's brows lifted. "So finding out your dad helped broker an arms deal and then profited from it, wouldn't be surprising?"

Alaric nearly choked.

Even though he had been expecting some dark crap on Mikael Erickson's computer, an arms deal wasn't exactly the first place he went. But was he surprised by it? He remembered what that monster had said about his ma. About wanting to hurt Rhea, *even in death.*

So, no, in that regard, he wasn't surprised.

"I'll need yeh to elaborate."

"I figured as much. Here's the details." She handed him a new little flash drive. This one was in the shape of a little Japanese onigiri. A rice ball snack.

"The long and short of it is that I found a few memos that help explained what, exactly, your father does for the king of Ashland."

Alaric furrowed his brow, confused. "What do yeh mean? I know what he does. He's the crown's chief financial advisor."

"Sure, but do you know what that *means?*"

"I guess I don't know his job responsibilities if that's what yer getting at."

Romy nodded. "Yeah, I am. He's a day trader, but with a fancy title."

"A day trader? Like for the stock market?" Then it hit him. He had remembered learning about this vaguely over the summer in one of their many tutoring sessions regarding the operation of Ashland's government. "The Ashland Investment Fund," he muttered.

Romy nodded, as if she too knew the ins and outs of his country's economics. Perhaps she did. She was a hacker and looking up stuff was kind of her thing. "Bingo. He trades stocks for Ashland's sovereign wealth fund and it looks like he takes a lot of his orders from the king. Obviously."

Alaric raked a hand through his hair again, sending his dark waves in every direction. "Yer not exactly explaining the arms deal part, Romy."

"Hold your boxer briefs, I'm getting there. Or is it just briefs?"

He stared at her.

"I was *joking*. Sheesh. So I found some memos that speak to your dad getting orders from your grandfather to buy stock in Tyrannus Tech, which is a weapons manufacturer based in the United States. I thought the name was familiar and I was right. There was another folder I opened for you by the same name. In *that* folder, I found records of your grandfather working with US and Russian dignitaries for the purchasing agreement to go through. As in, he helped broker a deal for Russia to purchase US tanks from Tyrannus Tech."

Alaric frowned. He understood the business deal, but that wasn't illegal.

Romy sighed. "Alaric, the stocks, remember. He purchased the stock in Tyrannus Tech *before* the deal went public and Tyrannus Tech's stock value went through the roof. It's stock manipulation and that's—"

"Illegal."

Alaric understood now. It was insider trading, or policy manipulation. Whatever you wanted to call it, what his father and grandfather were doing was illegal.

Some people could see it as a victimless crime, and sure, it wasn't *murder*, but it was still criminal. The market was a house of cards, built on nothing more than the perceived value of money. It was complex and intricate and manipulating it to benefit one entity over many brought instability due to unfairness and depreciation.

It also didn't help that this illegal activity revolved around weapons manufacturing. You didn't have to be a stock market genius not to feel great about that deal.

Alaric's stomach soured.

He'd believed this of his father, but his grandfather? The man wasn't a kind, loving grandad—he'd been perfectly comfortable sending away his grandchildren for sixteen years—but Alaric had, at the very least, seen King Leander as a ruler who cared about his country.

Technically, that was still true.

He was growing their sovereign wealth fund, making their country richer by the day, by the hour. But was it right? Was that what Ashland wanted in a king? Money and prosperity over ethics and morality?

"I won't say anything," Romy said, in the quietest voice he'd heard her use yet.

At that, Alaric looked down at her, raising an eyebrow. "This coming from an ethical hacker?"

Romy hesitated, then gave him a small smile. "Well, it *is* rare that you can prove stock manipulation... and this would make headlines."

"Maybe, but it would hurt the people of my country," Alaric said, his voice hard.

"That's why I won't say anything. You have my word, and it may just be the word of a hacker, but—"

"I trust yeh."

She blinked up at him. "You do?"

"Ethical, right?"

Romy grinned, moving her hands to her hips. "Are you *sure* you don't want to make out?"

With a roll of his eyes, Alaric turned to head back to the dorm, shoving his hands in his pockets. "G'night, Vasquez."

"Sweet dreams, Durham."

In his pocket, Alaric squeezed the little jump drive, wondering if an illegitimate child and an insider trading scheme was just the tip of the iceberg when it came to Mikael Erickson.

The only thing he *did* know? Sleep wasn't happening tonight.

# 18

## SADIE

Emmeline and Oakley were asleep, and Trang was, as usual, doing something on her laptop. Her pale face illuminated by the blue light of the MacBook Pro balanced on her thighs. Sadie sat at her desk, hunched over her tablet, staring at the blurry PDF.

It wasn't like it had slowly come more into focus since the last time she'd looked at it, but *Peaceful Sea* called to her like a lighthouse beacon back home. Like the lights on the Durah cliffs, warning of danger, death, and homecoming.

Her fingers pulled at the name *Scealan* on the glass screen and zoomed in.

Prime Minister Rosing had said that it had been treason, and that Leander had made a difficult decision that had saved Ashland but destroyed a family.

Practically speaking, Sadie had uncovered the

secret to this document. There was no need to really look at it anymore. Yes, she'd found evidence of treason, and the resulting executions, but what was done was done. Could she really use this discovery to prove her worth as heir apparent? Was it something she could use to blackmail King Leander and ensure that her title was not passed over to Titus?

Somehow, she doubted it. So why was she still staring at this?

With a frown, Sadie glanced back at the notes on her phone. The notes she'd typed out from her time with the prime minister. Some of what he said just hadn't made sense. Especially the very last part. *He has tried to make up for it in you.*

How could he try to make up for it in her? Did he mean by accepting Sadie as heir apparent? An outsider to the Eldana bloodline? It was far-fetched, but...

Sadie scrolled back up to the date of the report. July 28th. Yep, seventeen years ago was how long ago Prime Minister Rosing had told her the coup had been crushed.

That's when she froze, her brain locking on that date in the top left corner. It was similar to...

Sadie flipped back on her tablet through the

images, back to the one that had changed her life forever.

The Ashland National Merit Scholarship Program memo had been drafted the very day he'd received this report. Was that a coincidence? It didn't feel like one.

Sadie bit her lip, her mind racing as she worked to connect the dots.

*He has tried to make up for it in you.*

The words kept replaying. Was the scholarship program Leander's repentance for killing a family and orphaning a girl?

*Wait.*

Her gaze dropped to the name scrawled in the bottom corner. The name that had been partially cut off. The name she had assumed had been hers. The name of the first scholarship winner who would one day get a chance at the crown.

*Aurelia Sad—*

Looking at it with fresh eyes, Sadie could tell that the name was not *Sadie*. What she thought had looked like an *a* actually looked like a *c*. And the d was actually the *e* and the *a* and the *l* rather squashed together. The rest was cut off by the picture.

No, the scrawled name...looked more like *Scealan*.

*He has tried to make up for it in you.*
In you.
In. You.

The earth fell out from beneath Sadie, and she shot to her feet.

Her tablet dropped to the floor, the glass edge cracking and spiderwebbing across the pristine delicate surface. She banged her knees on the desk's legs, jolting the entire piece of furniture and causing a book and a jar of pens and pencils and knickknacks to fall and spill across the rug.

"Sadie?" Trang asked, pulling down her headphones and looking at Sadie with confusion, almost concern.

Sadie felt like she couldn't breathe. Everything was closing in around her. But for the first time, she didn't want to be pulled out of her spiral. She didn't want to come crashing back to reality. She wanted to be locked in this place between suspecting and knowing. Because if she knew, she worried it wouldn't break her this time. It would *erase* her. She needed... to run.

Gasping, heaving, Sadie fumbled for the doorknob.

It couldn't be true. Even if it was written in his own handwriting. Even if he jotted down the winner's name before it had ever happened.

Even if the days of those two memos matched. Even if—

She could *not* be the orphaned girl from the treasonous plot after which Leander created the scholarship program to ensure the daughter of his enemy had a *legitimate* chance at the crown when her father had not.

She had her own family. Her mah, her grannah...

Her mah who had died by suicide. Her grannah who'd suffered dementia. Her dah whom she'd never known, only read and reread his journal full of silly little poems and writings. She'd believed those things were all hers, but there was no one left for Sadie to ask if her mother and grandmother had been hers by blood.

If her thought process made sense, then that meant her whole identity was a lie. Her whole *life* was a lie.

*Princess Aurelia.* Prime Minister Rosing might have been old, but he hadn't acted senile. He'd been sharp. And having been around a senior with memory loss, Sadie was able to tell when their mind was slipping.

Prime Minister Rosing had called her that because he knew her real name.

*Aurelia Scealan.*

Finally, Sadie wrenched the door open with shaking hands. She ignored Trang's whispered shout and just started running. Her bare feet slapped against the stone floor as she took off through the castle corridor.

Her breath, the wind in her ears, the pounding of her footsteps—it blocked out thoughts, so she was concentrating only on how her body ached and the sounds of time racing to catch up with her. For the first time, Sadie could understand why Alaric ran that day. And kept running.

If she stopped... everything would catch up to her and she wouldn't be *Sadie* anymore.

A voice called to her. It was gentle and coaxing, but gruff somehow. An Irish brogue she knew unreasonably well.

"Cailín, oy, cailín... *Sadie*."

The world came rushing forward in a blur of color and sounds. Gone was only her breath and the sound of wind and waves, and the pounding of her feet. Now, it was the hard footsteps on stone, the angry muttering of someone much larger than herself, the dim lights of the castle corridors.

"What have yeh done, cailín?"

When Sadie realized who it was, where she

was, when time was suddenly moving around her and she was no longer blissfully numb, she tried to hobble away.

*Hobble?*

With a gasp, pain originating from her feet seemed to explode through her system. She looked down and blisters and blood, along with little pebbles and tiny broken branches, decorated her poor feet.

"Oh my god," she whispered. Where had she gone? Where had she run? Down to the beach with no shoes? That would explain the little pebbles and the sweat coating her body.

She could not let Alaric see her like this. It would just reinforce what he'd always believed. That she's weak, not capable of handling herself, let alone be queen.

It was saying something that even after all she'd discovered tonight, his opinion was still one of the things holding space in her heart. Like it wouldn't be displaced by anything else. Even something as humongous as finding out she might, potentially, be the daughter of a traitor executed by the man who had practically adopted her.

She limped away faster.

"Oy, oy, what are yeh *doin*?"

Alaric's hand grabbed her arm, his fingers wrapping around her bare arm. She was wearing a sleep shirt with a cartoon manatee that said *Oh, the hu-manatee!* and a pair of plaid boxer shorts.

"Nothing!"

"Yer wandering out of bed at three o'clock in the morning in yer pajamas with fecked-up feet. Definitely not nothing."

Sadie refused to look at him. "I'm *fine*."

Alaric stared at her like she'd truly lost it. And perhaps she had.

"Luv, why are... Jaysus Christ. Yer wee feet are bleeding. How long have yeh been... Yeh know what, screw it."

Before Sadie could react, Alaric bent over and placed his shoulder into her stomach, then stood, flipping her over so she hung halfway down his back.

She gasped. "Alaric! Put me down!" she hissed as all the blood rushed to her head.

"Yer clearly upset. And until I determine how best to fix yeh, yeh'll stay right up here."

Sadie was about to argue, and pound her fists against Alaric's broad muscular back, but the moment her feet left the ground a wave of relief flooded through her. Her feet had hurt *so* bad and now it was... less so. She went quiet and fell against his back, breathing in the scent of his well-worn hoodie. The clean detergent scent, and a hint of his own—like mint and fresh rain—calmed her racing heart.

His arms wrapped around her bare legs, and Sadie felt her entire body flush with heat. His hands were careful not to touch anywhere she wouldn't want him to, but that didn't stop her from feeling embarrassed. Nor from feeling like her insides had turned to butterflies.

She didn't ask where they were going and was surprised when they arrived at the infirmary.

"It's probably locked," she muttered.

"Hush," he commanded, and judging from his movements, Sadie guessed he was digging into his pocket. Then the sounds of a lock being picked echoed through the corridor.

"Are you seriously breaking in right now? You carry around *tools*?"

"Since I was thirteen. If it makes yeh feel better, yeh can't see it so technically yer not a witness."

"No, that doesn't make me *feel* better."

Unbelievably, the door clicked open, and Alaric dropped her onto a hospital bed after shoving one of the curtains aside. Well, dropped wasn't entirely accurate. He was surprisingly gentle.

With one look at her, though, he barked out a laugh. "Yeh look like a tomato."

"Because all the blood rushed to my head, you jerk."

"Better that than yer poor feet," he muttered, grabbing a first aid kit by Ms. Martinez's station and bringing it over to her. "Lemme see."

To her utter shock, he knelt down and, with nimble fingers, he started to pick off the pebbles and other debris left from the path down the village and the beach. It was pretty gruesome—she'd been cut in several places and blisters had burst at the bottom of her feet. But he didn't even grimace as he cleaned her off with warm water and soap and a washcloth.

Mesmerized at his careful, methodical movements, Sadie didn't dare say a word.

"How's that feel?" he asked softly, as he applied rubbing alcohol to sanitize.

"Stings," she whispered back.

He huffed. "I'd say so."

She *nearly* started crying right then. His gentle voice and even gentler hands were nothing like the Alaric she'd had in her head the last nine months. They were closer to the Alaric who took sharp things away from her when he didn't want her hurting herself, or who always worried about her slipping and falling. Who was always so... protective.

And yet, he's the one who hurt her the most.

More than Titus, more than Emmeline, even. His lack of faith had drilled into the crevices of her heart and refused to come out.

"I thought you hated me," Sadie said after a long moment of him using Q-tips to dab antibiotic cream on her open sores.

Alaric glanced up at her, her bare foot resting on his thigh felt so intimate. But... felt right too. His dark eyes held hers for a long moment, then he looked back down at his work.

He let out a puff of air, almost like an exasperated laugh. "Yer blind, Sadie. Blind as one of those butt-ugly fish yeh love in the bottom of the ocean."

Her face flushed. "And *you're* as rude as ever."

"Can't improve on perfection."

Sadie tried to yank her foot away, but he held on by her ankle, giving her a hard look. "Let me finish, cailín. If yeh won't tell me what happened, let me do this at least."

"Why do you even care?" Sadie snapped, trying to get her foot free.

He sighed. "Yeh really can't see it."

Sadie let out a growl of frustration, but Alaric suddenly surged upward, planting his hands on either side of her thighs. "I am *no'* messin', Sadie. Yer feet are wrecked. If yeh didn't already have a tetanus shot for school, I'd wake Ms. Martinez up to deliver one. Yeh've freaked me out and I won't let yeh leave me like this. If yer too blind to see it, I'll spell it out. I care about yeh. Whether yeh want me to or not. So hold still and fer the luv of God, stop fightin' me."

His hot breath was at her collarbone. His broad shoulders hunched like one of those massive athletes ready to tackle something. He looked threatening and yet, Sadie had never felt so safe. Or so breathless. Her heart hammered as she searched his angry, harsh, handsome face.

Not for the first time, she wished she wasn't so damn attracted to him.

"My whole life is a lie," she blurted out suddenly. She hadn't planned to tell him. It was too raw, too new. But Alaric always had a way of drawing things out of her. Those eyes of his…

Alaric sat back on his heels, his dark brows furrowed with confusion. "What?"

Sadie glanced away and rubbed her hands up and down her bare arms. Wordlessly, Alaric stripped off his hoodie and handed it to her. She took it and held it to her chest, like it was a stuffed animal rather than a jacket.

"Revenge... do you really believe in it?"

It was a question that had been circling in her head. Leander had stolen a future from her. He'd had her parents killed. She *hated* him for that. And she hated him for other things as well. She wanted him to pay for that crime. For murdering parents she'd never know...

However, before she'd realized that *she* was the biggest loser in this tragedy, she'd found herself agreeing with Leander's actions. Her parents could've started a civil war.

Was it the right call to end their lives to prevent an insurrection? Maybe not. But she was starting to realize that to govern a nation, you had to live your life in shades of gray.

It didn't stop her from wanting Leander to answer for taking her parents from her.

She felt Alaric studying her, but she kept her gaze on her wounded feet, afraid of his answer.

"No."

Surprised, she looked up, blinking at him. "No?" She thought he'd said that he had, once.

He shrugged. "The giant, Durah, and the sea, right? It only caused more bloodshed for her. It's not like it brought Ashland peace. So I doubt it would bring yeh peace. It might for me, not for yeh."

"You remembered my story?" Sadie asked. She'd told him nearly a year ago. It was the little rhyming fable her mother—her adoptive mother—had loved to tell her.

Alaric's stormy gaze searched her face. "I remember everything that's important to yeh, cailín."

Hot tears pricked her eyes and suddenly she was spilling her guts.

Out came everything. *Everything.*

Why Titus had started dating her. What Emmeline had done. What she'd planned at Hibernia and what she'd pulled off with Oliver. Her falling-out with Trang. Her fake relationship with Titus. Her struggle in being heir apparent with the king's advisory council. The memos she had snapped pictures of. And then... her conversation with the former prime minister of Greenland, his revelation, and her suspicion. That she might actually be Ashland's very own *Anastasia*. It sounded preposterous. So categorically bananas that she couldn't look him in the eye.

Her throat was hoarse from talking and her skin burned with the shame of how she'd just bared her soul to him. Once again.

All because of some sweet, beautiful words.

God, hadn't she learned her lesson?

"Yer not a lie, Sadie."

Sadie lifted her head, blinking at him, then flinched as his rough thumbs started wiping away the tears across her cheeks.

"Whoever yeh are, however yeh came to be that person...that's not a lie," his voice was gruff, and Sadie was beginning to realize that's how he sounded when he was clogged with emotion. "Yer ma. Her love for yeh wasn't a lie. And yer love for her, it's real?"

"Of course it's real," Sadie whispered.

"That's all that matters," he said.

Sadie tilted her head up, focusing on the low infirmary lights. The halogen glared into her retinas as she blew out a shaky breath. It was in this place where she'd been paralyzed with grief after losing the journal, the last piece of her family.

Those feelings, her grief, her love, her pain, had all been very, very real.

Alaric was right: Sadie Aurelia or Aurelia Scealan. Adopted or not, her past was her own and there was no truth that could take those experiences away from her.

Alaric was silent as he peeled open the Band-Aids and carefully placed them around her toes. One by one, he taped them on each of her feet—five total—and his face got stonier with each one he placed.

They didn't talk as he found slippers for her to wear from the infirmary closet, and they didn't talk as he put away the first aid materials and cleaned up their mess. They also didn't talk as he walked her back to her dorm, even though she very much expected him to leave her at the infirmary door.

When they reached her dorm, she hesitated, then started to hand him back his hoodie.

"I never asked... how come you were out so late. Did something happen to you too?" Now in a clearer headspace, she was curious.

Alaric made a face, scratching the back of his neck. "Another night, cailín. Yeh need sleep."

Sadie frowned. "Wait, what is it? What happened?"

He blew out a breath and scuffed his sneaker against the marble. "Nothing happened *to* me. But let's just say I have no trouble believing any of the shite yeh told me tonight."

Oh, Sadie was deeply curious now, but his stern look conveyed that was all she was going to get.

"Alaric... everything I said..."

Her frenzied confessional had been so liberating, but it had also made her vulnerable. What would he do now with all this information?

He started to turn away. "Don' worry. Tonight never happened."

She stared up at him. He just wanted to pretend that all of this *didn't* happen? Sure, she wished she hadn't been quite so forthcoming but all that he'd done, all that he'd said...it was meaningful to her. She didn't want to forget.

"Alaric—"

He suddenly surged toward her, his large hand cradling the back of her head. Her heart thudded as his fingers twirled into her mess of a ponytail and tugged her hair, tipping her neck back to force her face to his.

His gray eyes bored into hers. Serious and so like the turbulent waves off the coast she loved. With his thumb, he traced her bottom lip. "Go inside, Sadie. Go before I remember that yer not in love with my cousin and I could kiss the hell out of yeh right now if yeh let me."

Sadie's whole body flushed, concentrated heat pooling in her belly, and she stumbled back into the door.

With a smirk, Alaric pulled away and glanced down. "Cute shirt, by the way."

She scrambled for the door handle and nearly fell backward into her dorm room. Chest rising and falling, Sadie leaned her forehead against the door.

And then locked it before she did anything catastrophically stupid like rip open her door and allow him to follow through on his promise to kiss the hell out of her.

She shouldn't want that. She *shouldn't*, but oh, Durah, did she. He'd be gentle when he kissed her at first. Like he had been while tending to her feet. But then he'd be rough, like her sea, pulling her into his tide and carrying her out far beyond the safe zone so she'd drown in him.

Sadie swallowed, lifting her head from the door. Wiping her thoughts clean. She was still dating Titus. *His cousin.*

Alaric had rescued her tonight, and she was glad she'd told him all those things. It felt more freeing than she could've imagined.

Except for the part where he had captured her once again.

# 19

## EMMELINE

Emmeline was in the middle of her Global Food Supply class when she received the email from Ilsa Halvorsen. The secretary had certainly taken her sweet time. Nearly a month had passed since the United Energy Gala and Emmeline was hours away from calling her grandfather to tell him about the affair.

But, ultimately, that wouldn't get her what she wanted, so she was patient. For the most part.

Her patience was definitely tested by forcing herself to focus on the data chart in front of her that showed the per capita kilocalorie supply from all foods by continent. While she cared very much about global food production and people's access to it, it was still hard to focus on black-and-white numbers when royal secrets sat in her inbox two clicks away.

Instead, she minimized her email and turned

her attention back to Professor Thuku, a Kenyan researcher from the UN FAO (United Nations Food and Agriculture Organization).

"The minimum dietary energy requirement, or MDER, represents the calories required to remain and sustain a healthy weight for a person's height. This key measurement helps us look at malnourishment in a population. On average, if the MDER is generally lower, you will likely find a nation suffering from hunger and limited access to food. I want everyone to pick a country with an at-risk MDER and conduct a thorough research analysis as to *why* you think that country is struggling. There is never one reason alone. The world is complex. I want to see that complexity in your presentations. Let's report back two weeks from today. Class dismissed."

Emmeline slid her laptop into her bag and darted toward the back door of the classroom. She stepped out into the hall and swiftly into an adjacent room, which happened to be one of the art studios. She dropped her bag on a stool and opened her laptop once again.

Immediately, she pulled up the memos and started sifting through them one by one. They were all... *boring*.

Mundane tax changes, government spending

budget approvals, court appeals—it was impressive how much Leander seemed to manage. Impressive or obnoxiously controlling. Perhaps a bit of both. It didn't seem practical to micromanage an entire government. Either way, it was clear that Ilsa had taken the lawyer tactic that Emmeline knew from courtroom dramas. She'd drowned her with documentation to hide or delay her from finding any useful information.

Reading her twenty-eighth memo, Emmeline finally felt the spark of something worthwhile.

This one dealt with a company called Rielson Enterprises. It referenced a virtually undetectable software that collected data via the company's internal network. Rather than needing to install it on someone's computer, it could be applied through the wireless network, and whoever logged onto that network would have all their data tracked and analyzed.

A scary idea, but not exactly surprising. Emmeline assumed there were many similar products out there.

The name of the company sounded familiar, not because she knew its product or saw it in the news but because she was sure she'd encountered it recently. Frowning, Emmeline pulled open an app she had that followed business mergers, acquisitions, creations, and closures. It showed that Rielson had been bought out by a different company, Hellion, whose name was also familiar. Feeling like she was a detective hunting down some kind of new lead, she opened the student council folder, full of proposals and information about the school's administration.

Pulling up the books, she paused when she saw a down payment to Hellion, her blood running cold. Almus Terra had purchased this software from Hellion, formerly known as Rielson. A less punctilious person would've missed the connection entirely, but not Emmeline.

She glanced back to Leander's memo. He'd ordered the purchase of stocks in Rielson days before this data collecting product was announced. It seemed to be a rather straightforward case of insider trading. A criminal practice when it came to stock manipulation, but practiced so often it was hard to nail anyone (especially an entire country) with such an offense.

What was *more* important was that, once again, Ashland and Almus Terra were linked. The connection was loose, and maybe she was grasping at straws, but she couldn't stop remembering the conversation she'd heard that night at the gala between her grandfather and Rhett Croft.

What made Headmistress Aquila weak? Why was her grandfather instructing Mikael Erickson to invest in a company that Almus Terra had bought from?

Was Almus Terra paying for this new cataloging (privacy-invading) software, or were they using another one of Rielson Enterprise's products?

There were too many questions to entertain, especially by herself. She could spin her wheels for hours and never get anywhere with these questions. She needed to talk to Titus. Maybe even Trang. They were the ones looking through the school's financials. Was this one of those ATA purchases that had them bleeding money? Was Ashland reaping the benefits?

But if she brought this to Titus, would he even trust her enough to hear her out?

*C'mon, Emmie, don't be a coward.*

So what if he turned her away as he had before? This was different from a year ago when she'd cornered him in the corridor and proposed an alliance between them to take down their rivals. This time, it was for the greater good and at least she'd be *trying*.

Decision made, Emmeline slammed her laptop shut and she was halfway to the door when it suddenly opened in front of her.

"Emmeline," Danica said, her eyes wide as she looked at her former friend.

Emmeline tensed, her arms cradling her laptop like a shield.

Danica's gaze softened. Perhaps she saw Emmeline for what she was: a wounded gazelle one limp away from having her blood smeared across the savannah, her carcass left for scavengers. That's how raw and vulnerable she felt nowadays. It was pathetic but, after experiencing real friendship, nine months of near isolation was torture.

It was like *Flowers for Algernon* but with companionship.

"I was just leaving," Emmeline said, starting to brush past Danica as soon as she'd stepped inside the studio. *I'm saying that a lot these days.*

"How are you doing?"

Emmeline stopped, her hand on the doorknob. She looked back at Danica with narrowed eyes. "You don't have to do that, Danica."

Danica blinked. "Do what?"

"Pretend. I don't need your pity," Emmeline said coolly.

"I'm not pretending."

Emmeline narrowed her gaze. "But you are pitying me."

Danica glanced away. *Nailed it.*

Emmeline blew out a breath. "I'm fine. Tell Oakley I...I'm following her advice, okay? I'll see you later." Then she ducked out of the room before she could put her foot even further into her mouth.

Alaric didn't look thrilled to see her. Granted, few people ever did, but today felt different. Alaric actually seemed downright *angry* at her.

"Who spit in your Cheerios?" Emmeline asked, hands on her hips as she tilted her chin to meet Alaric's intense glare.

"What are yeh doin' here, Emmeline?"

Emmeline frowned, shifting her weight from one platform sneaker to the other. "I came to talk to Titus."

"He ain't here. Text him."

"He doesn't respond to my texts."

"Wonder why," Alaric growled, starting to close the door on her.

Emmeline slid her shoe between the frame and the door, stopping him from shutting her out—literally. "What the hell, Alaric? Are you mad at me?"

Alaric's dark gray eyes flashed. He stepped back and pulled the door open, revealing the empty dorm room.

Catching the hint, Emmeline stepped inside.

"Okay, what is it? What did I do?" she demanded.

Emmeline had ignored it until now, but Alaric's treatment of her had been all over the place since near the start of the semester. In fact, before the United Energy Gala, he'd been... considerate? For Alaric. They both took Experimental Energy and Market Research 101 and after their classes, Alaric had lingered to talk about the material. Then after the gala, he seemed to avoid her. Even shooting her dark looks on occasion. To her, Alaric's behavior had always been rather predictable. They weren't friends, but she felt like she understood him. Until recently.

"Let's just say I finally know why yer no longer friends with Oakley."

Emmeline's lips parted, her stomach sinking, her heart fracturing.

The one thing she had appreciated about Sadie was that she hadn't spread their drama around the whole school—though Emmeline had suspected that had been more for her own preservation than Emmeline's. But Oakley, Danica, and Oliver had kindly kept that incident to themselves as well. Again, likely more for Sadie's sake than Emmeline's.

All to say, she wasn't *surprised* that Alaric knew, but why now? Why did Sadie—because it had to be Sadie—tattle on her now?

Her face flushed with the words she was about to say. "So what do you want from me, Alaric? An apology?"

"Sure as shite not to me."

"And I'm sure as shit not apologizing to *her*."

"Are yeh for real right now?"

"I am *not* apologizing. She stole my crown. She stole *everything* and *everyone* from me," Emmeline hissed, trying not to raise her voice. "And if she wasn't strong enough to be in the game, then that's on her. I did what I had to do. Can you honestly say you thought she had it in her to be queen? I mean, come on. She was a ball of fluff! I was doing her a *favor*. I was doing Ashland a favor."

Alaric stared back at her as she breathed hard, her words flying out as if they were escaping a prison. She didn't fail to notice how his own complexion had paled, his gaze darting away as if in guilt.

"What yeh did was wrong, Emmeline. And I thought better of yeh."

Emmeline reared back as if she'd been slapped. For whatever reason... That. Fucking. Hurt.

As bad as knowing Oliver's opinion of her. And Oakley's.

Alaric was her rival. They were only cousins, not friends. And yet... hadn't family always been her true goal? She had *wanted* Alaric and Titus to be like brothers to her. She had only ever viewed them as rivals because she was so desperate to get her parents' attention. She'd thought she'd accomplish that by becoming heir apparent. She was starting to realize it wouldn't have mattered anyway.

"You...you don't get to pass judgment on me," she gasped, like she was jumping into an icy ocean. "Remember that night I had you pulled off a cop car? Remember how you almost ruined yourself? *I* helped you then. Were you spiraling because of Sadie too?"

She was yelling now, her emotions toppling over like a rockslide, crushing her at the bottom.

Sadie. Why was it always, always about *her*?

"Sadie isn't perfect, okay? She might be Miss Goody Two-Shoes, but she's using Oliver!" Emmeline cried, her voice nearly cracking. She sounded unhinged, which was so unlike her it made her unravel even more. She was coming undone and she didn't know how to stop it.

"She's obviously leading Titus on when she

doesn't really like him—how could she? And she's not good for Ashland. The council is going to eat her alive. Why can't anyone be on my side, for once?"

"Yeh don't think I want to be on yer side? Yer my SISTER, for Christ's sake. I want to be proud of yeh!"

It was like a bomb had gone off in the dorm.

A dirty bomb with shrapnel that pierced flesh and shredded hearts.

Silence settled between them, around them, like the world had just pressed mute.

For the first time, Alaric looked stricken. Like something had actually *surprised* him for once. "I...I mean...cousin."

Emmeline's heart felt like it stopped. Long enough for her to be presumed dead. And yet, her chest kept rising and falling with her rapid, unsettled breathing. She took a single step away from him, the backs of her knees brushing against a lower bunk bed.

"No," she whispered, "...you didn't."

That wasn't a slip of the tongue. That wasn't a stumble. Or an error. That was something he'd said out of rage, out of the depth of his soul, exploding like her own confessions from seconds before.

The truth.

Alaric drew his hands down his face, scrubbing his cheeks, and sighed. "Aye, I did. Just a blunder."

"Liar," Emmeline said, her skin beginning to prickle. His face had proved it. The horror at what he'd just said. What he'd just *admitted*.

Emmeline's mind flashed to the sight of Ilsa buttoning her blouse in her father's room. She knew her father had affairs, so was the possibility all that ridiculous? Had she been naive to think her mother had been faithful?

Alaric met her eyes and was it her imagination? Or did she see similarities between the two of them? Like their height or their sharp cheekbones. Their volcanic tempers and their bitter temperaments.

In his gaze, she saw the answer. The regret of wanting to hide this from her. Of not wanting to hurt her because… because…

Emmeline wasn't a princess.

Her knees gave out.

"Emmeline—hey!" Alaric darted forward, grabbing her by the shoulders and guiding her onto the bed right behind her.

He was saying something, but Emmeline wasn't hearing it. Her brain was short-circuiting with this information. There was no doubt who each of their mothers were, obviously, and if she and Alaric were brother and sister then it could only mean that Mikael Erickson was her father. Neither her mother nor her father were royal by blood. *She* wasn't royal. *She* was the bastard.

Dimly, she heard clips of words, like *computer files* and *paternity tests* and *STR loci*.

She wanted to yell that it couldn't be true, that he didn't know what the hell he was talking about, but Alaric wouldn't make up this kind of lie. From his reaction, he'd never had any intention of even telling her.

It...it had to be true.

"I think—I think I'm gonna be sick."

Instead of dodging out of the way, Alaric helped her up and rushed her to the bathroom. He held back her hair as she barfed into the toilet.

It was messy and disgusting and there was nothing princess-like about it. Her nails clicked against the rim of porcelain as she gagged and coughed. Finally unable to retch any longer, Emmeline sat back on her heels. Alaric handed her a wet washcloth and she rubbed her mouth until her skin turned red.

Alaric was silent for another minute, then grumbled, "Like brother like sister, I guess?"

A kind of hysterical laugh bubbled up inside her at the memory of when their roles were reversed and *he* was puking his guts out in front of her, which then quickly turned into gut-wrenching sobs.

"Aw, Emmeline," Alaric said, pulling her against his chest, which then made her cry even harder.

Why did everything she want slip away from her? Who was she kidding? She didn't have a family, and she never would. Everything she'd done to become heir apparent had been *pointless*. If King Leander knew the truth, he might've never allowed her on the throne. At least Alaric had been Princess Rhea's son. She was the bastard daughter of two cheating assholes. She had burdened her soul and ruined her friendships for nothing.

Perhaps that's what hurt the most. That it didn't matter how hard she tried, or how hard she yearned, it was never in the cards for her.

Emmeline would never be loved.

She clung to Alaric's shirt and drenched it with her tears. She didn't even realize when he moved her from the floor of the bathroom to his bed, but the next thing she was aware of was him pushing his covers over her and saying in the softest voice she'd ever heard, "I'm gonna get yeh some tea. I'll be back, yeah?"

Emmeline just buried her face into his pillow. It smelled like him. Like rain and mint.

Her brother. It was a strange thing that something that sounded so wonderful could also break her heart into teeny tiny pieces.

The door closed and another few tears rolled down her cheeks and the bridge of her nose to dampen the pillow.

She couldn't help but wonder...was this how Sadie felt? When she'd thrown that book into the fire? Had she felt like she'd just lost everything, or had it been even worse?

With that thought, Emmeline couldn't help but say to herself, "I deserve this," a feeling she whispered into the empty dorm room.

At some point while Alaric was gone Emmeline must've drifted off because she woke to a soft touch down her arm.

At first, she thought it was Alaric himself, but the touch felt different. Softer, more careful, more tender, more *reverent*. And the scent wasn't of mint and rain, but of herbs and old books.

Her heart stuttered.

*Oliver.*

His fingertips were gliding across her exposed

arm over Alaric's bed covers. It was nothing more than a soothing caress. The kind of touch a child might receive from a parent. Even though the comparison was strange, the feeling was not. She felt cared for.

If he was touching her like this, then he couldn't hate her.

It wasn't like having parents who loved her. And it wasn't like having friends who trusted her and had her back.

But *this*... this tiny movement down her arm, it was enough for now.

# 20

## TITUS

When Alaric had texted him to stay out of their dorm for a couple hours, Titus didn't question it. He didn't *want* to know what was happening in there. If Alaric had walked in on Seb and his girlfriend (which happened far too often) or if Alaric himself had a girl, it was better that Titus didn't know.

So he stayed in the student council room for longer than he'd intended, going through more of Trang's financial analysis. The girl was incredibly thorough, and admiring her work was a bit like admiring a symphony. The way she'd connected so many dots from raw numbers and data points amounted to a work of art.

A work of art that made his stomach turn, but impressive nonetheless.

The finances seemed to get worse every month, like some hidden fee uncovered or some new purchase that the school had to make to keep up with the greenhouse sustainability features. Trang did her best to identify the source of every cost, why it was needed and for how long—one-time purchase or ongoing. She factored in depreciation and a bunch of other accounting practices that he was largely unfamiliar with.

Brain fried, Titus was about to shut his laptop when the sound of an incoming email made him pause.

From anyone other than Headmistress Aquila, he would've ignored it for later. But he was literally the student council president. In many ways, his role was just as important as any other member of her staff.

He opened the email and started reading. Subject line: **HIBERNIA UPDATE**. With every word, the unsettled feeling in his stomach grew and grew until he sat there nauseated, and for once, it had nothing to do with his RA medication.

Hibernia was canceled.

That was the update. As far as Titus could tell, the winter ball was nearly as old as Almus Terra's current iteration, which was almost a century. Why was it just...canceled?

More importantly, how could they afford to

cancel such a massive fundraiser—which largely bankrolled ATA's Scholar track—considering the school's financial crisis? Had they abandoned the scholarship model altogether?

Well, there was one way to confirm his suspicions. Titus snapped his laptop shut and stood up. Too fast.

That. Bloody. *Hurt*.

With a groan, Titus staggered slightly, catching himself on the edge of the table.

Today was a bad day. Over the last (almost) year since his diagnosis, Titus had begun to understand how this disease struck. He had good days and bad days, and worse days. On bad days, the pain wasn't something that could be stopped with medication, it was just something to tolerate and somehow manage. The stiffness through his limbs, the fatigue through his body, the pain radiating from his joints... it wasn't an easy thing to hide.

Especially from Sadie, who was around him more than any other person, being his fake girlfriend and all.

It was also getting tiring to hide. He wanted to be able to explain to people that while he may not *look* sick, he still *was* sick. Living with chronic pain wasn't like he telegraphed illness all the time—there was no constant IV in his arm, or hollow cheeks, but he still felt like crap. It would make things easier when his classmates wondered why he couldn't fence during gym period, or why he struggled with the stairs. He needed to be able to use his disease as an explanation, not as an excuse. It should be such a simple thing, and yet it wasn't.

Especially in the eyes of his terrible parents, and his narrow-minded grandfather who only valued the *strong*. And yes, King Leander meant *physically* strong.

"Shit all," Titus grunted, slowly beginning to stretch himself out, flexing his hands, rolling his ankles, curling his toes, rotating his neck, and bending his knees. He was grateful he didn't have to do this coming out of a class. In those scenarios he either pushed through the pain, or he waited until all the rest of the students were out of the classroom to do his stretches.

When he was finally done, he hoisted his bag onto his shoulder, moved slowly down the stairs, and turned in the direction of Headmistress Aquila's office.

Was she going to be happy about him barging in, once again without an appointment, and demanding answers? No, but he didn't care.

She had said she was working on a solution and canceling Hibernia was hardly a step in the right direction.

It took him far too long to finally reach her office and at the sight of yet more stairs another wave of nausea hit him—this one courtesy of his RA.

Before he took the first step, his phone buzzed in his pocket.

It was Sadie, answering a text he had sent her a couple hours ago: **We haven't been seen together a lot lately. There are going to be rumors if we don't step up the dates. Unless that's what you want?**

Her reply, **I'll see you at dinner**, was short but clear: Yes, she still wanted to maintain their fake relationship.

At least she wasn't making it miserable for him anymore. Instead, she seemed grateful that he stayed with her, which is what both the Ashlandic people and the advisory council wanted, *and* she no longer seemed to be punishing him by poking at his guilt. But, for whatever reason, she had been rather absent as of late.

Titus also wondered if being with her hurt less because he was finally...losing interest?

He thought of her at the gala. Stunning, and

yet no more beautiful or radiant than at Ashland's summer victory reenactment for Eldana Day. But during the summer, he had felt a hollow ache in his chest. The distinct pain of kissing her and knowing she felt absolutely nothing as a result.

Recently, their movements were like those of actors in a play. Fluid, well-rehearsed, but meaningless except to their audience.

With his reflections about Sadie having distracted him from the painful trek up the stairs, he took a moment to collect his breath before he knocked on the door.

Titus was not out of shape. He swam nearly every day, which did wonders for his joints and built up every muscle group in his body. But that didn't stop this disease from sapping his energy.

He pictured himself disappearing into a tiny puff of smoke, then rolled his eyes at his own absurdity. Maybe Trang's weird sense of humor was starting to rub off on him.

"Come in," Headmistress Aquila's deep, regal voice called through the door. She glanced up from her laptop, which was connected to her large secondary monitor. She wore glasses that reflected the blue light of her screen. "Ah, Titus. Take a seat."

Titus shut the door behind him and sat in the same chair from that fateful day over a year ago where he'd met his cousins, his grandfather, and Sadie for the first time.

Headmistress Aquila stood up from her desk and sat across from him, reaching for her kintsugi Japanese tea set. To his surprise, she tipped the teapot and poured him a steaming cup. It looked green or white, not his preferred English Earl Grey, but tea was tea, and he wasn't about to refuse.

Clearly, this time, she'd been expecting him.

"You got my email."

"What's going on, Headmistress? You can't really be thinking of canceling Hibernia."

Headmistress Aquila sighed, her dark brown shoulders rising and falling with the movement as she lifted her own cup to her lips and blew on the hot tea. "I'm not thinking of it, Titus. I've *thought* about it. It's done."

"You can't be serious."

"I most certainly am."

"Why?"

"I don't need to justify—"

Titus curled his aching hands into fists, feeling what little patience he had fly out the window. This came on a bad day. Where he was exhausted and in pain and just didn't have the strength to handle a disappointment like this.

"Respectfully, Headmistress, you *do*. As student council president I am duty-bound to advocate for my classmates. Canceling Hibernia will affect them all. Just tell me the truth: This isn't your decision. It's the board's," Titus said, his tone anything but respectful. "The real reason we're getting rid of Scholars is that we can't afford them. They don't *want* to fund them anymore. They can't take away your choice to have Scholars so they're making the school bleed money to force your hand. Am I right?"

Headmistress Aquila stared at him. She may have expected his appearance in her office following that email, but not his theory, and definitely not his disrespect.

For a long moment, she continued to regard him, her dark eyes assessing him. "I am going to give you grace since you're feeling very frustrated right now, which I do understand, but I will not tolerate such an attitude from one of my students. Am I clear?"

Titus winced. She was right, of course. And it was extremely unlike him to go off like that.

He met his headmistress's gaze. "I apologize, Headmistress. I *am* frustrated, but that's no excuse."

The headmistress nodded in acceptance. Her next words were gentler, but with no less gravity. "Whether you believe me or not, Titus. It is *my* decision to cancel Hibernia, not the board's. And the reason is simple: We can't afford it."

"It...it's a fundraiser," he said dumbly.

She leveled him a look that matched the stupidity of his statement. "And yet, it still costs money to put on. I'm sure you remember your budget from being on last year's committee."

"It was an absurd amount, but the return also quadrupled the investment," Titus argued.

Headmistress Aquila gave him a sympathetic look, one that made Titus's cheeks blush in shame. This was *her* school and yet he was continually pointing out the obvious. He was sure she didn't want this. Sure, she was trying with everything in her power to look at solutions.

"I just mean..." Titus spanned out his hands, adding, "I'm trying to understand."

"You're not the only one," she said with a deep frown. "I am still looking at options, but Almus Terra is a unique school. In obvious ways to be sure, but also in how we are structured, funded, and run. We stand independent from any country, yet we're not privately owned either. We're made up of a board that controls nearly every aspect of our financial operations. This academy is literally built and sustained on the generosity of people who believe in its purpose and their responsibility to the world and its future."

"So the board *is* forcing our hand? I was right?" Titus asked, anger rippling through his whole aching body.

Zuri Aquila's look darkened, her chin tucking in and her gaze sharpening with annoyance. She set down her tea cup and settled back, posture perfect as always. "They're certainly not doing us any favors. They're united in the belief that problems can be solved with fewer students."

"Cutting Scholars," Titus said, disgusted. She wasn't admitting he was right, but...she wasn't saying he was wrong either.

The headmistress drummed her fingers on the arms of her chair. "You're smart, Titus. I see now that you care about this school more than I ever thought you would, so I will confide in you on this. Again, it is my decision to cancel Hibernia. But I am doing this for the Scholars. If this is to be their final year, I want it to be their best. I am taking that budget and giving the student council permission to disperse it to the organizations that need it most."

To the Scholar-majority organizations, she meant.

Gut sinking, Titus knew he was losing this argument. "But...but what Hibernia could bring in..."

"Would not be enough to sustain our scholarships for another year."

And the board was dead set on having them gone.

Slowly, gingerly, and aching, Titus got to his feet, shouldering his bag. Maybe if his RA wasn't making him feel absolutely knackered today he'd stay longer, try to figure out what the headmistress was attempting to do with the board and how he could help. But he wasn't sure he could be upright much longer. The fatigue was drilling into him like a rig looking for oil.

"Thank you for seeing me, Headmistress. I promise I'll make an appointment next time. And...I *am* sorry for the way I spoke to you."

She looked up at him, her gaze kinder than he deserved. "Thank you, Titus. I can't be too angry about it. It's nice to see where your heart lies."

Titus made it to the second staircase away from the headmistress's office and down by the admin hall before he had to stop.

The joints in his feet were screaming at him, his entire body needing a much longer rest.

Maybe he could've kept going if the news he'd just received hadn't been so devastating.

How were they supposed to fight a board who controlled everything? Though it seemed foolish now, he hadn't realized that Almus Terra was subjected to the whim of people's charity to such an extent. He had assumed it was a global institution, but, practically speaking, there was no "world government" to fund Almus Terra. It relied solely on a board composed of politicians and tycoons across the globe that believed in ATA's mission.

And what if that mission...started to change?

Titus lowered himself onto the staircase, sagging against the wall and focusing on breathing in through his nose, and out through his mouth. The pain radiating through his body was making him nauseated, though that could also be a side effect of his medication. He'd had nothing but a granola bar for lunch, which had been foolish, but he needed the time to finish his Advanced Political Rhetoric essay.

"Titus?"

He lifted his head from the hand that he'd buried into his thick blond waves.

Trang stood at the bottom of the steps. She'd

changed out of her uniform and wore high-waisted jeans and a cropped T-shirt with a velociraptor that said "Raptor ~~Daddy~~ Mom." Her silky black hair fell over one shoulder as she tilted her head, taking in his strange location: halfway down the stairs, leaning against the wall, with the dejection of a man who just lost his entire life savings.

But instead of making fun of him, she started up the steps and dropped right next to him. She crouched forward with her hands on her knees and shifted toward him. He regarded her warily.

Then she crossed her eyes and attempted to touch her tongue to her nose.

Titus let out a bark of laughter. "What are you *doing*?"

"Seeing if laughter really is the best medicine."

"Cute."

A slight flush colored her pale cheeks and Titus wondered how she took that word. He was strangely okay with however she wanted to take it.

"Is it working?" she asked.

Unconsciously, Titus began massaging his knuckles as a small breath of laughter escaped his chest. "Maybe? But to heal me completely, I might need Alex Horne and Greg Davies to follow me around every day."

"What if I can't hire the *Taskmaster* hosts to stalk you?"

Titus was impressed she'd even known the obscure British comedy show he'd been referring to, and it made him smile even wider. "Guess I'll have to figure out another way to survive."

"You can talk to someone," Trang suggested. Her voice was so quiet he knew she was being serious.

Had she guessed that something was wrong with him? They'd been spending more time together in this mess of financial discovery. He'd noticed that Trang was more observant than Sadie. Or maybe she just watched him more carefully than Sadie did.

A few weeks ago, even, the simple notion that Sadie didn't pay attention to him would've devastated him.

Now, though, he didn't mind. He liked the idea of Trang watching him instead. Of knowing something was different about him.

Right this minute, her gaze was on his hands and how he massaged and stretched his fingers.

Finally, he said, "Not yet."

For a moment, Trang watched him, then she nodded and started to get up.

His hand shot out and grabbed her wrist.

Slowly, she sat back down but she looked somewhat uncomfortable this time.

"Sadie...should I get her for you?"

Titus's jaw worked in annoyance. Once again, he wished Sadie would free him of their relationship. But he'd stay true to his word and let it be her decision. In the meantime, whatever this... *thing* that was blooming between Trang and him, it would be tainted forever if she thought he might be open to cheating on Sadie in any way. Even emotionally.

Could he tell her that it was all fake? Would she believe him and keep it to herself?

He trusted Trang, but it wasn't just his secret to give up. So he dropped her wrist and said, "No, she's busy. Sorry, you can go. Just...misery loves company, I guess."

Trang nodded but, surprisingly and to his great relief, she didn't leave.

He was silent for a beat before he said, "You know I'm not a bad guy, right? At least, I'm trying really hard not to be."

"Titus, if I thought you were a bad guy, I wouldn't be sitting here," she said, bumping his shoulder.

Then she moved so close he got a whiff of her shampoo, and it smelled of peaches. It smelled so good that it was slightly disorienting, and he wondered if he should've let her go to resist a temptation that was just beginning to rise.

"Good to know," he rasped, his hands flexing at his sides.

# 21

# SADIE

Sadie dragged her big toe through the crystal teal water of the Mediterranean Sea as she listened to Titus. The expression on her face not fully portraying the horror she felt inside.

It had been a strange week.

First, she'd found out that she was secretly the daughter of an enemy of House Eldana, who had been assassinated for their treasonous plot to dethrone the king, and she'd been given a new family because of it, then later, a *legitimate* chance at the crown.

Hours after that, she'd discovered that the boy she'd thought was rooting against her might have secretly been pining for her.

Currently, Titus was filling her in on everything going wrong with Almus Terra and the Scholars.

He'd told her about the threats to scholarship

students a month ago when he got the first email from Headmistress Aquila. But the idea of eliminating Scholars from Almus Terra was so unimaginable to Sadie, she hadn't *really* believed it would come to pass. But, she supposed, that's precisely when the worst things happened, wasn't it? When something sounds too evil to come true.

With Hibernia canceled, it now felt very much like a real thing that could actually happen. Guilt weighed on her, heavy and suffocating. She'd been so self-centered. Entirely focused on her fragile status as heir apparent and what she could do to prove herself to Leander that she hadn't even checked in about Titus's efforts to preserve the heart of their school. Sadie had fallen in love with Almus Terra long before she walked through its doors, and eons before she'd set her sights on Ashland's throne.

Ashland was important to her—of course it was—but so was Almus Terra. And she no longer believed that she alone could properly rule her country. Titus and Alaric were smart, strong, and capable, and she believed they were proud of their heritage and would rule Ashland well. So why was she clutching her crown so desperately?

Because of her pride?

It was more complicated than that, but the question didn't stop Sadie from thinking: If she hadn't been so distracted with Ashland and her own goals, could she have been more helpful to Titus lately in trying to save Almus Terra? And Trang, and Oliver, and Danica, and Jacob, and all their Scholar friends? Or was that her own arrogance in thinking she could solve everyone's problems?

"You haven't said a thing in ten minutes," Titus said, stabbing his spoon into his gelato cup and setting the melting sweet cream aside.

"It's a lot to think about," Sadie admitted. "I'm sorry you've been doing this on your own."

"Not on my own. Trang's been helping."

"Right," Sadie said, feeling a bit odd that the two of them were working so well together. Not because she felt jealous and territorial when it came to Titus, but because she felt jealous and territorial when it came to *Trang*. It had been ten months since they'd had their awkward falling-out, but the pain of losing her friend hadn't gone away. It had merely been suppressed. Before Emmeline's manipulations had driven them apart, she'd started to really love Trang. Almost like a sister. Thinking about how well Titus and Trang seemed to be getting along in their common goal made her jealous. She wanted to feel close to Trang herself.

She shoved a spoonful of lavender honey gelato into her mouth to stop herself from saying anything she'd regret.

"And Emmeline wants to help," Titus added, his tone light, but careful.

Sadie shot him a glare.

"I know." He raised his hands. "I haven't trusted her with anything. But, Sadie, I think she really does care. Remember, she's super into Oliver. And she really was friends with Danica. As shitty as she was to you and me, she loved them. I think she still does."

"If she's even capable of love," Sadie grumbled. Though even as she said the words she felt guilty. Sadie hadn't been immune to Emmeline's loneliness this year. Even Sadie had winced when she'd seen how Emmeline's parents so blatantly ignored her at court functions back in Ashland. Sadie basically hated Emmeline, and still that had been hard to watch.

"She's smart, Sadie. No, she's brilliant. She could be a solid ally if we want to save the Scholars."

Sadie said nothing, stirring her gelato until it was reduced to creamy goop.

"Just think about it."

Truthfully, Sadie didn't have to think about it. She was already feeling guilty over her self-involvement, and she knew what her answer should and would be. She just needed time to admit it out loud.

Just like she'd needed time to process who she really was.

The more Sadie had thought about it, the more she'd agreed with Alaric's words. So what if her mah and grannah hadn't been related to her biologically? It hadn't made them love her any less or vice versa. She'd been loved so much better than any of the heirs by their biological parents. The life she'd lived hadn't been a lie. It had shaped her into the young woman she was today. Coming to terms with King Leander executing her father hadn't been easy, but she didn't believe revenge was the answer, nor could she entirely write off his decision. He'd protected Ashland against a civil war. Likely saved countless lives.

But that didn't make her forgive him. She could understand his actions while still hating him for taking her family away. She could feel both things.

Just as she accepted that Emmeline would be

a strong asset, without forgiving her for what she'd done. People were complex and both things could be true.

Neither Sadie nor Alaric had been in the student council room since the Hibernia planning committee had met there just under a year ago. Unlike Emmeline and Titus, they had never run for the student council, even after Titus took over as president. Despite that, Alaric made himself right at home, as if he'd been lounging on the plush armchairs and watching his favorite show on the massive projector screen every weekend.

He crossed right over to the fridge, took out a sports drink he liked, and offered Sadie one. With an amused smile, she shook her head.

"You're here early," she said, dropping her bag on the long conference table and looking around the decadent circular room.

"I knew yeh'd be here early, and I wanted more time alone with yeh."

Sadie flushed at his boldness, then quickly turned away to pull out her laptop, pushing hair behind her ears out of nerves.

It had been almost a month since that night. Three and a half weeks since her world had once again been turned upside down in more ways than one. She'd met with Alaric only a couple times since then, all immediately following their shared classes, a seemingly innocent discussion by their desks as their classmates filed out so as not to incite any rumors.

Innocent by school social standards perhaps. Not innocent in the eyes of the crown.

Alaric had told her about Ashland reaping the benefits from an insider trading arms deal between the US and Russia. He'd explained in hushed tones that he'd stolen files from his father's computer and that a specific correspondence proved the blatant stock manipulation and borderline war profiteering. The stock manipulation then reminded Sadie of the Ashland Investment Fund and her conversation with Oliver who, she'd later found out, had gone to Emmeline for help.

It hadn't surprised or angered Sadie that Oliver had gone to Emmeline, but it did, unfortunately, further reinforce everyone's point that Emmeline would be useful.

Which was what led them to today. To this meeting.

"Are yeh sure about this, cailín?" Alaric asked, crossing to her and leaning against the table.

"Yeh think we can really work together? We're a far cry from a football club, I'd say."

Sadie raised a brow and shot him a smirk. "Good thing we're not shooting for the Premier League Trophy."

"Aye, then what, pray tell, *is* our goal, cailín?" He leaned closer, his breath warm against her ear and neck.

Sadie looked up at him, his handsome face and stormy eyes were so close that it made her stomach flip. All she would have to do would be to lift herself on her toes and—

Quickly she turned away, feeling flustered and foolish.

No. *No.* She'd had bad luck with princes so far. So what if Alaric might have been pining for her, and had watched out for her, and knew how to weave sweet words together that hit her right in the heart?

*He still doesn't believe in you.*

But when he looked at her like that—curiosity and respect in his gaze—she wondered if that were still true.

"It—"

The door clicked open and Sadie and Alaric both jumped apart.

It was Titus, with Emmeline behind him.

Sadie felt her cheeks heat like the rocks of Vesuvius as she took in her ex-boyfriend, now fake boyfriend, staring at his cousin, who was far too close for friendliness.

Alaric glared right back at him.

But Titus didn't rise to the bait. It didn't even seem to bother him very much. He simply strode into the room and dumped his bag on a seat while Emmeline stayed in the doorway.

She looked from Alaric to Sadie, then back to Alaric. "What the hell is this?" she asked sharply.

"A trap, obviously," Alaric deadpanned, the barest hint of a smile on his face.

Emmeline's eyes blazed. "I can see that, asshole."

"Come now, Emmie. If I'd told yeh Sadie wanted to meet with the three of us, yeh would've never come willingly. I would've had to haul yeh in here by yer toenails."

"You know me so well," she sneered, then spun around and started for the stairs.

*"Emmeline."*

Even Sadie flinched at Alaric's sudden sharp tone. The way he said it made it feel like the two were closer than Sadie would've thought. But what was more surprising was the way Emmeline stopped. Like she actually listened to him.

Emmeline turned, her eyes narrowed with irritation. "What?"

"Fifteen minutes. If yeh don't want to stay after fifteen minutes, yeh can leave."

Never in a million years would Sadie have thought that simple request would've worked, but it actually did. Flipping her hair, Emmeline returned, closing the door behind her and dropping herself into one of the chairs. She crossed her arms, looking downright furious.

"Fifteen minutes," she said between clenched teeth.

Alaric looked back to Sadie as if to say, *The floor's all yours.*

But when Emmeline's, Titus's, and Alaric's eyes all fell on her, it was like she was back at the threshold of Headmistress Aquila's office. That life-altering day over fourteen months ago where she thought she'd met the three most beautiful, intimidating people in the world. Even after all she'd been through, Sadie still didn't feel like she was *enough* next to them.

Emmeline made a dismissive clicking sound with her tongue and started to push herself off her seat.

"Hibernia," Sadie squeaked suddenly, then cleared her throat. She clenched her fists. After all, she had faced her king and an entire room full of the world's most powerful people and emerged victorious.

"I thought I might tell you how I won heir apparent at Hibernia."

Emmeline and Titus both stared at her. Alaric, still leaning against the table with his arms folded, simply smiled at her.

Sadie shot Emmeline a smug look. "It'll be more than fifteen minutes."

Nearly half an hour later, Emmeline and Titus *still* hadn't spoken a word. It had been a good six minutes of total silence, and Alaric, having already heard the story once before, was on his phone playing Fruit Ninja.

Emmeline kept shooting him looks that could kill, and it seemed like every time she *wanted* to say something, she'd stop herself and press her lips together.

Titus just stared at the floor, swiping his fingers over his mouth and jaw. Occasionally he rubbed his hands together and would glance warily at Sadie. As if she were about to steal all *his* money and donate it to charity.

"Well," Titus finally said, "that explains a lot."

As if her cousin's words broke a spell, Emmeline leaned forward and narrowed her eyes. "Why are you telling us *now*?"

Sadie shrugged. "It's not exactly a secret."

"That's not what I asked."

"Because," Sadie forced herself to meet Emmeline's gaze, "that's only what *I* was able to pull off, with Oliver's help, of course. Now imagine what the four of us could do together."

Emmeline raised her brows, her lips parting.

Titus's expression did the exact opposite. His brow furrowed and his lips pressed into a thin line.

"What are you saying?" Emmeline asked, disbelief in her voice.

"I'm saying that two things the four of us all love are in trouble. Almus Terra and Ashland. Alaric has already found irrefutable proof that King Leander and Alaric's father orchestrated blatant stock manipulation for Ashland's sovereign wealth fund—"

Emmeline flinched and the move was so obvious Sadie paused before Alaric subtly nudged her to continue.

"And the Ashland Investment Fund holds the pensions of our citizens. If Leander played the stock market and lost, he'd lose the livelihoods and security of Ashlandic citizens. He's gambling with people's futures and doing so illegally. And Almus Terra? We all love this school, and we all have friends here who are Scholars—"

This time Sadie purposefully looked away, knowing that Emmeline *used to* have Scholar friends.

"And now, thanks to the diabolical school board, Almus Terra will cease to exist as we know it at the end of the school year, when scholarships are phased out. We can't let that happen."

There was a stunned silence that settled over the student council room that made Sadie's cheeks burn.

"Look, I know how ridiculous this might sound..."

"I don't think you do," Emmeline interrupted coldly.

"Emmeline...," Titus started.

"No, I'm sorry, but she's just as naive as the day we met," Emmeline snapped. "I'll admit how she pulled off Hibernia is impressive. But it was only made possible through leverage she already had and Oliver's genius. She also did all that to achieve one singular, selfish goal."

"A singular, selfish goal *you* were after," Sadie shot back.

"I'm not denying that," Emmeline snarled, "but I am saying that was child's play compared to what you're proposing. You want us to... what? Rescue our country from the clutches of a greedy king and financial savant while we *also* figure out how to save our school from practically expelling the brightest minds here?"

Emmeline's cheeks were flushed, her eyes glassy.

Sadie was partially stunned at her words, but she wasn't allowed to linger on them before Emmeline launched into her next tirade.

"That's one of the problems with you, Sadie. You don't live in the real world with everyone else. You have this idea of how everything should be but not the guts to make it happen. Your stunt at Hibernia wasn't easy, but it was straightforward. You gave money away to charity—you didn't have to make any kind of sacrifice or hard decision. I mean, do you even realize what you're proposing?"

"She's got a point," Alaric said softly.

Sadie shot him a glare, feeling betrayed by his statement. He was the one who'd stood behind her on this idea. Of bringing the four of them together, to see what they could really accomplish. They'd been rivals by King Leander's design. But it didn't *have* to be that way. Sadie had finally started to see that.

Alaric raised his hands. "All I meant is that... going against the king? That's not just us disobeying Granddad, Sadie. It borders right up against treason."

*Not borders*, Sadie thought, *we're right on top of it. Defenestration is treason.* She wasn't about to say it out loud to prove their point, however.

Emmeline rolled her eyes. "I think it's generous you're even entertaining its feasibility. King Leander didn't get to be the most successful king in Ashland's history by being stupid enough to let four teenagers trap him into... what? Giving up his throne? This isn't Scooby Doo."

"Yeh've been quiet, cousin," Alaric said suddenly, his dark gray gaze going to Titus. "Anything to add?"

Titus blinked, almost as if he was surprised that Alaric cared about anything he had to say. He straightened in his chair and cleared his throat. "I'm in."

Emmeline scoffed. "Of course you are."

"I didn't stand up for the Scholars last year and

I should've," Titus said, his gaze cutting to Alaric and then over to Emmeline. "I'm not going to make the same mistake twice. I'll be damned if they're eliminated under my presidency."

"And Ashland?" Sadie asked, her heart flipping in her chest. Titus was the one who'd told her about the Scealans. Part of her wasn't sure she would have ever discovered her true identity without him. Not to mention, she probably wouldn't have been able to hang onto the title of heir apparent this long if not for his help. She knew he loved his country, but could he be convinced not to just disobey his grandfather but to actively work against him?

Titus sighed, then looked away. "I have to admit, that part seems unlikely, Sadie. As Emmeline said, Leander's a force. Trying to remove him from the throne seems impossible. Even just trying to get him to stop committing crimes with the Ashland Investment Fund—he has no reason to listen to us. There's no way. But you—or one of us—will take over soon. We just need to wait—"

"Waiting isn't good enough," Sadie snapped, her tone vicious.

Silence stretched in the room. Embarrassed by her outburst, Sadie folded her arms and looked away.

Emmeline latched onto her rage, smelling blood. "This is about more than stock manipulation or people losing their pensions. This is personal. What did Leander do to you?"

Sadie shook her head. No. She wasn't going to get into that here. Not when she'd only found this news out for herself a few weeks ago.

"If you won't be honest with us, how can we even work together?" Emmeline sneered.

"So you can use what I tell you against me? I know better than to trust a manipulative bitch!" Sadie exploded, her shout echoing through the room.

Emmeline jumped to her feet. "See! What a *joke* to think we could work together. I am out—"

She stopped short at the sight of Oliver Jackson standing in the doorway.

Sadie had asked him to give her thirty minutes before joining the meeting, hoping that would be enough time for the heirs to come around. With Oliver being her closest friend, she'd turned to him first before even going to Alaric with her idea of bringing the heirs together as a "team."

God, it seemed so silly now. What had she been thinking?

Emmeline's hands clenched into fists as she stared at Oliver. Sadie could see them trembling.

"What are *you* doing here?" Emmeline snapped, her voice nearly breaking.

Oliver stiffened, like he'd been slapped. "I was asked to be here. I'm helping out a friend."

"She's using you, *again*," Emmeline cried.

"Hey!" Oliver shouted back. "You don't get to decide that for me. I'm my own person, Emmeline. I give my help because *I* want to. Respect me enough to know the difference."

Emmeline slammed her mouth shut, still looking furious except now there were tears in her eyes. "Then you're making the wrong decision. This family is like a plague, and it will infect you too." She shook her head then grabbed her bag. "I'm leaving. I'll only make this worse."

Oliver stepped in her path, his expression much more gentle, like he was approaching a feral cat.

"Emmeline, just...wait a minute, okay? I know that's how you feel, but it's not true. You've been managing your own portfolio since you were eleven, you *immediately* recognized the Ashland Investment Fund, and you figured out that second insider trading deal with Rielson and its connection to Almus Terra. You're the smartest person I know. We need you."

Everyone's heads snapped back to Emmeline, and she flushed. Sadie wondered when Emmeline had talked to Oliver about this discovery, as well as how she'd figured it out in the first place, but that wasn't important right now.

Looking at Oliver, Emmeline sighed, her countenance appearing entirely defeated.

"You may need me, but you don't want me," Emmeline swallowed, tightening her grip on her bag. "More importantly, I don't belong here. I'm not one of you."

Sadie could feel Alaric suddenly tense beside her. Titus tracked it too and he looked back at Emmeline.

"What's that supposed to mean?" Titus asked.

"It *means*," Emmeline hissed like a viper cornered, ready to strike, "I'm not royal. There is not a drop of Eldana blood running through my veins. Alaric isn't the bastard, *I* am."

The breath froze in Sadie's lungs. And for the first time today she looked, *really* looked, at Emmeline.

She wore no makeup. Her hair was greasy at the roots and brittle at the ends. Her outfit was just a T-shirt and joggers, all wrinkled, and her eyes were practically bloodshot.

Oh, how the perfect princess had fallen. Perhaps Sadie should've felt good about that, and she was at least a little satisfied to know that Emmeline had been humbled.

But Sadie knew too well how it felt to lose something. An identity. *Family.*

And she would not wish that on anyone. Not even Emmeline.

Unsure exactly what she intended to do, she took a step toward Emmeline. "Emmeline..."

"Shut up, Sadie," Emmeline said, but it wasn't said in anger. It was more of a cry, like a plea. "Please...just leave me out of this. I am so done with this family. I am done trying to be a part of something I never had any claim to."

With that, she dodged around Oliver, tears already coursing down her face, and fled down the steps.

It took only a few seconds for Oliver to snap out of his shock, and chase after her.

"Bloody hell," Titus whispered, running a hand through his blond waves, looking stricken.

Sadie swallowed, twisting her hands in front of her, her own throat feeling clogged and tight.

"Relax, cailín," Alaric said, placing a gentle hand on Sadie's anxious fingers.

"Relax?" she asked, stunned. Seeing Emmeline unravel was like witnessing a natural disaster unfold on TV. You didn't experience the devastation yourself, but you felt its ripple effects in waves of anxiety.

"She'll be back," he said.

His words were so confident, Sadie believed him.

# 22

# EMMELINE

She'd thought she'd be okay to go. It was just supposed to be a meeting with Alaric to talk about the stock manipulation scheme they'd discovered from their stolen access, and then they'd meet with Oliver to see what, if anything, could be gleaned from the different instances. Honestly, she hadn't expected much to come of it. Especially considering that she'd already told Oliver a lot of what she'd found.

The whole "My grandfather committed insider trading" had been her explanation as to why she'd been lying in Alaric's bed crying herself to sleep. She'd blamed her tears on being upset about that discovery and her added stress about fighting with Oakley.

It was clear that Oliver hadn't bought it, but he was kind enough not to pry.

But today, if she could simply pass off the

information she had to Alaric and Oliver, they could take it to Trang and Titus, and the four of them could do with it whatever they wanted. She could offload what she knew and go back to being alone and miserable.

Except that her *brother* was a lying *asshole* who did whatever his precious Sadie wanted.

How dare Alaric trick her? How dare he presume to know what was good for her?

But telling them the truth had felt freeing. Even telling Oliver. That she wasn't a princess. That she'd lost the one thing that might've redeemed her in his eyes.

Well, now he could just pity her and move on like the rest of them.

And not being an Eldana? That was a tidy excuse not to have to work with any of them. Not to be a part of their little team.

Once again... not to be a part of anything.

It was a relief, really. Except... why did her heart speed up with hope when footsteps followed, racing after her?

Why did her stomach do crazy flips when Oliver's deep voice called her name? "Emmeline, wait up! *Emmeline!*"

Emmeline didn't stop, though, not until she felt his warm grip around her arm, tugging her back. Her feet shuffled and stumbled. She was wearing fuzzy socks outside the dorm—that's how much she didn't care—and they slipped in her Birkenstocks.

Oliver held onto her arm, his breathing only slightly elevated, as he glanced around the hall. Then, with a gentle pull, he guided her into an empty room nearby. It was a teacher's lounge, and Emmeline was surprised that Oliver would be so bold as to go anywhere off-limits to students.

They stood just beyond the door. His one hand was on the doorknob, while the other one was still on her arm.

Finally, he dropped his hands to his side and looked at her. "That's why you were in our dorm that day. That's why you'd been crying."

*Yeah, and I pretended to be asleep for an extra twenty minutes just to feel your touch on my arm—how pathetic is that?*

Emmeline swallowed. The words spilled as easily as tears down her puffy cheeks. "I'd just found out. Alaric told me. He's my brother."

Oliver's brows shot up toward his hairline, disappearing behind some rogue twists that fell over his forehead. "You...I mean...wow."

There was a long stretch of silence as Oliver

processed that information. Finally, Emmeline turned to walk toward the back of the lounge, dropping herself on the puffy leather sofa that smelled like coffee.

"Thanks for caring, Oliver. But you can go. They need you up there to even have a chance at pulling off whatever they come up with." She lifted her head to give him a small teary-eyed smile. "You're the secret weapon no one sees coming."

But he didn't go. Instead he crossed to the sofa and sat down next to her, leaving no space between them. The left side of his body was pressed against hers, from his shoulder to his thigh, all warm and solid against her, and Emmeline closed her eyes at how good it felt.

She blew out a breath. "Seriously, Ollie, just—"

Suddenly Oliver was holding her.

His arms, lean and strong, wrapped around her without hesitation. He pulled her in tight, and there was nothing tentative about it. Oliver Jackson knew how to hug.

In fact, with the exception of maybe Oakley, Emmeline was sure she'd *never* been held like this. With a fierce determination to impart something important, something she didn't dare name, so as not to disappoint herself.

More tears leaked from her eyes, rolling down her cheeks and jaw and dampening Oliver's shoulder. She made a sound in the back of her throat as her hands scrambled against his back, holding him in return, squeezing his shirt into her sweaty palms.

When Alaric had told her the truth about her father, and the lie her mother lived with every day, Emmeline had cried for the loss of a family she'd thought she'd had.

Now, she cried for never having one.

It was a familiar pain, a familiar ache, and perhaps that's why it hurt so bad. Why she couldn't stop the torrent of tears. She was so *tired* of it.

"It's okay, Emmeline. I'm here," he said, breathing against her ear, holding her tighter, as if he were trying to either squeeze out all her tears or fuse her broken pieces together.

"I wanted them to love me," she wept, saying the words that gutted her, that ripped her apart to be so vulnerable and weak. "I didn't care about being queen. I didn't care about being a princess. Not really. I just wanted them to love me, and I did...I did such horrible things for their love. For my love."

The awful truth. She'd loved her parents. Despite them sending her away, despite never showing any interest in her, despite it all. She'd been willing to sell her soul for their love.

"They don't deserve you, Emmeline," Oliver said, the side of his cheek pressed in her hair, his large hands brushing gently up and down her back. "I've always thought love should be given freely. But after everything... they need to earn yours."

Slowly, Emmeline nodded, realizing the full scale of how royally she'd screwed up. Oakley had given her love freely. Even Oliver had, in his own way. And instead, she'd turned her back on the few people who'd never needed anything from her at all, while Emmeline had given all of herself for the love of people who treated family like a game of chess.

Then again, perhaps it was a good thing she'd been sent away. Seeing her parents now, who knew what kind of monster she'd have turned out to be. Definitely worse than who she was now. Though, maybe, that wasn't saying a lot.

Finally, when Emmeline's tears had subsided and she was borderline dehydrated, Oliver sat back and lifted his shirt to wipe at her tears, even though there was a perfectly good roll of paper towels on the counter a few feet away. Emmeline blushed as the hard planes of his stomach were revealed, the shadow of the contours of his abs making his brown skin appear darker and sexier. Emmeline blushed so hard her ears felt hot and when Oliver lowered his shirt with a chuckle, she wasn't sure if he was laughing at her or at himself. The glimmer in his warm eyes told her that he was at least a little aware of how much he affected her.

"Listen...I know it's complicated but—"

Sensing where this was going, Emmeline started shaking her head. "I can't. Going back up there, working with them, it'll just remind me that I'm not one of them. Besides, they don't want me—"

"*I* want you," Oliver said.

Emmeline sucked in a breath, her puffy eyes widening at his words.

"I mean," Oliver rushed, his cheeks darkening, "I want you to be a part of this. I want your help. I know we need it."

With a sigh, she scrubbed a hand over her blotchy cheek, up into her wild, messy hair. She just didn't see how she could work with Sadie. And being with Titus and Alaric? Would she just resent them for being part of the family she'd wanted so desperately? God only knew how outrageously jealous she could be.

"But I don't want you to do anything you don't want to do," Oliver said quietly, hearing her unspoken fears. "And please believe me when I say I won't think any less of you if it's too much. But..."

Emmeline lifted her gaze, waiting for him to finish, her heart thundering just knowing he was fighting this hard for her.

"Yeah, you made mistakes... but you're not going to fix them by bailing, right? Maybe this is where you can earn their love."

Emmeline considered his wise words. How he came to be this smart and this good was an utter mystery to her. Surely *his* parents were the gold standard.

The idea of Sadie and Titus ever loving her was laughable, but Alaric? Her brother? He'd been angry with her, but he hadn't seemed to hate her, even after learning the whole truth.

Finally, Emmeline lifted her gaze to his and whispered, "Would it help me earn *your* love?"

Her words were bold, and they couldn't be taken back.

Oliver's eyes widened.

Perhaps he knew how she'd felt. Like Alaric's crush on Sadie, hers also had been difficult to hide. But now it was out there.

Oliver practically choked on air as he stuttered over his words. "I, you, I mean—"

God, he was so cute she could die.

Emmeline looked a mess—her hair, face, clothes, and, hell, even her nails were unpolished, so what on earth had possessed her to put her feelings out there like that?

She was such a fool in love.

"Sorry, ignore me," she said, wiping again at her eyes.

"I can't do that," Oliver's deep voice seemed to resonate in her soul, and she peeked over at him.

The look he gave her was heated, but it was still Oliver so the next moment he dropped his gaze, as if suddenly shy from his admission. Then he glanced back up and held her gaze as he slowly moved in, his forehead brushing hers.

Unable to stand another second of holding herself back, not after he'd been so sweet to her. She closed the distance and kissed him.

It was soft and gentle. Barely more than a brush, really. Just enough to punctuate her feelings for him.

Yet, as innocent and as chaste as it was, Emmeline felt a surge of desire rise up inside her. She wanted to throw her arms around his neck and fall into his embrace and take deep lungfuls of his lovely scent. She wanted the taste of him on her tongue and she wanted his hard chest against her soft one. His lips were smooth, full but firm, and just this tiny kiss had her crazy for more.

What a mistake. She was a disaster around him.

She sat back, taking in his somewhat dazed expression. He blinked a few times and swallowed quickly, a hint of a smile on his lips.

Her heart somersaulted at that tiny smile. Like he'd enjoyed that small taste of her too.

"Thank you, Oliver," she murmured.

His brows pulled together in confusion. "I... I didn't do anything."

She huffed out a breath. "Yes, you did. You're right. Maybe I can try to fix this."

"You mean you'll do it then?" His face brightened, unreasonably so, and that alone made her want to say yes.

Even so... she felt like she was slipping into something far more dangerous than a competition for a crown—an alliance.

She mustered up a small smile, choosing to ignore the fact that he'd never answered her question. "I'll do my best."

# 23

## ALARIC

"I didn't know the school had a dungeon. Did *you* know they had a dungeon?" Jacob asked as Alaric paced in front of the castle wall.

"Well," Alaric said, narrowing his eyes at the spot that Titus had said to look for amidst the climbing ivy, "it *is* a medieval castle. So, yeah, I assumed they had a wee dungeon."

Though when his cousin had suggested the dungeon as a location for their first official meeting with everyone (a group that Oakley obnoxiously referred to as the Terran Protection Squad), he'd thought the bloke half mad. It was located under the north-facing part of the castle, right below the ballroom and the west wing. To get there, Alaric and Jacob had to go through a rather narrow wooden door crisscrossed with black iron bars to the northwestern part of the bailey. It made sense that Alaric had never really noticed it before, being largely sectioned off by a row of well-manicured beech trees.

Finally, he found the iron rung behind a cluster of ivy and pushed inward. The stone door creaked open, revealing a staircase. He raised his brows.

"Yeh've got to be feckin kidding me."

"What?" Jacob poked his head in, and his eyes widened. "Neat!"

While most dungeons would have sconces along the walls, the Almus Terra dungeon was strung with fairy lights. Gold lights had been hung on the walls of the staircase, complete with fake branches and various-sized bulbs to make the descent more ethereal.

Jacob followed behind Alaric as they headed down the steps, nearly vibrating with excitement. Alaric punched a keycode Titus had given him into another door at the bottom of the stairs and stepped inside.

It was *technically* still a dungeon, but apart from it being underground and surrounded by stone walls, it looked more like a modern lounge at a five-star hotel.

Expensive plush rugs with glass tables, crystal vases with rare flower arrangements, modern art on the wall, butter-soft leather sofas and armchairs, a full barista coffee station, more fairy lights, a massive flat-screen TV, three gaming consoles, a turntable playing soft lo-fi jazz, and a pool table.

"Jaysus," Alaric said.

"Rich people, amiright?" Oakley said with a big grin, walking up to Alaric and Jacob with a little espresso cup in her hand.

"I'm sorry to break it to you, Oak," Jacob said, wide eyes still taking in the scene. "But you're rich."

Oakley patted Jacob on the shoulder, "Ah, Jakey, there are rich people, and then there are *rich people*. I'm the regular kind. Meaning, I don't hoard money for 'student council operations' to build a freaking clubhouse in the dungeon."

It was then that Titus walked up, his hands in his pockets, casting a sheepish look around. "To be fair, Calixa only showed me this place right before she graduated and I honestly didn't know what to *do* with it."

"Well, we found a use for it. Can we please get started?" Emmeline said impatiently from the front of the room, standing before a projector where her laptop was plugged in.

Oakley rolled her eyes while Alaric smothered a small smile.

Emmeline had turned a corner in the last week. Though she and Sadie still maintained a healthy distance, Emmeline had dived headfirst into this so-called protection squad. After her talk with Oliver, she had returned to the student council room just as Alaric had said she would. She'd then proposed inviting into the fold not just Oliver and Trang, but Jacob and Oakley as well. Sadie and Titus had stared at her, shocked at the sudden about-face, but they had no real objection.

She'd also clarified that her involvement in this group was in service of Almus Terra and Almus Terra alone. If they still had eyes on Ashland or moves against Leander, she honestly wanted no part of it.

Sadie wisely hadn't argued, and neither had Titus.

Alaric had a feeling his sister might come around though. Emmeline might not want anything to do with Ashland right now, but she'd given so much to the pursuit of winning over her family. That wasn't something she could abandon without closure.

Now, she stood in a white oxford button-down, wide-leg navy pants with heels, her hair glossy and wavy. Alaric could tell she wasn't quite back to her old self, but she was getting there. The full-blown presentation certainly seemed to be helping.

"Chill out, Emmeline," Oakley said, her tone stern but not churlish. "Let Alaric and Jacob use the fancy coffee machines. Everyone *else* has lattes."

Emmeline pursed her lips and held up her hand. "Five minutes then."

Oakley grabbed Alaric by the arm and guided him over to the self-serve Italian espresso station with the fridge full of creamer and shelves of Ethiopian beans.

"I'm surprised yer here. I figured yeh'd still be on no-speaking terms with her," Alaric muttered under his breath.

Oakley hummed in the back of her throat as she set the machine to brew. "I care about Almus Terra. And, well, she did invite me."

"In person?" Alaric asked.

"In person," Oakley whispered back. "To be fair, it wasn't hard to seek me out. We *are* roommates."

"It was plenty hard for her, yeh know that." Alaric said in a low tone.

Oakley hummed again, tracing the steamed cream into fancy latte art in the hot black coffee.

"Maybe it should be hard. Maybe she deserves that."

"Fine," he said with a sigh.

"But...maybe there's hope," she said as she handed him the coffee.

Alaric made a face at the latte art. "Yeh think I drink lattes?"

Oakley stared at him. "Do you hate everything pure and good in this world? What's your take on puppies or the *Fast & Furious* franchise?"

Alaric rolled his eyes and walked over to the couch, taking an open seat beside Jacob. He tried not to notice that Sadie and Titus were *still* sitting next to each other. Force of habit, he supposed. They didn't really have to keep up pretenses here, but technically Emmeline, Oakley, Jacob, Trang, and Oliver didn't know they were fake-dating.

Even Alaric was still having trouble processing it.

Honestly, he felt like a proper tool since Sadie had confessed everything to him that fateful night. She'd poured out her heart and soul in telling him everything, from Titus using her and Emmeline destroying her father's journal, to her current identity crisis.

And the only thing he'd been able to think about? *It was fake.*

She didn't love Titus—turns out she barely liked him. And from what he could tell, Titus was dating Sadie partly out of guilt for what he'd done to her, and also because it had been ordered by the king.

Alaric honestly had half a mind to finish what he'd started with Titus last year on the fencing mat. But that would only cause Sadie trouble, and since she didn't seem particularly hurt about it anymore, he let it go.

Instead, on that night, Alaric's head spun with hope. Hope of *finally* acting on feelings he'd been harboring for over a year. He'd listened to her then, in the infirmary, and replied with tenderness, which had been the bare minimum. Then he'd hustled her off to her dorm.

If they'd stayed up much longer, he would've hauled her against him and kissed the hell out of her. And when he threatened her with the possibility? He couldn't help remembering her sharp intake of breath, or how her pupils dilated with excitement.

Great, now he was thinking about *that*.

"Okay, let's get started," Emmeline said. "So, we all know—"

"Sorry, sorry, I'm here!"

All heads turned in the direction of the door.

Romy stood at the threshold wearing ripped jeans and a *Mortal Kombat* T-shirt holding her laptop. Her gaze roamed around the room as she mouthed *Whoa*.

When Jacob had suggested inviting Romy to the group as well, Alaric had very nearly objected. But his logic overruled his anxiety when it came to inviting the girl he had practically rejected to work alongside the girl he was actively pursuing.

That awkwardness aside, Ramona Vasquez wasn't merely an addition to the team. A hacker with her skills? She was the biggest tool in their arsenal. A no-brainer addition.

He only hoped she'd keep the drama to a minimum.

"You can get a latte *after* the presentation," Emmeline snapped. "Have a seat, Ramona."

"Ooookay," Romy said, her eyes still wide at the fancy dungeon as she walked in and took a seat, wedging herself between Alaric and Jacob.

Unable to stop himself, Alaric glanced at Sadie—who quickly looked away, the tips of her ears pink.

"I'm going to cut the intro and get straight to it," Emmeline announced, eager not to get interrupted again, "The board of Almus Terra has been forcing the school to take on vendors that have been bleeding the school dry in expenses. We've been spending more than what's coming in from tuition fees and our endowment. They're doing this to force Headmistress Aquila to get rid of the scholarship program. By the end of the school year, the first- and second-year Scholars will be forced to leave Almus Terra forever. If you need proof, here's extensive research from Trang. It's thanks to her we're even here, honestly."

"Yah! Go Trang!" Oakley shouted, leaning over and squeezing her roommate's shoulders while Trang went scarlet, sinking into her couch cushions.

"Titus is the one who pulled me in," Trang muttered, her gaze shooting to Titus, then Sadie, then quickly away.

"Learn to take credit where it's due, girlie," Oakley said.

"Evidence of this endeavor is summarized in slides four through eighteen. Before we get into planning, I want to share an important piece of information I uncovered," Emmeline continued. "If you remember, I told everyone not to text or email about this group. Use only word of mouth, that's because of this company—"

Emmeline clicked through to a slide with a logo that said *Rielson Enterprises*.

"This company created a product called Enyo that was recently purchased by Almus Terra to track everyone's digital footprint across our wireless network. In other words, the board can likely track our user activity. So, default to using your cellular data instead of the school's Wi-Fi to do anything the board might not approve of."

"You're shitting me," Oakley hissed, her voice deadly. "They're *spying* on us?"

Trang raised her hand. "Uh, how do you know it's this product? I didn't see that or Rielson on the books yet anywhere."

Emmeline glanced at Sadie, then back to Trang. A look of discomfort crossed her features. "Oh, it's there. Just under a different name because Rielson was recently bought out and renamed. So what's in our books is the same company under a different name, which leads me to my next slide." The presentation switched to a slide with a picture of a business executive that Alaric recognized immediately.

"Hey, Alaric, isn't that the guy who was looking to recruit me?" Jacob asked.

"His name is Rhett Croft and he owns about a hundred different entrepreneurial ventures," Emmeline said with a nod. "I overheard him and Ashland's king speaking at the United Energy

Gala. They were talking about Headmistress Aquila and er... I pulled some strings and got some details about a recent insider trading stock deal where King Leander got an early tip about Enyo—anyway, that part isn't as important. What's important is that Mr. Croft bought Rielson Enterprises and renamed it Hellion."

Oakley hit her fist on the sofa arm. "Holy shit, girl. Do you think he was selling that product to the headmistress when we went to her office on the first day of school?"

Emmeline shrugged. "Could be. Either way, we need to be careful with what we're doing on the internet. No searches, no emails, I mean we can't send—"

"Oh, chica, I got you," Romy interrupted, smacking on her gum. "We can use my network."

Everyone turned to look at the hacker.

"You... have your own Wi-Fi network?" Emmeline asked.

"Totally. And my own server. You can't trust public networks. That is like... rule numero uno in hacking, my friends."

"Now that you mention it," Oakley muttered. "Something is always whirring under your bed."

"It's also why I sleep in the nude. Servers get hot."

Oliver choked on his latte.

"Unbelievable," Emmeline grumbled.

"What about Ms. Reyburn?" Alaric asked.

Emmeline raised a brow. "What about her?"

"She's the Cyber Security teacher and head of IT," Romy said.

"I know who she is," Emmeline said with an exasperated sigh, "but if ATA is using Enyo, she was probably the one who helped install it. It's not exactly a product you'd want people knowing about. It's literally spyware. We can't rely on her as an ally."

Alaric frowned, knowing Emmeline was right, but finding it unlikely that Ms. Reyburn would condone such a product. She seemed like a woman who wouldn't want to spy on her students—then again, she always did know what they were up to in class. But Alaric had assumed that was her own eagle eye, not a piece of software purchased for the academy.

"Um," Sadie raised her hand tentatively. "Just to clarify...you're saying this product, Enyo, can trace and document everything we're doing on Almus Terra's Wi-Fi?"

"That's exactly what I'm saying," Emmeline said with a frown. "Though I don't know when Enyo was implemented on the network. It was purchased at the beginning of the year, but it could've been a month ago, a week ago, yesterday, or it could be getting installed tomorrow. Unfortunately, the student council doesn't have anything to do with IT policies and procedures. Like Alaric said, that's entirely Ms. Reyburn and her staff."

"Honestly, I don't know how the headmistress could sign off on this. It's a complete invasion of privacy," Oakley said, as she leaned back and crossed her arms and legs.

But Alaric was watching Sadie. She had gone noticeably paler and it was hard to focus on anything but the way she twisted her hands nervously in her lap, or how she gnawed at her bottom lip.

The group spent a long time talking about ideas and theories on how to "fix" Almus Terra. Was it about finding more money? Cutting costs? Somehow dismantling the school board? But how would they even go about that? Not to mention, time was running out. After their fall break, which started tomorrow, they only had six weeks before they were gone for winter break. Once they found a solution, who knew how long it would be until it actually took effect and saved the Scholars.

When Emmeline wrapped up the meeting, each person having been assigned their respective "homework tasks," Alaric trailed Sadie to the vintage record collection that she'd decided to inspect before leaving. He crouched down beside her and pulled an old Bing Crosby record out and pretended to look at it.

"What's wrong, cailín?" he asked quietly.

"I googled myself," she said.

"...So?"

"I googled *my real name*," Sadie said, her tone more urgent, gaze still on the records. "Or... what I think is my real name. Aurelia Scealan. That...I mean, should be fine though, right? Even if that Enyo product documented that. It wouldn't like...get back to Leander."

Alaric was quiet, processing the information. Emmeline had said King Leander had known about the product Enyo, so there was likely some connection between him and ATA's purchasing it. Leander had used this school to suss out his heir, so who's to say he couldn't use it for other things...like spying on his grandchildren and heir apparent?

After a long and heavy moment, she looked up at him, her big hazel eyes full of worry. "Right?"

There was no use worrying about something that couldn't be changed. "It'll be grand. Just a wee search query."

He took a nonchalant sip of his cold latte to get rid of the lie's taste on his tongue.

## 24

## TITUS

"I'm supposed to do what now?"

"Dip your hands into the melted wax," Dr. Sharrad instructed again, patiently. Always patiently.

Titus made a face and made no move to roll up his sleeves. Dipping his hands into the liquid hundred-fifty-degree paraffin wax wasn't high on his to-do list this morning. He needed to get to the dining hall, put something in his stomach, take his meds, and then make his way to his first class, which happened to be at the other end of the castle. Brilliant.

It was early though. Barely six-thirty in the morning and the scent of Dr. Sharrad's strong Turkish coffee permeating the school's infirmary was comforting and familiar by now.

And he needed comfort after their whirlwind trip across Ashland during fall break. Their latest royal PR tour had them traveling all over the kingdom for four days straight. They didn't even set foot in Heres Castle and took a six-hour flight from the west coast of Ashland straight to Toulon on the last day. It had been exhausting.

Unfortunately, being away from Heres Castle didn't give Titus a break from his mother. Several members of the royal family had accompanied the heirs to really convey, "Look at the 'one big happy family tour,' the royal edition."

Total bullshit.

Emmeline had barely *looked* at her so-called parents, Alaric's father wasn't even there, and Titus spent the whole time trying not to roll his eyes at every passive-aggressive, controlling statement his mother made.

But he was back now, and it was a relief to feel at home once again at ATA.

The school's chief physician sat on his favorite black leather rolling stool and took a long sip from his mug that read *Blood of Students*.

"I sure as shit didn't buy that wax for myself, Titus," he said, hiding a smile behind the mug's rim.

Dr. Sharrad was patient, but Titus had long since known that he could be sassy as well.

With a glare, Titus unbuttoned his sleeves and

pushed them up his forearms. When he still hesitated, his doctor set down his mug, and held up his hands, wiggling his fingers. "Would it help if I told you that I've tried it myself and it feels great? Makes your skin baby smooth too."

"Because that's what every bloke wants. Baby smooth skin," Titus grumbled.

Dr. Sharrad chuckled. "You'll just have to trust me on this."

Titus did. Over the last year, Dr. Sharrad had been his lifeline, and he knew how insanely lucky he was to have a doctor so focused on his treatment. Dr. Sharrad may not be his official specialist for his RA, but, as ATA's chief physician, he was very invested in all the students' personal health concerns and had been working closely with Dr. Konkin, Titus's rheumatologist, to provide Titus with the best care possible.

It was actually nice to know that he wasn't getting special treatment because he was a prince, but simply because he was a student at Almus Terra. He knew several Scholars who were regulars here with conditions like asthma, epilepsy, and type 1 diabetes.

It was strange to think that around this time last year he'd just returned from his first trip to Ashland during fall break and he was slamming the laptop shut on Dr. Konkin, refusing to hear any more about this disease. Now, he couldn't be more grateful to the doctors who had actually *listened* to him.

Grimacing, Titus plunged his hands in. Heat seeped through his skin and directly into his stiff, sore joints. "Fuuuuuck."

The true effect of the wax wasn't immediate, but Titus couldn't deny how good the warmth felt, penetrating his muscles and tissues.

Dr. Sharrad snorted. "Language, Titus. Now take them out."

Titus obeyed quickly because it was quite hot, lifting his hands from the liquid and letting the excess drip off. A nice thick layer of wax coated his hands like an extra layer of skin. Dr. Sharrad quickly slipped the plastic gloves onto Titus's waxed hands and wrapped the plastic in towels.

"Keep it on until the warmth fades then we can peel off the wax and you can head to breakfast. We can do this as often as you like. I'll make sure Ms. Martinez knows how to use the machine. I suggest at least once a day with how often you're typing. The wax will ease your inflammation. We'll resume whenever you return from winter break."

Titus nodded, slowly rolling his shoulders. "Whatever you say."

Dr. Sharrad tapped Titus on his forearm. "I mean it, Titus. Don't be a tough guy. Listening to your body is lesson number one with any illness, especially this one."

It took effort to forgo a disrespectful scoff. Titus was sure he'd never been labeled as a tough guy in his life, but the point was taken anyway.

After a few minutes, Dr. Sharrad helped remove the towels and plastic gloves and Titus peeled off the wax. The sensation was strange but not unwelcome, and sure enough, his hands were left feeling smooth as silk.

Titus grabbed his bag and hoisted it onto his shoulder. "Thanks, Doctor."

"Titus?"

Titus stopped at the door and his doctor regarded him, concern in his eyes. "I hope you don't mind me saying this, but every time you go to Ashland and come back, I find you in worse shape than when you left."

"I won't miss my meds, Doc. I'm a lot better at them now." Even with the traveling schedule of the tour, Titus had been very diligent in discreetly taking his medication. He hadn't been able to afford *any* downtime.

"I'm not talking about your medication."

His mother's face flashed through his mind

and dread settled in his stomach. Unfortunately, he knew exactly what Dr. Sharrad was talking about.

The next month and a half went by in a flash for the students. Especially without any Hibernia to plan for. They were able to concentrate entirely on their studies and their finals, and—in the case of the Terran Protection Squad—on different ways of trying to save the school.

None of their ideas had proved fruitful yet, but the Ashland royals and their friends were nothing if not thorough. By the time they were all leaving for winter break, they had stored several gigabytes of information on Romy's private server. From research into Rhett Croft's businesses and their board members, to how the school bylaws operated, searching, desperately for any loopholes.

With nothing to show for their hard work, Titus, Alaric, Sadie, and Emmeline boarded the flight back to Ashland for another break full of draining PR events, council meetings, and court functions.

Winters were brutal in Ashland in a way that even someone who'd lived in England all his life couldn't fully comprehend. Titus thought he knew cold, then he'd step into the courtyard of Heres Castle and the icy wind coming off the cliffside would take his breath away. Sometimes, he would wake up in the middle of the night in his dark, ornate bedroom, and hear the wind howling and screaming against the glass windows decorated in frost. Once, he saw the water coming from the Durah cliff face pushed back up into the cliffs by the sheer force of the brutal wind. A reverse waterfall. Seeing something like that...it made sense why people would believe in old folktales or pagan gods of nature.

Ashland was an interesting country in that it didn't have a singular religion that it identified with. It had been an isolated country for so long, with its own gods and folktales, that by the time Christianity, Judaism, Hinduism, Buddhism, and other world religions came to its shores, not a single one dominated enough to really shape the country's cultural identity. That was why their winter break in Ashland wasn't stacked with church visits or Christmas festivities. Instead, it was full of PR events, state dinners, and balls. Basically, the same programming as the summer months, but with ice and snow and yeti-strength wind.

Which led to much relief for Titus when he

and Sadie were forced to attend the advisory council meetings once again. At least these were inside.

It was during their second council meeting since the start of their break, four days since he'd received a one-word reply from Trang, that he knew he could wait no longer.

He had to talk to Sadie.

Over the last couple weeks, his conversations with Trang had dwindled down to nothing more than questions requiring simple yes or no answers about the school's financials and the investigation from their Terran Protection Squad efforts. She was distancing herself from him. He was dating her roommate, after all. Titus knew how it had to be.

Trang's silence, though perfectly reasonable, was driving him *up the wall*. He'd never had the intention of doing anything with Trang other than simply accepting her help, but now...

Yeah, now it was different. *Felt* different.

When Lord Eggfarts finally concluded the pointless meeting that Leander had once again deemed not important enough to attend, Titus grabbed Sadie's chair, stopping her from pushing back and standing.

"Can we talk?"

Her gaze flitted around to the old men getting up from their seats.

He stood, jerking his head toward the door. "Not here. Come with me."

So Sadie followed him down the hall and down the staircase and left into a corridor of old, polished suits of armor and battle crests from civil wars of the ancient houses.

"Titus, what's this about—"

"I want to break up. Please."

His voice was low, soft in the empty hall, but still the words were so sudden that Sadie jerked back, blinking rapidly. "Oh," she breathed.

Titus waited a beat while he tried to gauge her reaction, but it was hard to tell if she was more surprised or more upset. "I'm sorry, I know I said that I'd wait for—"

"Titus, stop," Sadie said with a sigh, dropping down onto a velvet settee between two suits. "You've been more than patient. I'm just...I'm just a coward. It's like you're this layer of protection around me. The second we break up, I know what will happen. Leander will make some excuse to dismiss me entirely and"—she clenched her hands into fists on her lap—"never in my life have I wanted to fight someone the way I want to fight him. I just know I'll lose. From where I stand right now at least."

"Not even Emmeline?" Titus teased, but Sadie didn't smile back.

She did, however, look determined. "We'll break up, I promise, but can I ask for one more day? Tonight..."

Titus nodded in understanding. Tonight was Durah's Winter Masquerade Ball, an event they had all been preparing for for weeks now. The etiquette, their attire, the dancing, the members of court. It was one of the year's largest, most outrageous events. He could understand not wanting to do anything public before tonight, where all eyes would be on the heirs, and especially the heir apparent.

"Yeah, of course. Later this month is even fine, but... do you mind if I tell Trang about us?"

It was rare that Titus blushed, but he felt it all across his face, even down his neck and across his shoulders. He tugged at his shirt collar, afraid to meet Sadie's gaze.

With a giggle, she nudged him. "Do I spy a crusshhh?"

"Please don't," he groaned.

Sadie reached over and tapped him on the

chest, right where he kept his phone in his jacket pocket. "Call her."

Titus huffed out a laugh and stood, taking out his phone. He started to head out when Sadie's soft voice stopped him.

"Titus?"

He glanced back. "Yeah?"

She smiled. "Thank you... for everything this year. I mean it. You're not a bad guy."

Her words settled something restless inside him. It was like he was finally able to breathe freely. Though he wasn't sure that what she said was entirely true, hearing it from her made him hope. Holding his breath, he pressed call and lifted the phone to his ear.

# 25

# SADIE

THE ALLURE OF A BALL GOWN HAD FADED. Not entirely, but just enough that Sadie didn't need to stare at herself in the mirror for twenty minutes as she got dressed for the event. Standing in front of a three-way mirror made her skin crawl. That could also be from last year's *incident* with Emmeline.

But this dress, she had to admit, was particularly extravagant. And, good lord, was it heavy. It had layers and layers of fabric, with heavy beadwork and jewels across the bodice. It was bright white and silver, reminding her of either the snow queen from *The Chronicles of Narnia* or the girl from Jim Henson's *The Labyrinth* with David Bowie.

White, silver, and jewels—her mask matched her dress. Tiny crystals dangled from the bottom of the mask, brushing her cheeks, which she knew was going to annoy her no end over the course of the night.

At least in this gown, her legs wouldn't be cold. Though she knew the ball was going to take place *inside* the ballroom of the massive royal yacht, she had no doubt she'd be expected to venture onto the deck for pictures, where she would surely freeze her royal ass off.

Since the royal family had been given suites aboard the yacht, she'd been able to wear heavy winter clothes when boarding and then change into her ball gown in her room. The vessel would return them to shore in the morning and they'd head back to the castle for their first free day of winter break. Even Leander accepted that they would likely need to recuperate after a night of revelry.

Such a kind man.

Sadie wasn't sure how she'd been able to withstand his company, given what she now knew he'd done to her parents. The more she thought about the assassination, the more she struggled. Couldn't they have been imprisoned instead? But Sadie knew the answer.

Wipe out the houses and there would be no more warring factions. History in Ashland would finally stop repeating itself.

And yet, Leander's blood must be laced with a drop of regret because he'd made it possible for Sadie, the last Scealan, to assume the throne. Or perhaps he did it to prove that his heirs would succeed over his enemies'. After all, there was no real way that Sadie would remain heir apparent. She'd been naive to think otherwise. She saw that now.

Still, she wasn't ready to give it up. What she'd told Titus was true…she'd been hiding behind his protection.

But no longer. If he wanted to pursue Trang, she not only gave him her blessing, she encouraged it. Because she'd believed what she'd said: He'd done a lot for her, and she wouldn't keep him away from his crush. Not to mention, she wanted Trang to be happy too. Her pride was the only thing holding her back from completely reconciling with her former friend.

So yes, tonight would be her and Titus's last event as a couple. They stood together now, side by side, as they greeted guest after guest.

The ballroom inside the royal yacht was magnificent, replete with Ashlandic heritage. Images of giants, wind spirits, and ice folk were woven into the decorations of sculptures, flower arrangements, and artwork. Nearly a hundred people occupied the space, dressed in equally expensive dresses and suits with matching creative masks.

"Don't look now, but Lady Cat-Oder's mask nearly fell into her drink," Titus muttered out of the corner of his mouth.

"You can't expect me not to now," Sadie whispered back.

He chuckled, eyes crinkling with amusement behind his peacock mask. His tux was simple and black, but complete with old-fashioned coattails, and a few peacock feathers sticking out from his jacket pocket.

Just then, a waiter came by with a tray of drinks, handing them to Sadie and Titus. "A rose cocktail for Princess Sadie, and a glass of scotch for Prince Titus. Imported liquor from one of our guests. The king requested you be seen drinking with these in hand."

Sadie and Titus dutifully took the drinks. It was just like Sadie's dress or Titus's mask—everything they wore, ate, and drank was closely analyzed. They sipped at their drinks for a few minutes before Titus interrupted their comfortable silence.

"I'm going to miss this."

Sadie glanced at him in surprise. "Really?"

Titus smirked. "It's been nice having someone to share the boring moments with."

"I guess you're right. Speaking of which... how'd it go with Trang?" she asked with a grin.

Though his mask hid most of his cheeks, she could see him blush underneath. "She ah... didn't answer. But I sent her a letter."

Sadie blinked at him. "A letter? Like, a *physical* letter?"

"Safer than an email or a text at this point," he said with a shrug. "Emmeline warned us not to do anything on the castle's network either..."

Again, Sadie remembered Enyo, the pictures on her phone, her research into the houses, and how she'd googled herself. That had been such a stupid move. But it had been almost two months ago at this point. Surely there was no cause for concern now.

"Well, a letter is more romantic anyway," she said, her tone teasing.

Titus rolled his eyes. "Enough, you."

At that moment, a couple approached from the dance floor and Sadie was somewhat surprised to see that it was Emmeline and Alaric.

As usual, Emmeline was stunning. She wore

a gown of dark gray, the color an accurate imitation of Durah's storm clouds off the coast. Like Alaric's eyes.

Sadie swallowed and turned her attention from the familiar color and instead took notice of how elegant and simple and *light* the mask looked, compared to hers. Emmeline's mask wasn't solid but a twining, intricate system of lines and curls.

Alaric had her by the arm, but his gaze was firmly on Sadie, those eyes raking from bare shoulder to bare shoulder. He was dressed in a tux similar to Titus's, but his mask was plain black with the phases of the moon in silver under the eyes.

"You two look bored out of your mind," Emmeline said. Then, with a glance at Alaric, she turned to Titus with a small smile, holding out her gloved hands. "Dance, dear cousin?"

"Love to, *cousin*." Titus gave Sadie a wink, then put his drink down on a nearby table. He took his not-cousin's hands and led her onto the dance floor, leaving Alaric and Sadie alone.

Without a word, Alaric plucked her own drink out of her grasp and set it on the same table. Then he held out his hand to her, his intentions obvious.

Sadie felt her skin ripple with heat. She had half a mind to refuse out of sheer nerves, but people were watching. It was just a dance. Expected, even, for her to dance with members of the court. Alaric was a prince, after all.

She placed her hand in his. Unlike Emmeline, she wore no gloves, and his palm and fingers were all warm and calloused and lovely.

As soon as they made it onto the ballroom floor, he pulled her close into the rigid waltz dance frame. They were closer than they needed to be, but she suspected he did that on purpose. As they fell into the familiar steps, Sadie couldn't help but marvel at how strange it was that they were both so *good* at this now. So natural. He'd been a rough foster kid and she'd been an orphan from a single-parent household. Now they wore finery and consumed food and drink more expensive than the cost of their entire upbringings... *in one night.*

Alaric leaned in, his lips brushing against the shell of her ear. "Yeh look like a wee polar bear."

Sadie gasped and nearly hit him, but he held tight to her hand as he pulled back with a giant grin on his face.

It was so handsome and boyish, Sadie felt

her heart leap. "Polar bears have fur, you ass. I'd never wear fur in a million years."

"Then what do *yeh* think yeh look like? A snowball?"

"Because I am round and white?"

"Or a marshmallow."

"If I jam my heel into your foot I'll be free to enlist a new dance partner."

Alaric laughed, his chest vibrating with the movement against hers. "Nah, cailín, we're too good together."

"Are you trying to flirt with me right now?"

"Technically, I'm trying to seduce yeh."

Sadie's cheeks flushed at the word *seduce*, fireworks exploding inside her with excitement and...longing.

*No. Stop it.*

She leveled him with a look. "By calling me a polar bear and a marshmallow."

Alaric sucked in air through his teeth. "Ah, admittedly, I'm doing a piss poor job of it."

*You're really not.* That was the scary part. Though his coquetry was hardly flattering, he was making her smile. In his arms, waltzing around the dance floor, it would be so easy to succumb to the fluttering feeling in her belly.

But Alaric had hurt her once before and so had another prince. Even though she had forgiven Titus, she wasn't entirely sure she was over the feeling of being played. Of being used.

Even if being used by Alaric Eldana sounded like a thing that her body really *really* wanted.

"I'm dating Titus."

"For show. And not for long."

Thinking about her conversation with Titus earlier, Sadie glanced away as he danced her toward one of the large windows that showed the moonlit seascape. *How can he know?*

"Says you," she muttered. Admitting that she would be officially single soon felt a bit like giving a dog a bone, so she kept it to herself.

"Aye, says me."

The music had moved into the next waltz, Alaric had his fingers on her chin, tilting her face up toward his, and she sucked in a breath. Thanks to his black mask, his gorgeous gray eyes were even more entrancing.

To her horror, she could feel herself actually leaning in. "What...what about Ramona Vasquez?" she asked, trying to remind herself why dating Alaric Eldana was *not* a good idea. Not even a choice. Though she hadn't seen

Ramona with him since that day... that wasn't to say he didn't have other girls to amuse himself with from time to time.

Though she felt guilty for thinking of him like that. He was nothing like Sebastian Bane.

Alaric frowned, but his gaze stayed on her, unyielding and refusing to be brushed away. "Yeh cannot blame me for trying to get over yeh, Sadie."

Her heart thundered. *Shit*, she believed him when he said that.

"Alaric—"

His eyes narrowed in challenge. "There was one kiss with Ramona, and I broke it off with her the night after the gala. I told her I'm still hung up on yeh. Which I am. I'm not holdin' back anymore, Sadie. If yer heart isn't his, it *will* be mine."

Sadie clenched her jaw, her heartbeat pounding in her chest like a wild beast banging on a cage. "Is that a threat?" Her fingers curled around his large hand, pulling it down so people watching wouldn't think she was cheating on one prince with another.

He seemed to catch himself and let go of her frame, stepping back. "A promise."

"Princess Sadie," a voice said behind them.

Sadie and Alaric both stepped away from the edge of the dance floor, Sadie turning about-face in a swirl of thick silvery-white fabric. A tall woman with short dark hair, rather striking in an all-black gown and simple black face mask that covered her cheeks, nose, and most of her forehead, stood alone.

"Princess Sadie," she said again, "May I have a moment of your time?" The woman addressed Sadie and yet her gaze was on Alaric.

It was hard to tell her features because of the mask, but Sadie assumed she was middle-aged. Was she a member of the court? Sadie glanced back at Alaric, and he took the hint. He gave a short bow and disappeared into the crowd.

Sadie turned back to the woman, whose gray eyes still followed Alaric's tall retreating form. "Yes, of course... I'm sorry, because of the mask, I can't tell who—"

The woman took Sadie's arm suddenly, not hard, but firm enough to startle her. It was something strangers didn't do—especially strangers toward a royal.

"Aurelia," the woman said, and Sadie's skin prickled, her breath hitching in her chest. "Please, don't be alarmed. The Operation Peaceful Sea report you have in your possession is, in fact, very real and if you're the smart girl I believe you to be, by now you likely know who you are."

Sadie stumbled in one of the thousands of layers of the dress, her thoughts falling over each other. *So it is really my name. From the memo. It's all true.*

To hear an absolute stranger confirm such a thing...what was happening? Who *was* this woman?

"Listen to me, delah," she said softly, and Sadie's heart tripped at the familiar Ashlandic term of endearment her own mah and grannah used to say. "Uploading that document to your cloud gives anyone monitoring that network access. You have been *far* too careless online. You all have. Get your hacker to cover your tracks and tell her to look into Virin Corporation."

Sadie's pulse spiked, her head starting to pound in tempo with her rushing blood. "Virin Corporation...the oil drilling company the king signed a deal with?" She knew it, of course, and hated it. The evils of offshore drilling ran deep.

"Please keep your voice down, Sadie," the woman whispered. "Yes, that's it. Follow Virin and remember, stay offline unless you can ensure your network is secure."

Before Sadie could ask anything else, the woman had let go of her arm and disappeared into the crowd.

Sadie stood there, completely stunned and still trying to process her words. Running after the woman was both impossible and impractical. Rather unexpectedly, the feeling of dizziness had snuck up on her and her dress was certainly not made to move fast in. Plus, the heir apparent chasing down a mysterious woman in black in the middle of a masquerade ball wouldn't just be noticeable, it would be newsworthy. She could make headlines or, at the very least, become the subject of a viral social media post.

Slowly, she moved through the crowd, many of the guests greeting her, and it took far too much of her concentration to greet them back. A few more minutes in the crowd and she was strangely hot.

Feeling overheated, she made her way to the double doors out onto the deck. It was freezing outside, which certainly took care of one problem, but it didn't really stop the deck from spinning. Why was the deck spinning? It hadn't been the waltz with Alaric, and she'd only had half a cocktail. She was a lightweight, sure, but not *this* light.

"Princess, a photo? Do you mind?"

A man with a press pass had followed her out and he smiled at her, innocently raising his camera.

"Actually, I'm not feeling—"

The man took her arm, and guided her around the bend of the deck, into the shadows and next to the railing of the cruiser. "Just under the moon here. Ah. Stunning."

If it would end this interaction soon... *One photo, then.*

Sadie tried her best to pose, even though her gaze was so unfocused she couldn't tell where the lens of the camera was. That should've been her first clue, maybe her third, but her brain wasn't working properly.

"No, no, just here, please," the man said, striding forward and taking her by the shoulders to position her.

He yanked her forward, teetering her off balance, and then shoved her backward. Hard.

Sadie didn't even flail as she went over the railing, down, down, and hit the icy waves below.

# 26

## ALARIC

It had been nearly impossible to take his eyes off Sadie that night. As much as he'd teased her, she looked beautiful. Yes, her gown was ridiculous, but it flowed from her pinched waist and made her look like a fairy-tale princess. Her shoulders, neck, and clavicle were enticingly bare, with a sprinkling of silver glitter. He should've been embarrassed about how *sparkles* caught his eye. But mixed with the light freckles on her soft skin? It was torturous.

He'd stepped away when the woman in black had approached her, but not for long. Like a moth to a flame, he'd circled back around the dance floor, hunting for another glimpse at her.

He was aware of how pathetic it was, but he'd long since stopped caring. Once, he might've had pride with this girl, far too much even. Not anymore.

Alaric scowled at the crowds, his sharp gaze scanning the faces and ball gowns until he saw her heading through the double doors.

Why the hell was she going outside? It was below freezing. Without even thinking, his long legs took him after her. She swayed slightly, her hand on one of the doorframes, before she disappeared through it. Unfortunately, he was halfway across the ballroom and he had to fight through crowds. But he was tall and could keep his gaze on the door, noting who went in and who went out. Sadie didn't come back inside after a few seconds, but a man in a tux with a camera and press badge around his neck went out.

Half a minute later, Alaric had followed in their footsteps. It was largely empty out on the deck, only a few couples bundled in thick coats and furs, and a quick glance told him Sadie wasn't out on the main deck.

With a frown, he stepped to the side, unsure which direction she'd gone. His neck snapped to the left when he heard a distant sound...a sound like a splash.

He remembered her swaying by the door.

Fear, colder than the sea below, gripped his heart. Alaric ran. He nearly slammed into the railing, his hands catching the frosty metal as he looked over the side into the dark waves below.

A white blob in the middle of the black waves.

*That damn dress.*

With more sense than he thought he possessed, Alaric stepped back and tore off his jacket, kicked off his shoes, and darted to one of the life preservers mounted to the wall every few yards along the side of the deck. The life preserver around his arm, Alaric took a running jump and leapt off the yacht.

The Ashlandic wind sliced through him and when he hit the icy waters, it stole his breath. He almost drowned right then, gasping and coughing, the shock to his system like *nothing* he'd ever felt. But he had no time to dwell on the cold, not if Sadie was going to live. Not if they were *both* going to live.

To his horror, Alaric couldn't find her in the waves as his frozen limbs started treading water. He thought he'd dived close to her—she couldn't be far.

*That damn dress.*

It was so heavy. All that fabric, all those jewels…

With a huge breath, Alaric dove beneath the

waves and sure enough, he could see white glowing under the light of the full moonbeams shining through the surface. Knowing he would need to abandon his life preserver, he let it go, hoping he'd be able to reach it when he came back up with Sadie in tow.

His powerful arms and legs cut through the water like swords as he swam toward her. He wished he was a better swimmer—that was Titus. Alaric was a strong runner, and now he'd give anything to have spent more days at the pool.

Miraculously, Alaric managed to make it to her before she sank too deep to reach. His arm hooked around her waist and he pulled and kicked to the surface. Their heads broke the water, and he thanked all the Ashlandic gods, all the Catholic saints, and even Buddha and the Hindu gods that she gasped.

She was alive, not drowning, just sucking in lungfuls of air and shivering and shaking so badly she practically jumped in his grip.

But *Christ*, was she heavy. Sadie herself was lighter than air, yet the dress full of water made her weigh what felt like an extra fifty pounds. Growling with frustration, Alaric ripped through her skirts, tearing at the tulle and layers and silky material until the white mass drifted away in the current.

Like a faithful dog, the life preserver had followed him, and he snagged it, then started kicking them toward the side of the ship.

"Hold on, luv, hold on," Alaric panted, every bone in his body vibrating with cold and adrenaline pumping through his veins.

Sadie only whimpered, coughed, and hacked and clung to his neck like her life depended on it, which it did.

It felt like an eternity, a *lifetime*, before Alaric managed to find the side ladder but in reality, it couldn't have been longer than eight minutes. But as each second ticked by, he feared hypothermia, of their body temperatures reaching the point of no return. Sadie was barely conscious. She was in shock, shaking, panting, nonresponsive, so he seized her by the waist and hauled her over his shoulder, then he grabbed the rungs and started climbing.

When he reached the deck, he thought he might die from exhaustion, but that was only his brain. His body was still moving, still fueled by the life-or-death adrenaline pumping through him. They weren't out of the woods yet. They needed heat *stat*.

Carefully, he managed to drop Sadie onto the deck and then jumped over the railing himself.

She'd barely touched the floor, before he was scooping her up and running into the first door he saw.

Again, luck or fate or gods were on his side, because it was a serving door, a back hallway that the staff used. Heat seemed to blast them in the face, and it nearly made him stumble and drop Sadie, shivering and nearly unconscious in his arms.

He cursed his lack of knowledge of the gigantic yacht and just started trying doors. The first one he found was a linen closet.

Good enough.

As gently as possible, he set Sadie down on the floor and started stripping. Just before he pulled his boxer briefs down, he grabbed a fluffy white towel from the shelf and wrapped it around his waist. Then he turned to Sadie, whose lips were blue, and still shaking so hard she was bruising herself. She didn't protest as he ripped the fastenings off the remains of her stupid dress. The one that had somehow both saved her and nearly killed her.

Propriety be damned. She could scold him later. She was going to die if she didn't get those wet clothes off and get her body temperature up. He peeled the dress away from her icy body and then wrapped several fluffy towels around her and started rubbing her limbs as much as he could.

"C'mon, luv, gotta get warm. Can yeh move? Try to move."

"It—it h-h-hurts," Sadie whined. Her lips were still blue, and she was still shaking something fierce, but there was life in her eyes again as she finally seemed to register him.

"I know, beautiful. But that means yer blood is moving. It's getting yeh warm again. Wrap yer arms around my neck."

Frankly, Alaric was starting to feel the same excruciating pain as the adrenaline began to wear off. Now that they were on the yacht, *safe*, his body was rightly punishing him.

*Feck*, he was *exhausted*.

He had never felt fatigue like this. Never felt like every bodily system he had was on the verge of shutting down.

With a soft whimper, Sadie obeyed, pressing her face into his neck and shuddering every few seconds, but he would take shivering and teeth-clacking over stillness. Over death.

God *damn it*, he'd almost lost her. *Really* almost lost her.

It was that thought that gave him one last surge of energy.

Simply getting her out of wet clothes and wrapping her in towels wasn't going to get her body temperature back where it needed to be.

Reluctant to let her go, even for a moment, he detached her arms. "I'll be right back. Try to dry your hair."

He stood and walked to the door, then poked his head out of the room, put two fingers in his mouth... and whistled.

Thirty minutes, a bribed staff member, and two mugs of hot spiced cider later, Alaric and Sadie lay in his bed with four extra blankets piled on top of the comforter. It had taken every ounce of strength Alaric had left to get them to this point, with precious body heat being passed between them under layers of covers.

It was only concern for her that kept him awake.

She had been too cold and out of it to argue about their current situation, but Alaric was starting to wonder when Sadie would realize that she wore nothing but one of his shirts and he wore only a pair of pajama pants and they were, well, spooning.

Her body was so small up against his. Small and fragile and soft. His arms cocooned her, and with his chest against her back, she could likely feel the pounding of his heart.

Given her state of undress, one would've assumed his quickened pulse was from arousal. It wasn't. He kept reliving the moment he saw her white gown in those black waves. Feeling her limp body in the water as he'd grabbed hold of her.

Wondering if he'd been holding a corpse.

But no, she was alive. Alive and wrapped in his arms, where she belonged. And he wouldn't allow himself rest until he was sure she was staying that way.

With gentle fingers, he moved her still-damp hair clinging to her back and pressed his face into the curve of her neck. He resisted the urge to kiss her there, careful not to make any moves in the wake of their trauma.

She made a soft sound in her throat, and he waited for her to speak. She didn't.

"Are yeh warm?" he asked finally. Even if she was, he wasn't sure he could let her go.

She was silent for a long moment. She hadn't said much except to answer important questions, like this one. He was about to sit up and check her expression when she finally whispered, "Yes... but I thought I'd never be warm again."

He squeezed her a little tighter.

"If you hadn't..."

Her fingers fluttered over his arm, before she took his hand and pressed it against her stomach as her whole body gave one more terrified quake.

"I'm here, cailín. Yer safe."

It was only then that she finally shifted in his arms. She hadn't moved since he'd taken the empty mug of cider from her hands and he'd pulled her into his bed with him. Her hazel eyes met his, wide and glassy. "Someone tried to kill me, Alaric. I'm not safe."

An intense stab of both fear and rage drove into his chest like a spear. "Tell me," he whispered, voice low and dangerous.

With a shaky breath, she recounted the moments since their dance. The woman in black's strange warning to look into Virin Corporation. Her sudden bout of dizziness and overheating. The man with a press pass and camera and how he'd shoved her over the railing.

"What did yeh have to eat or drink?" Alaric asked.

Sadie's brow furrowed, then her expression cleared with realization, her lips parting. "A cocktail made specifically for me—you think it was spiked?"

A muscle in Alaric's jaw twitched as he grinded his back teeth. "No one here would risk pushing someone overboard unless they were sure they wouldn't be able to fight back."

"That woman said the Operation Peaceful Sea report is real and she found it because I synced it to my cloud. That means she somehow has access to Enyo, Alaric. Which means other people must too. If there was insider trading, then maybe Leander made some kind of deal that gives him access to Almus Terra's Enyo program so he knows about the report and my search history. It's like she was... trying to warn me before this happened." She paused and lifted her gaze to his. "Alaric, don't lie to me. This was a murder attempt, wasn't it?"

Alaric studied her face. It eased something inside him to see that her lips were no longer blue, but pink and full. He forced his gaze away to check the flush of her freckled cheeks and her expressive eyes. Most of her makeup had been washed away by the briny sea, but the mascara was stubborn and rimmed her eyes like those of a raccoon. Still beautiful, though. He wiped at a smudge with his thumb and she let him, still staring up at him like he had all the answers.

He didn't. He wanted to believe that his

grandfather would never attempt to murder an eighteen-year-old girl. But now that Sadie knew the secret of her ancestry...she was a threat. A danger to the peace he'd tried so hard to maintain for decades. Not only was she the daughter of an ancient rival house, she had access to every facet of Ashland Court and politics. She was his *heir apparent.* An enemy kept too close.

The absolute arrogance of this man to give Aurelia Scealan a shot at his throne, believing she would never, in a million years, triumph.

But she had, and surely, he was regretting it now. Perhaps enough to kill her.

The press pass, the spiked drink, even her heavy dress that would guarantee she sink and make her drown faster if hypothermia didn't kill her first...

"Aye, I think it was," Alaric said, his gruff voice as gentle as he could make it through the blinding rage roiling through his chest.

"But he's *king*. He could simply dismiss me as heir apparent. What kind of a threat am I to him? I'm noth—"

"Yer not nothing." Alaric took her face in his hand, smoothing his thumb over her freckles. "Yeh proved yer brilliance at Hibernia when yeh held millions of dollars hostage over the most powerful people in the world. Yeh *are* a threat, Sadie. Imagine if yeh went public with the news of yer identity and the facts of yer parents' assassination? Yeah, Leander has brought peace and stability to Ashland, but his people still suffer. He is not beloved by all. Yeh know this and yeh wanted to become queen to help *everyone* access the things yeh believe in: health care, food, education. If he dismisses yeh as heir apparent and yeh were to come out with the truth? He'd have an enormous uprising on his hands. The people love yeh. They would back yeh. Whether yeh realize it or not, cailín, yeh have the power to *incite change.*"

With every word, Alaric could feel Sadie's pulse quicken. He felt the change in her breath, cradling her face, her heartbeat so close to his own. She looked up at him like she was seeing him for the first time all night, even though they'd never been physically closer.

Then her expression shuttered and she shivered. "Because of who I am."

Alaric studied her again, this time trying to understand why that look had disappeared—the one that made his breath catch. "Aye, because of who yeh are."

Her gaze lowered and she started to pull away,

but he caught her around the waist. "Where do yeh think yer goin'?" he practically growled.

She shivered again. "Back to my room."

"No."

"Alaric—"

"Sadie, *no*. Yeh haven't stopped shivering, and someone here tried to kill yeh. Like yeh said, yer not safe."

He was glad they would be back at Almus Terra the day after tomorrow. He couldn't imagine trying to keep her safe in Heres Castle, where every single person was under the king's control. Anyone could make an attempt on her life. It made his grip on her hip and waist tighten.

"We can't sleep in the same bed, Alaric. This is entirely inappropriate," she said, her face flushing scarlet, finally saying the quiet part out loud.

"Why? Scared I'll do something to yeh?"

Sadie met his gaze, challenging. "No."

He smirked back at her. "Then there's no issue. But like it or not, we're on a wee boat and there's no fireplace. Blankets and body heat is the best way to keep yeh warm."

Sadie glanced away and he really wished she would stop blushing so much. "I could take a warm bath..."

Alaric lifted himself up, dropping an elbow

next to her head so he loomed over her. "I just saved yer life, *cailín*. I'm not saying yeh owe me anything. But yeh scared me half to death. Please, humor me and *stay*."

Sadie stared up at him, their faces so close, and her gaze jumped to his lips. Ah, it would be so easy to lean down and capture hers. But. She had yet to address his feelings. Tonight was only about keeping her safe, warm, and within his reach. Nothing more.

Slowly she nodded and he settled back. Now that he knew she wasn't going anywhere, he felt he could finally stop battling the exhaustion that had come with the crash of adrenaline.

Before he could situate them back into their spooning position, she grabbed his wrist. "Alaric."

"Hmm?"

"Thank you for saving my life."

"Stay with me, cailín," he murmured, his head hitting the pillow. "That'll be thanks enough."

As he was drifting off, he felt Sadie's fingers slip between his own, and something in his restless heart slid into place.

# 27

## TITUS

Titus had just finished pulling his Tom Ford cable-knit sweater over his head when a knock sounded at his door. Thinking it was one of the staff delivering breakfast or morning tea, Titus answered, "Come in."

But instead of a maid with his tray of Earl Grey, Emmeline stormed through, her gaze raking over his bedroom like she was looking for something.

"Uh... can I help you?" he asked.

"Have you seen Alaric? He's not answering in his room." She squinted into Titus' yacht bedroom, miniature when compared to the standards of the castle, snooping like her brother might be hidden in the closet. He nearly thought she was going to step forward and look under his bed.

"Not since last night. It's eight-fifteen,

Emmeline. We were supposed to sleeping in this morning."

"Yes, but since *when* last night?"

Titus searched the dregs of his memory. That scotch had hit him harder than most drinks. Alcohol coupled with his RA meds was a bad combination, but it had been unavoidable last night. At least he'd had something in his stomach to cushion the blow.

"I don't know," he answered finally. "Since I danced with you and he danced with Sadie, maybe?"

Emmeline blew out a breath, a piece of her long honey hair fluttering in front of her. "Yeah, same. But that was like ten-thirty. Leander wouldn't have let us leave earlier than midnight."

It was odd, he had to admit. Also, he'd searched for Sadie for a while after that point before asking Ilsa where she was. Ilsa hadn't known and when he'd seen Leander a bit later, his grandfather had made no mention of Sadie whatsoever. Like she didn't matter in the least.

"Sadie was missing too," he said.

"I noticed. You don't think they...went off and hooked up somewhere?" Emmeline asked, glancing at him, as if to gauge his reaction.

Titus searched for any hurt or jealousy

spiraling through him at the suggestion. To his relief, he found none. Instead, there was only anxiety about when Trang would finally receive his letter and how she might respond to the truth and his... confession.

"Sadie wouldn't do that," Titus said, and, because he'd known Alaric at least long enough to judge his character about these sorts of things, he added, "and neither would Alaric."

"Oh, just admit it: You're not really dating," Emmeline said, her words dripping with exasperation.

"And I would admit that to you, why?" Titus shot back, crossing to his dresser to put on his wristwatch—and subtly slide his medication behind a lamp so she wouldn't take notice of the orange pill bottle.

"For God's sake, Titus, do you think I give a damn anymore? I'm illegitimate. Even if Leander found out and didn't care, *I* still do. I was only after the crown to make my parents happy and lo and behold, they're pieces of shit."

There was something in Emmeline's voice, a noticeable crack, that made Titus raise his gaze to look at her in the mirror of his dresser. She was looking away, her eyes glassy.

In that moment, Titus forgave her—not that

she'd asked him to, that wasn't really Emmeline's style, but she probably wanted his forgiveness without admitting it out loud.

It was an easy thing to do, surprisingly, when he saw how much they were alike. They may not be related by blood, but holy hell, they were practically twins.

She had worked so hard to make her parents love her, notice her, to be part of their world, and for them to be proud of her. Simple, basic needs for any child. Titus was the same. He'd loved his parents. In fact, he hadn't told anyone about his RA because he *still* didn't want to disappoint them.

They were terrible people. He shouldn't care what they thought. But they were his *parents*. It was written in his DNA to love them, to want their approval.

"Yeah, me and Sadie—it's all fake," Titus said at last, stepping away from his dresser to face her. "But it's helping her, and I wanted to at least do that. We're calling it off in the next few days though. Staging a whole fake breakup."

Emmeline lifted a brow at him. "So you can finally date Trang?"

Titus coughed into his fist. "That wasn't exactly—"

Just then another knock sounded on his door. Maybe *that* was his breakfast. He hoped he could get rid of Emmeline in order to eat and take his meds before they docked and headed back to the castle.

Again, not his much-needed breakfast, but his grandfather's head secretary and personal guard. "Captain Kendrick," Titus said, "Is...something wrong?"

Kendrick's stoic face betrayed nothing. "His majesty would like to see you. Please come with me, Your Highness."

Titus glanced back at Emmeline and her face mirrored his worry. Why would the king need to see him at this time? And him alone? Stress bloomed in his gut, making it churn with nerves. He turned back to Captain Kendrick, who stepped back and gestured for Titus to join him. Titus shut the door on Emmeline, still in his room, and followed the captain.

The yacht was big enough that it hardly felt like they were on the water. Only the sea from the windows gave him any indication that the boat was moving back toward the shore. It was also big enough that it took several minutes to reach the king's suites and during that time, Titus ran through a series of possibilities in his mind.

Had his grandfather found out about his RA? Was this going to be where he disowned Titus and took away his title as heir? Disowning him was unlikely from a publicity standpoint, since Leander would be condemned as ableist and elitist and dickish, but quietly removing him as an heir was a *real* possibility.

"You may go in," Captain Kendrick said when they reached the large door.

Swallowing hard, Titus stepped inside, and the first thing he noticed was that Sadie was in one of the chairs opposite Leander, who reclined in a massive wingback chair that resembled his throne.

Sadie looked a mess and... terrified.

Her hair was wild and full of tangles and her eyes still had remnants of makeup around them. But what nearly made him choke was that she was wearing a man's dress shirt and enormous pajama pants that had to have been rolled a few times to be able to stay on her waist.

His mind went utterly blank with confusion.

"Titus, take a seat," Leander said, his voice cold. Titus could now see why Sadie was terrified. Fury seemed to be rolling off the king of Ashland in waves, as choppy and wild as the sea outside the window.

Titus took the seat next to Sadie and he noticed how she actively avoided his gaze.

"We seem to have a situation on our hands," Leander said, his voice quiet and calm. But Titus could hear the rage simmering underneath. "Your girlfriend was found in your cousin's bed this morning."

*Holy hell.* Emmeline was right.

Even if his retort to her had been to keep up the pretense of their fake relationship, he'd still believed what he'd said. That Sadie and Alaric wouldn't...

Still, he knew Alaric had feelings for Sadie. And he had feelings for Trang. Now that Sadie knew he was over her, had she felt free to act on whatever feelings she had for Alaric?

"Your Majesty, nothing hap—"

"Not another word, Sadie."

Titus glanced at Sadie, and she shot him a panicked look, as if to say *please believe me.*

"Titus, do you have anything to say to this shocking and reprehensible news?"

No, he really didn't. Just like Trang, Alaric wouldn't have made a move without knowing the truth of their fake relationship.

"Well," Titus said slowly, trying to choose his words carefully. "Sadie and I are dating under *your* orders, sir. It's not as if we're in love. She's free to—"

"Don't," Leander snarled, "finish that sentence. She is not free to do *anything* without my approval. She is my *heir apparent* or have the two of you forgotten that?"

His words were dangerous now. Low and sinister.

"Luckily, we have paid off the servants who witnessed their tryst, all of whom signed an NDA," Leander continued, "but in case anyone saw that *dance*, for instance, we must make it clear that the two of you are as strong as ever. I cannot have it leak that my heir apparent is cheating on my grandson with my other grandson. What kind of fool would that make of me?"

Again, Titus glanced at Sadie, who shrank in her seat, as if to make herself as small as possible. He couldn't blame her. Leander looked truly terrifying.

"Which is why…next month, we will announce your engagement."

Every muscle in Titus's body seized up, while Sadie's jaw dropped like a cartoon character's.

Leander stared down at them both, as if daring them to protest.

Because what else could they do? A royal

engagement was an extreme reaction to a situation that hadn't even made the news.

"Gran—Your Majesty," Titus said, trying to control his voice from sounding choked. "With all due respect, that... it doesn't make sense. No one has even heard—"

"I will tell you what doesn't make sense, Titus," Leander said. "What doesn't make sense is when I've ordered you to maintain this relationship for the good of Ashland and yet you're both disloyal. Do you know what crumbles empires faster than economic disasters? Social ones. This, for example." Leander lifted his arm and clicked a remote Titus hadn't even noticed he'd been holding. The TV turned on and a news story flashed to the masquerade ball last night.

An Ashlandic news reporter spoke into a mic, dressed in a thick fur coat over an evening gown, "Princess Sadie looks like a true fairy tale come to life in a gown designed by Christian Siriano. She's spotted with her boyfriend, Prince Titus. The couple has been dating for a little over a year and there are rumors that an engagement could be imminent, but an unnamed source at Almus Terra Academy has documented the couple fighting—"

The distant, shaky cell phone camera showed

Sadie and Titus on that fateful day in the bailey, where they *had* been arguing.

"—about their different upbringings. We all know Prince Titus grew up with a silver spoon in his mouth, living in a multimillion-dollar London townhome and attending Eaton, while Sadie grew up in working-class Farach, raised by a single parent and a senior citizen. This class tension highlights a much larger problem in our country and others: the disappearance of the middle class. While not all millionaires are royals—"

Leander turned off the TV and Titus shifted his gaze back to him, understanding dawning.

This intervention had nothing to do with Alaric or any potential rumor. Marrying him off to Sadie was an answer to a political and economic problem that Leander had ignored for most of his reign, even amplifying it in many ways.

It was ridiculous, the idea that such a problem could be addressed by the matrimonial binding of two people from two different worlds, and yet there would be no arguing.

"This will be announced in a press conference in five weeks' time. Titus, you're dismissed."

Later, Titus would ask himself if there was anything more he could have done in this moment...but right *now* he found nothing.

Looking at Sadie, he rose from his seat and left her. He swore he saw her trembling. But if he stayed... it would likely only make his grandfather angrier.

Titus stepped outside and immediately he was grabbed by the arm and hauled down the hall into an empty room. At first, he thought it was Captain Kendrick, but no. It was Alaric.

Alaric looked as unhinged as Titus had ever seen him. His dark hair was more wild than usual. He wore flannel pants and was bare-chested underneath a zip-up hoodie. He wasn't even wearing any socks.

"Is she all right?" he rasped.

"She's freaked," Titus said, pulling his arm from his cousin's grasp. "I've never seen him so pissed, Alaric. What the *hell* were you thinking?"

"It's not like that! It's—" his voice was nearly a shout before he caught himself. With a deep breath, he ran both his hands through his wild hair. "Yeh don't understand. We did *nothin'*, but I know it looks bad."

"It doesn't just look bad, Alaric, it looks like something very specific happened," Titus said, thinking of Sadie and her wild hair wearing Alaric's clothes.

"Feck, feck," Alaric swore, out of breath, his

fingers digging into his scalp. "Titus, she fell off the yacht."

Titus stared at him, sure he'd heard wrong. "What?"

"She fell off the fucking yacht. Into the sea. I heard the splash, I went in after and managed to get us back on deck and into a linen closet to dry us off. I bribed a servant to get us to my room without being seen and I made sure she didn't—that we both didn't—get hypothermia. We were jus' keepin' warm and we fell asleep in my bed."

Titus pressed his fingers into his eyes. "Do you *hear* yourself? Do you know how insane that sounds?"

"It's the fecking truth," Alaric growled.

Titus stared at him in utter bewilderment. His face was completely serious, even *frightened*. It was unsettling to see Alaric, of all people, afraid. But how could he believe such a story?

With nothing left to say, Titus ripped the door open but as soon as he stepped into the hall, Sadie came barreling toward him, her hair still a mess, her hazel eyes wide with a terror that mirrored Alaric's.

She grabbed fistfuls of his sweater and whispered fiercely, "I need to talk to you."

# 28

## ALARIC

Alaric leaned against the door, ensuring that no one could walk into the room they'd commandeered while Sadie told Titus *everything*.

There was a tiny jealous piece of him that wanted to be the only one she told all her secrets to. But that was stupid and selfish. He'd already been stupid and selfish enough for one day.

As Titus had said—what the hell had he been *thinking*? Keeping Sadie in his bed, dressed like that, knowing it would look like nothing but the obvious. He should've at least set some kind of alarm to wake them up so she could get herself out of his room and back to hers.

But, no, he'd been far too exhausted and too unsettled to think of such a normal thing. Truth be told, he was still worn out. The toll of fighting the frigid sea had done a number on his body and all he wanted to do was crawl back into bed and sleep for a week. At the same time, however, one of his stewards bringing in his morning tea and finding Sadie and him in the same bed, half-clothed with legs tangled, not to mention the nightmare that followed, had him on edge.

Even if it had been the best sleep of his life.

But the infamous "morning after" would live forever in his memory. The steward rushing out before Alaric and Sadie had even been fully awake. He'd found her some pants and he pulled on a hoodie just in time for the king to come bursting in like they'd committed some act of treason.

Alaric had barely been able to hold himself back from attacking his grandfather then and there. Sadie had nearly died at the command of this odious man.

But Leander had been flanked by Captain Kendrick and two guards. Alaric was a good fighter and could take down punks in an alleyway—no problem. But a high-ranking ex-military operative like Kendrick and other trained soldiers? Not a chance.

So, he'd held back as Leander took Sadie away.

For thirty minutes, he'd nearly lost his mind thinking of her alone with that...murderer. But now she was here, right next to him, and he felt like he could breathe again.

Halfway through her story, Titus had slowly backed up, his arm fumbling for a chair. They were in some kind of place where the crew of the yacht did administrative work.

When she was done, Titus looked at her with a mix of horror and disbelief.

"Do you... need to see a doctor?" he asked finally.

"Oh, um," Sadie pursed her lips, blush coloring her cheeks. "I think I'm okay, Alaric took good care of me."

Warmth exploded in Alaric's chest, and he bit on the inside of his cheek, hard, so as not to smile like a fecking tool.

Titus nodded, seeming to accept this, then glanced at Alaric. "Sorry I made assumptions."

There wasn't anything to apologize for—the evidence had been damning—but Alaric appreciated it, nonetheless. Though part of him was still angry at Titus for using Sadie to get ahead, it was becoming harder and harder to hate his cousin.

Titus sighed and dropped his head in his hands. "Christ, I cannot believe this."

"Which part?" Alaric muttered, folding his arms. He likely didn't have much time before Leander would demand the whole yacht be torn

apart to find Alaric so he could get *his* lecture from the king.

"I mean...everything? Sadie being a Scealan is unfathomable on its own, but someone trying to *kill* her by shoving her overboard?"

"Not *someone*. It's obvious who has the motive and the means to—"

Titus made a sharp gesture against his throat. "Seriously? Lower your voice and pray no one walking by heard you. Look, I don't need to be convinced this family is screwed up, but for now at least, I think she'll be safe."

"What makes you say that? Because we're returning to Almus Terra tomorrow?" Alaric asked.

"Not...exactly," Titus said, his gaze shooting to Sadie.

Sadie looked downright miserable. No, more than that. She was fraying at the edges and Alaric couldn't blame her. She'd nearly been offed last night and had every right to be freaking the hell out right now.

Wringing her hands, Sadie said in a hushed voice, "The king wants to announce...our engagement."

*Our engagement.*

Suddenly it was like he was drowning in the

Labrador Sea again. All sounds muted, the indescribable cold seeping into his bones and bloodstream.

Logically, he knew Sadie and his cousin weren't in love. That the engagement ordered by their king was just that—an order. But the idea that it could potentially happen...

"I should go," Alaric heard himself say. "Leander will be looking for me."

"Alaric..." Sadie's fingers grazed his arm but he stepped back, opening the door.

"Stay with Titus or Emmeline, Sadie. Don't be alone. The whole day. Promise me." He forced his gaze to meet hers.

She looked as if she wanted to say more but maybe she felt the emotion in his eyes, because she didn't argue. "I promise."

Without another word, Alaric left to collect on his grandfather's lashings.

Alaric sat at a pub. Not unlike the one he'd gotten sloshed at the night he'd seen Titus and Sadie kissing for the first time in the castle gardens. Except this time, he was completely sober.

A pint sat in front of him, untouched, his dark gaze locked on the flat across the street.

It had been a long, *long* day, but miraculously,

he was here. Just a few yards from the home of the man who'd shoved Sadie overboard last night.

Part of him couldn't believe the man was still alive after clearly failing to complete his assignment. But Alaric had seen him enter the flat just ten minutes ago.

He glanced down at the message string on Discord between Romy and him. Before leaving school for winter break, she'd set him up with some special double-encryption software that would allow them to communicate freely. The possibility of their conversation being tapped was low, but still there.

After getting the verbal beating of his life from his grandfather with phrases like *"Can't you keep it in your pants?"* and *"I should let your father deal with you,"* Alaric had docked with the rest of the court and once they reached Heres Castle, he'd gone straight to the Royal Guards' admin offices. Using the special USB drive loaded with Romy's signature blend of spyware, he'd given her direct access to the guards' servers. From there, she'd worked her magic.

In three hours, she'd found the guest list to the masquerade ball last night.

In twenty minutes, she'd cross-referenced the people with press passes with the staff directories of news outlets in Ashland and the surrounding countries.

That narrowed suspects down to a Mr. Richard Warren. A man...who did not exist. Except everyone alive left some digital footprint, and to get into the ball the man had to be photographed. Using CCTV footage, Romy ran a facial scan that identified the man as Richard Warren, who had several aliases. One of which rented an entire flat in Durah for only four days.

*Who* did that?

Paid hit men, Alaric supposed.

Alaric was out of his depth, but he'd come this far. It was a miracle the man hadn't disappeared from Durah already. But the saving grace was that he'd likely been waiting to get paid and hadn't known that Sadie had survived. He was probably packing up now, about to catch a flight out of Ashland, maybe for the rest of his miserable little life.

Alaric left money and his untouched pint on the table and headed out of the pub. To avoid recognition, he kept his hood up and wore a medical mask, like he had a cold. With his unruly dark hair casting shadows over his brow, he was virtually unrecognizable, and he needed to keep it that way.

His phone went off—Romy again. *You shouldn't be doing this, dumbass.*

True, this was beyond foolish. While he could be approaching a professional hit man, he very much doubted it. For one, would a professional assassin be so easy to find? The man wasn't a sniper, for God's sake. He'd pushed a drugged girl off a boat. In fact, Alaric suspected this was just a normal guy being used by the Eldana family to tie up loose ends. If Sadie's body was found and foul play was suspected, they'd tidily pin the murder on this poor sap.

*Not poor*, Alaric reminded himself; this evil son of a bitch was perfectly at peace with killing an innocent girl. Truthfully, Alaric was more concerned about walking out of this flat a murderer, rather than being murdered himself.

Using his lock-picking tools, Alaric easily got the door open. He walked up a decrepit staircase that reminded him of his old flat back in Dublin and came to the door at the top of the steps. He also got that one open without any trouble—which meant he clearly wasn't walking in on a Jason Bourne type.

In fact, the man was *asleep on the fecking couch.*

The flat was small and moldy and sparse and there was a suitcase in the corner and five empty bottles of liquor on the table. Warren was probably trying to drink away his guilt.

With light steps, Alaric came to the couch. For the second time that day, he imagined killing a man. Putting his hands around his bare neck and squeezing, or taking the pillow and smothering him in his drunken sleep...

Apart from his father and grandfather, Alaric had never hated anyone so much. This man had almost killed the girl he loved.

He *loved*.

It was a strange, twisted moment to acknowledge the intensity of his feelings, but par for the course for Alaric. He wasn't a gentle guy, and he never claimed to be. He was his father's son. Angry and vengeful.

But... he was his mother's son too. If he ever wanted her to be proud of him, if he ever wanted Sadie to love him back, he could not bloody his hands.

Deep down, he also wanted to believe that it wasn't in him. But, again, his father was a son of a bitch and his grandfather had been willing to kill as well. Leander didn't pull the trigger, but he ordered the shot. That lack of humanity—it was in his DNA.

The only thing he could see clearly now was

this: If ever there was someone to kill, it would be this man sleeping before him.

Alaric grabbed the man by the collar and slapped him hard across the face.

Warren awoke with a cry, clutching his cheek and reflexively trying to curl into a ball. "No, no, please, I'm innocent, *please*."

For a brief moment, Alaric hesitated, the reaction not what he expected. But that was his mistake. Warren suddenly threw himself off the couch and tackled Alaric, his flailings half-crazed, drunk, and desperate. After swiping at Alaric's face, he threw a punch into Alaric's side with all his might, but he was still weak compared to the sturdy nineteen-year-old who'd been street fighting since he was ten. Alaric drew back and threw an elbow at the guy's head, holding back just slightly so as not to knock the guy out cold.

Warren cried out in pain and his body went limp. With a grunt, Alaric pushed him fully onto the disgusting floor, grabbing him by the throat and pressing his knee to his chest.

Oh, how easy it would be to just squeeze a little harder.

The man stared up at Alaric with wild eyes, nails scratching at Alaric's hand on his throat. It had been a pathetic attempt. The scuffle only served to give Alaric a bruise in his side, but it had dropped Alaric's hood and sent his mask askew, a fact that he only realized after Warren choked out three words.

"Please, my lord."

*Lord.*

It wasn't the first time Alaric had faced the fact that he looked like his father, Lord Mikael Erickson.

"I did *everything* I was told. It's not my fault she survived. It's not my fault."

Was the man drinking because he'd failed? Alaric felt that urge to squeeze even stronger now.

As if sensing Alaric's murderous fury, Warren started sobbing, fat tears and snot collecting on his ruddy face. "I know I failed you twice. But have mercy. Your wife—she must've found out somehow. I did everything you asked back then, too. Have mercy."

Alaric's grip slackened as his lips parted in shock.

*Your wife?* Could he... could he be referring to Alaric's ma? Does *failed twice* mean that he hadn't been successful with not just one, but *two* murder attempts? The first being Alaric's mother? But that wasn't possible. Princess Rhea was dead. Regardless of that, she hadn't died from foul play, it had been walking pneumonia, according to the reports.

He'd even seen her name carved into the rock by the sea. In line with ancient Ashlandic tradition, her ashes had been dispersed into the salty waves before Alaric had even turned two. This man was drunk and half-delirious. In his mental state he couldn't be trusted with his own name, let alone the truth about something as big as the crown princess's death.

He'd heard enough. Alaric reared back and punched the man dead in the face. Warren grunted, his eyes rolling back in his head, his nose breaking and blood running down his lips. Alaric shifted the unconscious man up against the threadbare couch so he wouldn't choke on his own blood and vomit, and then got to his feet. He straightened out his hood and his mask, and then he left the flat, his fist throbbing.

Emmeline tightened the wrap on his hand, enough to make him wince. She clicked her tongue and didn't look the least bit sorry about it.

His sister was *pissed*.

Alaric had told her what happened. At least, most of it. The only thing he'd left out was *why* Sadie had been shoved overboard. The secret of

House Scealan was not his story to tell, but Alaric saving her and finding the man who'd done it, well, that was *his* tale.

"You could've died. Twice."

"I wasn't going to let her drown, Emmeline," Alaric said, rotating his hand that was covered in a wrap to help his bruise heal.

"And the hit man's flat? You assumed too much that he was going to be just a regular man. What about the Royal Guard? Captain Kendrick? Leander has the entire military—"

"To prevent things like a coup," Alaric snapped, "not to murder an innocent girl. Especially not his heir apparent. Yeh think a trained assassin would be hired for that? No, they'd want someone they could pin her murder on."

At that, Emmeline went quiet. "You're still an idiot," she said after a long beat.

"So people keep telling me," Alaric said with a sigh. "Speaking of...can she stay with yeh tonight?"

Emmeline scowled at him. "Is that the only reason you came to me about all this? So I can babysit your girlfriend?" At his face, she quickly added, "You know I'm not going to say no. Someone tried to kill her. I don't like her, but I don't want her hurt. I'm just saying—I want you to tell me things."

Alaric's shoulders relaxed. "I *am* telling yeh things."

"Because you want to, or because you have to?" she asked.

"Both. Why can't both be true?"

Emmeline sighed. "Fine then. I still hate you putting yourself in danger. You're...you're the only real family I have, Alaric." Her voice was soft, so soft it startled him.

Without overthinking it, Alaric reached over and pulled her close, placing a warm kiss on her forehead.

She looked up at him with watery eyes, and he gave her a smile.

"See yeh at dinner, sis."

On his way back to his room to change for their final dinner in Ashland, Alaric received another Discord notification. Expecting it to be Romy, he pulled it up.

Instead, it was a new friend request. **WomanInBlack.**

Immediately Alaric thought of the woman in black from the masquerade that Sadie had told him about. He hit accept and a message popped up.

A news report from twenty minutes ago. **Unidentified Man Found Murdered in Durah Flat.**

Alaric didn't have to read the article to know who the man was, and he didn't need to be a detective to know his father must have paid Warren a visit right after he had. Lord Erickson must not have been merciful.

The **WomanInBlack** sent another message.

> You were nearly caught. If you need information, contact me next time. Stay safe.

# 29

# EMMELINE

*This shouldn't be so awkward. We're roommates for heaven's sake,* Emmeline couldn't help but think.

Yet, sitting in her bedroom in Heres castle with snacks from the maids, acting like it was some kind of pajama party, was uncomfortable as hell.

Sadie sat in one of the plush chairs, hugging her knees to her chest and wiggling her bare toes against the edge. Emmeline was brushing her teeth for an unnaturally long amount of time, her synapses firing in every different direction.

She'd lived with Sadie in the same room, or at the very least, the same two castles for nearly a year and a half and this was the first time she'd ever felt compelled to talk to her.

Finally, Emmeline ducked her head and spit out her toothpaste. She wiped her mouth and poked her head out of her bathroom. "Warm enough?"

Sadie's head shot up like a dog hearing the word *treat*. "Oh, yeah. I'm fine."

The room fell quiet again as Emmeline dropped herself onto the bed, taking a knitted throw blanket and drawing it across her lap. Out of the corner of her eye, she studied Sadie.

Okay, so the girl was stronger than Emmeline had ever given her credit for. If Emmeline had gone overboard into icy waters, she'd be in the trauma wing of a hospital right now.

"Do you...wanna talk about it?" Emmeline asked.

Sadie blinked at her. "With you?"

Emmeline blanched. Okay, she deserved that. "Never mind," she muttered, reaching for one of the dozen useless throw pillows to toss off the bed.

"I didn't mean it that way."

"Yes, you did. And it's okay. If I were you, I wouldn't want to talk to me either. Ever."

Sadie was quiet for a minute, then she finally blurted out, "Why did you hate me so much? Because I was winning the crown? Do you want to be queen that badly?"

Were they really going to talk about this? Emmeline heaved a deep sigh. This was part of the reason she'd been nervous about tonight. Oakley and Trang weren't here as a buffer, there was no longer this impenetrable barrier between them.

"Titus and Alaric," Emmeline finally said.

Sadie blinked. "What?"

"They were supposed to be *my* family, Sadie. My cousins. They could've been like brothers to me. And instead, they only cared about you. Only saw *you*. Yeah, you were winning the crown and potentially stealing my chance to finally make my parents care about me. But really, I hated that you took *them* away. It wasn't your fault that our grandfather—I mean, *their* grandfather—pitted us against each other, but you were easy to blame. Not just that, but you had Oliver's friendship, too, and I..."

Emmeline blew out a shaky breath, feeling her throat tighten with every word.

"Anyway, I know this is majorly overdue and I'm not asking you to accept it because I wouldn't but...I *am* sorry. For everything."

When Emmeline finally looked up, she was shocked to find that *Sadie* was the one crying.

"I'm so scared. I keep seeing the black water all around me and then I can't breathe, and I can't move and—"

Emmeline surged up from the bed. Wrapping her arms around Sadie's shaking body, she held her tight.

Tentatively, Sadie returned the embrace. It was weak, but it was there. Emmeline thought of how utterly warm she'd felt when Alaric had done the same to her. How wonderful it was to have a person care about you.

"You can say it," Emmeline said softly.

"I thought I was going to die," Sadie whispered.

Emmeline held her a bit tighter. "You're alive though. Alaric saved you. I'm here tonight. I won't leave you."

Sadie sniffled, then Emmeline felt her tearstained cheek rest on her shoulder. After a long moment, she mumbled, "I still kind of hate you. For what you did. But I think I hate you less."

Emmeline swallowed. "Yeah."

She hated herself for what she did, too, but she also knew that if given the same choice, she'd likely do it again. It wasn't the right thing to do, but it was what Emmeline had chosen. Now, though, she was able to let it all go. That final tether connecting her to the hope of having loving parents... snapped forever.

It wasn't in the cards for her, and maybe that was okay. She could try to build her own family. One she chose.

The two girls fell asleep in Emmeline's king-size bed, facing each other, knees nearly touching. And for the first time in her life, Emmeline slept knowing she wasn't completely alone.

Almus Terra Academy's observatory was donated by the United States' NASA program back in the late 1980s, but it was surprisingly well maintained for being over forty years old. Emmeline had only been there once: during her first day tour with Oakley. Astronomy wasn't really her thing, so she'd never had a reason to go back—until today. It was under Oakley's suggestion that they keep their meeting places inconsistent—rumors could start if other students started noticing the Ashland heirs consistently going into the northwestern part of the bailey every week.

"So what you're saying is that there's this mysterious 'woman in black' who knows everything we're doing?" Oakley dug her hand into the bag of cheddar puff rice snacks that Jacob held and popped a few into her mouth. "And she's guiding us like... Mufasa's ghost?"

"I feel like Rafiki is the better analogy here," Romy said, clacking away on her laptop. She hadn't stopped typing since they'd all arrived back from break, and no one had wanted to interrupt her to ask her what she was working on.

Oliver also had his laptop up and he was sitting next to her, his gaze shooting over to her screen every once in a while. As a programmer, Oliver was just a hop, skip, and a jump away from being a hacker, and it seemed he was starting to develop an interest in hacking skills.

"You're both wrong. She's like Aragorn at the Prancing Pony," Trang offered.

"Let's refocus," Emmeline said, though she wasn't mad about the detour. Their collective vibe was slightly defeated, since they'd all returned from winter break with no better ideas or outcomes to save Almus Terra.

"Virin Corporation," Jacob said, testing the name around a mouthful of cheddar puffs. "That's a lead, though, right?"

"It definitely is." Emmeline drummed her fingers on the clean white table as she gazed up at the domed ceiling. "I know the Ashlandic people aren't happy about the deal with Virin either.

Someone cornered me over the summer about it," she said, remembering the woman and her brazen daughter.

"I already have a news alert in place," Romy said. "We'll all get notifications on our private secure network should anything happen with Virin."

"Can't you... dive deeper?" Sadie asked.

Romy looked up from her computer and fixed her brown eyes on Sadie. Emmeline, Alaric, Titus, Oakley, Trang, Oliver, and Jacob all exchanged looks as they felt the tension in the air rise.

"And how do you propose I do that, Princess?" Romy asked, raising her brows. "Hacking into their system could take me months. We don't have that kind of time. Unless you have a whistleblower employee who could get me backdoor access."

"Sorry," Sadie said quickly. "I don't know how this works."

"Clearly," Romy muttered.

"All right," Emmeline said. "Look, you're both right. Hacking into Virin won't work, but a news alert isn't enough either. Any more ideas?"

Oakley shot her an appreciative look—or at least, that's what it looked like to Emmeline, but maybe she was just being optimistic.

"I did as much research as I could into the origin of Virin," Sadie said as she sent them all a document over Romy's secured network. "Don't worry, I covered my activity—I read your guide," Sadie said, looking at Romy.

Romy had painstakingly prepared a guide for them all to follow, on how to use the private network and her servers, as well as how to cover their digital footprint.

"Wait...," Oakley said suddenly, scrolling through Sadie's report. "Virin is an entity of Etropy?"

"Was," Sadie corrected. "It bought itself out a couple years ago."

"Etropy was an energy company started by Rhett Croft," Oakley continued. "He backed out not long after its creation and sold it to some other rich pricks. I only know because my first-year roommate was a C-Suite whose dad bought Etropy."

"Croft is linked to Virin?" Titus asked. "Maybe we really should be looking at *him* then. He was at the school. More importantly, he's had his hand in nearly every company we've looked into that's bleeding Almus Terra dry."

"Oh! I can contact him and pretend I'm interested in that internship," Jacob offered, his eyes bright with excitement. "Maybe do some spy—"

"Don't you *fecking* dare, Jake," Alaric growled.

Jacob shrank in his seat and Emmeline shot Alaric a glare, then she turned to Jacob and said, much more gently, "Alaric doesn't want you to get trapped, Jake. Not with a man like Croft."

"But what *is* he like?" Trang asked. "We know he buys and sells billion-dollar companies like they're Monopoly properties, but other than that, who is he? Is it possible he's just a bored philanthropist?"

Emmeline thought back to the conversation she'd overhead at the gala at the Singapore Sky-Park. "No, he's more than that. If he was just interested in business, why was he talking to the headmistress of our school, or the king of our country?"

"You mean you think he has a different agenda?" Titus asked.

"I'm saying it's clear as mud. Remember Hibernia? That was a front for a trade summit. These people don't do anything in black and white."

Titus was silent for a minute. "Sebastian said something weird on the plane ride home from Singapore. He said that his father *owed* his victory to Croft. But I know for a fact that Croft backed his opponent. I thought he was just hungover, but now..." Titus shrugged.

"Wait, are you saying you think he tampered with the UK's elections?" Oakley asked, her eyes wide.

"I don't know—that's just what he said." Titus responded.

Oakley slammed her fist into her palm. "Well, we should find out, damn it."

"I can talk to Sebastian." The words were out of Emmeline's mouth before she could take them back.

Everyone's gaze swiveled to her.

The idea of talking to Sebastian repulsed her, considering everything that had transpired between them last year, but he talked easily, especially about himself and his family.

"You think he'll just tell you something like that?" Titus asked with a frown.

Emmeline shrugged, but there was a trace of shame. "He's told me stuff before."

"I don't think it's a good idea." Like watching a tennis match, the group's looks shot to the other side of the room, to Oliver.

In rare form, he was scowling.

Emmeline raised her brows. "Sebastian is largely harmless."

"But what if he tips off Croft or something?"

"I doubt he's that close with the man," Titus interjected. "Seb didn't even talk to him at the gala."

"There's no harm in prodding. Let Emmeline shoot her shot," Oakley said simply, ending the argument then and there. "Okay, what's next?"

They moved on with the meeting, but Emmeline was highly aware that Oliver kept scowling at her until they left before that evening's astronomy class.

Thursday nights were one of the few times of the week that Emmeline had the dorm room to herself. Every week, Oakley and Danica had D&D, Sadie had "fake date" night with Titus, and Trang had a multiplayer online game in one of the school's computer labs. Emmeline could play the *Bridgerton* soundtrack as loud as she wanted while doing yoga poses in the center of the floor. There was something about doing sun salutations to Vitamin String Quartet's rendition of Sia's "Cheap Thrills" that made her feel powerful.

So when there was a knock on her door she didn't hear it the first time and, on the second, much louder knock, she nearly tripped in her haste to answer it. Her only thought was that it could be Alaric to tell her more about the WomanInBlack he'd been messaging over the last couple weeks. Sometimes the woman would answer his questions, and sometimes she ignored him completely. He complained about it constantly.

Just to Emmeline, it seemed, since he now refused to talk to Sadie about, well, anything. Why, she hadn't dared to ask. She had no idea what was going on between them, and she had no desire to find out. Never again would she meddle in Sadie's love life. Especially if it had to do with her brother.

"Hey—" she opened the door, a little sweaty and breathless from yoga, and nearly slammed it shut when she saw that it was, in fact, *not* her brother.

"Oliver."

He stood there, clutching his bag, his gaze on her face. Then it traveled downward, to her Lululemon sports bra and tight yoga pants. Eyes wide, they shot back up. "Sorry, this... this a bad time?"

She was sans makeup, her hair was a mess, sweaty, not wearing a shirt and it was *Oliver*, but... Well, shit. She'd enjoyed his gaze raking down her body way too much.

With a smile, she stepped back to let him inside. "Not at all. Just taking advantage of the space without any roommates."

"O-oh, you're alone then?"

Emmeline pressed her lips together to hide a smile as she tapped her phone to turn down her Bluetooth speaker, now blasting Duomo's version of "Wildest Dreams" by Taylor Swift.

"Don't worry, Ollie, I won't jump you."

Oliver huffed. "That wasn't why I—listen, have you seen Sebastian yet?"

Emmeline took a towel hanging from the bedpost and wiped down the glistening sweat across her clavicle. Oliver's gaze tracked the movement.

"No. I'll talk to him over the weekend."

"Don't. I mean, you don't have to. I know what he meant about the election."

Both surprised and extremely confused, Emmeline lowered her towel. "Pardon?"

"I... er... did some digging. Romy has been helping me, and I've been getting better and I just thought... to save you some time." Oliver pulled out his tablet and flipped it around to give it to her.

The screen was a bunch of text and graphs and Emmeline was far too distracted to read it properly. "What am I looking at, Oliver?"

"Prime Minister Bane's opponent hired a digital advertising firm to run targeted ads throughout the campaign. The firm is owned by—"

"Croft," Emmeline muttered. The name was printed in Oliver's report, but she would've guessed it anyway. He owned *everything*.

"But Croft's firm tanked the campaign."

"What? How do you know that?" Emmeline asked, her brow furrowing.

"Data analysis. It also helps that the Elections Act of 2022 introduced certain transparency requirements for online political ads, so I was able to pull a lot of information because of that. The Online Safety Act of 2023 has also influenced how political advertising is regulated online, so—"

"Never mind, I believe you," Emmeline said, her lips twitching with a smile at this brilliant, adorable nerd. "So, you think Croft's firm tanked the campaign on purpose and Croft offered his endorsement as recompense, but the campaign had already done its damage to secure Bane's victory."

"That... is my assumption, yes," Oliver said, adjusting his glasses on his nose.

The damning knowledge that Rhett Croft had, in fact, tampered with an election was lost on her in that moment, in light of the obvious.

"Why did you do this?"

Oliver blinked at her. "Why..."

"This must've taken you most of the night. Why did you do this?"

"To...to help."

Emmeline took a step into his space, her chest nearly brushing his. "You did this so I wouldn't talk to Sebastian."

Oliver's cheeks darkened, but he didn't step back.

"Because you didn't *want* me talking to Sebastian."

Happiness, no, *giddiness* soared through Emmeline like a dopamine high. He was jealous. He didn't want her talking to that big-headed British brat!

But then, just as fast, the thought occurred to her that Oliver might expect her to manipulate Sebastian with a hookup, as she had in the past. As he had *witnessed* in the past.

She stepped back, her face flushing, her heart hurting. "I wasn't going to *seduce* him for this, Oliver."

"I know that!" Oliver said, a little too loudly. So loudly she almost jumped. She'd never heard him raise his voice like that. "I know that," he repeated quietly. "I just...didn't want him anywhere near you."

Emmeline's heart melted. It was a gooey mess on the floor between them. He could've stepped in her heart puddle and tracked it all over the castle and she'd still be happy about it.

"You don't have to worry about him, or any other guy," Emmeline said softly. "I like *you*, Oliver. If that wasn't already clear."

Oliver rubbed at his neck, avoiding her gaze, his jaw set. "Yeah... I think I know that."

He *thinks*. He did step on her heart a little with those words. But she wasn't mad at him for it. She'd done some shitty things—especially to Sadie, his best friend. She didn't expect him to fully trust her yet.

Especially not with his heart.

Emmeline handed him back his tablet. "Thank you, Oliver. This made me happy."

He blinked down at her. If he was expecting her to make another move, he would be disappointed. Emmeline had already laid out her feelings several times and she wasn't going to force them on him if he wasn't ready for it.

Slowly, Oliver nodded. "Right. Then, I should go."

"Unless you want to stay and watch me finish yoga. I wouldn't mind."

Oliver nearly tripped getting to the door, but

a nervous laugh escaped him anyway. "Later, Emmeline."

"Bye, Ollie."

Once he was gone, Emmeline returned to her yoga mat but didn't do any more poses. Instead, she just listened, beaming, to Archer Marsh's version of "Give Me Everything."

# 30

## SADIE

"Explain this one to me again," Sadie said, tapping the end of her pen on her notebook. The same notebook filled with notes about the ancient houses of Ashland that was now also filled with stock market operations.

Emmeline paused, chewing her kimchi fried rice and glancing away from her own stack of international law books to look at where Sadie was pointing. The two of them both ignoring the strange looks from their classmates at the sight of known enemies eating together. Talking. Acting friendly.

It had been nearly one full month since arriving back at Almus Terra. Since nearly dying off the coast of her beloved Ashland. The nightmares of the dark waters and the black sky above her had finally started to fade, but she still woke up shivering some nights. Those nights, Emmeline, being a light sleeper, woke up with her and they would escape into the hallway, down to the student kitchens to fix hot chocolate or hot cider and talk.

They weren't friends, both of them hesitant to label this new tentative relationship. But considering their lives were so intertwined, and that they were, for the first time, on the same side, they felt like partners. At least members of the same team, or, as Oakley referred to it, squad.

"Which one? Oh, pump and dump?" Emmeline asked.

Sadie rubbed her brow. "Yeah, I swear I'm trying."

In the last couple weeks, Emmeline and Oliver had both started teaching Sadie the ins and outs of the stock market. It was a wonder, really, that Sadie was so good at economics but so bad at the stock market. She understood complex economic theories, the concept and the importance of free trade, but the minute she delved into bear and bull markets, all her intelligence flew out the window. Perhaps the animals were too distracting.

"Sadie, I've been studying the stock market since I was eleven, okay? Don't expect to understand all this crap in two weeks. A pump-and-dump stock manipulation scheme is when you buy a ton of stock in a company so the price of that stock becomes ridiculously high, making the company look desirable, which then tricks others into investing in the stock. Then you sell all the stock you bought in that company once it reaches a peak. Another way of explaining this is just that it falsely inflates a company's perceived worth for the benefit of making more money, which then makes the market unstable because it's not based on—"

"Truth. Yeah, I get it." Sadie shoved her dinner plate away and pressed her fingers into her eyes, feeling a migraine coming on. She wasn't even sure why she was trying so hard to understand stocks—it wouldn't help them save Ashland. But she hadn't been able to let go of her concern over the Ashland Investment Fund. Like Emmeline, she now tracked the AIF daily, looking for any significant changes to it, of which there were none, really. Emmeline tried to tell her that nothing was out of the ordinary. But why did she feel so restless about it?

*Because people's pensions are in there, for one thing.*

That was a terrifying thought—but ruining people's pensions is something Leander would do everything in his power to prevent, not cause. Besides, Sadie had other things to worry about: like the king who tried to have her killed, Almus Terra eliminating the scholarship program in a little less than four months, and the boy whom she'd unwittingly started to fall for hadn't looked her in the eye since he'd held her in his arms all night.

Admittedly, that was another thing she should not be worried about. Against her better judgment, Alaric had wriggled his way into her heart. Though, more accurately, he'd punched his way into it. In some ways, Sadie hated how cliché it was. Her falling for her rescuer. But if she was being honest, she'd admired him from the start. His logic and cynicism in their original International Econ debate had forced her to rise to his challenge, his passion and heart had won her over in his student rally for the Scholars, and the small gestures he'd made in passing, showing that he was always looking out for her.

And when he proclaimed that he'd steal her heart?

Alaric already had it.

He just couldn't know about it. Not yet. Nor could anyone else. She was still dating Titus, and their engagement was to be announced *tomorrow*.

A press conference was to be held at Almus Terra and even though none of it meant anything to Titus or Sadie, it would still force them together. Force them to act like they were in love. There would be a kiss involved for sure.

She couldn't blame Alaric for staying away. Not because he was necessarily angry (God, she hoped not) but because it would be painful for him if he really liked her, which Sadie was starting to believe he really did.

Although it still bothered Sadie that Alaric didn't believe in her. That night, in his bed, she thought maybe he was saying she, Sadie Aurelia, had the power to incite change. But the next moment she realized he was talking about who she *really* was. Aurelia Scealan. That name, that identity alone was an image strong enough to spark a revolution. That's what he'd been trying to tell her.

Another piece of her heart had chipped off then. The disappointment in hoping he'd thought of her as someone who could fight for her country and achieve great things.

Instead, he'd only been referring to circumstances beyond her control.

But she couldn't help wanting to ignore everything else and act on her impulses. He'd held her that night, kept her warm, saved her life, stolen her heart, and it was only the next morning she'd been able to admit to herself that she wished he *had* tried something. She wished he had kissed her without reservation, and they could've lost themselves in each other.

Now it felt like that might never happen.

As much as she wanted Titus and her to be free, she couldn't shake the feeling that their relationship was the only thing keeping her safe at the moment.

"Oh, you're kidding me," Emmeline suddenly whispered, breathless, next to Sadie.

Sadie blinked, having forgotten where she was, momentarily lost in thoughts of Alaric. A distraction that plagued her too often nowadays, especially in class.

"What?" Sadie asked, glancing over to see Emmeline staring at her phone.

Frowning, she took her phone out as well and in the same second, she understood Emmeline's reaction.

It was a Virin news alert, one that made Sadie see red. *After eight months of drilling,* the simple headline from the Associated Press read, *Virin Corporation is forced to pull out of the Ashlandic Coast with no oil to speak of.*

"They drilled...for nothing?" Sadie's memory flashed through all the insipid council meetings about what "good" their partnership with Virin would do. How it would bring oil and money and jobs to Ashland.

Already there were reports of damage to their native marine life and fishing industry because of the seismic blasting and drilling, which so many Ashlanders had been worried about. All of this destruction, for nothing.

"Yes," Emmeline said in a small voice, "but that's not what I was talking about. Sadie... I think I know why that woman wanted us to watch Virin."

Sadie lowered her phone to see Emmeline's pale face. "What do you mean?"

Emmeline grabbed her bag and pulled at Sadie's wrist, abandoning her fried rice. The two girls nearly ran from the dining hall. They found one of the empty classrooms on the seaside of the castle. Seeing the peaceful turquoise of the Mediterranean made Sadie's heart hurt.

Since that night on the yacht, she was now scared of the open water. But it hadn't diminished her love of it. Like so many things, both her love and fear of something could coexist.

When Emmeline shut the door behind her,

she yanked out her tablet and pulled up a stock tracking app. "Sadie, look. The Ashlandic Investment Fund just increased by eight hundred *million*. They sold their shares of Virin and turned a massive profit just this morning."

Sadie stared at her, not following.

To her credit, Emmeline didn't look exasperated when she explained, "It's one of the stock manipulation tactics—false information. Leander likely *knew* there was no oil there. Or he suspected it. But the premise of finding crude oil... that's huge. Everyone invested in Virin. They thought it was going to be the next Exxon, or whatever. Leander let the investment grow and right before this news story was released, he sold his shares this morning. This isn't a major story yet. Once it becomes one... everyone will jump ship. But Leander gets to take home the profits."

If that were true, it was reprehensible for a million reasons. But the one Sadie cared about most was the sea. It had nearly taken her life, but still she loved it. It held all her memories of her mah and grannah. The trips to the dock, the passing of ships, the small but modest Durah aquarium her mah had taken her to for her eighth birthday, or the stuffed sea lion her grannah had gotten her. She'd spent a full year working on the Ashlandic

Sea Mammal Conservation's web presence before her heir apparent duties proved to be too much.

The ocean was a part of her. A part of every Ashlander. Just another thing that made her Sadie Aurelia.

It made her furious. It made her *brave*.

Just like that day before Hibernia. She'd been broken and torn down and *angry* enough to actually do something to make a difference. Lately that fierceness had faded. Her worry over being replaced as heir apparent, her need to prove herself, her desperation to know who she really was, and the fear of nearly disappearing beneath those waves... it had all been so much.

But threatening what she loved? For sheer profit?

Sadie was ready to be that girl again.

With shaking hands, more from anger than the anxiety of what she was about to do, Sadie took out her phone, then navigated to the social media account where she had the most followers—over ten million—and handed it to Emmeline. "Film me."

Emmeline stared at her for a beat before she clocked Sadie's determination and held up the phone. "Go."

Sadie looked straight at the camera. "Hey,

everyone. Sadie here. Unfortunately, I have some sad news. And I wanted you to hear it from me first. Prince Titus and I have decided to go our separate ways. We feel we're better as friends. Entering this world was scary at times but I'm so grateful I had him by my side. Though we're very different people, I will always have the highest respect for him. More importantly, I wanted to make an announcement to my fellow Ashlanders about our beloved waterways. Earlier this morning it was discovered that Virin Corporation, an oil company that's been drilling for eight months in the Labrador Sea, reported that it has found no oil. They made a grave miscalculation, and our fishing industry as well as our marine life have paid dearly for it. There is no excuse. As next in line to Ashland's throne, I promise that I will never sacrifice our most precious resources for profit. There is *always* another way. Princess Sadie over and out."

Emmeline dropped the phone, her fingers flying across the screen. Breathless, she asked. "You want to see it?"

Sadie shook her head. "Post it."

With a few more taps, Emmeline looked up, biting her bottom lip. "It's up. I can't believe you led with you and Titus."

At that, Sadie rolled her eyes. "Our breakup will be shared five hundred times more than me posting about an oil-drilling company—depressing as that is."

Sadie's phone suddenly started going off.

Emmeline grimaced, holding it up.

King Leander.

Sadie sucked in a breath, but it was too late to back down now. She knew this might have just incentivized Leander to find a more creative way to remove her as his successor, but she had finally *done* something.

This entire time, she'd been sitting on her hands as heir apparent, investing in the potential of power in the future. So she could make real change when she became queen. But what if she never got the chance? What if she never got the crown?

She had *some* power *now*. And the future had to start someday.

Her heart pounding, she took the phone. "Your Majesty."

"You are finished, Aurelia," he hissed.

Sadie drew in a sharp breath at the name. Leander's voice was the arctic.

"*Done.* Tomorrow, instead of announcing your engagement, I will name Titus heir apparent. Believe me when I say: Your life is over."

The line went dead, and Sadie slowly sank into her seat, her adrenaline fading.

"Sadie? What did he say?" Emmeline asked tentatively. But Sadie didn't reply. She didn't say anything or do anything for a long time, her mind spiraling.

It wasn't panic, or grief, but maybe something close to shock. She had given up almost two years of her life to this. Sacrificed so much, worked so hard, dated a guy she didn't love, worked herself to the bone, chipped away at her very soul—all to be the heir apparent she thought her country needed her to be.

In a single post, she'd destroyed it all.

It was the outcome she had been prepared for, and yet, it didn't hit her until this moment. Had she made the wrong call? Should she have endured Leander's game a little longer?

Had she failed her people by being too brash? Had her righteousness cost her country the change it so desperately needed?

Her one consolation was that after getting to know Alaric, Titus, and even Emmeline—she no longer believed she was the only person who could save Ashland.

"Sadie?"

"Saaaadieeee."

"Cailín."

Hearing her special nickname, she finally looked up, surprised to see Titus, Trang, Alaric, Emmeline, and Oliver all standing around her, concern on their faces.

Her friends. They'd showed up.

It was that realization that helped her focus, helped her breathe again. She still doubted what she'd done, but she couldn't take it back now, and she wasn't sure she'd want to, anyway. What good would she do if she simply stayed silent when she had a voice? She just had to trust that Titus would take her place and fight for Ashland, that he would refuse to be Leander's puppet.

Though her gaze lingered on Alaric a beat too long, she finally turned to Titus, who sat next to her. "I'm sorry I didn't give you a heads-up," she said, her voice sounding funny to her own ears.

Titus smiled and placed a hand over hers. "You were brilliant, Sadie. Bloody brilliant."

"At the press conference tomorrow," Sadie forced the words out, "he's going to name you as heir apparent."

Her ex–fake boyfriend set his jaw, then released her hand. He stared at her for a lengthy moment, and Sadie could tell that a thousand different emotions and thoughts were going off inside him. He suddenly stood, yanking on his already perfect blazer to straighten it. "I understand."

Sadie didn't know what that meant but before she had time to ask him about it, he was out of the classroom.

"Oliver and I are going to man your socials. Field the comments, okay?" Emmeline offered, getting up and shouldering her bag. "And you should plan to post again when your title is revoked tomorrow."

"Right, okay," Sadie said. "Thanks, Emmeline."

She nodded, then it was just her, Alaric, and Trang. Alaric looked as if he wanted to say something, and Sadie wanted to hear him say anything—anything at all, but Trang surprised them both by saying, "Alaric, can I have a word with Sadie?"

He nodded, then paused at the door. "Cailín, remember, be—"

"I'll be careful. Thanks," she said.

With what Sadie thought looked like reluctance, Alaric left.

Trang cleared her throat. "You and Emmeline seem...better?"

"We worked a few things out," Sadie said softly, then she looked over at Trang, tears already forming. "Something I wish I'd tried to do with you a year ago."

Trang held up her finger, voice quivering. "No, you don't get to apologize first. I'm supposed to do that."

Sadie shook her head, her hair whipping around her cheeks. "God, Trang, *no*. I should never have thought you could—"

"You were devastated. You might've believed anyone could—"

"You're not anyone!" Sadie exploded. "You were my best friend. We were becoming like sisters. Trang, I miss you."

Trang's eyes filled with tears, reflecting Sadie's own. "I miss you too."

"I'm actually jealous that you and Titus have become close. Jealous that *he's* been close with you. I want that."

Trang threw her arms around Sadie and the two girls squeezed each other tightly. As if to make up for lost time.

"You have that. You have me," Trang promised her.

Sadie pulled back. "You should know...Titus wanted to break off this relationship a lot sooner.

He didn't want you to think he was cheating on me with you. We haven't felt that way about each other for a while now."

Trang blushed deeply, placing her hands over her reddening cheeks. "I got his letter. I've read it a dozen times, hoping it was true, but if it wasn't... I just couldn't do that to you. I think I'm starting to like him, Sadie."

"Well, he *already* likes you," Sadie whispered, nudging Trang gently with her shoulder. "Thanks for having my back. But I mean it: I one hundred percent support the two of you."

"Of course you do," Trang said with a smirk, "because you have a thing for Alaric."

Sadie pursed her lips. "It's not supposed to be that obvious."

"Maybe it's just obvious to me. When are you gonna tell him?"

"I... I don't know. Not for a while."

Trang frowned. "Why?"

"It's not a great look for me to suddenly go from one prince to the other. People will be even more obsessed with the idea that I'm some sleazy princess who got kicked out of Royal Court."

"Sure... but that's not the only reason, right?" Trang hedged.

"Okay, fine. *Fine.* I'm scared," Sadie finally

admitted. "The last time I dated a prince, he broke my heart. But with Alaric? I don't know if he'd just break my heart…I'm scared he'd shatter it. When he said he didn't believe in me, I was depressed for a month. If I'm being honest, it was what he said to me that night that drove me to Titus. He has this power to build me up or tear me down and I can't…" She let out a shuddering breath, as Trang squeezed her hand. "I just lost my crown, I don't think I can afford to lose my heart, much less my faith in myself."

# 31

## TITUS

Titus had imagined this moment since he was eight years old. He could still remember the day his guardian at the time had told him words he'd never forget.

He was a prince, destined to become the king of Ashland.

It was a position he was entitled to and groomed for. He had sacrificed so much. Worked himself to exhaustion, suffered stomach ulcers from stress, and grown to hate the parents who had laid their expectations on a young boy who had nearly crumbled under the weight of it all.

Certainly, everything he'd gone through had to mean something, right?

That's what he'd always thought. Until today.

Titus sat in the hallway outside the castle's main keep—the room used for the welcome banquets, school balls, assemblies, and graduation—listening to the press gather inside. The chairs were set up, the podium, cameras, mics, and teleprompter all good to go. The Eldana royal family had even made the trek to Almus Terra for this one press conference. He'd seen his mother and father only briefly before they took their respective seats. Why bother to greet their son and tell them how proud they were? He was finally going to become the first in line for succession. He was going to become *king*.

Absently, Titus pulled out his phone and looked at the text string he had up on his phone. Trang had finally reached out to him. At last. It was short and simple, but it made his chest ache with hope.

**Good luck today. Let's talk later.**

Next, he pulled up his social media and checked Sadie's last post. The one where she'd bravely stood up for Ashland, defying Leander despite knowing how terribly dangerous his grandfather was.

He respected her for that—admired her really.

Her post had already received a million shares and a million likes. She'd been featured in news stories, with her speech used in sound bites and original audio. Followers and fans were quoting her words, echoing the many unjust and difficult things in their countries. Things they wanted to change.

*There is* always *another way.*

Titus clenched his jaw and set his phone to silent, tucking it back into his pocket. Automatically, he began massaging his knuckles. They were throbbing today, but he could take the pain as long as it didn't come with overwhelming fatigue, though the two almost always went hand in hand. Whatever his pain levels were, he just needed to have his energy intact.

"We're about ready for you, Prince Titus," Ilsa said, her bright smile forced.

Titus glanced up at the woman who had stood as the liaison between him and his grandfather for nearly two years at this point.

Emmeline had told him Ilsa was sleeping with Prince Frederick. And though she'd used it once to help her get information, she hadn't weaponized it since. Instead of being angry, she now just felt pity for Ilsa and Prince Frederick. Whatever their relationship could possibly be, it would always be rooted in lies. And lies were poison, corroding anything good or believable.

How could someone live like that?

Lies were like the traitorous white blood cells in his bloodstream, eating at his joints and tearing him up from the inside out.

And he'd had enough, thank you very much.

Carefully, Titus got to his feet, making sure not to groan like an old man. He took a moment to bend his knees and stretch his joints—he shouldn't have been sitting for so long. But he was worried about being too tired once he got to the podium.

"Thanks, Ilsa," he said, following her toward the side door that would lead directly into the path to the platform.

"Do you remember how this is supposed to go?"

Titus didn't even have a chance to respond before Ilsa was explaining it again for the fifth time.

"The king will make a statement about how sorry he is to hear about the end of your relationship with Sadie and will then explain that the reason for the breakup was actually because of changes within our political landscape. While Sadie Aurelia has been doing a fine job as heir apparent, he has come to see that she lacks the resolve, integrity, oversight, and ability to make sacrifices for the greater good. Through it all, you have been by her side and shown the king you are ready to take on your birthright. It is with the will of the king and the approval of his council that you ascend to become first in the Eldana line of succession."

It was nearly Leander's speech verbatim, and Titus wondered if Ilsa simply read it that many times or if she'd written it herself.

"You will then be called to graciously accept the title and thank your grandfather for his leadership and wisdom and though you still care a great deal for Sadie, you both agree that it would be better for Ashland if the two of you parted ways now."

It was laughable, the idea that any ridiculous explanation such as this would be accepted by the public. People were going to lose their minds. Titus and Sadie break up and Sadie releases a video directly criticizing Leander's policy—then a day later she's denounced as heir apparent and her ex-boyfriend ascends the throne? None of it screamed "amicable."

But if they thought *that* was dramatic, it was nothing compared to the bomb Titus was about to drop.

"Just read from the teleprompter," Ilsa advised, adjusting her headset. "You're on!"

Then she practically shoved him through the door. He emerged to a round of applause, while his grandfather beamed from the platform, arm outstretched, welcoming his new heir apparent.

Swallowing hard, Titus mounted the steps and ignored his aching knees. He got to the platform and accepted the awkward embrace from his grandfather.

Lights had been set up on the sides of the platform and they beamed down on him, making it hard to see the crowd. But her face stood out anywhere. His mother sat with his father, back ramrod straight, her narrowed eyes on Titus. Neither looking proud, nor happy. But... even if she had been, nothing would have changed what Titus was about to do.

As the applause died down among the crowd of reporters and Ashlandic court members, Titus's gaze shot to the teleprompter. At the blandishments he'd been instructed to say.

"Thank you, Your Majesty," Titus read. "With my whole heart, I accept this great honor. I love Ashland for many reasons, but the way our country's leadership is passed down is one of them. We look at the best and brightest to guide our people through the turbulent waters of global conflicts, economic crises, and societal pressures.

Even if that person is not of royal blood, we give them that chance."

Titus paused, his hands gripping the sides of the podium. "Ashland values the strong," he continued, going off script, "and if there is one thing you can be sure of it's that my grandfather is strong. He looked for that quality in his heirs. He found it in me."

Titus slid his gaze away from the teleprompter. "People of Ashland, and the world, I have one more announcement to make. Fifteen months ago, I was diagnosed with the autoimmune disease rheumatoid arthritis."

Gasps and a series of flashes erupted from the crowd below him.

Titus kept his gaze focused ahead. It didn't matter how his parents reacted, or his grandfather, this was about the truth. *His* truth. He wouldn't lie to the rest of the world about who he was anymore. He would not pretend to be this effortless golden prince when he was sick and in pain but still worthy of people's respect and belief in his abilities. He could be *both* things.

"I live with a chronic illness and my days are not always easy. They're difficult, and painful, and that may seem like a weakness to others, but I promise you it's not. Because your ordinary is my extraordinary. I am still learning the limitations of my body, but I can tell you that I value strength now more than ever. Strength of character, resolve, dedication. Living with this disease requires resilience I didn't know I had until it tested me. I stand before you today with faith in myself and a promise to the people of Ashland: I will be strong for you. Thank you."

As soon as the last two words were out of his mouth, reporters started jumping up from their seats, shouting questions.

A large hand clamped down on Titus's shoulder in a death grip. Leander was smiling but it did not reach his eyes. To no one but Titus, Leander looked murderous.

Distantly, Titus wondered if Leander was now planning his own grandson's demise—a watery grave just like Sadie's.

"Thank you, yes, we will release information about my grandson's condition in the coming days, assuring everyone rheumatoid arthritis is—"

But Titus didn't get a chance to hear what his grandfather thought of RA. Captain Kendrick was guiding him down the platform and through the same side door. He practically yanked Titus down the hallway and into another staff corridor and antechamber, surrounded by stone, and away from anyone who could overhear.

"Stay," Kendrick growled.

Then he left.

Titus didn't relish being treated like a dog, but he knew he'd be forced to face the music eventually.

But instead of his grandfather coming through, it was his parents.

When he saw how livid they looked, Titus finally realized how utterly shameful their reaction was.

He wasn't some irresponsible teenager—he wasn't drinking, doing drugs, or getting girls pregnant. All he wanted was to take care of his body. To feel better and accept his sickness as a part of himself and *live*, but on his own terms. At least when it came to his health.

It was such a little, tiny thing to ask.

"We should disown you for that," his father said, cold gray eyes boring into Titus like knives.

"Go ahead," Titus said, his voice not even angry, just hollow. Just tired. "I'm sorry, by the way. I'm sorry you cannot accept that you have a sick kid. I'm sorry you cannot accept that I have a chronic illness, and I will have it all my life and that it's not part of your fucking plan."

"Titus!" Lady Calliope gasped, reeling back in horror.

Titus ignored her. "I have spent nearly three years listening to you tell me that everything is okay—but it's not. I'm not *okay*. But I'm not fucked up either. I have rheumatoid arthritis, whether you accept it or not, and I will not let you make me feel like a failure. How I choose to share this disease with the world—and how I rule in this body—will be on *my* terms. Mine and no one else's. Because none of you deserve my allegiance, I forced your hand. And I won't apologize for it. You should've told your father, your king. You knew about my disease. You could've told him about my RA at any point but you didn't."

He was breathing hard, his chest rising and falling with exertion from finally getting those words out. To his father—this larger-than-life man who never smiled at his son. Who never said *well done* or gave him even the smallest measure of kindness.

Somehow, Titus had looked up to this man. When he was eight years old, finding out he was a prince, he'd worshipped his father. But over the years...he began to fear him. He was through with being scared.

"Are you done?" his father asked coldly, the signature Eldana gray eyes like dark ice.

Titus blew out a breath. "Yes. I'm done. I'm so done with the both of you." He looked up and met his father's gaze, anger finally outweighing the fear of him. "You're a cruel father, and she's a terrible mother, and it took me this long to finally understand why. You're *jealous* it's your *son* who has the chance to become king, and not you. And you're *bitter* that your own father deemed you unworthy of his crown. But not me."

Somehow Titus knew what was coming before he'd even said the words. Magnus reared back and punched him right in the face. Thankfully, Titus turned just in time, his father's fist only hitting his left eye and cheek instead of smashing and breaking his nose. He staggered from the blow, sucking in a shallow breath.

"Magnus!" Calliope shrieked.

"You're a worthless, ungrateful child and I regret the day you were ever born," his father said calmly. Clearly.

The pain radiating through his face was nothing compared to the pain echoing through his chest. And yet...the words were liberating somehow.

Titus stared at the ground, leaning against

the stone wall, as the footsteps echoed out of the chamber. At the last moment, he looked up and his eyes locked with his mother's. He wasn't sure, but he thought, maybe, there was regret there.

It didn't matter now though.

Titus slid to the ground and he stayed there until the light from the windows faded and shadows fell across his face, dark enough to cover the beginnings of the bruise below his eye.

His hands felt good—they always did after the wax. His joints didn't feel too bad, all things considered. Especially since he'd sat on that hard stone floor for a good two hours before he finally got his ass up and went to the infirmary.

He was surprised that his grandfather hadn't made a punishing appearance, but there was a high probability that Leander couldn't even stomach looking at him. Perhaps, for the second time in Leander's life, he had been blindsided. You'd think he would've learned his lesson with Sadie, but no.

Titus sighed and shifted the ice pack on his face. He'd asked Dr. Sharrad and Nurse Martinez for some privacy after they'd patched him up to the best of their ability—but there was nothing to be done for the broken pieces inside him.

"Knock, knock," a familiar voice said from behind the infirmary bed's curtain.

Titus's stomach did a weird somersault. He didn't want Trang seeing him like this, but... *she was here*.

Her head poked through the curtains and, immediately, her gaze went to the shiner on his cheek.

"Can I come in?" she asked.

"You kind of already are," he said with a small smile.

"I'll take that as a yes, then," she said, slipping between the curtains and sitting next to him. Close too. Her thigh was right up against his.

A memory of him next to Sadie in the infirmary came back to him. It felt... like a *lifetime* ago. He'd been a different person back then. Or at least, a different version of himself.

As Trang took the spot next to him, his gaze shot to her chest. Not in a leering way, but in a *holy hell she's wearing the shirt I got her* kind of way. The words "It's Accrual World" were in bold print and his mouth twitched at them. He looked back up at her face. Silky black hair hung down in pigtails, electric blue eyeliner swiped across her eyelids, a dozen bracelets, and sunflower earrings—she was beautiful in her details.

"What you did...," she said softly, "was amazing."

Such simple words. Powerful ones though.

If only... if only they had come from his parents. But there was no more room for ifs anymore. Trang was here with him. *She* mattered. Her words meant everything in that moment.

"Yeah?" he said, a small smile tracing his lips. "Made you fall for me, then?"

"Yes."

The ice pack slipped from his hand, dropping to the floor with a thud.

"To be fair," Trang said, scooping up the ice pack and wiping it off on her T-shirt and then tenderly holding it to his cheek, "I was already about 78.25 percent there."

Titus stared at her, mumbling, "That's oddly specific."

The smile she gave him was breathtaking. "I don't joke around with numbers or with feelings." Still holding the ice pack to his cheek, Trang slipped her free hand across his jaw, tilting his face down. Softly, so softly, she touched her lips to his.

With this permission, Titus surged forward, his hand scooping behind to cradle her neck, the smooth pieces of her hair sliding between his fingers, as he kissed her back. The ice pack tumbled from her grip and she gasped against his mouth.

"Titus—your face!" she half-laughed, half-protested, all of it muffled.

"Don't care," he murmured, kissing her again, and again.

But her giggling was infectious and though he wanted nothing more than to continue kissing her possessively—he chuckled, too, and buried the good side of his face into her shoulder, holding her close.

Her body relaxed against his, her arms coming around his wide shoulders. Gentle fingers threaded into his blond waves as she stroked his hair.

It was a gesture he didn't know he needed. A kind of love he thought he'd never have. Something that felt... unconditional.

After a few moments, he lifted his head, and their eyes met. This time, the moment felt different—charged. Her lashes fluttered closed, and he leaned in and kissed her slowly and deeply. Every breath and brush, gentle and sweet, and even when Titus's bruised face began to ache as Trang cupped his jaw and demanded more from him, he didn't pull back. Because this pain? He relished it.

# 32

# EMMELINE

"Did you know?" Emmeline asked.

From the look on Sadie's face, she figured… probably not. The three of them, Emmeline, Sadie, and Alaric, sat in the state room where they'd once taken their dysfunctional family portrait for the announcement of the Ashland heirs.

They'd sat in the crowd along with the media and the rest of the Royal Court. If anyone found it odd that Sadie was there, watching her replacement in action, they didn't say anything. Of course, it would've been a bigger story if she *hadn't* been there.

Finally, as if she'd just registered Emmeline's question, Sadie shook her head. "I…no. He didn't tell me. He might've tried to once, but… God, there's so much that makes sense now. I thought it was odd he was taking so many vitamins."

Emmeline looked to Alaric, and he shrugged as if to say, *Don't look at me.*

Well, now Emmeline knew why Titus had a second phone and what secret he'd gone so far to protect. Sadie's pale face and wide eyes indicated that she was *also* putting two and two together.

*Damn.* Now Emmeline felt like an even bigger bitch than before—and the bar was already pretty high. Inadvertently, she had threatened to expose his disease. Given the timeline, he'd likely been diagnosed just a few months before she blackmailed him. And Titus had probably been going through a sea of emotions—worry, fear, self-doubt, even shame because of their messed-up family's views on perfection. It had been his decision to share that information, on his time and not a moment sooner. And she'd forced his hand.

Her own ruthlessness was only slightly mitigated by the fact that he'd been dating and using Sadie for his own purposes, but still—to use his illness against him...

No doubt about it, she was going straight to hell.

She honestly felt nauseated at the moment, but she kept the guilt to herself—nobody needed to focus on *her* feelings right this second.

"Do we...know where he is?" Sadie asked softly. "It's been a couple hours. I'm worried."

"In the infirmary," Headmistress Aquila said, stepping into the room. She wore a dark purple pantsuit with a stunning shimmery silver blouse, her long braids done in one large thick braid that hung down her back. "It seems he needed to be treated for a black eye."

"*What?*" Alaric growled at the same time that Emmeline and Sadie gasped.

"Dr. Sharrad said he won't say from who," Headmistress Aquila said with a sigh. "Let me be clear: If I thought it was Leander, he would be banished from my school. But he was with me the whole time, along with members of the ATA publicity staff. We're working on a press release on Titus's sudden...announcement. It will be very beneficial, I think. Autoimmune diseases aren't very well-known, and this could do some good in shedding light on how a chronic illness like RA affects an individual. With his permission, of course."

"Can we go see him?" Sadie asked.

The headmistress cocked an eyebrow at her. "It's the infirmary, Sadie, not a hospital. You don't need my permission...though, Trang Nguyen is reported to be with him."

"Did his parents leave?" Alaric asked. There was a distinct edge in his voice that the headmistress heard as well because she frowned.

"As I understand it, they are down at the docks, getting ready to board. The ferry is set to return them to Toulon, along with the press, in a couple of hours. They should get back to the mainland by sundown. Alaric, you are not to leave this castle, understood?"

Alaric had already been walking toward the door when Zuri Aquila's words stopped him in his tracks. He turned back, a murderous fire in his eyes. "What, he gets to hit his kid and just walk away?"

"I never said that, but you must think big picture. What Titus did today was very brave. Do you want a story about the crown prince of Ashland hitting his son to overshadow your cousin's announcement regarding his disease? Because that is what would happen."

Alaric's jaw worked as he clenched his fists, the muscles in his large arms flexing with restrained aggression. Finally, he released his fists and stepped away from the door.

"May I go to the docks, Headmistress?" Emmeline suddenly asked.

Sadie, Alaric, and Headmistress Aquila all turned to stare at her.

"I just... want a chance to say goodbye to my parents. I didn't get to, that's all."

The headmistress studied her for a moment then gave a short nod. "Hurry down, then. It won't be long before they depart."

With that, the headmistress turned and started to leave the state room, then gave a gasp of surprise. "Don't just stand there eavesdropping, you two—go in, for heaven's sake."

Sheepishly, Oakley and Oliver ducked inside.

"We heard you three were in here," Oakley said, shooting a look at the door as their headmistress shut it behind them.

"Titus is in the infirmary?" Oliver asked, his dark brows pulled together.

"Trang is with him," Sadie said.

"Oh, aces. Good for them," Oakley said with a nod, like she'd known all along the two had a thing for each other.

As much as she wanted to stay and talk through Titus's announcement and the implications of it, Emmeline needed to get down to the docks. She knew it was going to be now or never to confront her mother.

Titus had shown such courage that it inspired her to face her own demons.

She could say over and over that she didn't

care about her parents and how they didn't care about *her*. But that would be a lie. She *still* cared. It *still* hurt. She wanted them to know how much they'd hurt her. And she worried that if she didn't confront them now, she would never get the closure she needed. That wasn't to say she still wouldn't need gobs of therapy. But at least this was a start.

She headed for the door, but Alaric quickly stepped in front of her. "Yer not going down there alone, Emmeline," he said.

"I'm fine, Alaric. It's not... they won't *hit* me."

At those words, Oliver suddenly took her hand. "I'll go with her."

Emmeline flushed, and though she felt like Oliver's bravado was entirely unnecessary, she squeezed his hand in return.

Oliver led Emmeline out of the room, through the admin offices, and past the castle gates and barbican.

"You really don't have to come," Emmeline said, "Alaric is just being overprotective."

*Like a brother.* Honestly, the thought made her indescribably happy. It also made her greedy. She wanted to go back to Titus and apologize. *Really* apologize for what she'd done now that she knew the implications of it. She wanted to grow closer with him. Even if they weren't related by blood, the desire for him to be her family hadn't gone away. If anything, it had grown stronger.

"He has every reason to be protective," Oliver replied gruffly, his hand squeezing hers again. "Someone should be by your side. And that someone should be me."

Emmeline's cheeks, neck, and ears all heated. "Careful, Ollie, you'll give a girl hope when you talk like that."

Oliver stopped walking and she nearly stumbled. He looked down at her, his eyes locking with hers. A shiver went through her spine with that look. For once, he wasn't the one blushing and looking away.

Emmeline swallowed thickly. "We need to keep walking," she said, tugging him along.

They were quiet the rest of the way to the little village. The docks were a straight shot down the main street and the island was so tiny that the distance was no more than a few blocks. Shadows stretched across the cobbled pavements, painting a picturesque scene of a quaint French Riviera town. Emmeline could see a cluster of people on the deck of the ferry, waiting to be taken back to Toulon.

But her mother was in a little boutique,

because of course she was. Emmeline could see her through the window display. She had enough time to *shop*—but not enough time to speak with her daughter. Unbelievable. And yet, believable.

Taking a deep breath, Emmeline started toward the door, but Oliver pulled her back, down a tiny alleyway, where no more than a few feet separated one seaside building from another.

"Oliver, what—"

Suddenly his lips were on hers. His large hands cradling her face as he kissed her. Fiercely.

Oliver's lips were everything she imagined them to be. Full and smooth and earnest. He kissed her like he was begging for something, not demanding it. His kiss wasn't harsh or punishing like Sebastian's, but instead warm and exciting. A kiss with a promise of more sweetness to come.

He had her pressed against the side of the building, the two of them hidden in the shadows with her mother on the other side of that wall.

When he pulled back, Emmeline blinked up at him.

For once, she had nothing to say. He had vanquished all her operative brain cells. Stolen all her words.

Oliver grinned, his mouth hitching up to one side in as close to a smirk as she'd ever seen on him. Then he dipped his head and kissed her again. On his fourth kiss, Emmeline drew up on her tippy toes, wrapping her arms around his neck and parting her lips on a soft moan.

"Em," Oliver groaned into her mouth as their kiss dissolved into something wetter, hotter, more intense.

If that was a new nickname, she loved it.

Her hands clawed at his back as he pushed her against the brick, her hair messy and getting tangled with every rough drag down the wall.

The tinkling of a bell echoed down the little alley. A shop bell. Emmeline pulled back suddenly, her head bumping against the brick.

She still had to talk to her mother, but... *but* this moment was everything she'd ever dreamed of.

Oliver stared down at her, his forehead close to hers, his glasses dipping down his nose, breath fogging up the lenses.

"I didn't mean..." His throat bobbed, the muscles in his dark brown skin straining. "I just... you were being brave, and so I wanted to be brave."

Emmeline blinked up at him, emotions threatening to melt her resolve into a pile of salty tears and skipping heartbeats.

"I've been dreaming of that," she whispered, "for almost two years. You don't need to be brave for me, Ollie."

His gaze softened. "Go talk to your mom. I'll be right here."

Emmeline gave him a smile, then slipped out of the alleyway into the shop. Where her father and mother were. Well, not her father. Prince Frederick. The bell must've been Prince Frederick coming inside, maybe to fetch Lady Chloe for the ferry.

They looked away from the store's modest inventory, surprised to see Emmeline.

"I'm glad you're both here," Emmeline said. "I'd like to speak with you about something important."

Lady Chloe tilted her head. "Oh, Emmeline, your hair is a mess, darling."

"Save it, Emmeline. The ferry will be leaving shortly," Prince Frederick said with a frown. It did not pass Emmeline's notice that he had a glass of an amber liquor in his hand.

"No, I won't save it, Your Highness," Emmeline said, taking care not to call him "Father." She didn't even want to call her mother "Mom."

"For the first time in my life, you're going to prioritize *me*, for just two minutes."

Prince Frederick's gaze sharpened with annoyance. Chloe just frowned.

"I will be filing for emancipation."

Their expressions didn't change much, except becoming more confused. Emmeline didn't expect them to know what that meant, exactly. But she'd still hoped for more of an emotional reaction. This would be the last time they disappointed her.

"Since your vapid stares are telling me you don't know what that is, let me explain," she continued. "Emancipation is for children to legally declare independence from their parents. From the moment you sign those papers, I will not have a mother or father, and *you* will not have a daughter. Since that's consistent with how you treat me anyway, I doubt you'll have objections. I would rather live my life without any expectations from you than continue to be heartbroken time and again. If the king disapproves, I don't care. Sign it anyway."

Emmeline's gaze slid from Frederick to her mother. "Do this and I will never ask you for anything again in my life. I don't even want your money. *Don't* do this, keep me bound to your rotten life, and I will make sure your affairs are exposed, Father."

Her gaze bore into her mother's. "And, Mother, you will do this for me...simply because I asked."

Chloe's look cleared with realization, quickly morphing into a display of real fear. She knew that Emmeline *knew*.

Chloe nodded, her earrings trembling with the force. Frederick looked murderous. "You dare threaten—"

"Freddy," Chloe said, grabbing his arm, "she won't be heir. We can keep this quiet. There's no reason not to give her what she wants."

Frederick snorted and tossed back the rest of his drink. "Spoiled brat just like her mother," he grumbled, then left the shop on unsteady drunken legs with the door slamming behind him.

There was nothing else to say. As much as that had *hurt*, it was freeing. On her way out, Emmeline stopped and looked back at her mother. "You should leave him, you know. You can do that."

Chloe blinked, then squared her shoulders. "Why would I ever go back to being a no one?"

Disgusted, Emmeline turned and left.

*Closure.*

Thankfully, Oliver was quiet as they walked back up to the castle. Emmeline wasn't sure she had it in her to speak yet. Not about her conversation with her parents, nor about what happened in the alley.

Their kiss had been... would it be cringey if she said magical? Because it was. Even now, she still felt his arms caging her in, his herbal, warm, cotton scent around her—so comforting, like a home she'd always wished she'd had.

It had given her the rush of strength she'd needed to go in and say what she'd needed to say in front of her parents. But their coldness had been ice water dousing Oliver's warmth.

Their lack of feeling for their daughter was heartless, and it reminded Emmeline of herself. Of what she'd done to Titus. And Sadie. Of what she believed to be within herself. Was she simply fighting against her own nature and the inevitability of who she was at her core? A bad person?

And if that *was* the case, she didn't want Oliver, who was so good, anywhere near her.

When they reached her dorm, Oliver went to pull her in for a hug, but she stopped him, her hands on his chest, his on her waist.

He looked down at her, confused.

"Oliver... listen... I like you, I really, *really* like you. But..." Tears pooled in her eyes as she stared up at him. So handsome, so hers. "I'm messed up. I'm lonely and I'm so *angry* about it.

I was willing to do whatever it took to get my parents to love me, and I hurt others along the way and I thought I was justified. I'm a bad person, Oliver. But you're good, and I am poison and I don't know that I—"

Oliver pressed his fingers over her lips, quickly brushing his thumbs under her eyes where tears had started collecting on her lashes. "Hey, stop it. You are *not* poison to me, Emmeline."

Emmeline just ducked her head, shaking it. Oliver's hands still cupped her face, as if he were trying to hold on to her.

"I thought you needed more time to trust me with your heart but now I think...I don't trust myself with it. I don't want to hurt you, Ollie."

"Emmeline..."

She pulled his hands away. "I'm sorry. I'm so sorry, just...give me time."

Before he could do anything else wonderful, like kiss her or tell her sweet things, she slipped into her dorm, shutting the door behind her and leaning against it. To her surprise, Oakley gave a squeak, jumping back so Emmeline wouldn't run right into her.

"Oak! Did you...hear?"

Oakley looked sheepish. "Well, I heard voices, and you were right there."

"Eavesdropping again?"

"I listen in on my friends because I care."

Emmeline chuckled, as a few tears trickled down her cheeks. Oakley's face crumpled with concern.

"Oy, Emmie..."

To her even greater surprise, Oakley drew Emmeline into a hug. The first one in well over a year. Which only made Emmeline cry harder.

"We're friends?" Emmeline sobbed, latching onto the word like it was the most beautiful thing she'd heard all day, which was saying something. With Titus's announcement, Oliver's borderline declaration of his own feelings...

And still it was Oakley who destroyed her.

"Yeah, Emmie, we're friends," Oakley murmured, rubbing circles on her back.

"My parents are awful. What if I'm just like them?" Emmeline whispered, her worst fear finally spoken out loud.

"We aren't our parents," Oakley said gently, squeezing her a bit tighter. "And because you're confronting that, you won't be. Also, you have maybe the nicest guy in the world smitten with you—clearly you must be doing something right."

Emmeline rested her head on Oakley's

shoulder and nodded, her words giving her hope, despite her fears. There was still so much doubt inside her, about what kind of person she was. But even that small detail was a far cry from who she'd been when she'd started at Almus Terra.

She didn't want to doubt herself, but she *did* want to question her own ethical choices. The moment she'd been completely confident in everything that she did was exactly when she lost sight of those she cared about. One thing was for certain: With the people she had in her life now, she felt she would be able to stay on the right path.

# 33

# SADIE

"You didn't have to stay with me this whole time," Sadie said, watching the sun dip below the horizon, the light reflecting across the sea water in the most beautiful of rays.

"The last time my prick of a granddad was around, yeh almost died. So yeah, I think I did."

Alaric was even more grumpy than usual, not that she blamed him. All three of them were still shaken by Titus's announcement. For nearly an hour together in that state room, they'd all been absorbed by their thoughts and, in Sadie's case, regrets.

She wished she would've paid more attention to Titus. The slow way in which he moved sometimes. His facial expressions that she now recognized as how he masked his pain. The pills he took at specific times.

Something had been going on. She'd just been

too self-absorbed and too angry at him to figure it out.

How alone he must've felt. How miserable.

God, she had punished him so badly for trying to protect himself.

"His actions aren't excused by his disease, Sadie," Alaric said softly, as if he knew her thoughts were spiraling about Titus.

He was, of course, referring to the fact that Titus had dated her under false pretenses.

"I know, but I was punishing him to some extent. I don't like that I did that."

"We can't be perfect all the time," Alaric said, smoothing a larger pebble with his thumb and whipping it across the water. The waves into their little beach made it hard to see where exactly the stone sank beneath the surface.

"Like you are?" Sadie asked, a hint of teasing in her tone.

Alaric turned and gave her a sharp look. On top of the rock, where she could see the docks and the ferry and when the king had finally left, Sadie hugged her knees to her chest a little tighter.

"I'm not perfect, cailín. Yeh know that."

Sadie didn't like the way he said it, but she also wasn't sure how to argue either. Alaric *wasn't* perfect, but that didn't keep her feelings for him from nearly overflowing. It had been almost two months since the masquerade ball, and they'd barely exchanged more than a few sentences. The only time they'd even acknowledged each other had been during the meetings on how to save Almus Terra.

Which they still weren't any closer to figuring out.

Trang had continued to audit the school's bookkeeping systems. Titus had met with Headmistress Aquila every week for an update on any solutions for their financial troubles. Emmeline and Oakley had been monitoring the stock markets to see if there was any strange correlation between Ashland and Almus Terra. Oliver, Romy, Jacob, and Alaric had been researching and using every cyber security and hacking trick in the book to see what they could find out about Rhett Croft and his many entrepreneurial endeavors.

Sadie, well, she hadn't been able to do very much. She helped where she could, but the biggest contribution she'd made was stirring up such a shitstorm on social media that the entire world seemed to be angry at Leander and Virin Corporation. The fallout from her post had been enormous. Other leading oceanologists, marine biologists, climate change scientists, and world leaders had jumped on her speech, expanding her story to tell their own.

Unfortunately, that didn't exactly help Almus Terra. And she truly wanted to save the Scholars more than she wanted to take down Leander.

He had ruined her life in a lot of ways, but that was in the past. She worried for Jacob's, Oliver's, and Trang's futures. Her friends who wouldn't be able to come back to Almus Terra if they didn't solve ATA's financial problems within the next *five weeks*.

So, Ashland could wait. She wasn't even sure she could do anything more at this point—though that gutted her to admit. Now that she was no longer heir apparent, or even a princess, really, what *was* she? She trusted Titus as Ashland's future king, but that didn't alleviate her concerns about what more damage Leander could inflict in the coming years before Titus assumed the throne.

She supposed she could figure out a way to reveal herself as Aurelia Scealan, daughter of revolutionaries who'd been assassinated at the hand of the king. Depose Leander sooner rather than later. But she didn't *want* a civil war or violence of any kind. It was one of the very few things that she agreed on with her king.

"What are yeh thinking about, cailín?" Alaric asked, dropping down on the rock next to her, though he kept a healthy distance from her side.

Even though she and Titus were officially broken up in every way now.

"How you promised that my heart would be yours, and then you avoided me for two months."

Alaric visibly flinched.

"Yeh were with Titus."

"That didn't stop you at the ball. And that doesn't mean you had to *ignore* me."

"Yes, it did," he grumbled.

"No, it didn't," she argued, hurt. She hadn't allowed herself to miss him before, but then he'd gone and shorn her defenses that night. He'd *made* her look at him again. Made her start falling for him again.

"Ah, here! It doesn't matter that it was fake, Sadie!" he exploded, surging up from the rock and pacing in front of her. "Just seein' yeh with him made me—"

He stopped, running a hand through his hair and sighing.

"I was a damn tool that night. A proper gobshite for not thinkin' about how it would look the next mornin', and knowin' people might be lookin' for yeh. I was angry with myself for bein' so selfish."

Sadie stared at him. He truly did look frustrated. Plus, his brogue always got heavier when he ranted.

"I don't blame you for that."

He paused, glancing at her. "Yeh don't."

Was that a question? She frowned. "I don't."

He walked over to her, sneakers crunching on gravel, and stopped so close that Sadie had to tip her neck back to meet his gaze.

"Then what do I need to do to get yeh to look at me how yeh used to?"

Sadie's heart skipped. "What?"

"I used to be able to read every emotion on yer face, Sadie. During detention, I'd make bets with myself on where yer mind was. What I could draw out. But yeh stopped lookin at me after…"

Slowly, Alaric's brows rose, his lips parting in memory. "That night. Outside yer dorm."

Sadie looked away, blushing. She didn't like that such a little thing still bothered her, and she wanted to deny it then, but she couldn't bring out the words.

Gently his hand guided her face back to his.

He was leaning over her now, his hand on the rock next to her hip, their faces just a few inches apart.

"I thought I was losin' yeh, cailín. It's no excuse for what I said. I was a feckin arsehole. But I didn't want to lose who yeh were. I didn't want yeh to become a royal hallion like the rest of 'em. I thought yeh'd go into this toxic world and change yerself. I should've known better. I should've known yeh could become queen and still be this amazing, passionate, kind person that I was fallin' in love with."

Sadie's eyes widened. "Falling—"

Alaric's fingers brushed over her lips, hushing her. "Yeh didn't think I believed in yeh. That night in my bed. That's why yeh said that. About who yeh are. I was referring to Sadie Aurelia, not Aurelia Scealan. Case that wasn't clear."

Her hazel eyes searched his gray ones—she could admire her sea in them. The Ashland Coast. Home. Where she was born, and where she would've died if not for him.

"Yeh still don't believe me."

"It's not that," Sadie whispered back, barely audible over the sound of *this* sea. The turquoise waters lapped against the pebbled shores, and she was reminded of their first detention. "I'm scared. Every person I've really loved with all my heart, I've lost."

"Yer not going to—"

"Don't say it," Sadie said, shaking her head. "Now that I'm irrelevant to the court, I'll likely go back to being a driftless orphan. You're still a prince. Alaric—" her gaze widened with realization. She couldn't believe she hadn't thought of this until now. What *would* become of her? Would she go back to Ashland alone? Always looking over her shoulder, wondering if Leander would try to have her killed again? She knew she should be concerned about *that* of course, but somehow not returning to Almus Terra seemed like the bigger risk. She loved this school. She'd found new purpose here, and she had discovered what she was capable of.

"I may not even be able to stay at Almus Terra next year. Leander will surely drop my tuition, and without a scholarship..."

Alaric's brow furrowed. "That won't happen, cailín."

"I can't do this," Sadie said softly. "As much as I..." She swallowed. "You have the power to destroy me, Alaric. If we start dating and I have to leave and I..." Alaric started to open his mouth, but it was her turn to place her fingers over his lips. "You will stay. You're happy here. I want you here. But being apart would be too difficult."

"Because yeh still don't really trust me."

"I told you, it's not—"

"Don't lie to me, Sadie. Yer capable of many things, but lying ain't one of them."

Sadie snapped her mouth shut, her heart aching at his expression—she'd seen him angry, frustrated, worried, smug, but this was the first time she'd seen him heartbroken.

"C'mon," he said after a long time. "Let me walk yeh back to the castle."

She wanted to protest but when he held out his hand, the words died on her tongue. Her traitorous heart wanted this, wanted him, even if it hurt in the long run to take it.

Because the hopeful, optimistic Sadie was long gone. There were only so many times she could break before the pieces of herself were too small to put back together.

But the way Alaric held her hand the entire way back to the castle felt like he would hold together every single shard of her.

# 34

# ALARIC

"Back again, Mr. Durham?"

Alaric looked up from the screen. Ms. Reyburn stood at the end of the computer lab row, the blue light of the screens reflected in her lenses. It was Saturday night, well past curfew. But Ms. Reyburn had never reported him in all the times she'd caught him, and this was the third time just this week.

With a sigh, Alaric leaned his elbows on the desk, nudging the keyboard and mouse as he dug his fingers into his dry eyes. Though he was technically using Ramona's, he liked the darkness and whirring sound of the ATA servers in the computer lab. It helped him focus.

Frowning, he glanced at the Discord chat from the WomanInBlack. She had been enormously helpful in breaking down cyber security walls blocking a list of board members he'd been investigating, but at the end of the day it all seemed *pointless*. He didn't even know what he was looking for anymore. He had to keep trying, though.

"Aye, and I'll be back tomorrow night," he muttered.

The Scholars were still doomed at the end of the year. And after Sadie had pointed out that she would likely be among that group, Alaric was more than just stressed. He was panicking. What could they do to force the board to lower the school's expenses? Was it even possible to remove them from power? But then who would fund the school?

"Hmm. Is there something I can help you with?" Ms. Reyburn asked.

Alaric glanced over at his Cyber Security teacher and nearly did a double take. She wasn't in her usual blazer and slacks that she wore to class, but in high-waisted jeans, a *Care Bear* T-shirt, and a worn leather jacket.

Alaric shoved his hands into his pockets as he slouched in the chair. "Yeah, get us a new school board."

"That takes money, I'm afraid."

"Everything does in this world," Alaric said bitterly.

To his surprise, Ms. Reyburn pulled out the chair next to him and sat down. "The headmistress told me what you and your friends are up to. Wanting to save the Scholars. If I can help, I will, Alaric. Though I suspect you're doing just fine on your own, considering your online activity has vanished entirely from the Enyo logs."

Okay, now Alaric was even *more* surprised.

"We're not doing *just fine*. We're stuck. There isn't anything we can do," Alaric spat, wanting to fling the computer against the wall. If only there was another Hibernia where they could hijack everyone's money and hold it hostage until their demands were met.

"Do you want to walk me through it?"

Alaric rubbed his temples. He didn't even know where to begin. It was like one of those police boards with photos of evidence and suspects and clues and red string everywhere.

He thought of the Ashland Investment Fund and his father and the king's stock manipulations, including the insider trading schemes with Rhett Croft; Croft's visit with the headmistress at the beginning of the year; and then Croft's conversation with Leander that Emmeline overheard at the gala.

Like a grizzled detective in a TV show, his gut

told Alaric that they were all connected somehow. Except there was no red string.

Alaric thought of Sadie down in those dark waters, all because she'd googled herself. "No offense, Ms. Reyburn, but you installed Enyo. I can't trust you."

Ms. Reyburn smirked and patted him on the shoulder. "Have it your way then. Good luck, Mr. Durham."

Ms. Reyburn left the lab, her boots clicking down the hall. A few minutes went by and Alaric received another message from the WomanInBlack.

It read, **It's easy for a hacker to get lost in the details. But sometimes the easiest way to break through a wall is to look for a door.**

Alaric scowled at the cryptic words. What the hell did that mean? Still, the advice brought up the thought of the lock-picking kit he always carried around. How he had to listen for the metals to disengage. Brute force never worked. Finesse did.

Alaric's gaze slid to the list of board members. Then back to his notes about the stock manipulations within the Ashland Investment Fund. He thought of Virin Corporation, Tyrannus Tech,

Rielson Enterprises, Zolans Industries—all connected to Rhett Croft.

British Prime Minister Bane was on the school board, and he had been elected because of Rhett Croft. Oliver had all but confirmed it.

They had guessed the connection was Croft before, but maybe they were looking for the wrong things. The illegal things. A man like Croft was careful with infinite resources. The red string wouldn't be in black and white but hidden in shades of gray.

Alaric sat back and cracked his knuckles. No more hacking, no more brute force. Time to pick at that metaphorical lock.

The red string began unfurling the following week in the form of a text from Titus in their group chat labeled Terran Protection Squad.

**EMERGENCY MEETING IN THE DUNGEON ASAP.**

Even though everyone looked stressed to some degree, Titus looked by far the worst. His black eye was nearly gone after four weeks, but there were dark circles under his eyes and his cheeks looked thinner, like he wasn't eating.

Being his roommate, Alaric knew why. Titus was up late into the night working with Leander and dealing with the repercussions of his press conference. Hearing the calls, Alaric knew that Leander's demeanor was so far beyond *pissed*.

The one good thing Titus had going for him, though, was Trang. She was in their dorm nearly every night, chilling. They were hiding their relationship from the rest of the world and, therefore, the school, but at least they got to be together behind the doors of their dorm rooms. Even Alaric had to admit, they were disgustingly adorable.

Titus sat on one of the couches, with Trang next to him, her hand in his.

He tried not to be jealous of them.

Over and over again, he had replayed in his head that conversation with Sadie on the beach. How fecking dense did he have to be not to realize what was really hurting her sooner? That night when she'd been tipsy, he'd played on a loop for months, thinking about how she had looked up at him with such hope and respect. And he'd crushed it with his bare hands.

Why had he not thought to clear the air sooner? Maybe because it involved admitting what a selfish bastard he was.

Feeling Sadie's eyes on him, he turned to meet her gaze. She looked away, and even though the exchange was fleeting, it eased something in him. She was still watching him. Despite what she said on that beach, he was hopeful. She still wanted him.

"We're all here, Titus," Emmeline said. "What's the emergency?"

Notably, Emmeline was on the other side of the room from Oliver. While Oakley sat next to her, chin on her shoulder. Alaric was relieved, at least, that his sister had her best friend back.

Titus glanced at Jacob, Ramona, then Oliver, and finally he looked at Trang, who watched him with worried eyes.

"Headmistress Aquila called me into her office this morning. The good news is that the Scholars will be returning to Almus Terra next year."

Silence followed his words. No one was cheering. From his tired, defeated expression, everyone could tell there was more to be said.

"Well?" Oakley said. "What's the catch then, mate?"

Titus heaved a sigh, his shoulders fell a little, and Trang rubbed his arm. "I don't blame the headmistress. She's doing what she thinks will save the school."

"Out with it, Titus," Ramona urged.

"She's selling Almus Terra," Titus said, "to Rhett Croft."

A shattering sound followed his words, and everyone glanced at Emmeline to find her coffee cup in broken pieces at her feet. Milk, coffee, and sugar all over her shoes and the hem of her pants.

Her words tumbled out in a whispered breath. "Oh my god."

Titus looked miserable, his expression mirroring everyone else's.

"What I heard at the gala." Emmeline looked ill. "The headmistress is weakening… that's what he meant. He was pressuring her to *buy the school*."

"Son of a bitch," Oliver hissed.

Everyone stared at him in surprise. No one had *ever* heard Oliver curse before.

Alaric clenched his fists together, a muscle ticking in his jaw. Considering his research over the past week, he wasn't exactly surprised.

"He's been coercing the board to increase their operating costs to make it impossible to refuse the sale. It's not the board who've been forcing her hand… it's Croft," Alaric said. It was what he'd started working on after his talk with Ms. Reyburn. He'd stopped looking at the obvious and started looking for the string. The thing that connected them all to Croft.

"How can you be sure of that?" Trang asked.

"We've been researching it," Ramona said after a beat. "Well, Alaric has mostly, and I've been double-checking his work. There's not a single board member who isn't under Croft's thumb in some way. Either they were able to start their business because of him, or they were elected or appointed because of him. It's buried in articles and historical business records... but it's all there."

"But... but why?" Jacob asked, his expression confused.

That was the question, wasn't it? First, it was *why* did Croft care to make all these connections to the school board? Now, it was why would he want to buy Almus Terra? He couldn't make money from a school. The only resource coming out of Almus Terra was...

Alaric froze.

His gaze shot to Jacob.

The young Tanzanian genius who had created the battery that put Zolans Industries on the map. That little contact card Croft gave him for Jacob. To offer him an "internship."

"The Scholars," Alaric said, his voice breathless. "He's after the Scholars."

# 35

## TITUS

For a long moment, there was only the sound of the coffee percolating in the espresso machine while Alaric's proclamation sank in.

"It's...it's not so bad, though, right?" Jacob asked, optimistic and naive in the way only a fifteen-year-old could be.

Except that wasn't fair. Age had nothing to do with it. Titus had probably been jaded at twelve, thanks to his strict tutors and the emotionally abusive parents he'd never even met.

He rubbed at his eyes again, and felt the tension in his chest lessen with Trang's hand on his thigh. For the hundredth time, he was thankful she was next to him. The last month since the press conference had been a nightmare. They were so close to the end of the school year and while he wanted to focus all his energy on saving Almus Terra, he now had a whole different set of responsibilities as heir apparent. Especially heir apparent with a chronic illness.

He'd known the fallout was going to be bad, but he hadn't prepared for *how* bad. Specifically regarding his family. The rest of the world was incredibly supportive, somewhat surprisingly. But there was an entire older generation in Ashland, Leander's generation, that questioned Titus's ability to rule, which is why they stayed up into the early hours of the morning responding to interviews and preparing press releases and public service announcements with information about the disease, as well as other chronic illnesses that were often misunderstood.

"I mean, we get to stay at Almus Terra," Jacob continued after no one had said anything for a good fifteen seconds.

"It's worse than shutting it down, Jake." Alaric's voice was gruff, hollow.

"That's a tad melodramatic, Durham," Oakley snapped.

"No, Alaric has a point," Titus said. "It's what I worried about when I heard the news. Croft would be able to control every aspect of the school. He could eliminate the student council, get rid of the headmistress, and control admissions and scholarships."

"And *use* the Scholars," Alaric added.

"Okay, I'm not following. What do you *mean* by that?" Oakley asked.

"Look at the companies in Croft's portfolio," Alaric said. "Zolans Industries, which exists because of a Scholar alumnus of Almus Terra—Imani Nyerere—who created the zol battery. The leading engineer used in the weapons defense contractor from Tyrannus Tech was also a kid from ATA. Takumi something from Japan."

"That could be a coincidence," Oakley said.

"Enyo from Rielson was developed by a former Almus Terra alum," Emmeline said. "Her name was Mina Volkov, and Croft bought Rielson and turned it into Hellion."

"Third time's the charm," Romy muttered.

"He would be using Almus Terra as a talent farm," Sadie said, her hazel eyes wide.

That was *exactly* what he'd be doing. Titus rubbed at his oncoming migraine.

Alaric nodded, his look grim. "Yeh should've seen the way Imani was treated at the Energy Gala. Croft was parading him around like a bloody pet. Not a brilliant scientist with a mind of his own."

Rather than ATA graduates starting their own ventures based on their vision, they would be subject to the whims of a narcissistic billionaire. But this man's end goal couldn't simply be money—of which he had infinite amounts—it was power. It was the influence that his businesses bought across the globe. The force and strength he could wield in every country on every continent. He was like a medieval conqueror, expanding his empire without checks or balances.

Titus took a deep breath, feeling every aching joint like individual nerves through his body. "I hadn't thought of the possibility of trapping the Scholars, but it makes sense. Privatizing the school isn't the answer," he said with a sigh, dropping his hands from rubbing his temples. God, he was tired. His grandfather was punishing him for announcing his disease without permission, but Titus wasn't going to roll over and take it. He was going to prove to his grandfather and the rest of the Eldana family that he *could* do this.

"But then what do we do?" Jacob asked.

Ah, the question they had all been trying to answer since before the winter break.

"We have to stop the sale," Emmeline said finally. "Headmistress Aquila may well know the risks of privatizing the school, but she probably doesn't know everything we know about Croft."

"Right. She may not realize that she's selling it

to an actual tyrant who wants an infinite supply of ATA students to make him billions," Oakley offered. "Not to mention the other shady shit he's been doing with the stock market."

"But what's the alternative?" Trang asked. "I hate the idea just as much as anyone. But this revelation still isn't going to save Almus Terra. The headmistress would only be in a worse position than before. It's a choice between Scylla and Charybdis."

Titus agreed with her, but he agreed with Alaric as well. He couldn't help but think the school should be shut down before the keys to the literal castle were handed over to Croft.

"Let's find out when the sale is happening," Titus said. "I think we can all agree that Headmistress Aquila should know what she's walking into. Right?" He glanced around at his friends.

Though their expressions were bleak, they all nodded.

Titus turned to Romy. "So, uh, could you—"

"Already on it, boss," Romy said, beginning to pound on her keyboard faster than usual.

"Are you seriously hacking into our headmistress's calendar?" Oliver asked, leaning over to peak at her laptop screen.

"Oh, cariño, it's already done. Do we want to

know where she gets her kickass power suits? I have her email receipts."

"I'm surprised Ms. Reyburn isn't stopping you," Emmeline said with a wayward glance. "You once said breaking into ATA's security is like breaking into Fort Knox. Shouldn't we be concerned it's so easy?"

"It's not easy," Romy scoffed.

Emmeline rolled her eyes. "You know what I mean."

"Reyburn's letting you," Alaric said, his arms folded. "Enyo or not, she knows what we're up to."

"I hate to agree that anyone is better than me, but I think you're probably right...Oh shit," Romy glanced up from her computer screen.

"What?" Titus asked.

"It's happening Friday."

"*This* Friday? As in, two days from now?"

She nodded slowly, biting her lip.

Oakley summed up everyone's feelings. "Well...fuck."

*Princeps Iuventutis.* Titus stared at the words in Latin under the student council crest. *Leaders Among the Youth.* The engraving was there, taunting him, reminding him that he had failed this school. He felt like a villain in that old TV show *Arrow*, where Oliver Queen would yell at some greedy executive, "You have failed this city."

*Wow*, Titus thought dully, *I must really be losing it*. He didn't particularly care about superheroes, but the show was one of Jacob's favorites and always seemed to be on in his dorm when he, Oliver, Titus, and Alaric would study for their classes or work on Terran Protection Squad efforts.

*Which were all for nothing.*

Emmeline poked her head over him, her long hair brushing his shoulder. "That posture can't be good for you, Titus."

Titus blinked at her. He was slouched far down in one of the chairs in the student council room, leaning back.

"Yeah, shouldn't yeh be using the fancy shite?" Alaric asked.

Titus squeezed his eyes shut. When had Alaric and Emmeline walked in? In the corner he could hear Trang's gentle breathing. She'd fallen asleep an hour ago on top of research books. He hadn't been able to bring himself to wake her up, so he draped his jacket over her shoulders and let her be.

"Ergonomic," Sadie said.

Sadie was here too. Of course she was.

"What?" Alaric asked.

"That's the word you're looking for. Ergonomic chairs."

"The headmistress is selling the school in less than five hours, and you're worried about my arthritis right now?" Titus said, his tone somehow both amused and annoyed.

"Well, we have to worry about it *now* since you didn't really give us the chance to earlier," Sadie huffed.

He'd received an earful from her post–press conference as well.

Despite everything going on, it truly touched him that the three of them seemed to care so much. Even Alaric.

*We've come a long way.*

"Have you really been here all night?" Emmeline asked.

"Don't pretend you didn't just come from the library with Oliver doing the exact same thing," Titus muttered, running his forearm over his tired eyes.

"How do you know that?"

He tapped his phone. "He texted me."

Emmeline plopped down in the chair next to him. "Snitch."

His lips quirked in a smile that quickly fell. "This might be the end of the line."

"Then we'll make sure the school shuts down instead," Alaric said.

"How? By planting some mysterious, unidentifiable mold? Bio-bomb the place?" Emmeline asked.

"That could be plan B," Alaric said.

Emmeline raised an eyebrow. "What's plan A?"

"Yeh don' wanna know."

"It's too bad we don't operate like the United Nations," Sadie said, her voice wistful, "instead of indulging the whims of rich people."

"To be fair, that's how Almus Terra started," Emmeline said. "Like the United Nations, it was the brainchild of a group of powerful people around the world. Alaric, what is plan A?"

"Yeh don' wanna know, sis," Alaric repeated.

"*Alaric,*" Emmeline growled.

But their voices faded into the background as Titus replayed a conversation he'd had nearly eight months ago, with the Singapore skyline in the background and a glass of baijiu in his hand.

"That's it," he whispered.

The other three heirs glanced at Titus, who was now fully upright in his chair. His gray eyes wide, his slacks and white button-down shirt wrinkled beyond ironing, his blond waves all over the place.

"What's it?" Emmeline asked. "The *mold* idea?"

Titus lunged for his computer. "Get out your laptops and go to this link I'm about to send you."

Titus truly did not know how he was currently standing. He hadn't even had time to shower. But at Trang's insistence, he'd stuffed his mouth with a ham and cheese croissant and swallowed his medication all en route to Headmistress Aquila's office.

According to the school's bylaws, in order for ATA to be officially purchased, the ownership agreement had to be signed by all members of the school board and the headmistress or headmaster of the academy. According to her calendar, Zuri Aquila was supposed to meet with Rhett Croft to sign at nine o'clock in the morning.

It was now 8:55.

They would be there by now...if not for Titus.

It was all these damn stairs. If ATA survived this, Titus was seriously going to look into how to make this school more goddamn accessible.

Pain raced through his foot and up his lower back as Titus went to mount the second to last staircase to the headmistress's office. He stumbled back and Emmeline caught him.

"Titus! Let's—let's slow down."

"We can't!" He swore, frustrated. Normally he didn't hate his body so much. He'd done a lot of work accepting this disease and his corresponding needs, but at the end of the day, he was slower than the others and he couldn't let his movements stop them.

"You all go ahead," he said, passing the tablet with all their work to Emmeline.

Before Sadie and Emmeline could protest, Titus felt a sturdy shoulder nudge under his arm and a firm grasp haul him up the steps. Alaric had Titus's arm looped around his shoulders and he gave his cousin an encouraging tug. "Nah, mate. We do this together."

Emotion clogged his throat, and he nodded. Pride didn't even factor into it. For the first time... his family was there for him.

"Yeah, thanks." His words were hoarse as Alaric helped him up the steps. This set and the next.

His cousin let him go in front of the door with the eagle knocker and Titus stepped back to tug down his blazer, hopefully concealing his wrinkled shirt. Then he glanced at the rest of the heirs and opened the door.

"Apologies, Headmistress," Titus began. "I know I promised to start making appointments, but this is urgent."

"Titus." The headmistress stood, her dark eyes wide. "Sadie, Alaric, Emmeline...what in the heavens..."

"Zuri, what is the meaning of this?"

Titus looked down at the average man sitting in one of the chairs pulled up in front of Headmistress Aquila's large desk.

Rhett Croft was exactly as Titus had remembered him from the gala, and the news stories from all the research he'd done over the last few months. Entirely unremarkable. An American accent unidentifiable from any cultural region of the country. Average height, graying brown hair, bland features. The only impressive detail was his three-piece suit complete with a chain on his vest.

Titus thought he looked like a prat.

"You cannot sell Almus Terra to this man," Titus said.

Headmistress Aquila's features darkened with rage. "Titus, this is unacceptable—"

"He's manipulated the board, Headmistress,"

Alaric interrupted. "Every single board member has been complicit in using more and more expensive vendors to keep the school running. Every time they increase our operating costs, it's been at *his* direction. They're all tied to Croft. He's orchestrated this entire buyout."

Titus had never seen their headmistress speechless until this moment. Her mouth opened and closed several times, before she jerked her gaze from Alaric to stare at Croft.

Croft was glaring at Alaric, his hands tight on the chair, but he said nothing. Denying it would be foolish since it would be easy enough to prove, especially given all the information they had collected.

But there was something beyond that in his face. A look that clearly said, *So what?* It was the arrogance of a billionaire caught in a crime. *Go ahead, charge me. I'm untouchable.*

"Headmistress, he wants to use Almus Terra's students," Emmeline continued. "His intentions are to employ them in his companies, to use every generation of Scholars however he wants—"

"Young lady," Croft said to Emmeline sharply. "My employees have every resource they could possibly want at their disposal. I will not sit here and have you paint me as some villain."

"What about Imani Nyerere?" Alaric asked. "His title is lead engineer. He's not making any decisions in how his battery is used, or—"

"He is in this for the science. That's all that matters to him."

"And Takumi Miyamoto? Did he want his engineering work to be used for two global superpowers to buy even *more* weapons?" Alaric almost shouted.

"Zuri, get these brats out of your office right now," Croft seethed, jumping to his feet.

Alaric slammed the side of his fist against the wall. "Up yers yeh—"

"That is enough," Headmistress Aquila commanded, her peremptory tone echoing through her office. "I understand your concerns, but this sale will still allow students to earn an amazing education they otherwise would not have access to."

"There's another way, Headmistress," Titus said, stepping forward and extending his tablet, ignoring the aching pain in his feet. "We can save Almus Terra. There might need to be changes. But we can preserve the purpose of the school. You told us over and over about how we affect the future of the world. *Pax in terra.* If you sell it, Almus Terra won't exist anymore."

"Zuri—" Croft began, but the headmistress threw up her hand, crossing to Titus to accept the tablet. She scanned the first few lines of the document they had spent the last five hours preparing. She raised her gaze to Titus, then to Alaric, Sadie, and Emmeline behind him.

"This is a proposition to the United Nations Economic and Social Council and the UN General Assembly. You're requesting that Almus Terra Academy be added as a specialized agency of the UN."

Her gaze was sharp, assessing, taking in the idea and considering its merit.

"A specialized agency of the United Nations is an autonomous international organization. It would be funded by voluntary and assessed contributions," Titus said, pride growing in his voice. "It wouldn't be a hard sell, Headmistress. Many of the countries who founded the United Nations founded this school after World War II. In some ways, we'd just be... making it official."

The idea had come to him from Sadie's words and his conversation back at the United Energy Gala with Madame DuPont. What if they didn't just operate *like* the UN, but as *part* of it? Organizations like the International Atomic Energy Agency and the United Nations Children's

Fund—were conceived to work toward a better future for the entire world. Working in over 150 countries and territories, helping to eradicate poverty, reduce inequality, acting as a catalyst for sustainable development, saving children's lives—all of the specialized agencies' missions were the same. And so was Almus Terra's.

*Pax in Terra.*

A hint of a smile touched the dark cherry red of Headmistress Aquila's lips.

Titus could feel the seed of hope plant firmly inside him. Almus Terra may change being formally associated with the UN. It might no longer be the same exact school it was now. But its mission would stay the same. The heart of the school would be protected. Besides, Zuri Aquila had clout with a majority of world leaders. They would not just let her keep her school, but allow it to flourish.

"It could take months, maybe a year or more, to make possible what you're suggesting," Croft hissed. "This school won't have the funding to stay open during that time."

Headmistress Aquila's head turned so sharply, her braids swung to her other shoulder. "You should know, sir, that I do not respond well to threats," she said, her voice as cold as ice.

Then she walked over to the desk, took the document that she'd been about to sign with an elegant ivory fountain pen, and ripped it down the middle.

"You are dismissed, Mr. Croft. Kindly never step foot in my school again."

# 36

# SADIE

Sadie had seen angry men before. Like the men whose money she'd held hostage at Hibernia. Or Leander upon discovering her in Alaric's room the night he'd tried to have her killed.

But she'd never seen a man quite as angry as Rhett Croft was right now. His bland features went ruddy with rage, while his arms and shoulders trembled from how tightly his muscles locked and his hands clenched and unclenched.

No one moved, nor said anything, for a good twenty seconds, the time seeming to stretch on for an eternity.

Finally, Croft adjusted the cuffs on his sleeves under his suit jacket and straightened his tie. The motions seemed to calm him down enough to be able to speak without yelling.

"You're making a mistake, Zuri. Almus Terra

would have the best technology available, the best instructors, the—"

"Please address me as 'Headmistress,' and I told you, your offer is rejected." Headmistress Aquila raised her arm toward the door. "Please leave."

With a growl that sounded almost feral, Croft got all the way to the door's threshold before he paused and turned back toward Titus.

"Your grandfather will be deeply disappointed in hearing this, Prince Titus. He had such high hopes for the three of you." His gaze flitted from Titus, to Alaric, to Emmeline. "Yet again, you have disappointed him. I will relish walking down this hall to report directly to him on your failure." With that, he headed down the steps.

Casting a look at Alaric and Emmeline, Titus frowned and then followed Croft down the steps, though much more slowly.

Sadie's heart pounded. Leander was *here*? Why? There could only be one reason, really. Their only connection was the shady stock manipulations all over the Ashland Investment Fund.

While Emmeline followed Titus down the stairs, Sadie caught Alaric's arm before he could go down too.

"This is why they started working together," Sadie whispered, her chest tight with understanding. "Leander introduced Croft to the school and all the board members, and in return, Croft helped him grow our country's sovereign wealth fund without needing a lot of capital to invest. It was a trade."

In order to start a sovereign wealth fund for a country, the country in question needed a surplus of capital. Ashland had never been a wealthy nation based on its resources. After years of civil war, its modest wealth came from its ports and its fishing industry. But with pensioners' funds and special stock market strategies, the Ashland Investment Fund had been able to grow. With Croft's help.

"Leander's here to deliver on his end of the deal," Alaric said, brow furrowed. "Let's pay the old man a visit. Shall we?"

He held out his hand to her.

Sadie looked up into his strong, handsome face. It was possible that all their futures fell apart after this. They had stopped Croft from buying ATA, a long-form operation engineered by Leander and then thwarted by his heirs. The king of Ashland did not tolerate insubordination. He may be getting older, but he was still healthy and strong for his age. He had time to find another heir. Perhaps a distant Eldana relative who would do what they were told. Like Sadie, Titus could be reduced to the status of a figurehead and then replaced whenever convenient. They would likely use his rheumatoid arthritis as a reason to dethrone him—make up some story about how he was too weak to rule such a strong, durable people. The idea of it made Sadie sick with rage.

"We saved Almus Terra, but what about Ashland?" she asked, her gaze searching his.

Alaric's lips tugged into a half-smile. "*Ashland is my homeland.* That night, after Hibernia, that's what yeh said. That none of us could compete with the sense of purpose that comes from true belonging. One way or another, cailín, yeh will save yer homeland. Maybe not today or tomorrow. But some day."

"You..." Sadie felt her pulse skip, like his stones across the coast, "you remembered I said that?"

Alaric's gaze softened as he repeated, "I remember everything that's important to yeh, cailín."

On her tiptoes, grabbing the strings of his hoodie, Sadie kissed him. It wasn't slow or tentative, and, yes, it was a little clumsy. But it was still perfect. Firm and warm and thrilling and smelling like mint and pine. She wanted to loop her arms around his neck, dig her fingers into the hair at the nape of his neck, feel the strength and warmth of his chest that she'd once felt against her back when he'd held her close all night long. Her stomach swooped like being dropped in a roller coaster and she gasped at the sensation, allowing Alaric to take control.

His hand caught her jaw as his mouth, hot and hungry, nearly devoured hers in response. But it was only for a split second then—

"*Ahem.*" Headmistress Aquila cleared her throat obnoxiously.

Sadie pulled back, her face hot like lava, but Alaric followed her, his forehead pressing against her temple as she turned her face to the side to avoid their third kiss.

She was grinning like an idiot, though.

When she'd faced Leander a year ago it had been because, more than anything else, she'd wanted to prove him wrong. There was nothing she wouldn't do for her country. But becoming heir apparent? Forcing his hand? She'd done those things out of desperation and rage. A coup based in spite and a warped sense of justice. She'd had nothing left to lose and *everything* to prove.

However, now she knew that Alaric believed she could make a difference. This time, when she faced Leander, she wouldn't be motivated by anger. It would be courage, plain and simple.

"Sorry, Headmistress." She ducked away and started down the stairs, catching Alaric's hand and dragging him behind her. At his deep groan, she glanced back at him. "We can't leave them to deal with the king alone."

Alaric mumbled something, probably related to her terrible timing, but his heavy footsteps hurried after her.

Emmeline and Titus stood at the end of the castle corridor, the stained-glass window of an angel with a dove shining gold, blue, and purple light on the floor and their gray Almus Terra uniforms. But it was Leander's voice that carried across the marble that gave it away.

"You forget your *place*. I am king, Croft."

"King of an insignificant country. I've built a global empire that's far more powerful than any nation-state."

The next moment, Rhett Croft practically flew back down the hall, barreling toward Sadie with such a demented, dark expression that Alaric quickly pulled her to his side.

"I will make sure security escorts him out the

castle," Zuri Aquila said in a low voice, then followed Croft, her heels clicking after him.

Sadie and Alaric joined Emmeline and Titus, their gazes all connecting as if to assure each other, *This won't be like last time. He can't pit us against each other anymore.*

Leander stood next to the mantle, looking into the cold ashes of a fireplace that hadn't been used since January. Lord Mikael Erickson stood off to the side of the room along with Captain Kendrick.

The king of Ashland looked up at Sadie and Alaric's footsteps and Sadie was shocked to see that it looked as if he'd aged another five years since she'd seen him last. He'd been looking older at Titus's press conference, but just the last few weeks seemed to have weighed him down with the stress of a decade.

"I was wrong...," he said, his gray eyes like looking down the barrel of a silver pistol, so dark and threatening they spoke of death. "I'd thought my children would always be my life's greatest disappointment. But no, it turned out to be my grandchildren. The heirs I had waited sixteen years for. I shouldn't be so surprised. Yet I had hope..." He looked back down at the fireplace, seeming truly mournful. "Such hope.

Now you have cost your country a favorable relationship with one of the most important men on this planet."

"You're the disappointment, Your Majesty," Sadie said, stepping forward. "How dare you play the stock market with the pensions of your citizens."

Leander gave a short derisive laugh, not at all startled to find they knew about his shady dealings. "Oh, Sadie. Still such a naive little creature. *Playing* implies the dual possibilities of winning and losing, and I *never* lose. Let's also not pretend there's anything to be done about my crimes. Whatever your feelings may be, I have grown the AIF and should you attempt to have my actions investigated, it could hurt Ashland and our economy and none of us here want that."

Sadie's hands curled into fists, hating that he was right.

He fixed her with a smirk. "People have tried to take me down before. Many, many times. And yet here I am, still standing."

Immeasurable arrogance and pride. Whoever went up against him lost. Including her parents. They'd tried to take Ashland back and they had failed. Leander believed she would be no different.

But *she* was still standing too.

Sadie raised her chin, defiant in her stance. "You lost at the Winter Masquerade Ball. When you tried to kill me... and failed."

He turned his head, steel eyes inspecting Sadie as if evaluating every childish freckle. Sadie felt every muscle in her body lock, prepping for the blow.

"What?" His gaze narrowed. "What the devil are you on about?"

Was he really going to try to deny it?

"The ridiculous dress, the spiked drink, and the photographer who pushed me over the side of the yacht," Sadie shot back. "Alaric saved me from drowning. That's why we were in the same room the next morning. Not that you'd believe us, but a news reporter might. It's not like I could prove the attempted murder, but a simple DNA test could verify that I have the blood of a Scealan. And it wouldn't be hard to believe that, like you did sixteen years ago, you tried again to eliminate any threats to your crown. But this time you weren't trying to quash an attempted coup but to kill an innocent teenage girl. Your heir apparent, in fact."

Leander had gone a new shade of white. The silver in his eyes seemed to darken to chrome as he processed every threatening word.

"You... know who you are," he rasped.

Sadie blinked, taken aback. That's not what she thought would surprise him.

"Sire—"

Mikael Erickson took a step forward, setting his tablet aside and for the first time, looking... nervous? Alaric's fingers wrapped around Sadie's wrist like a warning.

Leander lifted a hand to silence his chief financial advisor. "When did you learn who you are, Sadie? How?"

"I found some documents in your drawer, then I had the good fortune of talking to the former prime minister of Greenland. And I put it all together."

Leander was staring at her, not unlike he had that night at Hibernia, when he was debating about giving in to her demands. "Smart girl," he muttered, rubbing a hand over his wrinkled jaw.

"If you didn't know I knew about my parents, then—"

Before Sadie could finish the thought, Alaric had crossed the room and grabbed his father by the shirt collar, slamming him into the wall. "Yeh son of a bitch it was *all* yer doin'—"

The force and strength of Alaric's sudden moves surprised everyone, including Captain

Kendrick, who started to intervene when Leander made a short cutting movement with his wrist, telling him to halt.

"I did what I had to," Mikael snarled back, grabbing Alaric's wrists, trying to shove his son away. "Her existence could destroy everything we have built. When Rosing ran his mouth, I made sure to monitor her activity and when the stupid girl *googled herself*—"

"You have access to Enyo," Emmeline said.

Mikael rolled his eyes. "Of course I do. It was my idea for Croft to sell the product to the school. After the sneaky brat made off with all our money at the trade summit I had to take precautions—"

Alaric shook Mikael so hard his father's head hit the wall, and the man winced. "Talk about her one more time, yeh fecking load of bollocks," Alaric said through his teeth, "and I'll toss yeh off the Durah cliffs myself."

Perhaps she shouldn't have been, but Sadie was stunned. Alaric's *father* was the one who'd tried to have her killed, and even though Sadie had always thought the man evil, through and through, she was surprised he'd acted independently from his king.

Taking in Leander's stricken expression, he must have been thinking the same thing.

But how had Alaric put this together so instantly?

"So it was *you* who found Warren? Pity you only broke his nose. You might as well have just finished the job for me," Mikael sneered at his son.

"Alaric," Sadie said softly, "what's he talking about?"

"I found the man who pushed yeh overboard, Sadie," Alaric growled, pressing his fists tighter against his father's throat. "He'd been hiding out in a crummy flat in Durah. He all but confessed to me that he'd been hired by my da, except I'd assumed he was working under orders of the king." Alaric shifted his gaze back to his father. "If I'd known it was all *yer* idea, I would've just tried to kill yeh then."

The more she processed everything, the more sense it made that it had been Mikael Erickson. She'd made a fool out of him at Hibernia, and given his cruelty toward his own son, and the daughter he refused to even acknowledge, she had no trouble believing he would send her to a watery grave.

"Alaric, please," Sadie said, remembering that day so many months ago when she'd held him back as he had trembled with such hatred and heartbreak. She hated that he still felt it. "Stop. You are *not* him."

A heavy moment passed before Alaric finally dropped his hands and stepped back, his chest heaving with deep struggling breaths. Like he'd just sprinted a mile.

It was then that Leander snapped out of his own shock, his gray eyes growing sharper with barely suppressed rage. He held out a hand toward Erickson.

"You...I will deal with you later. Kendrick, guard him."

The captain saluted and took up a stance between Alaric and his father, but Alaric just made a disgusted noise in his throat as he joined Sadie at her side.

"Now, *Aurelia*," Leander began, his voice firm and commanding, like the one he used in all of his media appearances. "You are free to come out as Aurelia Scealan. It is in your right, and I am not in the business of killing minors to protect my crown. Despite what you had thought me capable of. However, you need to know what you'd be unleashing with this information." He dipped his chin, meeting Sadie's hazel eyes. "Chaos. Do you *know* what your parents had concocted? They had plans to blow up energy plants and military bases. An attack on the Durah port to weaken the country's economy as well as infrastructure. Civilian lives were on the line. Even if that's not your intention, what if you are mythologized into a figurehead to start some extremists' revolution? Do you think it would be peaceful, Sadie?"

No, she didn't. Sadie knew her country's history. Though she wanted to believe in a more peaceful world, a generation with hope and cooperation, she feared the worst.

"If people were truly happy, there would be no cause for a revolution," Sadie said. "I'm not saying that's the answer. But if you had been a better king and listened to the people and what they *need*, my existence wouldn't be such a threat."

"You have quite the gall to be lecturing me. I have given everything to Ashland. My blood, sweat, and tears, my soul, my family...because of me, there hasn't been a war in seventy years. No other monarch in Ashlandic history can claim that. This country, it would be *nothing* without me."

"Always a flair for the dramatic, Father."

Everyone turned toward the new voice at the doorway. A woman, tall, with short black hair and wearing dark gray slacks and a simple white button-down with purple heels, leaned against the doorway with her arms crossed.

She looked familiar to Sadie. The curve of her lips and her short black hair and striking gray eyes... it was the woman in black from the masquerade. But the rest of her face was familiar as well. Like Sadie had seen her in passing over the last year.

It wasn't until Alaric said, "Ms... Reyburn?" that Sadie recognized the woman as the professor of Cyber Security as well as the head of Almus Terra's IT.

Her small smile grew wide. "Actually, I'd prefer *Mah*, but we'll get there."

# 37

## ALARIC

Alaric felt like he'd fallen into the Labrador Sea again. The shock that ran through his system was the same. Every nerve ending in his body was alive and firing.

"What's the matter, husband?" Ms. Reyburn said, dropping her folded arms and walking into the room. "You look as if you've seen a ghost."

The room was silent. Sadie's hands had found Alaric's arm, and she was squeezing him tightly. He wasn't sure if it was for his benefit, or hers.

Alaric glanced at his father and confirmed the truth in her words. Because while everyone else looked at his teacher—a woman claiming to be his mother, Princess Rhea—like she was a dead person come back to life, Mikael Erickson was the only one looking at her with nothing but hatred.

That's when he remembered the words from

Warren, sniveling on his disgusting floor. *"Your wife—she must've found out somehow."*

And then his father's own words about his mother. *Even in death.*

He had wanted to hurt her, punish her, even in death because he *knew* that she wasn't really dead. That he'd tried to have her killed, but as with Sadie, he'd failed.

The real reason Alaric had been abandoned, sent to live in foster homes and become part of a system that almost made him untraceable was because Erickson hadn't wanted his mother to find him. At least, not easily.

Emotion built in him like a pressure cooker. His mother... could this really be his mother? She didn't look like her photos, but if her husband had tried to kill her, he didn't blame her for going through a few cosmetic surgeries to alter her appearance.

"Rh-Rhea," a wizened voice said from a few feet away.

Alaric watched as his once proud, strong, and impenetrable grandfather seemed to wilt before his very eyes. His hands shook so badly, the tremors seemed to go up his arms and all the way down his spine. Captain Kendrick abandoned his post next to Alaric's father and rushed to help his king down into a nearby chair, while Leander could do nothing but stare at his long-lost daughter.

"Is that... really you?"

Rhea's gaze softened ever so slightly as she looked down at her father. "Yes, Dah."

Leander made a choked noise as he raised a trembling hand to his mouth, his gaze raking over her from head to foot. Rhea let him take her in, but she didn't go to him.

Rhea looked over at Alaric, offering him a small, sad smile. "You've grown up so well, Alaric. I hope you'll give me a chance to get to know the man you've become. I'm sure you have questions. All of you."

The crown princess of Ashland turned slowly to address the four heirs. "First, I apologize for deceiving you since my arrival at Almus Terra. As soon as the press release came out about the four of you, I made every effort to find a way into the school. I wanted to be as close as possible now that my search was over."

"You... you'd been looking for us?" Titus asked, his brows furrowed with confusion. "*All* of us?"

"Of course I have," Rhea said. "I never supported my father's ridiculous idea to send the three of you away. It's not that I didn't want to protect you from the court and the media. On that front, my father and I agreed. But to separate you from your parents? Never." The final words she directed to Alaric, her eyes shining with emotion. "My father floated the idea to me when you were born. But I told him we would only be separated over my dead body. I didn't realize that would be so literal."

"LIES!" Erickson boomed, the first word he'd said since the wife he'd tried to murder had suddenly appeared. He surged forward and Kendrick stepped in front of him. "Be honest, Rhea. Tell them what you were *really* planning. Against your own father. Treason!"

Rhea drew herself up. "It was not *treason*, Mikael. Dissolving the monarchy and creating a parliamentary system to give our citizens a voice is not a coup when a member of the royal family has the power to do it."

The words fell like an atomic bomb—silent, history-altering.

Princess Rhea had wanted to tear down the monarchy. She had likely been working behind the scenes to see if that was possible.

"Ha! You're no different from the Scealans. Your father had finally brought this country peace. Economic prosperity. I would not see it ruined because of some preposterous notion that the people can rule themselves," Erickson said, with a sneer. "Your ideals were foolish, and you were nothing but a naive little girl with no respect for your family or your father."

"So you would *have me killed*? The mother of your child?" she asked calmly, piercing Erickson with an icy glare.

For the first time, Alaric could see what Sadie meant about his eyes. How they were like the sea and storm clouds off the coast of their home. He saw the storm in his mother's eyes in that moment.

"Not long after I had Alaric, I started noticing myself growing weaker. It was easy enough to test my blood and trace the poisoning back to you. Especially since you tried to poison Emmeline when she was *two years old*! Your own daughter, Mikael. Neither one of us died to absolve your sins."

"What?" Leander said, his voice dropping. "What did you say?"

"You think I didn't know you slept with my sister-in-law?" Rhea continued, her fierce diatribe picking up speed. "It was so obvious the way she looked at you. Not that I minded you having a distraction. But then you tried to have me smothered mere days after I confronted you about the poison, and I had no choice but to escape the castle. Thanks to people I trusted I was able to fake my death and start a new life. Once I found out you went through with the plan to send the children away, I tried to find them. To at least stay close and make sure someone was giving them the love they deserved, but you kept them well hidden. Especially Alaric, you bastard. For sixteen years I searched, learning from every honorable cyber security analyst and digital hacker I could find, looking for them. Not to mention pulling as much dirt and documentation about you as I could. I've been hacking into Ashland's systems for nearly two years at this point. I felt that I finally had enough information. I wanted to come back sooner, but then Sadie was named heir apparent and I worried for her safety since she wasn't of your precious Eldana line. Only later, thanks to the girl's own sleuthing, did I discover how *truly* vulnerable she was as Aurelia Scealan."

It was then Alaric realized how Rhea had pieced together Sadie's true identity. As Sadie had assumed, the woman at the masquerade ball had access to Enyo. Of course the head of IT would. She had been following all their digital activity, likely to watch over them. She'd found Sadie's research into Operation Peaceful Sea and with her hack into Mikael Erickson's personal computer, she was able to work out the truth. Just as Sadie had.

"I thought it would be smarter to keep a low profile until I knew what you had planned, darling husband," Rhea continued, flitting her wrist dismissively. "Turns out our son foiled your plans anyway."

For a long moment, no one moved. So many questions had been answered and yet Alaric had about a thousand more. His heart hammered in his chest as he stared at the woman who'd loved him once. Who loved him still, it seemed. The woman who bounced him on her knee as a baby and squeezed his chubby cheeks.

Leander then stood and nodded to Kendrick. The captain of the royal guard seized Erickson, wrestling his hands behind his back, and Mikael let out a vengeful howl that seemed to shake the golden picture frames and crystal china.

"I've been *protecting* you, Leander!" Erickson shouted. He struggled enough for one arm to escape, and he pointed at his wife with a shaking finger. "She wanted to destroy your legacy and the Eldana line! I'm the only one who truly loved you. Who believes in what you were doing!"

"You commit adultery, poison your daughter, try to murder your wife, and then have an innocent teenage girl thrown into the sea?" Leander's voice trembled with emotion. Strangely, it seemed to hold grief, instead of rage. "I loved you, too, Mikael, like a son. My two others are lazy, weak, selfish creatures, but I gave you Rhea. My pride. And you betrayed me. Betrayed Ashland. You'll be put to death for this."

"No!"

Everyone turned to look at Emmeline, who stood there, stricken. Tears collected in her eyes. "Your Majesty...there's been enough death."

Sadie's hand squeezed Alaric's, and she spoke up as well. "Emmeline is right. Let him stand trial, Your Majesty."

Leander glanced between the two of them, looking tired and old, and he simply nodded. Captain Kendrick marched Erickson out of the state room like a prisoner of war, and Alaric knew it would be the last time he ever saw the man. Except, perhaps, at his trial.

Rhea turned to her father. "Dah, we have much to discuss. But first I want you to know I am not here to take back the throne." She turned to Titus and placed a hand on his shoulder. "You have an exceptionally fine heir apparent, and—"

"Actually," Titus said, his expression serious, "becoming king is what my parents always wanted for me. Not something I chose. I'd like more time to figure out what, exactly, I want for myself."

If Rhea or Leander were surprised to hear the prodigal son say such a thing, they didn't show it. Princess Rhea simply nodded. "You will have time. You will *all* have time. For now, I ask for a few moments to speak with my father. Alone, if you don't mind."

With a gentle tugging on his arm, Alaric followed Sadie, Titus, and Emmeline out of the room.

The moment the door was closed, Emmeline, having spent too much time with Oakley lately, said the words everyone was thinking.

"Holy...fuck."

The four of them had been allowed back in the headmistress's office. Headmistress Aquila was dealing with the fallout of Croft's departure as well as getting more campus security to assist Captain Kendrick in detaining Lord Erickson at the docks while Leander and Rhea discussed the future of their country in one of Almus Terra's state rooms.

Between the four of them, they hadn't said much, all of them reeling from the reveal of Princess Rhea.

"This could change everything," Titus said softly.

"It already has," Emmeline muttered.

"How..." Alaric cleared his throat. "I'm having trouble... believing it." Even though he'd seen his own eyes staring back at him and, deep down in his soul, *knew* that woman down the hall was his mother. "How did no one know that the *crown princess* had faked her own death?"

"People knew," Sadie said. "They had to. But they must've loved Rhea to have gone to such lengths to make her look dead on a doctor's table and then get her out of the country. Remember, we don't bury our dead or hold wakes. We cremate them and send their ashes into the sea. With a cremation, it is easier to fake a royal's death in Ashland than in most countries."

"Do you really not want to be king, Titus?" Emmeline asked softly.

Titus shook his head. "I don't know what I want. I've lived my life entirely for my parents, but this year... it's really made me question things. I thought achieving this title would justify everything I went through but no—not if it doesn't make me happy."

"Could... could a parliamentary system really be possible?" Sadie wondered out loud.

"That is my hope."

The four of them all turned in their chairs to find Rhea at the top of the steps. She gave them a kind smile, one of assurance and comfort. One that felt very much like a mother, in Alaric's opinion.

"Do you three mind if I speak to my son for a few minutes?"

They all glanced back at Alaric before quickly getting to their feet. Sadie leaned down and kissed his cheek before joining Titus and Emmeline down the steps. The door shut behind them and Alaric was left alone with his mother.

The room seemed to go on for miles even though there couldn't have been more than twelve feet between them.

"I'm sorry, Alaric."

Alaric was shaking his head, his pulse hammering. He didn't know if he could do this. Face her. The memory of her room still lived in his heart, the framed photographs of him on her desk.

He'd been loved.

He looked up, and tears were steadily rolling down her cheeks. She brought her hands to her mouth and nose and gave a choked sob. "My baby boy. I worried...I would never see you again."

He saw then that she'd kept it together as long as she could. Now, like a dam, her love and loss were crashing down, threatening to drown both of them.

Alaric got to his feet unsteadily.

She sniffed and wiped at her eyes, visibly pulling herself together. Her next words were steady, but fast. "I'm not going back to Ashland immediately. I'm still a teacher here. I'll stay on, finish up the semester, make sure Enyo is purged from ATA's servers and help Zuri find my replacement. But...but maybe we could meet up, from time to time, when you're free. Between classes. I know your finals are coming up..."

Alaric noticed she was twisting her hands in front of her stomach. A nervous habit he recognized from a certain redhead. His mother was nervous before him, worried they wouldn't have a relationship when Alaric had long since given up the hope of having loving parents.

But that didn't mean he didn't still want them.

"I have a question."

Rhea wiped at her eyes again, looking somehow hopeful and scared at the same time. "You can ask me anything."

Alaric took out his phone and swiped through his photos. He stopped when he came to the ones he took in her room of him as a baby. "Did yeh really have to dress me up in this sailor outfit? It's brutal."

A laugh escaped her, one that was part disbelief and part sob and part hiccup. "Trust me, there were many worse sailor outfits."

"Ah, fair play," Alaric said, tucking away his phone and shoving his hands into his pockets. "Then yeah. I'd like that."

His mother gave him a brilliant smile, and though it was still hard for Alaric to believe that something like this had happened—that his mother was alive and standing in front of him asking to be part of his life—he was choosing to believe. Because believing in something good was worth it.

Sadie had taught him that.

"I need to walk Leander back to the docks. See my vile husband off," Rhea said, turning toward the door. "Zuri said she'd clear out a room for the five of us to have dinner. Me, Emmeline, Titus, you, and Sadie. Do you think they would like that?"

Alaric followed her down the steps. "I think it's grand."

He started to walk her toward the admin offices when he paused, spying a ripple behind the tapestries, a pair of familiar Converse underneath. "I'll see yeh at dinner, then."

Rhea smiled and nodded, then continued walking as Alaric doubled back and pulled at the tapestry of the Xinhai Revolution to find Sadie behind it.

"What are yeh doin', cailín?"

Wisps of hair floated around her face thanks to the tapestry's sudden movement and she stared up at him with wide hazel eyes. Sadie licked her lips. Lips that he'd now *finally* tasted.

"I wanted to check on you... but I also didn't want to interrupt."

Alaric grinned, stepping into her space, backing her up against the stone castle wall. She'd waited for him because she was worried, and she'd hidden because she hadn't wanted to interrupt his time with his mother.

He had time to get to know Rhea. All the time in the world, hopefully. But it was Sadie he could no longer wait for.

He let the tapestry fall behind him, casting them both into darkness.

"Alaric—" Sadie protested.

Here, in the shadows of the sunlit hallway, hidden by layers of textile and history, he cupped her cheeks and dipped his head down to kiss her until she was breathless.

For the second time, she gasped against his lips and for the second time he took advantage, coaxing a deeper, hungrier kiss from the girl who had driven him mad for nearly two years. The one who stole his heart in the span of an economic debate. The princess and heir he fell for so desperately and wholeheartedly that he'd jumped into the cold deadly sea for.

Sadie pulled away and he groaned in response. Was she stopping them again? Before, he could understand, but not now. He wasn't ever going to stop kissing her.

"What about your mother?" Sadie whispered, her panting breath loud in the muffled sound of the fabric surrounding them.

"Gone. We're having dinner with her later."

"Oh. Well, Leander—"

"She's making sure they get on the damn ferry."

"They're leaving? So then—"

"Sadie, fer once in yer life, stop arguing with me and let me kiss yeh long enough to forget yer own name."

"You're taking too long—"

Alaric swallowed her words, so sassy and demanding it set his blood on fire. He was pretty sure by the fifth kiss she was struggling to remember all three of her names when the tapestry was ripped back and sunlight illuminated them both.

"Behind my *antique tapestries*?" the headmistress shrieked. "You have dorm rooms for God's sake!"

# 38

# EMMELINE

It was her fifth time reading over the press release, and still Emmeline was having trouble believing the announcement was really live, in pixelated black and white.

> **BREAKING NEWS: ASHLAND'S CROWN PRINCESS RETURNED FROM THE DEAD**
> By Rosemary Guidry
> *Published: May 1, 7:30AM GMT-5*
>
> DURAH, Ashland (DAFB)—Surprising both her father and the entire world, Crown Princess Rhea has returned from our beloved sea, proving that there is, in fact, life after death. Less than two years after her son, Alaric, was born, Rhea discovered a plot to poison her and man-

aged to escape before the treacherous deed could be fulfilled. She escaped to Scotland and, after multiple surgeries to alter her appearance, has been living there under a new identity. Unconfirmed sources will not yet say how and why Rhea chose to come forth now, but the culprit behind her poisoning is, apparently, in custody and still under investigation for a slew of crimes against the crown. Working with her father, King Leander, Rhea discusses a peaceful transition back into court life. It is surmised that she will take the throne from her father for a time before Prince Titus is old enough and ready to take his crown. But even that is questionable with Rhea's return. Rhea was known in her younger years as being too radical for her father, but there was no question that her people adored her. What will Rhea do once she has the crown? What will become of our beloved heirs?

Nearly a week after their dinner with Crown Princess Rhea and Emmeline was still asking herself the same question. What were their futures going to look like? For once in each of their lives, there didn't seem to be a predestined path lined with abusive parents, a stern governess, death and grief, and the burden of feeling alone and adrift.

Perhaps she should be freaking out. Having this much freedom was often scary, but she wasn't scared at all. She was *thrilled*.

It helped that Rhea was absolutely wonderful. Honestly, she'd been the exact kind of mom Emmeline had dreamed of. She told them all about her life from when she was a child to her early university days and getting engaged to Mikael Erickson, the man her father had trusted and loved like a third son. She had been sick as a younger child and teenager, aggravated by Ashland's outdated medical practices and their failure to recognize celiac disease. It was a doctor at Almus Terra, back when *she* had attended, who finally helped her identify the disease and set her on the right diet—an experience that she and Titus had much to discuss. By the time she returned to Ashland to get married to Mikael, she was well and strong but because of her history of illness, it was easy for her symptoms from the poison to go unquestioned.

Rhea didn't dominate the entire conversation, even though her life in Scotland, attending university, and training at huge software companies, was absolutely fascinating. More than once, Rhea would joke about how physically close she and Alaric had been. Just a few train rides and ten million people between them.

Alaric seemed to be more at peace than Emmeline had ever seen him. He grinned and laughed with his mother during dinner, and he hardly ever let go of Sadie's hand under the table.

When it was over, Titus left feeling confident about his decision to relinquish his crown to Rhea for the time being, and hearing Rhea's tentative plans for a parliamentary system in Ashland brought Sadie to tears. There would be no doubt it would take time to alter their country's path, but Leander had been permanently changed by the betrayal of his chief financial advisor and the shock of his beloved daughter's return.

The unthinkable had happened: He was willing to relinquish his crown prematurely. Emmeline rather suspected nothing other than the fierce love he'd had for his daughter would've allowed him to do so.

Emmeline, for her part, had been stunned when Rhea had stopped her on the way out of dinner and hugged her fiercely. While the other three lingered down the hall waiting for her, she'd shared a quiet conversation with her half-brother's mother.

"I want you to know, Emmeline," Rhea said, her voice tight. "I think of you as mine. Chloe... she never wanted to be a mother. But I knew you were Mikael's daughter, and I... I did love him once. I spent many hours with you and Alaric in my arms humming you both to sleep. I just wanted you to know. In case, well, you ever needed to know. You were loved. And you are still. You and me, we both survived."

Emmeline couldn't speak. Her throat had closed up, but Rhea seemed to understand.

Thinking back on that moment, Rhea's offer had meant everything to her, but surprisingly, she felt no need to try to establish a relationship with Rhea right away. For now, Emmeline was content with her friends. More than content, truly. She was overjoyed with them.

Not to mention, she was a little frightened to hope for too much in another parental figure after she had just closed her heart and dissolved all hope for her biological parents. But that wasn't to say in the future that she wouldn't find comfort in Rhea.

So, for the moment, she wanted to focus on the family she'd found and made for herself.

"DONE!" Oakley shouted, slamming her laptop shut, tossing her hands up into the air and waving them dramatically.

The move jostled them both enough on the bed that Emmeline's tablet slipped from her fingers onto the pillow.

"And how do you feel about it?" Emmeline asked with a grin. Oakley had spent the last three weeks preparing an internship application for Malachite Inc., a specialty research firm in new energy and climate change, located in northern France.

They had checked and double-checked that it was not, in any way, affiliated with Rhett Croft.

"Oh, I'll ace the interview. No question. And then you can come visit me and Danica in Amiens on special weekends," she said, squeezing Emmeline's arm. "Unless, you know, you're too busy hooking up with Ollie."

Emmeline made a face. "Don't make it sound so crude."

"How would you prefer I say it? Canoodling?"

"That's even worse."

"Ollie, any preferences?"

Oliver sat on the floor with his laptop, opposite the bed where Emmeline and Oakley had been working. He glanced up, his dark eyes drifting to Emmeline and she felt that familiar thrill every time their eyes connected.

"Uhhh... I don't have any preferences," he said.

"Boys *always* have preferences," Oakley replied.

Emmeline snorted, though her face was flaming with heat. Her relationship with Oliver was so new. After the day they'd saved Almus Terra and Rhea had come to rescue both her family and Ashland, Emmeline had struggled about when to tell Oliver that she felt she was ready to give in to their feelings and trust them.

In the end, Sadie, of all people, had been the one who'd convinced her to go for it.

The day after Leander left, while they'd been getting ready for classes in their shared dorm like any other day at Almus Terra, Sadie had said softly, "I'm really proud of you, Emmeline. Lord Erickson didn't deserve your mercy, but you gave it to him anyway."

At the time, Emmeline had just thought that, no matter what, she didn't want Alaric, or herself for that matter, to hear about their father being put to death. It was that simple.

But it had made her think... maybe she really was trying to be the good person she aspired to be. That she felt like her friends deserved.

Every day, she tried to be someone worthy of them.

She playfully kicked at Oakley with her fuzzy socks. "Go. Find Danica. Tell her you finished the internship application she completed two weeks ago."

"Are you kicking me out of my own home so you can hook up? Sorry—canoodle?"

"Yes," Emmeline said.

Rolling her eyes, Oakley blew Emmeline a kiss and winked at Oliver, then closed the door behind her.

Oliver immediately shut his laptop and set it aside. She giggled, finding it adorable that the only time he ever shut his computer *so* quickly was when there was the possibility of kissing Emmeline.

He moved up onto his knees and Emmeline crawled forward on the bed, their kiss perfectly synchronized, as if they'd done it a thousand times instead of just a few.

Oliver's touch always made her melt, but nothing had compared to the moment where she'd found him in the computer lab to tell him she wanted to make this work and he'd pushed her up onto the lab desks, turning a fantasy into a reality and rewriting old history.

"Have you considered it?" Oliver asked, pulling out of their kiss, breathless.

Emmeline bit her bottom lip. "I dunno, Ollie. Meeting your parents... spending the summer with you. It feels big. We *just* started dating."

He gripped her hands, pressing them to his cheeks. "It is big. But my feelings for you are big. They want to meet you, Em. It doesn't have to be for long. I know you have a bunch of stuff in Ashland to work on. But... I want them to know you."

Emmeline considered it. It was true that she didn't want to wait a whole summer to see Oliver again. And it wasn't like she had princess duties to worry about anymore. But Rhea had promised all of the heirs a home at Heres Castle, including Sadie, for however long they wanted. They all planned to finish their schooling at Almus Terra and then find their own path in the world. If that path was coming back to Ashland to help build a new government, then that was definitely a possibility.

"A week," she said with a smile, kissing the tip of his nose.

He grinned at her, a huge toothy smile that made her feel like nothing ever had before... she didn't know she could ever be so happy.

There was a knock at the door and Oliver moved back while Emmeline straightened her shirt. They *knocked* at their dorm now. Ever since Oakley had walked in to find Trang straddling Titus with his shirt off.

"All clear," Emmeline said, smothering another smirk as Oliver adjusted his glasses.

Sadie burst into the room, a huge grin on her face, Alaric right behind her. The two had become nearly inseparable, but Emmeline guessed it was mostly Alaric following Sadie around like a lovestruck puppy. Though Sadie seemed just as smitten with him, to be sure.

"Sea turtles!"

"What?" Emmeline asked, confused.

"There are sea turtle eggs out on the Toulon beach near the harbor. Professor Parmeno is letting a group of us take the ferry to go out and get some pictures. Do you want to come?"

Sadie was nearly bouncing up and down on her heels. She wore a T-shirt with a giant squid that read "You're Kraken Me Up!" tucked into wide-leg holey jeans and white sneakers. Her red hair was loose and wavy, but she wore very little makeup nowadays. Somehow Sadie had only let her princess days give her confidence, without changing the core of who she was.

Slowly but surely, the two were becoming close and Sadie's own casual style was starting to influence Emmeline. Without needing to be perfect all the time, Emmeline found she enjoyed athleisure almost as much as her brother did.

"Titus and Trang are already out by the barbican. We're going to walk down together. Where's Oak?" she asked, glancing around the dorm room.

Emmeline stood and slipped on her own shoes, a much comfier pair of Hoka sneakers, and slipped her hand into Oliver's, as natural as breathing. "With Danica. They're probably celebrating the end of their application process for their internship."

"Oh," Sadie said, hesitating. "Should we see if they want to come?"

"Luv, the ferry is gonna leave in thirty. We have a short window," Alaric said, his voice patient, a hand on her lower back, guiding her out the door.

He was so much gentler lately. As if Sadie had tamed whatever restlessness had lived inside him for so long. Of course, it could be that he was starting to get to know a parent—a loving, worthy parent—for the first time in his life.

"Oakley will be fine," Emmeline assured her. "She's Australian. I'm sure she's seen sea turtles."

"Is that a *Finding Nemo* reference?" Alaric whispered.

Emmeline snorted and elbowed him.

"To the turtles!" Sadie said, pointing to the sky with an enthusiasm that Emmeline noticed had been buried for the last year and a half.

Trang and Titus were waiting for them right outside the castle gates. Titus, too, no longer looked like a future king of Ashland. Instead, he looked... *happy*. He wore simple jeans, sneakers, and a T-shirt with an old Monty Python sketch on it. Something about coconuts.

As the six teenagers started down the path from the castle toward the docks, Emmeline tilted her head up to the blue, blue sky. In front of her, Sadie gushed to Alaric and Trang about the life cycle of sea turtles. Next to her, Titus and Oliver talked about their upcoming final for their Industrial Development class.

"Titus, what's the update on the UN-sanctioned specialized agency process?" Emmeline asked once there was a lull in the conversation.

Another thing that Rhea had done, with her father's approval, was offer to fund the Scholars for another year while the school's UN application went through. While Emmeline knew that Headmistress Aquila had to be dealing with

Croft's temper tantrum, with ATA now under observation to be brought into the UN, there couldn't be anything done to the school that would cause concern.

"They want the student council to visit the next UN General Assembly in the fall," he said with a smile. "It's pretty promising."

"It'll happen for sure," Oliver said, his fingers slipping between Emmeline's.

Emmeline cocked an eyebrow. "So confident."

"With the four of you involved?" Oliver said, pushing his glasses up farther on his nose, "That's just statistics."

Leave it to Oliver, her brilliant Scholar, to look at past data to predict the future. But with the castle gates behind their backs, and the world at their feet, Emmeline needed no guarantees.

# ACKNOWLEDGMENTS

Parting with characters is one of the hardest things for an author to do. Which is why I'm incredibly grateful I got an extra book to hang out with them. Originally, *Royal Heirs Academy* was a one-book deal. My amazing publishing team saw there was more of this story to tell, and here we are.

I'm used to writing standalones (eleven, to be precise) so this duology was a wonderful, unexpected challenge. At first I was more than apprehensive, I was flat-out terrified. Thank you to my awesome agent, Masha Gunic, for taking a late-night freak-out call as I prepared to turn in a ten-page synopsis for my first book two, and thank you for so much more. Without your guidance and the rest of Azantian Literary Agency, this series would not exist. The support, care, and energy you have shown for my career has lit a fire within me that has me always working on another project, another story, another cast of wonderful characters. Ours is the partnership every author hopes for, and I'm eternally grateful I get to experience it.

Of course, Almus Terra Academy would not even exist without my sweet, talented editor, Jessica Anderson, who had the brilliant prompt: *What if we created a fictionalized version of this real school where royals go?* I remember first reading that *Vanity Fair* article about UWC Atlantic and having ideas spark like fireworks. Jessica, you gave me more than just a two-book deal—you gave me years of precious memories with these characters and fans of the books. I cannot thank you enough for your vision, guidance, and red pen.

Publishing a book is not easy. Trying to make a book stand out and connect to the right booksellers and influencers is *especially* not easy. Kelly Moran, my fantastic publicist, and her marketing colleagues worked so hard getting these books to readers. Additionally, my production editor Marisa Finkelstein, copy editor Diana Drew, proofreaders Dassi Zeidel and Bunmi Ishola, and production coordinator Martina Rethman—I really appreciate your careful eye. And where would a book be without its cover? The stunning cover art by Deanna Halsall and design by Patrick Hulse have helped make this series a success. My gratitude to everyone at Christy Ottaviano Books and Little, Brown Books for Young Readers for your support and love of *Royal Heirs Academy*.

In writing this fictional series I didn't shy away from real-world references. That's because I want the issues in these books to feel relevant to teens, even if the glamorous world at ATA is out of reach. Topics like the sovereign wealth funds and insider trading in stocks required research and help from someone much better versed in economics than me. Thank you, Trent Hill, for your help in brainstorming this plot line with me and your continued mentorship.

Special thanks to Gina Orlando for her review and feedback in helping me write Titus's arc with his chronic illness. Again, much love and gratitude to Jodi Meadows and Kara McDowell for their blurbs, and Kristy Boyce, who is an absolute sweetheart angel sending me picture after picture of my book at various bookstores as she traveled for her own *Dating and Dragons* tour. And to RuthAnne—you are an AMAZING critique partner and friend, and I look forward to our writing retreats so much.

To OWL Ink, the awesome group of ladies I spend all my Thursday nights with—Caitlyn, Kayla, Devon, Emily, and Catherine. Our weekly goals and meetings give me life and inspiration, and I'm so glad we found one another.

All the love to my Swiftie Book Club at Red Stick Reads: Alison, Alex, Amanda, Bea, Lara, Ashley, Melissa, Ashlyn, Jamie, and Madison. Plus, the owners of RSR, James and Tere—I adore you both.

I have some pretty amazing friends who not only buy my books but show up unannounced at book launches (looking at you, Lindsey Whitlow), travel with me on writing trips and take care of me when I'm sick (*ahem*, Meaghan Kosman), and are there for me every step of the way. Christa, Kourtney, Kelly, Meaghan, Johanna, Lindsey, Bridget—y'all are, without a doubt, the best friends a girl could ask for.

Finally, to my beautiful family, thank you for being so dang proud of me. Without your confidence in me, these words wouldn't be here. End of story.

# CELEBRATING 100 YEARS OF PUBLISHING

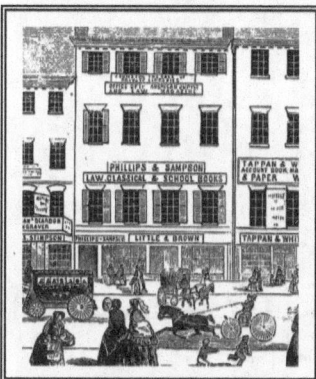

Dear Reader,

You may have noticed the words "Little, Brown and Company" on the title page of this book and wondered what they mean. Well, Charles C. Little and James Brown were the founders of this publishing house, and the "and Company" is all the editors, designers, marketers, publicists, salespeople, and more who help produce each book and bring it to readers like you. Little, Brown was founded in Boston, Massachusetts, in 1837, and some of its early publications included *The Writings of George Washington* and *The Works of Benjamin Franklin*. The catalog grew to feature works by Emily Dickinson and Louisa May Alcott, among many other notable authors. In 1926, recognizing that the literature we read when we are young has a deep and lasting influence and requires expert curation, the company appointed an editor to lead a dedicated children's department.

In 2026, Little, Brown Books for Young Readers celebrates one hundred years of excellence in publishing. Today, we are a division of Hachette Livre, the third-largest publisher in the world, and we are based in New York City. Our staff has grown from a team of two to more than one hundred people. And with the changes in technology, our books are read by more readers, in more ways, and in more countries than ever before. However, one thing has not changed: our commitment to providing a supportive home for all creators and superb stories for all readers. Thank you for being one of them.

*Megan Tingley*
Megan Tingley
President and Publisher

To learn more about Little, Brown's history,
authors, and books, please visit LBYR.com.

# LINDSEY DUGA

is the author of *Royal Heirs Academy* as well as several other YA novels and middle-grade ghost stories. With a passion for history and mythology, she's always been fascinated with royalty across cultures and fantastical worlds. She lives in Baton Rouge, Louisiana, with her family and dog, Delphi. She invites you to visit her online at lindseyduga.com and to follow her @LinzDuga.

www.ingramcontent.com/pod-product-compliance
Lightning Source LLC
LaVergne TN
LVHW031534060526
838200LV00056B/4490